To Shoot a Sinner

Lydia Margett

The characters and events portrayed in this book are fictitious. Any similarity to real persons, living or dead, is coincidental and not intended by the author.

Lamond House Press books may be purchased for educational, business, or sales promotional use. For information, please email the Special Markets Department at contact@lamondhousepress.com.

ISBN-13: 979-8-9941837-1-7

Cover design by: Fitter Fang

Library of Congress Control Number: 2025926985

*To Johannes,
love of my life and husband-to-be.*

And see ye not that braid, braid road
That lies across that lily leven?
That is the path of wickedness,
Though some call it the road to
Heaven.

THOMAS THE RHYMER

Chapter One

Outskirts of London, England

March 1818

Charlotte Aston hardly ever got enough sleep—a commodity she valued above all others. It was worth its weight in gold and, like gold, was all the more precious when one did not have enough of it.

This morning—if one could even call it that—Charlotte found herself more desperate for sleep than she had been in years, and that was saying quite a lot. In fact, she would do anything short of murder to be back in her warm, soft bed at this very moment. Instead, she was standing in this desolate field, her boots caked in mud and escaped tendrils of hair plastered to the back of her neck in the cool morning mist before the first birds had even begun to sing.

A voice sounded from somewhere in the mist, and Charlotte turned, raising her pistol into the oncoming dawn. There was another shout, and she fired, the sound of the pistol echoing in the morning stillness. Then everything went black.

∞∞∞∞

Benjamin Scarsdale was bored to death of duels. Granted, it had been years since he had been roped into such a stupid endeavour. But there had once been a time in his life when his youthful arrogance had practically begged for the young, equally arrogant toffs of London to call him out.

He had participated in at least five as the primary duellist and around the same number as a second for the few idiots he counted as friends. He had always known it was foolish. Even in his wilder days—if one could call the years of scraping and clawing his way up from the gutter, wild. Frenzied. Desperate. Determined. All might have been better descriptors.

The one that currently had him standing in a god-awful field in what could be called one of dear Mother England's most miserable glooms to date was the kind he abhorred the most: a duel over a tart.

He also knew for a fact that the tart in question could not care less about a duel being fought over her—if she knew about it at all, which she probably did. Word travelled through the back streets of London faster than a bullet.

That was part of the problem. Honour, he could understand. The defence of a woman, he could understand. This was neither of those things.

Chapter Two

The previous night

Benjamin threw back his fourth…fifth?…scotch of the last few hours. He had lost count and, if he were honest with himself, really could not hold his liquor the way he had in his young, hard days. This scotch was far finer than the blue ruin of the London gin houses he once had cause to frequent. But the fine peat-rich elixir of the verdant Scottish isles—each glass worth more than he could scrape together in a year in those lean days—sat more ill in his gut than those cheap spirits ever had.

At the ripe age of thirty—an age he had never expected to reach—he was starting to suspect this was the beginning of a precipitous geriatric decline.

Benjamin looked out over the den of Elysium, the sumptuously appointed gambling floor churning with monied patrons, elite and suspect alike, rubbing elbows under his roof, trying to account for each of the drinks that had led to his current state.

The first had been a toast, poured jovially in his study, shared with his only two friends in the world, Jonathan Bradford, the Duke of Wells, and Alexander Burke, the Marquess of Elkington.

Really, he had been happy for Elkington's news—though he knew things that would likely have even his besotted, devil-may-care friend reconsidering his situation. The three of them had shared another toast before Elk left. That made two drinks.

The third had been poured by a conciliatory Wells as Benjamin handed over the thick roll of banknotes that he had been certain he would not lose when he had wagered them weeks prior. He had not thought Elkington would be snared so quickly, though he knew he could find no better woman than Elsie Wylde, a woman with secrets all her own.

He did not like to admit that he had been wrong. But more than that, the news of their engagement unnerved him. It was not that he was not happy for his friend—in fact, he was relieved the man had finally come to his senses. But knowing what he knew of the lady in question, which was more than anyone else in London—likely the whole of the British Isles—he was certain it would not turn out well for either party in question. The knowledge hung heavily on him. It was a familiar weight, but not so comforting as it had once been.

Wells had left shortly after. That was when Benjamin had poured the next drink. Four. There must have been another between then and now, for the tumbler in his hands was still three fingers full. It was probably his fifth.

That was why he felt this gnawing emptiness in his chest. It was not because he had seen his friend happier than he could remember. And it was not because he had proven himself ignorant in the course of others' relationships; he had just misjudged the situation. It happened—usually to other people, not him—but he could accept that.

It was then, as he stared down at the amber liquid in his hand, considering tossing the contents back and seeking out a server to refill it, hangover-be-damned, that a familiar face on the floor caught his attention.

Patrons of Elysium were free to come as they pleased, but a fashion had emerged among some of the regulars to wear concealing face masks—it added to the mystery and allure of it all, he supposed. Following that set, it had become common practice for anyone attending the club to don at least a black domino, though the more ostentatious the mask, the better. It was because of this fashion that the unmasked face stood out so much more clearly. Sucking in a frustrated huff, he set the tumbler on the rail and made his way down onto the floor.

"Jasmine, what are you doing here?"

The beautiful, shapely woman turned, a charade of innocence stamped on her beautiful, hard face. Like most prostitutes who worked the London streets, Jasmine had all the feminine charms that tempted men to their disgrace. But she also had the same weathered toughness beneath it all. The reality beneath a beauty that had seen the truth of life's savagery and survived.

"Wot d'ya mean, sir?"

"Do not *sir* me, Jasmine. You know you are welcome to come as a patron, but none of this." He did not begrudge her the work, but he would descend the basement steps into the pits of Hell rumoured to lurk below his establishment before he let his club become a brothel.

She opened her rouged mouth again, likely to argue her case, but Benjamin held up a hand. "You can stop by the kitchens to grab something for your sprogs, but then be on your way, please."

Her dark eyes scrutinised him for a moment longer, calculating her odds of getting what she wanted, then she shrugged, a secret, expert smile taking over her face as she passed by, her clean, rough hand daintily passing over his chest as she made her way towards one of the concealed side doors on the edge of the rotunda.

"Alright, *sir.* If that be all…" She let the teasing words hang behind her. "You always know where t' find me."

He gave her a wave as she flounced off in the crowd, men's eyes devouring her as she passed. Normally, he would have dismissed her flirtation without a second thought. Years on the street had made him circumspect in his dealings with women—he had seen what the diseases could do. But the gnawing hole in his gut made him hesitate. Some contact—any warmth at all, even if purchased—might lessen its hold.

A shove from behind had him whipping around, the spirits slugging through his blood, unsettling his balance. The offender was a young, corny-faced lad glaring up at him from a mask haphazardly skewed across his face. Benjamin stared down at the smaller man for a moment, uncomprehendingly. The boy did not even look old enough to have been let in the doors. He would have to have a word with Harvey. If he had started letting children into his hell, so help him…

"What are you about, sirrah?" The boy's voice was cultured; a gentleman's whelp then. A bothersome type.

"Rethink your question." Benjamin rubbed the bridge of his nose. The dull throb of too much drink had settled between his eyes, and he was too old to be spoiling for a fight. He wanted to find his bed.

The lad glared. "I say! Who do you think you are? Throwing out another man's sport? I already paid for her. I have half a mind to give you what for, you grotty little man."

Benjamin just stared, completely uninterested in the arrogant little prick.

"I expect compensation! This is common thievery!" The lad was working himself into a lather, the uneven tone of his skin under his domino turning an unflattering shade of red.

"Get out."

Benjamin's voice was low. They had already attracted a crowd. From the corner of his eye, he could see another young buck, surely this boy's companion on their ill-advised evening of revelry, pushing through the crush.

"Freddie!" The newcomer's voice was still cracking.

Children. When the other boy arrived, Benjamin felt a flicker of recognition pierce through the throbbing in his head. This was a lord's brat. He knew his father. But he could not pin the man's name or face in his muddled mind. He never let his control slip like this. It was foolish and messy.

"Freddie," the brat muttered. "We should go. Come." He pulled on his arm.

"Listen to your friend, boy." The dismissal in Benjamin's voice must have struck a chord in the milksop before him.

"I say!" Freddie was flustered, and even to Benjamin's diluted eye, soused. "I will not go. I will have satisfaction!"

The trembling youth beside him let out a bleat at that, his eyes as big as saucers when they turned on Benjamin, as if hoping he had not heard his friend's challenge.

"Rowley is my second." The fair-haired youth blustered

and took an equal hold of his friend. "Send yours to discuss particulars. I will see you at dawn."

The slight slur of his words undermined the effect of the outraged stand as much as the tottering way he leaned on his friend as they turned to take their leave. Benjamin would wager his right arm that the boy would not make it to the field.

Still, he absently waved a hand, done with the idiots before him, and returned to his office, instructing a passing server to track down Wells.

∞∞∞

Present

Benjamin had no choice but to agree to pistols at dawn. How unoriginal. As the challenged, it was his prerogative to choose the weapons, but Wells had taken one look at him and declared swords to be out of the question.

Benjamin was sure he fared somewhat better than his pickled opponent, but he had acquiesced.

He regretted his capitulation now, though. His head was throbbing, and he hated the wet, all-permeating drizzle that seemed to come from up, down, left, and right, all at once, making his beautiful wool overcoat smell of wet dog.

What was the point of this misery? There was no sense in such a worthless display. Standing in the damp, pointing guns at one another, was an empty gesture of manliness that smacked of deluded privilege. The idiot standing across from him did not know the price of life—how capriciously fate could have it leaking out of your guts in a back alley after years of miserable scraping and enduring. He could feel the cold cobbles beneath his face—could feel the heat of his lifeblood soaking through his clothes.

He meant to teach this foolish boy a lesson, at least, or else the morning would be a complete waste indeed.

And so at the indicated moment, he turned, took aim at the figure across the field in the mist, and fired.

Chapter Three

Earlier that morning

"Lady Charlotte. Lady Charlotte. Please, you must wake up."

Charlotte groaned as she was shaken forcefully from her sleep. When she opened her eyes, she was met with the darkness of her room, illuminated only by a single flickering candle. Why, in God's name, was someone in her bedchambers?

"Please wake up. You have to help Freddie."

At her baby brother's name, she bolted upright, panic replacing the grogginess.

"Why? What has happened to Freddie?" Charlotte looked frantically around the room until her eyes fixed on Rowley Calthorpe, her brother's best friend.

"You'd better come see for yourself, my lady."

Rowley stood and held the candle aloft so she could find her wrapper and slippers. She followed him through the familiar halls of her family's London townhouse.

Their only house. It hardly needed a locational qualifier when all the other family holdings had long gone up in proverbial smoke. And even this house was teetering perilously close to alternative ownership. It scarcely even resembled the home it once was, with all its trappings of elegance stripped away in the hopes of fetching a passable price.

In the last two years, since their father, the eighth Earl of Elford's passing, their country estate had been forfeited, their extensive stables auctioned off, and every memento of their family's past brilliance pawned; and still, there was no money.

Charlotte managed to make ends meet, but just barely. She had ensured that the solicitors, before they had to be dismissed, secured a stipend to provide for her youngest siblings' tuition at Eton. She did not want Marcus and Henry to be left with no resources in the world, and as she knew, education was worth all their former properties put together.

In the first year, she had managed to economise the household well enough. There had always been enough food, and she was able to retain a few of the core staff. Now, however, they were down to nothing. No butler, no cook, and the single maid-turned-housekeeper, turned beast-of-burden, had quit three months ago.

In the last year, things had gone from pinched to dire at an eye-watering speed. She had sold everything of value they owned and tried to take in mending, though her own skills with a needle and thread made such an endeavour completely unproductive. She had taken to pretending not to be in residence so that her old friends and acquaintances could not realise the depths to which the Aston family had fallen.

Finally, she'd applied for a job at the newspaper. She'd paid the last of her week's grocery budget to a young actor to go to the paper and act as her stand-in, presenting her writing samples as his own and promising to submit timely editorials as long as he could do so by post.

Blessedly, the newspaper had desperately needed fresh new writers, and Charlotte was paid a modest sum for each weekly editorial she submitted. While not extravagant, the steady flow of income allowed her to keep food in their bellies and a roof over their heads. She thought she had come up with the path to their salvation and that nothing could endanger them again.

She had been mistaken.

She knew that now, standing over the prone figure of her brother, Frederick, the current Earl of Elford. He was sleeping, sprawled on the bare carpet of the drawing room floor.

She had stood like this, watching him sleep so often as a young girl. Her mother had died when she was young, and her father had remarried a kind but rather flighty woman four years later. When Freddie was born, Charlotte thought he was the most angelic creature she had ever laid eyes on. He had their father's light colouring with lovely starry blue eyes and soft, delicious cheeks. She could stare at him for hours.

The young man lying before her was a ghost of that darling boy. He had stretched out and become gangly but not very tall—a product of his lifestyle, she was sure. Their father had been a tall and imposing man. Looking at him now, it was like looking upon a stranger. Freddie already had the paunch of a much older man past the bloom of youth, and his face was gaunt and sallow, no doubt from the countless nights of revelry and the excess of drink.

He smelled foul, and his clothes were in tatters—though they were far too new and fine for their modest budget. Charlotte had to close her eyes briefly to curb her anger at his careless excess. It had been this reckless behaviour that had gotten them into this mess to begin with, and they had quarrelled abominably about it many times.

But as the Earl of Elford, Freddie held the purse strings, however unjustly, and he did not take kindly to his elder sister's waspish attempts to control him or his birthright.

"What happened to him?" She spoke to the room at large, though only one of the other inhabitants had the power of speech at the moment.

"He had a bit too much to drink." Rowley cringed an apology and fidgeted beside her.

Rowley Calthorpe had always been a kind boy and stood to inherit a sizable marquisate in the near-to-distant future. Still, despite his wealth and influence, he was a timid and malleable creature that could be counted upon to support Freddie's foolish schemes.

"I can see that. But why would this concern me?" She did not look up from Freddie's washed-out face.

A beat of silence followed. "He challenged someone to a duel."

"He *what?*" Charlotte nearly shouted into the dark room.

Rowley did not meet her eye.

"Who did he challenge? When is it to be?" Charlotte held up her hand before Rowley could explain. "And before you start, I do not wish to know why. For any reason you could give is too foolish for words."

"He challenged Mr. Benjamin Scarsdale. And the duel is tomorrow. Today. In a few hours, actually."

Charlotte felt as if the floor had shifted under her, and for a moment, the entire room seemed to tilt on its axis.

"*Benjamin Scarsdale?* The gaming hell owner?"

She had heard of him. A memory from her recent investigations for an editorial pressed itself upon her mind.

"'*E was one of us once.*" *Claire, the washing woman, saw Charlotte's interest pique as two boys chased by, one threatening the other with some nebulous justice to be meted out by an omnipotent Scarsdale.*

Charlotte's pencil suspended above her notepad as the curious image settled in her mind.

"*Rough-like. 'E rose up from the streets. No family to speak of. Mean fighter, easy thief. But 'e also knows it all. Everyone's secrets. No one knows how. 'E just sees you and knows. And if 'e 'as your secrets, 'e 'as your soul.*"

The woman, really no more than a girl, spoke with her voice lowered, her words getting lost in the steam that bubbled out of the cauldron where she stirred her morning's laundry. Her tired grey eyes alight with something more—reverence, fear, awe.

Charlotte had seen enough of the streets by then to know the power of a folk hero. A figure steeped in legend and myth—and no small amount of danger—gave the people something to hope for, something to whisper about to pull through the dreary days and rough winters. It did not much matter how real the character truly was—it was about the story.

"*I saw 'im once.*" *The girl's tone pulled Charlotte closer.* "*Thought I was dreamin'. It was when I first started. Slept right here in the courtyard under the eaves. It is wondrously warm. Steam does not cool until after dawn, if you can believe. But it was nearly dark still—not even time for the new girls to start the fires up. And I seen him. Thought it was a spectre, the shape coming out of the fog. But then 'e was real—solid. I didn' touch him, so I can't tell y' 'ow I know—but I was sure. There is somethin' so solid about 'im. And done up in fine clothes. The finest I'd ever seen. But there was blood on 'im. I closed my eyes then. Pretended I was still asleep."*

Charlotte's breath was high in her chest, and her pencil was still suspended above the pad. Something about the girl's voice told her this was not the kind of thing she should write down.

"I did not want 'im to know I had seen 'im. 'E'd use my secrets against me. Not that I 'ave so many. But still, they're mine. Benjamin Scarsdale is not the kind I want takin' note of me. Master o' London's Secrets, they call 'im." Despite her words, there was respect in her tone. Charlotte knew not to prod further. The residents of St Giles were loyal to this man—whoever he was. And she was not fool enough to involve herself with such a figure.

Rowley had the decency to look even guiltier than he already did. "Scarsdale. The very one. Though I do not know if it is proper for a gently bred lady to know so much of him."

"I would imagine it is not proper for a gently bred lady to know much of what I know, Lord Calthorpe." She took a steadying breath. "It is lucky that my brother saw fit to drink himself into a stupor. You will have to call off this foolish duel, for it is clear he cannot attend, let alone stand upright and point a pistol at someone."

For some reason, her mind did not conjure a picture of this man lying before her on a duelling pitch. Instead, she saw in her mind's eye the cherub-faced boy of his youth, brandishing a toy pistol above his head as if he were playing highwayman with the indulgent stable hands at their father's country estate. The image made her want to cry.

"It is funny," she said bitterly, "for once, Freddie's drinking will save his neck."

Rowley somehow looked more chagrined, and he danced back and forth from one foot to the next, as if he were standing on a bed of hot coals. At that moment, it looked as if he might indeed prefer to be standing on hot coals.

"Rowley, what aren't you telling me?"

The poor boy looked as if he would cast up his accounts on the carpet beside her stinking brother. "You see… I already met with his second. And… And…" He could not get the words out.

"And what?" Charlotte could not stand another moment in suspense.

"And he also made a wager. With another young buck at our vingt-et-un table. He said that Freddie was too in his cups to make it to the duelling field. And Freddie bet him he was wrong."

The tragically comical picture of Frederick as a little boy evaporated, and an icy calm overtook Charlotte.

"How much did he wager?"

"Three hundred pounds." Rowley named the sum, looking down at his shoes.

Charlotte felt herself sit hard on the settee. It should have been reupholstered at least a year ago. The signs of age and wear were showing, and bits of frayed red thread poked out at the seams. For some reason, that was all she could think of—how dismal this little settee looked in the flickering light of a too-expensive candle.

Three hundred pounds would destroy them. She would have to take the boys out of school. They would need to sell the house. Perhaps she could get them a modest flat if she doubled her editorial work. But she was not naïve enough to believe there were no other debts of her brother hovering just out of sight, ready to be called in when it became clear their house of cards had truly fallen.

There was only one thing to do.

Charlotte stood. "I will go in his place."

Chapter Four

Present

It had been years since Benjamin had felt such grudging respect for a man he met on a duelling pitch.

Usually, a man foolish enough to demand satisfaction in the form of a duel was a certain breed of popinjay. The toffs liked to play at danger and valour, though anyone with a true sense of honour and dignity would respect the value of life and limb and seek to resolve their conflicts in a more civilised manner—despite the archaic standards of gentlemanly conduct.

Of course, pot and kettle and all that, considering the fact that he was also on the duelling pitch. But Benjamin Scarsdale did not issue duels. He merely respected the summons, however asinine he might believe it to be. He knew the value of his life and never sought to take another. Not again.

That is how he knew he had only clipped the lad in the shoulder. The lad who, surprisingly, had done the truly noble thing and shot in the air when another man had aimed directly at him.

Thinking back through the haze of scotch to his encounter with the boy the night before, he could not reconcile the arrogant, entitled young man with the stoic figure that had stood across from him moments earlier.

He would never in a million years have guessed that the whelp would raise his pistol to the sky. Why even call a duel in the first place if he would not try to extract his pound of flesh? Had Benjamin misjudged him? He had always had such a keen eye for a person's true character. Hence why he had so few friends.

Benjamin mulled over this thought as he and Wells stood by their horses, waiting for the surgeon to announce that the boy was still living. Normally, Benjamin made a point of hightailing it out of the site of a duel. It did not do to risk further trouble by being caught in the illegal activity, and, in his experience, his challengers were usually willing to let the matter rest after realising how close to death they had actually come.

However, the surgeon did not wave the customary all-clear. Instead, instructing the scrawny young man who had acted as the boy's second to kneel in his place, the surgeon stood and hailed Benjamin and Wells over.

How eminently strange, Benjamin thought to himself. In all his duelling experience, he had never seen the good doctor do this. Even if someone got hurt—never fatally at his hands, of course—he bandaged them up or arranged for them to be taken home to be tended to properly. Now, the doctor's severe face contorted in an odd mix of confusion, censure, and—was that discomfort?

"What is it, Doctor Price?" Wells always insisted on enlisting his own personal physician, citing a disinclination to lose his best friend and, more importantly, business partner to a quack's malpractice.

"Um, Your Grace." Price's hands fluttered from his bag to the prone patient beneath them.

"Is he dead?" Benjamin felt a flutter of panic, followed by a familiar wave of nausea. Cold cobblestones. The stench of the streets. Blood.

"No. Not dead, sir."

"Well, out with it, Price. My bollocks are going to shrivel up and fall off if I have to stand out here in this soup much longer." Wells shook his coat, sending a shower of dew droplets down on the patient below as if to emphasise his waning patience. "If he is not dead, and is not likely to be soon, then I say our business is done here."

The good doctor glanced back down at the prone figure and the boy kneeling beside him, holding a cloth down on his compatriot's shoulder to staunch the wound. He looked like he could have been the one shot. The pallor of his face was alarming.

"Yes, Your Grace, of course. He is not dead. But *he* is a *she*."

Benjamin felt like his eyes must be bulging out of his head as he stared at the doctor. He must have heard him wrong. He looked back down at the figure below them. The boy was dressed in the usual trappings of a country gentleman. The breeches, boots, and riding coat all spoke of a young man of means dressed for a morning ride. But looking closer, with the doctor's proclamation ringing in his ears, Benjamin could see the truth unveiling itself before him.

The legs in the trousers were shapely and long, longer than

a typical lady. The glimpse of hips that showed between the flaps of the long riding coat were rounded and tapered in a surprisingly elegant and enticing way. Benjamin snapped his gaze up further, unable to believe his eyes. The coat and tunic obscured most of her torso, but where the young boy held his hands at her shoulder, Benjamin could see a delicate collarbone and smooth expanse of neck.

Then the doctor pushed the injured lady's crushed bicorn hat aside.

What truly arrested him was the young woman's face. It was shockingly lovely, and he found himself implausibly enthralled.

Her nose was long and sharp in a wholly unfashionable way. However, combined with the upwards tilt of her wide eyes, though currently closed, and her high-arched, almost invisibly light eyebrows, they created a strange elfin effect that made his chest squeeze.

Before he could fully examine her features or his reaction to them, the boy kneeling beside her let out a strangled cry. Benjamin's eyes snapped back to the boy's hands, and he jolted in alarm to see rivulets of thick, red blood seeping from under the cloth pressed to the wound.

Snapping his eyes back up to the elfin queen's face, he noted the pallor that invariably indicated a serious loss of blood.

"Doctor Price, I believe it is your job to keep the injured duellist alive no matter their gender." Benjamin did not like the unwelcome feeling of panic that beat in his chest, and he strove to quash it with his ever-useful armour of brutal efficiency.

Not wasting another moment on Doctor Price's uncertainty, Benjamin swept the young woman into his arms and began marching back through the field toward his horse.

"Follow me to my townhouse. Doctor Price, I expect you to be ready to operate the moment we arrive. You!" He nodded to the boy over his head. "Bring her mount and yourself to Hanover Square. You have some explaining to do."

∞∞∞∞

After a brief yet informative interrogation of the pitiful boy that he now knew to be Rowley Calthorpe, the heir of the Marquess of Ashley, Benjamin returned to check on his guest. His still unconscious guest.

"Why has she not awakened yet, Doctor?"

Price was washing his hands in a bowl of already pink water that sent a twinge of anxiety through Benjamin. The doctor had clearly fished out the bullet and sutured the wound while Benjamin was downstairs with the future Marquess, but he had hoped that after the short procedure, Charlotte would have come to again.

Charlotte. Charlotte Aston, daughter of the late Earl of Elford and sister to the current. Disconcerting that he had already taken to calling her by her Christian name in the privacy of his own thoughts.

They had met once before. It was at some *ton* function the likes of which he rarely, if ever, attended. As the not-so-secret bastard son of the Marquess of Winden and the notoriously cutthroat owner of a number of pubs, hells, and warehouses, he was not exactly a society hostess' ideal guest. Still, his close connection with two ducal titles and the most eligible bachelors of London society, Wells and Elkington, had earned him entrée into the ranks of high society, if only grudgingly.

Where had he met her? A ball? A musicale? He could not recall. Honestly, he could hardly recall Charlotte.

The only vague impression of her he could conjure was of a disinterested wallflower who, when they were introduced, seemed so distracted searching the crowd for her kid brother that she had hardly given him a second glance.

Not one lacking in female attention, despite his disreputable birth and more disreputable dealings, he had dismissed her as quickly as she had him.

Now, however, looking down at her pale face and bandaged shoulder, tunic cut away to reveal both slender shoulders, Benjamin could not imagine having ever pried his eyes from such an otherworldly beauty.

Even now, wounded and rain-dampened, she looked regal. Her high forehead looked pinched even in sleep, as if she carried the weight of the world on her shoulders. Her hands clasped over her chest could have been holding the hilt of a sword over her prone form. A warrior ready for battle.

Even her hair, braided around her head—likely to hide under her cap—looked like a crown of gold against the pillow. His pillow. When they had arrived, he had carried her up to his own chambers and laid her on his own bed. Why had he done that? There was a surplus of unused rooms in this house. Why had he unthinkingly brought her there?

His surprise was feigned. He was lying to himself. This had been intentional. A part of him—a base and delinquent part—was desperate to see her laid out in his bed, even if it was only for a moment.

He stood still now, while Price fished through his bag of medical debris behind him. He could not lift his eyes from her lovely, angular face.

And if ye dare to kiss my lips. / Sure of your bodie I will be.

The stanza came unbidden to his mind. Upon the initial accumulation of his wealth, he had taken to collecting old books and manuscripts. Anyone on the streets knew money could buy food, power, security—but it was not until he had those things that he saw what it could really grasp hold of—knowledge. It was a secret luxury he allowed himself; the quest for knowledge for its own sake was a heady drug only the truly wealthy could enjoy. He could wield his business and his reputation like a weapon, but he always felt the threat of the streets breathing down his neck. It was only in the reading, the amassing of knowledge, that he caught glimpses of what life could be beyond his world.

He had felt especially drawn to folkloric literature, so rich in mystery and tradition that it made him feel worlds away; another man in another time. It was a balm to the soul of the young boy scrounging for tuppence when others his age—his own flesh and blood even—were being read stories safe in their beds. A life he had tasted and lost.

He had not thought about that feeling in years. The hobby had faded with the growing realisation that this quest for knowledge could be even more valuable. The knowledge of others. Secrets. Things they did not want others to know. That was the truest power. He could use the knowledge of another to bend them to his will.

He had never imagined he would recall much of the content of the books he read. Ultimately, his mind for figures and people had built his empire, not old prose fading into obscurity.

And if ye dare to kiss my lips. / Sure of your bodie I will be.

He could not even think of where he had read it. Perhaps he had made it up. Still, the thought was alarming, and he floundered for rescue. Wrenching his gaze from sleeping Charlotte, only then did he realise Doctor Price had been speaking to him.

"I apologise, Doctor. What was that?"

Price gave him a curious look, but was so out of sorts himself, he just shook his head and repeated himself. "She came to briefly when I was extracting the bullet and screamed and thrashed so hard, I thought she would strike me." There was genuine fear in the doctor's eyes. "So I gave her a draught of laudanum before I continued."

"Gave her?" The idea of Price forcing the sedative down a frantic Charlotte's throat sent a surge of protective fury through him. The poor woman did not know where she was and who she was with. Let alone being awakened with such agony. She must have been half mad with fear. Benjamin knew the feeling well.

"Yes. I could not otherwise have finished the operation. And without the proper staff, I might add." Price looked simultaneously apprehensive and affronted. He clearly knew the power Benjamin wielded but also felt the indignity of serving someone of such dubious birth.

All that considered, he was an excellent doctor, and Benjamin recognised the invaluable service he had provided in saving Charlotte's life. From a wound he himself had inflicted.

"Thank you, Doctor Price. You will be compensated generously for your impeccable efforts." Benjamin suddenly felt devilishly tired, and he waved a hand in the air, dismissing the man.

He stripped off his wet outer garments and rang for a footman to take away the bloody remnants of the doctor's work. Once a fresh jug of water appeared on the washing stand, he sponged off the grime of the morning, including some of Charlotte's blood, and stood with his back to the hearth.

Despite her considerable height for a young woman, she looked so small in Benjamin's bed. Her white face shone in the dim light of the room, and he felt it calling to him like a beacon. His mind was numb from the shock of the morning, or perhaps the excess of the night before was catching up to him. Either way, he could not muster the aloof resistance that had become second nature over the years. Walking over, he sat on the edge of the bed opposite her.

It was such a large bed, and she was bound to be unconscious for hours still. On top of that, it *was* his bed. Where else would he be able to rest his head? He was very tired.

Of course, he could sleep in one of the other chambers—though they were likely not turned out for an occupant. He could go to Elysium, where he kept rooms that he occupied far more often than these, but that would be such an effort. It would be no effort at all to lie atop the covers here beside Charlotte. It would only be for a moment to rest his weary body. It was not so improper as all that. And what did he care of propriety, anyway? He was Benjamin Scarsdale. The most renowned rogue in all of London.

Before reason could win out, he shifted his legs upon the bed and pillowed his head on his arm. As sleep quickly dragged him under, he watched the fading form of Charlotte Aston beside him until a lingering thought caught at his mind: he could stay right here, forever.

The thought was so jarring that the hard-fought exhaustion pulling at his limbs vanished in a rush of panicked adrenaline. He fixed his gaze on the canopy of the bed, trying to calm his jackrabbiting heart.

Chapter Five

Charlotte woke gradually as if she were surfacing from the bottom of a lake. Her mind was sluggish, and she could not filter through the jumble of her thoughts—some dreaming, some awake.

When she finally managed to peel her eyelids open, it took many moments to realise the deep green silk damask stretched over the canopy of the bed was wholly unfamiliar to her. As she looked around, she saw that the other parts of the room were equally foreign. The tastefully reserved yet clearly rich quality of the decor spoke to a wealth that she had never experienced herself. Even at the height of their family's finances.

Her sluggish brain took in the surroundings with detached admiration, as if she were watching from far off, somehow through someone else's eyes.

After a few minutes of concerted effort, she began to take stock of her bodily sensations. Her whole body felt stiff and sore, as if she had ridden a horse across all of England. Then the true pain hit her. Her shoulder felt as if it had been lanced through with a hot poker. She gritted her teeth against the immediate agony and closed her eyes, trying to focus on her breath.

That was when she felt something warm in her hand. She flexed her fingers gingerly, and the movement sent tremors of pain through her shoulder.

It was solid. Her hand was wrapped in something warm and solid. She flexed her fingers again, trying to make sense of the sensation.

Finally, she opened her eyes, blinking away the grit of bad sleep.

It was a hand.

There was a hand in her hand. Or, more accurately, her hand was held in another. Another hand that was, she realised belatedly, attached to a long, muscular arm, which was, in turn, attached to a grown man lying beside her, dead asleep.

Panic rocketed through her, and she shot up in the bed, the pain and fear making her swift but clumsy. She jumped out of the bed, distantly relieved that her clothes seemed to be intact, though the neck of her tunic hung looser than she remembered. Frantically, she grabbed the closest thing to her and flung it at the large sleeping man.

The sound of shattering porcelain echoed in the quiet room, and Charlotte felt a splash of cold water down her arms as the water pitcher connected with the man's torso.

Within a single breath, the strange man was on his feet, vaulting over the bed toward her as he pinned her to the wall, a knife drawn and pressed into her neck.

In all this, Charlotte had not even managed to let out a scream. Fear knocked the breath from her lungs—or maybe it was the force of the towering man pinning her to the silk-lined walls.

He stood there for what felt like an eternity, chest heaving and eyes clearing as he shook off the remnants of sleep and battle instinct. All of a sudden, he stepped back, and Charlotte sagged against the wall.

She could not feel her face. That seemed strange. Then, a wave of fiery hot pain ripped through her shoulder, and she only just managed to grab the basin of the fallen water pitcher before she cast up her accounts.

∞∞∞∞

Benjamin stood watching Charlotte retch violently, unsure of what to do. He felt off-kilter himself, still not totally sure if he was dreaming or awake.

She had attacked him! He felt absurdly impressed—maybe even proud. But the shame that followed those feelings quickly drowned them out. He had attacked her back.

Living on the streets all those years ago had honed a vicious animal instinct within him. It was either kill or be killed, and despite the years of living in relative safety and civility, it was clear that instinct had not faded with time.

Even though Charlotte's drawn face as she leaned her head back against the wall drew him towards her with a tugging sweetness, he took another step back, pocketing the switchblade he kept on him at all times. Something in him screamed to protect her, to comfort her, to wipe the beads of sweat from her brow. Instead, he moved over to the window, looking out while she put herself to rights again.

The evening had set in the square below, and carriages rattled past, already ferrying their passengers to evening entertainments.

"What happened?" she mumbled, her voice weak.

30

"You were shot, Lady Charlotte. In a duel. You were brought back here to receive emergency medical treatment for the resulting bullet wound."

Silence met his proclamation, and he looked over his shoulder in a gesture he hoped seemed nonchalant to check that she was still conscious. She was. And she was regarding him with wary, assessing eyes that made him turn back to the window.

"Who are you?"

He tried to ignore the twinge of disappointment he felt at her lack of recognition. It was just his pride. "Mr. Benjamin Scarsdale, at your service."

He turned and sketched a vaguely mocking bow. Whether he was trying to mock her or their circumstances, he was not sure. In precarious situations such as this, it was vital to maintain the upper hand, and in all his years of pushing his way to the top, Benjamin had learned the power to be had in making one's opponent feel small. Shame was a universal motivator.

It seemed, however, she had not registered his tone as she looked up at him with alert, intelligent eyes. Those warm brown eyes were a shock. He would have thought a woman of her colouring would have light eyes—blue or green—but hers were a soft, honey brown that were even more enchanting in their unexpectedness.

"You shot me." Her deadpan proclamation was almost enough to make him laugh.

"Ah, yes. Guilty as charged." He raised his hands and gave a contrite smile, trying another tactic. "Though I also rescued you, I hasten to point out." Perhaps charm would win him the upper hand.

"And brought me to your home," she looked around the room, "and your bed chamber; I presume?" The comment was an accusation.

"Nothing untoward has occurred, I assure you, Lady Charlotte." He was growing defensive. For God's sake, he'd saved her life. A bit of gratitude would not go amiss.

"You attacked me with a knife," she continued. "Was shooting me not enough for one day?" She was still sitting on the floor, and the gaping top of her tunic revealed her shoulders in a supremely distracting way. He hated himself for noticing it.

"You attacked me with a pitcher. While I was asleep and defenceless, I may add."

Charlotte looked pointedly at his pocket, where he carried his knife, and arched a nearly invisible eyebrow. "Defenceless?"

How could she manage to be sardonic at a time like this? Benjamin wanted to laugh. Or kiss her.

No.

Where had that come from? Granted, she was uncommonly beautiful. But he needed to regain control of this situation. Thoughts like those led only to ruin. He would not be ruined.

∞∞∞∞

Charlotte was ready to throttle the man standing before her. He had the audacity to participate in a foolish duel with her idiot of a brother, shoot her, bring her to his bachelor home, hold her at knifepoint, and claim to have rescued her?

If her shoulder had not been screaming in pain, she might have just marched across the room and delivered an incredibly deserved slap. As it was, though, she could barely see straight. The lingering effects of what she assumed to be laudanum did not help matters much either.

All she really wanted to do was crawl back into this man's bed and sleep forever. However, the powerful sense of self-preservation she had honed over the years since her father's death was rearing its head, and she struggled to push herself off the floor.

In two easy strides, Mr. Benjamin Scarsdale was at her side, helping her to her feet with a surprisingly gentle touch. She tried to shake him off, but the movement caused a pain so acute that she just collapsed further against him.

He was only half a head taller than her. Unusual. Most men of the *ton* could only just meet her eyes straight on. He was also strong and sturdy in a way that made her want to lean in more and allow him to support her weight. He smelled of warm spices and sun-dried laundry. She wanted to press her nose into his shoulder and inhale.

With that alarming thought, she stiffened and held herself as far apart as she could without completely disengaging. She did, unfortunately, need his help to remain upright.

"If I could impose on your generosity," she emphasised the word with obvious irony, "a little more, Mr. Scarsdale, I would request the loan of a carriage to return me to my home."

Mr. Scarsdale shook slightly beside her, and she wondered if he was laughing at her. "I am afraid that is not possible. The doctor requested that you remain abed for at least a week, if not longer. You cannot risk getting an infection before the wound heals."

At the mention of the wound, her shoulder throbbed, and

her vision blurred again slightly. Her mouth tasted foul and tacky. She wanted nothing more than to drain a pot of tea and lie down. By sheer willpower, she remained upright.

As if reading her thoughts, he reached for a glass on the bedside table. "Here, drink this. The doctor left it for you." He handed her the tea, and she drank deeply, frowning as the liquid washed over the film on her tongue. It was cold. How long had she slept here in this man's chambers? Did she stink of blood and sick? Why was the latter more concerning to her at this moment than the former?

She straightened her spine. "That being said, I would prefer to stay in my own bed for that amount of time. I can hardly remain here in the home of the most notorious bachelor in London."

He did not need to see how out of sorts she felt standing there in the deceptively safe circle of his arms.

"Notorious, am I?" He seemed almost gleeful at the comment.

"I think you are well aware of your reputation. I imagine you have gone to significant efforts to cultivate it." She did not mention the darker reputation she had heard tales of on the other side of town. The one she suspected he had come by without need for cultivation. The one that had street urchins and washing women whispering behind their hands and watching for shapes in the fog. Charlotte allowed him to lower her back onto the edge of the bed. "I would only like to preserve my own." Her head felt fuzzy again, and the bed beneath her was soft and warm.

"I do not think any gentleman wishes to be notorious." He had dropped his voice to a soothing tone and gently leaned her back onto the pillows.

"Pfft you ar' hardly a gentleman." Charlotte only just got the words out before her eyelids drooped closed again.

"Rest easy, Charlotte," a soft voice said from all around her, and with that, she slipped back into the welcome embrace of sleep, full of indignation.

Chapter Six

This was completely unacceptable.

Benjamin had spent the past few evenings visiting the gentleman's clubs and gaming hells of the London elite and was now sitting in his own office in Elysium, reading through the establishment's ledgers.

Until this week, the young Earl of Elford had been just another irresponsible fop wasting away his new inheritance. Such specimens were the bread and butter of gaming establishments such as his own, and Benjamin had never had cause to begrudge them their fun. They had made him a rich man.

Frederick Aston, however, was beyond the pale. In the last few years, he had racked up considerable debts at almost every fashionable establishment in London—and many of the unfashionable ones as well.

As far as Benjamin could tell, the Elford estate was completely bankrupt. He could not fathom how the Aston family maintained their current residence and kept the two youngest Astons enrolled at Eton.

What was more concerning to Benjamin was that, as far as his investigation could tell, the man who held the vast majority of the young earl's debts was Baron Reuben Deering.

Cold cobblestones. The sharp tang of the docks. Hot blood seeping through his collar.

Deering was a grasping and vindictive man who resented his status and seemed set on making it everyone else's problem. He owned a mildly successful shipping company, but he made most of his wealth in the contraband goods he sold and other underhanded dealings he conducted with the more dubious businessmen of London.

Deering was detestable for a number of reasons, but Benjamin's hatred of him was far more personal. Reuben Deering had killed his sister.

∞∞∞∞

It had been three days since Charlotte had seen Scarsdale. He had not returned to his room since she awoke the next morning, and instead, a young, sweet-faced maid sat in the corner.

"You have to help me return to my home, Lizzy. This arrangement is wholly inappropriate." Charlotte had sat in the hip bath as the young woman gently patted a damp cloth over the tender, puckered skin of her shoulder.

"Yep, don't I know it? You are as fine a lady as I have ever seen, and you should not be having dealings with such a man." Content that her wound was well cleaned, Lizzy moved oto scrubbing the dried mud and filth from Charlotte's arms. "But honest as I can be, my lady, there is nothing you should be doing to turn down such help." She eyed the wound again, giving Charlotte a pointed look. "From what I can figure, which ain't much since it is none of my business, you have found yourself in a spot of trouble. And miraculously, that man has seen fit to see you out of it. In luxury."

The maid waved a hand around the well-appointed chamber, which Charlotte had begun to consider her prison. "Of course, I would never refuse to help you leave if you truly wish it. But I would sure as be sacking myself. And I need this job, my lady. My brother is in the workhouse. With this job, I can get him out."

Charlotte rested her head on her bent knees, still soapy in the lather that she staunchly refused to recognise as the same scent that had so pleasantly clung to Benjamin Scarsdale's neck. She did not want to be the cause of Lizzy's unemployment.

"Honestly, I am still pinching myself that I got this job. I have never been a lady's maid before. Never even known one."

Charlotte snapped her head up at that, jolting her shoulder and pulling a groan from between her clenched teeth. "You have not had this job long?" She had assumed Lizzy was just one of the household staff.

"No, m'lady. Just got hired yesterday. My cousin is the cookmaid. She came and found me at work and dragged me straight here to interview. And just like that, I was hired." The woman shrugged her thin shoulders. Her frame was not one that was made to be thin.

Charlotte blinked. How strange. Had Scarsdale really not had a single maid in residence that could have managed the duties of a lady's maid, even a temporary one? Had he set out specifically to find someone to look after her in her convalescence? And after she had thrown a pitcher at him, no less?

"Where did you work before this, Lizzy?"

"Lifetime of jobs, m'lady. But most recently, I worked as a seamstress."

Charlotte nodded, watching the girl's nimble but scarred hands wring out the cloth and lather the soap once more. "Wasn't such a bad place as all that. Better pay than usual. But nothing like this. I can have James out in two weeks at this rate."

She set to scrubbing soap into Charlotte's hair with none of the finesse of a practised lady's maid. Charlotte did not mind.

"I will not leave, Lizzy," Charlotte spoke to the ceiling as Lizzy poured warm water over her hair.

There was a beat of silence, and Lizzy's freckled face appeared above her. "You mean that?"

The hope in the woman's eyes angered Charlotte. How dare Scarsdale play them both like this? Charlotte would have to leave. She had her own family to protect. But she could not condemn Lizzy to the same fate. She would not do that to Lizzy or her brother.

"You have my word. I will not leave unless I have to. And if I do, I will ensure that you are not dismissed on my account." It was a bold promise to make. Bolder still, since she had no idea of the character of the man she was dealing with. But she had fought her way forward time and again. She was sure she would manage something.

Over the last few days, Charlotte and Lizzy had spent most of Charlotte's short, weary days in each other's company. Somewhat to Charlotte's surprise, healing from a bullet wound was deeply exhausting work. Her torso had bruised considerably, and an unflagging ache settled in the joints around the wound, even though Lizzy kept it scrupulously clean, and the doctor, on his brief daily visits, proclaimed it to have not yet festered.

It had been over a year since she had the luxury of a lady's maid, and while Lizzy's gentle care was lovely and appreciated, her companionship was the real boon. The two ate together and read together—Charlotte read out loud to Lizzy, who said she preferred to listen—and they quickly grew comfortable in each other's presence.

Finding companionship with the staff was nothing new for Charlotte. Her childhood had been lonely after her mother died of cholera when she was young. Her father was affectionate but distant, unsure of what to do with an inquisitive young girl.

Then he remarried. His new wife, Veronica, was young and well-bred and, necessarily, wholly unfamiliar with small children. When first Freddie, then later on, the twins came, Charlotte was acutely aware of her alien status in the home. It had felt as if her father finally had a family again, and she was a tolerated relation.

As much as she loved her darling little brothers, she had never felt fully part of them. She had found some solace in the companionship of the staff. While she did not fit into their world either, they had been kind and patient, allowing the young lady to ease her loneliness by passing the time with them, despite the breach in propriety. Charlotte knew not all servants would have been so tolerant of her, and she appreciated Lizzy's openness all the more for it.

Over the days they spent together, Charlotte slowly pried information from the woman. Apparently, she had only been hired the day of the incident. In fact, the butler had sought her out through her cousin, the cookmaid, and she had not yet met Mr. Scarsdale. There had apparently not even been an opportunity for such an introduction since, according to Lizzy, Mr. Scarsdale had not so much as set foot in the townhouse since she had been hired.

Charlotte felt embarrassed by the relief she felt at the declaration. The idea of the sweet, pretty young Lizzy living and working in the same house as the dangerous…handsome man had sparked unwanted jealousy in her, and a contrary surge of protectiveness for her new friend. Not that she truly suspected Scarsdale to be the type of man to take liberties with his staff. He was arrogant, but in her limited estimation of him, she did not feel he was entitled.

Despite Lizzy's welcome company, by the end of the third day, Charlotte was so pent up and anxious that she could hardly sit still. She had taken to pacing the room with her arm in a sling.

This unexpected reprieve from her usual toil was quickly growing into a serious concern, and her mind was conjuring up countless avenues of ruination for her and her family.

First and foremost, had it become common knowledge that she was staying in Scarsdale's home? That alone would spell the end of the Aston family—or at least her involvement in it.

Second, did Freddie know what had happened? Had news of the duel leaked into the circulation of *ton* gossip? If it had, and anyone knew that Freddie had not made it to the duelling pitch, his bet would be forfeit, and Charlotte could not imagine where she might find the resources to recover from such a blow.

This led to her greatest concern: the bullet had lodged in her right shoulder. She could not write. How would she be able to pay for even the bare necessities? What if she lost her position because of her missing submissions? She had precious little stored away to protect them from immediate starvation in a worst-case scenario, but it would not last them long enough for her to get a new job. She certainly could not keep the enrolment office at Eton happy when they were already breathing down her neck for the twins' latest tuition payment.

Somehow, the last few payments had never reached the school, and now they were in arrears. Charlotte could not imagine where those carefully guarded cheques had gone. She did not want to examine the genuine possibility that her idiot brother had discovered their existence and rerouted them to his own pocket. Her little golden Frederick could never be so selfish.

These worries swamped her, and she was trying to outpace them in her circuitous path beside the window when the door opened.

"Lizzy, dear, do you think you might be able to pen a letter for me?"

"I have never been called Lizzy before, but if that is what it takes for you to call me dear, then please, by all means, carry on."

Charlotte whipped around, arm bouncing painfully in its sling.

"Mr. Scarsdale." Charlotte was frowning. Had he been this handsome the last time she saw him?

"What are you doing out of bed? You should be resting."

His dark hair was shorn unfashionably close to his head in the same way orphans' and prisoners' were to keep lice at bay. Somehow, though, on him, it looked soft and tempting to the touch, while simultaneously accenting the hard planes of his face.

He wore impeccably tailored evening clothes and held an elegant walking stick in one hand. Charlotte had always detested the gentlemanly accessory for its uselessness, but she suspected Scarsdale's was more a weapon than a crutch or affectation.

"I was not expecting you." She stood taller, rolling her shoulders back and wincing at the pain.

"No, I suppose you were not. Here I am, though. And though I imagine I cannot tout even a fraction of the usefulness of a 'Lizzy,' I would gladly offer my services as her stand-in. I do know how to read and write—if only passably."

Charlotte worried her lip between her teeth. She did not want Scarsdale to know of her business with her employer— or even that she had an employer—but desperation won out, and she nodded her head.

He swept over to the writing desk in the room's corner, folding his tall, athletic form into the elegant wooden chair, and pulled out a sheet of foolscap and a quill. She watched him with no small amount of reticence until he looked up at her and nodded expectantly.

She sighed and rubbed her good hand over her face. Why had she not learned how to write with both hands? How shortsighted of her.

∞∞∞

"Dear Mr. Keiler." Benjamin's hand paused at the masculine title. Who was Mr. Keiler?

Charlotte continued on, unaware of his pause. "Please accept my apologies for not keeping our agreed appointment on the fourteenth of March. I found myself indisposed and unable to send word. I am writing now to assure you that it will not happen again, and I hope you are not opposed to continuing our agreement. Sincerely, Aston."

At that, Benjamin looked up again. "Why do you sign with only your surname?"

He knew the question to be impertinent considering the private nature of the correspondence. But he could not fight the prickling irritation at the idea of Charlotte maintaining an illicit "acquaintanceship" with some man. And what was this missed appointment? God, if it were anything close to the salacious ideas he was already conjuring up—and surely it must be, for no respectable unwed lady would ever maintain a correspondence with a man who was not her brother or father—then he was perversely glad their little duel had caused her to miss the torrid rendezvous.

She did not look at him but instead kept her clinical gaze out the window. "So he does not realise I am a woman."

Thank god. The relief was perverse, and he kept his face impassive so she might not see how such a strange admission had doused the flame of envy in his chest. But why would she be concealing her identity in a private correspondence? Alertness pricked his ears; the familiar feeling, like a bloodhound on a scent, that there was a secret to be rooted out. Her tone brooked no further questions, and Benjamin made a show of sanding the ink and folding it into an envelope.

"Anything else?" He hoped so. This woman was proving to be far more intriguing than just the sister of a good-for-nothing earl. She had secrets. Big ones. He itched to unravel them.

Charlotte closed her eyes for a moment as if she were in pain again, and Benjamin longed to reach out and take her hand in his. The impulse was most unwelcome and made him irritable.

"Well?" He regretted the sharpness in the word.

"Just one more, please. I would not ask if I could do it myself." Her voice was small and strained, and he wanted to bash his own head in for his brusqueness. You could take the boy out of the gutter, but you could never wash that gutter stench off the boy.

Without a word, he pulled another page from the drawer and poised his quill above it.

"Dear Mr. Roberts and Mr. Finch of the Eton College tuition office, I apologise again for the missing fees for pupils, Marcus and Henry Aston. I have located the misdirected funds and am forwarding them to you forthwith. Sincerely, Frederick Aston Earl of Elford." She had her face pressed against the windowpane and did not look over when she finished speaking.

"Do you make a habit of not signing your own name to your correspondence?"

Charlotte closed her eyes. "Mr. Scarsdale, might I ask that you keep the contents of these letters to yourself? Or better yet, forget them altogether?"

"Charlotte." She did not seem to notice that he used her Christian name. "If you are in trouble, I can help you. You need only ask."

At that, her head whipped around to look at him directly. "I do not need charity. I have it under control. Thank you, Mr. Scarsdale."

"You may call me Benjamin if you'd like."

"That would be the height of impropriety."

"More improper than sharing a bed?" He grinned at her stormy expression.

"I did not agree to that arrangement. In fact, I requested to be returned to my home upon regaining consciousness."

Benjamin was relieved to see the fire return to her eyes. He did not like the defeated way she had looked out the window while she dictated her letters.

"That does not change the fact that you have been sleeping in my bed every night since then, my dear." He said it to provoke her, but the idea of her in his bed sent a thrill through him, culminating in a way that made him glad he was seated behind the desk.

"Sir, I once again would request the loan of a carriage to return me to my home."

He had pushed her too far.

The idea of sending her away from the safety of his home had anxiety chasing away the thrill of desire. "That is not necessary, Charlotte. You and your reputation are safe here."

"I no longer wish to trespass on your hospitality, *Mr.* Scarsdale." She emphasised the formal address. "If you do not loan me a vehicle, I will just hire a hackney cab."

She was bluffing. He knew for a fact that she had no money on her person, or likely in her possession at all, to pay for a hackney.

"It is not trespassing. I am the one who shot you, after all."

"Indeed, you did. But I consider the debt repaid. I would feel far more comfortable in my own home now."

"No." Benjamin was growing frustrated. He felt the situation slowly rolling out of control, and he did not like not having control.

"Excuse me?" Charlotte's lovely, faint eyebrows shot up in an almost comical expression of disbelief.

"I said, no. You may not have the use of my carriage because you will not be leaving here tonight, tomorrow, or any time before your shoulder has fully healed." He sounded dictating even to his own ears.

She gaped for a few moments before finding her words. "You cannot hold me hostage."

"I am not."

"Then what do you call keeping me in your bed chamber against my will and using the fate of an innocent woman to coerce me into staying?"

Benjamin frowned at that. "What the hell?"

"Lizzy. You will sack her if I leave? That is coercion."

"I will sack no one. I never sack my employees."

Despite the endless swirl of speculation about the myriad cruel and debaucherous acts people suspected he had done—a hazard of the reputation—that accusation pricked his anger. He knew what a job meant. Knew it was the line between a full belly and a cold gutter. He did not allow people to cross that line on his account.

His statement seemed to surprise Charlotte. She stood silent, her large brown eyes watching him from a too-drawn face. She needed more rest. Had Price been by today to check her stitches?

"As for the rest, I call it good sense." Benjamin stood and made a show of smoothing out his evening wear. "Now, I am going to Elysium. I expect you here when I return tomorrow."

With that, he turned and left the room, marching down the stairs to his waiting carriage.

Chapter Seven

Benjamin stood in the middle of the bustling little street that led to the heart of the Seven Dials. Mangy stray dogs chased each other around, fighting for scraps of rubbish that had accumulated in the gutters. Mangy stray children did much the same, weaving in and out between carts and washing women, startling caged chickens, and angering the few shop owners who tried to shoo the ruffians away from their goods—knowing full well the threat of the light fingers of the small, ill-clad, underfed urchins.

He had been one of these urchins—years ago now—but it never seemed long enough. The stench of the street was more familiar to him than his own skin. It was part of him. He wore it like a film—never able to scrub hard enough to rid himself of the grit and grime of the memories of his years alone. After Delia had died, he had tried to hold on to odd jobs. But the longer he lived on the street, the further he fell. He had spent years scraping himself back up from scrounging through these gutters. He had done things he was not proud of—anything to survive. And now he had.

Hell, some might even say he had thrived. But no amount of time, money, power, or distance he put between himself and those days could help him escape.

And now, here he was again. Back in the Dials. The last place he wanted to be.

It had not been hard to find out who Charlotte's Mr. Keiler was. The head of the Times' editorial columns. It had surprised him to discover that the man was a professional. A journalist. He had expected a fine lady of the *ton,* like Charlotte Aston, would be writing to a decorator or some haberdasher or other. Though perhaps not considering her family's financial state. But he would never have guessed she was in contact with the papers.

Even more surprising was *why.* He had sifted through the columns under Keiler's purview and found different pieces ranging from the latest in European horse racing to the political foibles of the Commons and Lords. It had been a weekly column about the state of London's working class that had caught his eye. Rather radical for the publication, but the times were changing. It was more than just the *ton* who paid for the news. There was certainly a market for the self-made merchants and businessmen of England. But even they would likely have no interest in the trials and tribulations of those on whose backs they made their money.

The column had drawn him in. The stories were first-hand accounts of the women and men he had struggled beside. Their lives on the streets. The horrors of the workhouses they toiled in. The brutality of the sicknesses that stole through their cramped quarters and took their loved ones and babes. He had no way of knowing these stories had any connection to Charlotte. The writer was listed as *Anonymous.* Not surprising considering the subversive nature of the contents. But something about the compassionate way the writer opened their writing to share someone else's voice had grabbed him. He would have followed up even if he were not hunting out Charlotte Aston's secrets. He had done this long enough to know that this feeling in his gut, this drive, could not be ignored and would lead to something valuable. He was never in a position to turn his nose up at something as valuable as a secret.

Now, however, standing in the roiling chaos of the mid-morning Towers Street, he was not so sure he wanted to follow this lead. He could turn around. He could go home.

But they had seen him. The grubby urchins had started swarming, whispering his name amongst themselves. He rarely went out to deal with issues on the streets anymore. He had enforcers for that now. Hired thugs who could wield physical might, so he could wield his knowledge. Blackmail was far more elegant than bloodying his knuckles. But that did not mean that in his leaner days, when he had been living hand to mouth, trying to build something, he had not carved out a substantial reputation. A reputation that seemed to have grown and taken on a life of its own, as legends in the back streets of London were wont to do. The beleaguered children stared up at him in awe, and as he made his way down the tight street, he felt gazes from stoops and shop windows follow him.

By the time he reached Annie's washhouse, his presence had preceded him.

"Thought I heard talk of some Master Toff lurking around here!" The rough Belfast brogue cut through the steam that filled the cramped courtyard.

Young women—some only girls—hunched over cauldrons of boiling water, stirring the murky contents with long wooden poles before pulling the washing out with their red hands, completely impervious to the scalding heat.

A short, round woman hobbled out from the back shop, pulling a laundry line taut above her head before slowly making her way over to Benjamin.

Annie Dolan was a termagant and always had been. There were no two ways about it. To some, she may have seemed an ordinary washing woman. As the proprietress of a relatively successful laundry service nestled deep in the wilds of St. Giles that served a low-earning, but wide class of clientele, she had far more influence than one might give her credit for.

As a boy, Benjamin had stuck to Annie's corner of the Dials, knowing that though she refused to take in orphans, she ruled her district with an iron fist and would not tolerate the outright abuse that many street youths endured. As with anything in life, the protection did not come for free. Anything that was filched on Annie's turf was to be deposited through the back slot of her shop. Her daughter-cum-secretary-cum-right-hand kept careful note of each deposit, and if you could get something good enough, there was a hot meal in it for you and a night sleeping in the safety of her gated courtyard. Benjamin had only managed it a few times, but he still remembered the relief of a night stretched on the cobbles beside the glowing embers of a wash fire. The knowledge that no footpad would knife him while he slept behind the locked gates.

"Annie." He could not help the smile that tugged his cheeks as the rough woman gave him an assessing look. "Glad to see you again."

"Hope you've not come to sleep on my floor again. Heard

tell of you running all the games in London. You've not fallen from grace again, have ye?"

The jab at his uncommon origins still hit home. He had arrived in London and landed on the streets within a year. Though he was just as down and out as the other boys running the streets, he had been different, and they had known. His diction and accent alone had signalled him as an outsider— one with less experience than they. Any difference, any weakness, was leapt upon and gouged out. He learned the hard way that if he wanted to make it—wanted to survive—he had best forget his lofty beginnings and keep his head down. It had been a lesson well learned.

He flexed his shoulders, conscious of the stares he was getting. "I have come to ask you a question. About a writer."

"A writer, ye say?" Her lilting voice was mocking, and she leaned against one of the poles that supported the intricate net of washing lines above her. "Not much use for a writer down here, have we?"

A chorus of faceless agreement came from behind the steam.

"A writer you may have spoken to."

He held up the old newsprint one of his scouts had procured. It was dated almost two years ago. But the story had sounded familiar. The columnist did not include any names in their stories. Like the author, the subjects remained anonymous. Somehow, this made their tales all the more intriguing. The reader could imagine themselves in their place. A woman who worked at the looms in a factory. A young hawker who slept behind the bakery in hopes of being able to steal a fistful of flour from the evening delivery to bring home to his hungry family. A night soil man. A fishmonger. And in this case, a laundress who had moved to London hoping for a better life and instead had been cheated by her husband and prospered anyway, running her own shop and employing girls and women on the street.

Annie eyed the paper and gave a nod. He knew she could not read. But he saw on her face that his hunch had been correct. "You spoke to this writer?"

"Aye." She nodded again and pressed her lips together. He would get nothing for free.

Benjamin fished a coin from his inside pocket, one that three different light-fingered thieves had already tried to slit. Pressing the coin into the woman's swollen red hand, she smiled at him.

"There's a good lad. Now, what do you want to know about this writer?"

"What can you tell me?" He knew better than to lead with questions. The best titbits were revealed when a person spoke, not knowing what he was looking for.

"Well, I suppose the most pertinent point was that she was a *she*."

Annie waited a moment, watching for a reaction to that news. But he did not let his expression change. Even as that alone confirmed his suspicions.

Nonplussed by his placid expression, Annie continued, "Pretty like. She was wearing nothing fancy. Workwoman's fare, same as the girls in the mills. Broadcloth—dark. Easy to wash, doesn't show coal dust or blood." She looked at a cauldron beside her, likely full of similar garments. "But there was somethin' 'bout her that seemed fancy. Spoke like you when you were wee. Fancy like. But not so bad as some toffs. Rate she was a governess a'fore the writin'. Or some such."

Benjamin was itching to ask more. He was almost certain it had been Charlotte.

"Blonde as all. Rare to see that colour on a grown woman. Funny face. Pretty—as I said. But strange, like."

Charlotte.

"And she came here to interview you two years ago?" He masked the eagerness in his voice. He was getting somewhere.

"Aye, just abouts 'suppose. Yes, it was when Lauren was looking at those new machines. I told her they were too expensive. Anyways, who needs a machine to wash when there are able bodies needin' employment?" Benjamin knew to interrupt her before she launched into more pontificating about the laundry industry.

"And you met with her once? Or more?"

"Oh, just the once. But you can ask some of the other girls. She spoke with them other times."

"Other times?" Just how often did Charlotte Aston make a habit of venturing into the stews?

"Oh yes, I had been seein' her around for probably a year already before she came askin' for my story. Thought it was a bit strange though. Who in the world would want to hear my story? Let alone write about it?"

"A year?" Benjamin was stunned.

"Oh, aye. Thought she was some charity worker at first. The way she kept speakin' with the ladybirds. Thought she was tryin' to turn them to Christ or some such. But no. She just spoke to them. Heard their stories and wrote some down. Strange gel."

Benjamin did not miss the look of respect on the woman's weathered face. Somehow, Charlotte had been venturing into the bowels of London alone to speak to the dregs of society, those everyone else in her circle ignored at best and despised at worst, and had taken down their stories to share with the world.

More than that, it seemed she had *charmed* them.

It had been a long time since someone had baffled him. After years of seeing desperation draw out the worst in people, and then more years teasing out the worst that they tried to hide, Benjamin considered himself a practical witness to the truths of humanity. He had not thought himself capable of surprise. But here he was, standing in the stews of his youth where Charlotte Aston had made her mark.

∞∞∞

"I do not think you have thought this through, Ben." Wells was pouring himself a glass of whisky from the sideboard in Benjamin's office.

"Don't call me that."

"It is your name, Ben, and I will use it. As is my right, being one of the few people who put up with you." Wells took a hearty swig of the amber liquid and sighed in an agitating display of unbothered aristocratic pleasure.

Benjamin grumbled at the stack of papers on his desk. Since leaving the Dials, he had been in a foul mood. He was clever enough to know that one source was never enough to get at every side of a secret and had spent the rest of the afternoon interviewing people who had been interviewed by Charlotte. By the end, he was warring with a riot of confused emotions.

He now knew for certain that she had begun writing long before her father's death. Nearly two years before. So it had not been the financial necessity that had driven her to be so careless with her safety, though after his rounds today, he was certain none of the invisible sentries of Covent Garden would have let a single thing befall her. The loyalty she elicited was as strong as that he had fought tooth and nail for his whole life—even more so for it having been given without asking. He wondered if she even knew the power she now held. The foolish woman. What if they had not taken to her? What if, instead of being flattered and touched by her interest, the ruffians of the streets had taken offence at the high-born lady swooping in and nosing around their turf? She would have been like a lamb to the slaughter.

But on top of all of this, he had discovered another thing about Charlotte Aston. A deeper, darker secret that someone had paid handsomely to keep hidden. It was the type of secret Benjamin Scarsdale specialised in. And for once, it was a secret he was not happy to hold.

With the disconcerting worries ricocheting inside his skull, he wanted nothing more than to polish off the bottle in Wells' hand and take to the playing floor. Maybe he would be lucky, and some overstuffed toff would be causing a scene. He was itching for a fight, and a fist to a reckless and titled fop's face would be supremely satisfying. What good was owning a gaming hell if he could not take advantage of such opportunities?

But alas, the reality of owning a gaming hell, or any number of profitable establishments, was staring him in the face. Papers on top of papers, piles of correspondence, invoices, customs sheets, ledgers, and receipts were the truth of all business. True success came from boring, tedious responsibility, and Benjamin was fully aware of the alternative.

"Don't you have something else to do?" Benjamin demanded. "If I recall correctly, you are my business partner, not just a silent investor. Though I would not mind you silent."

Wells laughed and sat in the chair opposite Benjamin's desk, propping his feet up on the polished mahogany. "You shot the girl. Of course, you feel some responsibility for her welfare. But I do not know if this is the way to go about it."

"Feet off my desk. I do not want to talk about Charlotte." Benjamin regretted his slip immediately.

"Oh, Charlotte, is it?" Wells thumped his booted feet on the ground and leaned forward, snatching the paper Benjamin was reading from the desk.

"Wipe that shit-eating grin from your face before I wipe it off for you."

"Your bark is worse than your bite, Scarsdale. I am not scared of you." Wells held the paper aloft, teasingly waggling his eyebrows. "Come on, let's have it. What hold does this Charlotte have over you?"

"I told you; I do not wish to talk about her." He snatched the letter back from his friend's hand and picked up his quill again.

"Even so. I feel it is my responsibility to tell you that, whatever it is you are planning here, it is not the way to go about it." When Benjamin did not respond, Wells continued. "Trapping the princess in the tower will not win you a kiss, you moron. In fact, that makes you the ogre, or maybe the wicked witch."

At that, Benjamin sighed and rubbed his forehead. "A bit early in the night to be spouting nonsense, don't you think?"

Wells waved a hand. "If you fancy her, *don't*." He frowned

down at the scotch in his hand. "Though you should hardly need my advice there. Women are trouble. Ladies are even more. I know you like to think of yourself as the Robin-Hood type, but she is not your problem. Return her to where she came from." He gestured to the letter Benjamin had just folded into an envelope. "You need to get out of this before you lose your bearings. It is deep water, my friend."

Benjamin just scowled. "She is a lady. And she is recovering from a gunshot wound, you idiot. I do not fancy her; I am simply rectifying the problem she has caused."

He tried to mask the defensiveness in his voice, surprised that the comment stung. He knew he was no hero. He did not consider himself to be anything resembling Robin Hood. And he hardly needed advice from the Duke of Wells. They may have grown up on adjoining estates, but their lives had never been remotely the same.

"I do not see why that needs to be done from your town-house. Send her home, wait until she recovers, and accept her effusive gratitude then. Ladyship aside, fancy her or not, a woman in your debt is a woman in your debt. Just do not go making foolish decisions."

Wells winked and wiggled his brows at Benjamin over his glass, briefly looking like the boy he had spent his childhood with—before his mother moved him and his sister to London. The reminder blackened his mood even further.

"You can be a real ass sometimes, Wells. You know that?"

"Takes one to know one, lady shooter. Anyway, you would not care for me so much if I were not."

Without responding, Benjamin stood and yanked the bell pull behind his desk. Within moments, a young footman was opening the door. "Yessir?" The boy's accent was rough and thick, fresh from the depths of the Seven Dials.

He handed the boy a pack of letters. "Boyd, see that this gets delivered posthaste."

The boy dipped a bow and closed the door behind him. "Yessir. Of course, sir."

"She won't thank you for it." Wells's voice was a warning Benjamin knew to be valid, and as he walked back behind his desk, he plucked the whisky from his friend's hand and downed the rest of the glass in one go.

Chapter Eight

Back in the foyer of Aston House, Charlotte clumsily felt around in the dark, looking for a match to light the stub of the candle left on the side table for just such occasions.

After Scarsdale had left the room, Charlotte immediately set about gathering her things to leave. Considering she had only had her brother's old clothes, it did not take long. She could not write a note to tell Lizzy where she had gone. And she did not stop to examine why she had taken Scarsdale at his word when he had said he would not sack Lizzy. It did not matter, his reputation. She had known it was the truth the moment he said it. Something in his eyes. Something in her gut. Anyway, it was not important. Lizzy's livelihood was safe, and Charlotte had no way of knowing when Scarsdale would return.

She briefly considered changing into the clothes from the duel and leaving the fine muslin gown Lizzy had dressed her in that morning, but the idea of reaching behind her to undo the buttons was untenable. She resolved to wear it home and post it back with a letter of thanks. Charlotte did not want to owe this man, or any man, more than she already did.

She had walked the blocks home. There was no money for the hackney she had blustered about. Charlotte was grateful for her brother's riding coat, for it protected her from a particularly strong deluge of rain and concealed her gender, which, even in the hallowed streets of Mayfair, was a considerable liability.

What should have been no more than half an hour's walk stretched into an hour and then an hour and a half, and by the time she slipped her key into the front door and pushed inside, she almost collapsed with fatigue against the bare marble of the foyer.

Gone were the days when a butler would be standing by, ready to fetch the servants to prepare a hot bath and a cup of tea for their wet and weary mistress. Instead, unable to find a match, Charlotte half-dragged herself up the stairs to her room and collapsed on the bed, too tired to even take off her coat.

∞∞∞

Charlotte dreamt the entire night of hot tea and strong, warm arms pulling her up from the ground. It was not until late in the morning that she awoke feeling too hot and too cold, all at once. Her mouth was dry, and her head felt like it was ballooning from her neck, swollen and thick.

When she pried her eyes open and tried to blink away the uncomfortable grit that seemed to have accumulated over the night, she was relieved to be met with the familiar sight of her own bedroom. She pushed herself upright and fought the wave of nausea that reminded her that a bullet had been dug from her flesh only days before.

It was probably time to change the bandage. She looked down at the coat and the crumpled dress she still wore. How would she manage that?

No, the wound would have to wait to be dressed and cleaned until her brother got home.

The idea of asking Freddie for help after all the trouble he had caused made her already low spirits plummet. Charlotte shook her head and pushed out of bed, ignoring the dizziness and pain that ensued. There was nothing to be done about it, and any amount of indulgence in her own woes would destroy the entire family.

With that sobering thought in mind, she made her way out of the room and down the stairs. The sound of voices down the hall drew her towards the study. Strange. No one but she had been in the study for ages—at least not since their father died.

As she drew closer, she could make out Freddie's voice. He sounded happy, but not in his usual, near-manic way. His voice was relaxed, truly joyous as it had always been before the mantle of the earldom had landed on his shoulders. That could not be good

Warily, Charlotte knocked and pushed the door open. Sure enough, Freddie was sitting on the edge of their father's desk —her desk, as she had come to think of it. He was holding a crystal glass in hand, raising it high in jubilation and sloshing its contents onto the unpolished wood of the floor where an expensive Aubusson rug had once lain. Better it stain the wood than reach his mouth, Charlotte thought uncharitably. Her mood had gone from bad to worse upon finding this scene.

"Freddie, is it not a little early in the day to be drinking?"

She hated the voice she used when reprimanding her little brother. Charlotte had never aspired to be the harping sister bent on ruining all his fun. But someone had to be responsible. Even before she passed from a slow, wasting disease, her stepmother, Veronica, had been more of a distant patron than a mother figure for the boys.

For once, Freddie did not seem the least bit bothered by her comment. "Ah, Charlotte! Lovely to see you! Where have you been?"

Charlotte gaped. *Where had she been? Had he really just asked her that? After she literally took a bullet for him?* She was seeing red.

Before she could snap at him, Freddie gestured to the high-backed chair diagonal from him. "Charlotte, may I present Lord Deering? Deering, my sister, Lady Charlotte. You have met before, haven't you?"

Charlotte's blood ran cold. Deering pushed up from the chair with an audible huff and turned, giving Charlotte a perusing stare as he gave the slightest bow. His mouth curled into something of a sneer after looking at her crumpled and dirtied ensemble. "Lady Charlotte, it is a pleasure to meet you again."

They had met a handful of times before at society functions. Every time, Charlotte had engineered a quick escape. The way Deering leered at her and rarely gazed above her neck made her instincts flare. Every lady of the *ton*—and certainly every one outside it as well—knew the look of a lech.

Somehow, Deering was worse. Something about him put her teeth on edge—as if he might leap out and drag her away by her hair, even in the middle of a ballroom. Or her study.

"Lord Deering." Charlotte returned the barest of nods. She

did not like this man in her house, and she did not want to talk to Freddie in front of him.

"Charlotte, I have wonderful news." Freddie seemed oblivious to any uneasiness in the room.

"Does it have to do with Lord Deering's visit?" Charlotte kept the man in question locked in her periphery as she addressed her brother.

"No. Yes, I suppose. Not really." Freddie had clearly already consumed a generous amount of scotch.

The scotch she kept in the larder for medicinal purposes, she suspected, considering they had not had the funds for such extravagance in months.

Freddie pulled himself back on track. "What I mean to say is, Lord Deering came here to clear a few debts on my behalf. Very generous, indeed." He raised his glass again in Deering's direction. "But just as we were settling in to discuss the matter, the post arrived, and it seems the debts have already been paid by someone else." He waved a handful of letters in his hand.

Charlotte could not conceal her shock and rushed to snatch the papers from him. "By whom?"

"I do not know. Some anonymous benefactor."

"A guardian angel, more like," Charlotte muttered under her breath as she read through missive after missive from various clubs and dens of iniquity. The sheer number of cleared debts was dizzying. She'd had no idea how bad their financial situation really was. "Freddie, this is unbelievable."

Out of the corner of her eye, she saw Deering's face contort. "I do not understand how this is possible, Lord Elford. I thought I held the majority of your debts." The tone of his voice had Charlotte taking another step back, warning bells clanging in her ears.

"I thought so too!" Freddie was still effervescent in his relief. "But it seems this mystery champion has negotiated even the ones you covered. I am sure you can recoup your payments forthwith."

Charlotte eyed Deering warily. He pressed his thin, grey mouth into a tight line, and she suspected he was barely holding his civility in check.

"Oh, be happy for me, Deering." Freddie jutted out his chin in the way he had as a boy when the maid packed away his favourite toy soldiers before he was done with them. Despite nearly two years as the earl, Charlotte still felt like her brother was playacting at being grown. A moody and recalcitrant boy dressing up and masquerading as a man, still completely oblivious to the reality of his position. "Our problems are solved!"

That was the wrong thing to say. Charlotte stood perfectly still as Deering pressed a long exhale through his nose, pursed his lips, and nodded. "Congratulations, Lord Elford. I will take my leave of you. Lady Charlotte." He gave her another skin-crawling gaze and then left without another word.

"Grumpy old coot." Freddie frowned at the door Deering closed behind him.

Charlotte stared at the door too, a foreboding feeling settling into her gut. A man like Deering would not be put off so easily.

"Can you believe this, Charlie?" She could not fight the small smile that came at Freddie's nickname for her. He used it only when he was especially elated, and it always made her heart warm. "What a stroke of good fortune! I knew my luck was coming in!" He clapped her on the shoulder, and she yelled out in pain.

"Why, Charlie, what is the matter? Did I hurt you?"

Charlotte sucked in a breath and closed her eyes until the room stopped spinning. "No, no." There were more important things to deal with. "Who would do this for you, Freddie?"

"I haven't the foggiest!" he chirped happily as he made his way to the sideboard to pour himself another drink.

Yes, Charlotte saw, it was the medicinal scotch. The household budget would not stretch for another bottle. Maybe a cheap gin. But she shivered at the thought of buying a bottle at a gin house. Something about the hold blue ruin could take on a person—she had seen it time and again during her writing. Children, starving because their mothers could not bear to spend on anything but the poison. The same mothers, who in moments of lucidity were consumed with shame at what the drink drove them to do. Maybe once in her younger days, she would have judged them for it. Would have hated them for their weakness. But she had seen enough now to understand. It was an illness. A sickness they could not fight on their own. A sickness she suspected her own brother suffered from. And so, as she watched Freddie pour another glass, she could not stomach the idea of replacing it.

"I tell you, Charlie, lady fortune is finally favouring me. First, that puffed-up cit Scarsdale calls off the duel—" He stopped as if he knew he had slipped.

"Called it off?" Charlotte's head snapped up from the letters she was sifting through.

Freddie just waved it off. "Not to worry, Charlie. It was never actually going to happen. It is just something gentlemen do. A code of honour. And Scarsdale issued the necessary apology before matters escalated. Right too. At least he has some idea of his betters."

Charlotte's head was spinning. Had Rowley cooked up this excuse to appease her brother's ridiculously inflated ego? Or had Benjamin really issued an apology to her dimwitted brother to conceal her own involvement at the price of his own reputation?

Freddie carried on obliviously. "And now this! Whoever the chap is, he'd better make himself known. I am of the mind to buy him every round of drinks he could ever want!"

"With what money?" Charlotte mumbled again, mostly to herself as she sifted through the open letters on the desk.

None gave any indication of who had settled the accounts. Only that the debts had been wiped clean, and Freddie's credit was once again restored. One proprietor had even signed below the note with a kiss. Charlotte saw the red lip colour below a postscript from a Missus Fannie Bulette, professing her hope to depend on Frederick's continued patronage.

She bit back her admonition. Of course, Freddie had run up a debt at a brothel. Likely more than one.

Freddie continued chattering away about the plans he had now that he was freed up, and Charlotte carefully stacked the letters together and put them aside in a neat pile by her other correspondence. There was another unopened letter left on the desk. She picked it up and saw the return address was the Eton tuition office. Her heart dropped to her stomach. They were going to expel Henry and Marcus. She had dreaded this letter for months now.

"Freddie." She held up the letter. "When did this one come?"

Freddie looked disinterested, clearly having dismissed anything that was not sent from one of his favourite haunts.

"I don't know. With the rest of them, I assume."

Charlotte ripped open the envelope and flipped open the letter. "Dear Lord Elford, We send our sincerest thanks for the deposit of Masters Marcus and Henry's missing term tuition payment, as well as your generous donation to the school. We look forward to hosting the young gentlemen for the remainder of their education and appreciate your continued patronage. Sincerely, Mr. William Roberts and Mr. Elery Finch."

She needed to sit down. Now.

"Charlie, you really do not look well. Shall I send for the doctor?"

"We can't afford a doctor, Freddie." Charlotte rubbed her forehead.

"What do you mean we can't afford a doctor?" Freddie laughed derisively. "Have you not been here for the last half an hour? Everything is paid. We are free!"

"Freddie." Charlotte could not summon the energy to be patient with him. "Don't you see? This just means we are in someone else's debt."

"Well, until the man in question comes a'knocking, I will consider it an act of divine benevolence." He wrinkled his nose and huffed like he did when he was a little boy. "Why do you always have to be such a dark cloud, Charlotte? We should be celebrating."

"I am not a dark cloud. I am pragmatic."

Normally, she would be angry at her brother's insult, but the wind had gone out of her sails, and she was completely exhausted, not to mention dizzy. When was the last time she had eaten? Did they even have anything in the house that was edible? She had not been to the market this week, so likely, no.

"Pragmatic or not, you haven't got the faintest idea how to have fun. I pity you, Charlotte." She looked up at him in disbelief. "I prefer to enjoy life. And I am going to do just that." Before she could conjure up a response that properly conveyed her frustration, Freddie had left the room.

"The fool." Charlotte shook her head and leaned back in the chair, holding up the letter from Eton and staring at the names she had only just dictated the day before to a man who most assuredly had not forgotten the exchange as she had requested.

There was only one thing to do now.

Chapter Nine

Benjamin had not been home to his townhouse since last night. He still felt like a complete ass for the way he had treated Charlotte, and he was not ready to face her justified anger yet. He was even less ready to face the spinning, gut-twisting sensations that her presence elicited. The loss of complete control he usually maintained over both himself and his surroundings was disconcerting, at the least, and dangerous at worst.

After returning from the Dials, he had slept half the afternoon in his rooms above his office but then came down to the club floor after waking and being unable to fall back asleep. The windows high above the carpeted rotunda were open wide to air out the building from the previous night, and the afternoon sun slanted in on dust motes, momentarily blinding Benjamin.

"You look like shit," Elk called from across the room where he was lounging on an ornate settee, book dangling from one hand.

"Good morning to you too," Benjamin grumbled, squinting over at his second, and last, true friend. "Aren't you supposed to be planning a wedding?"

Alexander Burke, Marquess of Elkington, had returned to London only weeks earlier after nearly three years of sporadic travelling throughout the continent and further afield, and had announced himself betrothed to the second-eldest daughter of the Earl of Ravenswood.

The Wylde sisters were well known in both Edinburgh and London for living up to their surname. Elsie Wylde was widely regarded as a true spinster blue stocking by the ton—the most disappointing thing a beautiful woman could be. How little they knew.

She and Benjamin had met at one of his first, more legitimate, soirees just as he was getting a foothold in the business of entertainment for the idle rich. She had proven an interesting acquaintance, intelligent and young—full of secrets. Secrets that Benjamin now kept—though unlike all the other secrets he traded in, he had no intention of cashing in on her currency. She did not deserve it, and neither did Elk.

Charlotte Aston did not deserve to have her secrets traded either. The thought flitted across his mind, and he shooed it away.

Though he would never admit it, it warmed his cold, hardened heart that Elsie Wylde had landed his friend. Or, more accurately, his friend had landed her. If only it did not stir this dark loneliness within him.

Elkington grinned the self-satisfied smile of a man happily ensnared. "Elsie's family has it well in hand. I think I just get in the way."

The idea of Elkington ensconced in a cosy domestic scene with his betrothed and their loving families shot a bolt of envy through Benjamin. He shook it off. Elkington and, more importantly, Elsie, deserved all the joy that had come to them, and Elk certainly did not deserve Benjamin's surliness.

"I apologise, Elk. Congratulations again. I am so happy for you and Lady Elsie."

"Thank you, Scarsdale." Elkington stood and clasped hands with Benjamin. "It means the world to hear you say it. I only hope you find such happiness."

Benjamin scoffed. "Marriage is for toffs and paupers. I have no use for it."

Undeterred, Elkington shook his head and looked wistfully up at the slanting rays of sunlight making their way up the wall. "Someday, a bonnie lass will come along and change your mind, just you wait and see." He gave the words a Scottish lilt, imitating his new fiancée's natural brogue.

Benjamin felt a prickle of frustration again. Why could his friends never understand that he was not destined for the lives they lived? He had fallen too low—had started too low—for that ever to be possible. "What is it that you are here for?"

"I am part owner of this place. What reason do I need to stop by now and again?" Elkington made a show of looking affronted.

Benjamin gave him an unimpressed look.

"Alright, I came to ask a favour." Benjamin laughed. There it was. "What say you to a few drinks and a chat with your old pal?"

"I say you just want to dip into my stores of foreign spirits before your leg is well and truly shackled. Though I suppose I can indulge it just this once." Benjamin clapped his friend's back, and they made their way across the floor to his office.

∞∞∞

The two men drank and talked together until the club patrons began filtering in. A knock on his office door broke their reverie, and Boyd poked his head around the door.

"There's a lady here, sir."

Benjamin did not sit up in his chair. "There are quite a few, Boyd. You know Elysium is open to women. As long as they have money in their pockets, I don't much care who is allowed in."

Boyd looked uneasy. "Yes, but she is not the usual type of lady."

"Butler and Harvey know not to let prostitutes in, my boy. Not to worry. It is not that kind of establishment." Boyd was an excitable type and had only been hired off the streets a few months ago. He was still settling into the change of clientele he saw.

"Begging your pardon, sir, but she is not a ladybird either. She is a *lady* lady. And a pretty one too if you look past the clothes." He looked like he thought he'd said too much.

Benjamin felt a trickle of unease at the boy's description. "Is she tall? And fair?"

Boyd nodded. "Like a fairy." He squinted his eyes. "Are fairies tall?" His brow furrowed in serious thought.

It was nice to see the moment of whimsy on the young boy's face. Benjamin knew only too well how quickly all flights of fancy were snuffed out in the cold, hard rabbit warren of the Dials. But the import of Boyd's statement quickly pierced the moment, making Benjamin's jaw clench.

Benjamin's chair gave a thud on the plush rug as he rocked it back onto all four legs. Boyd jumped. "Don't worry, lad.

You are not the one in trouble." He ruffled the boy's hair as he whisked past him into the hall and out onto the gaming floor, Elkington close on his heels with an anticipatory gleam in his eye.

"Who is this fairy of yours, Ben?"

"She is not a fairy—I mean, she is not mine. Not my fairy."

Elkington had the good sense to hold his tongue, but he watched with a barely suppressed grin as Benjamin scanned the already-packed gaming floor.

Amongst the swirling tide of masked revellers, it took no effort at all to spot Charlotte Aston's bare face in the crowd. Not that it would have anyway, Benjamin thought, taking in her rumpled appearance. She was still wearing the dress he had bought for her and passed on to Lizzy. Though he had the surreal feeling that he could have found her beautiful face even if he were blindfolded.

She locked eyes with him only a moment after he'd found her, and she squared her shoulders, meeting his gaze straight on. She looked ready to march into battle, his elfin queen. *No*, Benjamin gave himself a mental shake, *not his*.

But she could be. The whisper of her secrets caressed his whirling mind, and he shuddered.

Charlotte began making her way through the crowd toward them, head held high, ignoring the stares of the other patrons.

"Ah." The one syllable from Elkington was far too knowing.

"Lady Charlotte, what a pleasure it is to see you out and about. But are you sure it is wise for you to be up so soon, considering your condition?" Benjamin fought to keep his tone cool, charming, and solicitous. He knew the leading statement would provoke her, and he was secretly gratified when her eyes flared.

"Your condition?" Elkington's voice was raised nearly an octave above his usual baritone as he arched his eyebrows and gave Benjamin a questioning look.

She scowled at both of the men. "I am not…expecting. He shot me." At her matter-of-fact declaration, Elkington's eyebrows shot up even higher, and then he tipped his head back and laughed uproariously. "Alexander Burke, Marquess of Elkington. Pleased to make your acquaintance…"

"Lady Charlotte Aston." Benjamin supplied, his throat grasping at the words as if he could keep her name to himself—and in so doing, squire the captivating woman away from prying eyes.

Elkington reached to take her hand in greeting, but she winced and shook her head ever so slightly. "Ah, yes. The gunshot wound in question. Well, in that case, I will take my leave of you. I imagine the two of you have much to discuss. Lady Charlotte, a pleasure."

"Likewise, my lord." She did not curtsy, as was customary. But she did give Elkington a tight smile—as if even the smallest of formalities were wearing down her last reserves.

She needed to lie down. And take some broth. Benjamin would have the cook make her something warm and fortifying. Maybe the housekeeper, Clarance, could mix her up a poultice and a draught of the sleeping herbs she had made en masse when some of the staff had come down with the grippe last winter.

Elkington started down the stairs behind Charlotte and had the audacity to look back and throw a wink at Benjamin. "Good luck," he mouthed before he descended the rest of the stairs, an unnatural buoyancy to his step.

Benjamin ignored him and mapped the dark smudges

beneath Charlotte's eyes and the hollows in her cheeks and forehead. Had he really seen her only yesterday? Her condition had worsened. And clearly, she had not stayed in his chambers at the house in Hanover Square, where she should be resting. Why had his staff not alerted him to her absence? He reached out almost unconsciously to offer her a steadying hand. "Really, you should not be—"

Charlotte interrupted him. "I am here to repay my brother's debt."

The words stopped Benjamin dead in his tracks. The steel in her tone matched that in her spine. He was not getting out of this conversation.

"Please follow me if you would."

Chapter Ten

She looked terrible.

Now that he was seated across from her by the fire in his office, a tea tray between them, he could see her more clearly. More wisps of hair had escaped her braided crown than could be called fashionable. Her brother's coat was still pulled over her shoulders, and Benjamin suspected it was because she could not actually remove it without help. The dress she had been wearing the night before was crumpled almost beyond recognition, and the hem was damp and muddied as if she had been trekking through the London streets all day.

More concerning than anything though, was her face. It was leeched of almost all colour besides bright spots of red high on her cheekbones that he doubted were painted rouge. She still sat with her back straight and both hands folded in her lap—where had her sling gone? She looked miserably exhausted.

"I will not insult either of us by beating about the bush." Her voice was steady and composed, though her gaze remained fixed on the fire. "I know you have bought up my brother's debts, and I am here to repay you."

Benjamin remained silent. He would not dispute her claim. He suspected she would not stand for it.

"As I am sure you are aware, we do not currently have the funds to pay back the whole sum. Or any of it, if I am being honest." She rubbed her forehead. It seemed like a habitual gesture—something she often did to rub away the burdens that had been unfairly dumped on her shoulders.

"So, I have come to propose an alternative payment." Benjamin's ears perked up at that, but he did not dare respond or even move.

"I have been working as an editorial author—well, journalist really—for a newspaper over the last year. I have some samples of my work here." She pulled a sheaf of papers from her coat pocket and passed them to him, their hands touching carelessly in the exchange, sending his pulse spiking. He took them and pretended to read over one while she continued. "I am a diligent worker, and I can carry out any correspondence, bookkeeping, invoice drafting, receipt duplicating—any clerical work, really. I know it would take ages for me to work enough to cover the debt, but I am committed to repaying you." She said the last in a rush as if she was worried she would not get the words out.

Benjamin was silent for a moment, assessing the woman sitting across from him, glowing in the firelight. "No."

Her gaze snapped to his. "No?" Her nostrils flared. "What do you mean, no?"

He steepled his fingers under his nose, affecting a nonchalance he suspected would infuriate her further. "I mean, no. It is not a terribly complicated word, and yet, you seem to take issue with it on a regular basis."

She was fuming now. He loved it.

"I take issue with your obstinate nature and heavy-handedness. You are not the King of England, sir. You have no right to meddle and control as you do."

No one had ever spoken to him like that. It was as if his reputation meant nothing to her in the face of her righteous indignation. It was careless, really, and Benjamin suspected she would not usually allow herself such a slip of her control. Which made him wonder—was her injury making her sloppy? Or was it something about him—them—which made her feel free enough to loosen the reins? It was an intoxicating thought that settled in his chest.

"No, I am not the King of England. Would not care to be either. No real power there." He waved a hand lazily and fought a smile as she watched it in baffled fury. "No, Charlotte, I say no because your plan is flawed."

She furrowed her brow at him, clearly unused to being told she was wrong. She went to cross her arms and stopped, sniffing painfully. For a moment, Benjamin lost his nerve. *This is who you are.* The Master of London's Secrets. He had not gotten here by being soft. Would not have survived.

"Flawed how?" She was not going to bend. Amazing woman.

Benjamin carried on as if nothing had happened. "For one, how do you plan on supporting your family outside of your work here? Surely you do not expect to be paid a salary on top of your debt repayments."

He saw her confidence waver, but he continued on. "More to the point, though, I do not need a secretary. I have all those tasks well in hand." At that, he saw her deflate slightly, her mind clearly spinning to come up with a solution. "However, I have another proposition."

She regarded him with wary eyes. He had not planned this. *Liar.* Ever since he had collected her secrets, he had been heading down this path.

He hated himself a little more for it every step he took, but the opportunity was too good to pass up. "I would like you to become my mistress."

She stared at him, jaw slack, shock written all over her face. He did not move. He did not even breathe. And then, she laughed. She threw her head back against the seat and laughed, loud rolling laughs that sounded like spring and heaven and the green countryside of his youth. He could not catch his breath, watching her laugh. It was as if her face broke open and a whole new woman emerged. A beautiful, angelic woman. He could not look away.

Chapter Eleven

After a few unsuccessful attempts, Charlotte reigned herself in. Her side was splitting from the force of the laughter, and her cheeks ached and burned. She had not laughed like that in a long time, not since she could remember.

She pressed her good hand to her stomach. "You cannot be serious."

"I cannot?" Benjamin Scarsdale regarded her curiously from across the hearth. He had not shifted position since his preposterous proposition, and his relaxed, lounging form looked like a panther resting in its domain—in control and always ready to pounce.

She swallowed another gulp of air. "Of course, you cannot. Gaming hell owners do not have unmarried ladies as their mistresses. It is absurd."

"I am hardly just a gaming hell owner."

He picked up a filigreed letter opener from the table beside him and rolled it negligently along the upholstered chair arm. She knew as well as the rest of London how much more this man was. There was no place in this city his reach did not extend—the whole of England, really. He was a dangerous man, and she would do well to remember that. Funny how easy she found it to forget all of that.

"Is this rule written somewhere? I admit I have never read of it myself." He drew the flat of his thumb across the blade. Her breath caught at the perfect display of controlled power and intimidation—and something else… Sensuality?

"Oh, my God. You are serious." All the laughter fell away, and in its place emerged an uncomfortable tingling awareness. Dread, she supposed.

"Of course I am serious. Do I look like a man to waste my own time?" One perfect dark eyebrow arched mockingly at her.

She could not find a response to that, so she shook her head.

"In payment of your brother's debts, I offer you the position of my mistress for…" He tilted his head, pulling the thoughts from the heavy air as he spoke, "A month." He set down the letter opener and plucked an empty glass tumbler from the small, ornate chess table that sat beside his chair, twirling it in his hands. Those strong, lethal hands. They could never be still. "Beyond that, I will pay you one thousand pounds in order to provide for your family after our arrangement has ended, so you may have time to find another means of income at your leisure."

Charlotte was speechless.

"I must say it would be a considerably smaller commitment than that of working off his debt by writing letters for me for the foreseeable future. But of course, the decision is completely up to you."

He regarded her with cool blue eyes. They were icy and predatory in a way that made her want to back into the chair's cushions—or lean forward.

This was madness. She could not seriously be considering this. Her head was swimming. The pain in her shoulder had begun to shoot down her arm and back, and the room felt impossibly warm, yet her hands were freezing.

She had no other options. This was the lifeline she had needed, cast out by the most alluring man she had ever met. How could she say no? How could she say yes?

Something of her thoughts must have played across her face, for he leaned forward, bracing strong arms on his legs, the expensive fabric of his superfine jacket and expertly tailored buckskin breeches doing nothing to conceal the raw power of those limbs. She had the sudden, queer impression that the two of them were playing a game of cards—the highest stakes game of cards she had ever played in her life— and he was about to lay down his ace.

"How is your Italian, Lady Charlotte?" His words were benign. His cultured accent almost lazy in its relaxed tone. A casual question, much more suited to a sun-dappled drawing room and a polite afternoon call.

Her mouth went dry. Her tongue was coated in heavy sawdust.

He knew.

How?

His lips quirked, as if she had asked the question out loud. His eyes were sharp and, if she were not sitting so close, she would say amused. But the emotion behind them was not nearly so straightforward. There was more there. Calculation. Power. She had the fleeting thought that anyone in her shoes might see the devil himself peering back at her.

And perhaps it was her own feelings she saw reflected back

at her. Deep behind all the cunning and subterfuge, she saw pain. Desperation.

"My Italian is passable. Though my education on the subject was cut short." She managed to force the words out, and she caught the fleeting spark of surprise in his eyes. He recognised her challenge then. Good.

He leaned back, and she felt herself drifting. Lord, but he was handsome. And perhaps he really was the devil. It was particularly hot in here. "I cannot give you a proper answer just now. I have to think on it." Her head felt fuzzy, and all the events of the day—of the week—seemed to finally be catching up to her.

She watched in wonder as he processed her answer. First, he looked pensive, then his face broke into a shocking, dazzling smile, and her heart skipped a beat.

"Spoken like a true woman of business." His face grew serious as if he were trying to rein in his reaction. "So you will consider it?"

"Yes, I will consider your offer, Mr. Scarsdale." The admission felt like a weight lifted from her shoulders, and she breathed a dizzying sigh of relief. Was she truly entertaining his proposition? His threat was clear enough. But she was not sure it even mattered. She was not sure it would have any bearing on her decision.

He took her left hand in his, placing a delicate kiss on the back and then the palm, sending shivers up her arm. She should not be allowing such liberties, a small voice in the back of her mind was saying. But she did not pay the voice any heed.

"Call me Benjamin, please."

"Then I suppose you should call me Charlotte. Though I

have not actually accepted your proposal." The word was wrong. "Proposition," she corrected. Her head felt full of cotton. She could not make her gaze focus on his face. "Did you slip something into my drink again?" She could feel the frown weighing down her eyes. "I am still furious about that, by the way."

"Charlotte, are you alright?" His voice sounded far away, and she felt his hand on her cheek, then brushing hair from her forehead. She frowned. The touch was surprisingly gentle, and she leaned into it.

"No, I am not alright. You shot me. Remember?" That was all she could manage before she floated away.

∞∞∞

"Infection has set in. The bandage should have been changed twice a day. It looks like this wound has not been cleaned in at least thirty-six hours." Doctor Price wiped his hands on a clean cloth after irrigating and redressing the wound.

"I did not know she had not been changing it. I did not even know she had gone home. She was not supposed to leave my townhouse." Benjamin felt especially defensive when Price glanced up at him through his thick spectacles. Those glasses—what was the use of a doctor who could hardly even see?

"Well, it doesn't matter now. Either the fever breaks the infection or..." He trailed off and did not look at Benjamin.

He could have throttled the old man at that moment.

"You will need to keep an eye on her. And try to keep her cool. She is in a lot of pain and discomfort. A cool cloth on the forehead will be heaven sent."

Benjamin just nodded. He did not trust himself to speak. He was furious. But he knew the bulk of the anger was directed at himself. And a bit at Charlotte. How irresponsible could she be? She was in no condition to be striking out on her own and wandering the streets of London at all hours of the night.

Doctor Price took his leave, and Benjamin stood above the bed, his bed—again—looking down at the sleeping woman. How had she—in so short a time—managed to upend his life so completely? He had to put his foot down somewhere. He would not allow her to push him any further from the fierce control he had spent his entire life cultivating. No, he would let Charlotte Aston into his bed, but he would not let her into his life—into his heart. There was no heart left for her, anyway.

With that resolution firmly in place, he sat in the chair beside his bed and dipped a sponge in the basin of cool, fresh water he had called for. He was in control.

∞∞∞

Charlotte wove in and out of bizarre fever dreams. She was laughing and chasing Freddie through a field. She was helping her stepmother with the twins. She was feeding her own children. She did not have children. She never would. Someone was firing a pistol at her. Lord Deering was breathing down her neck. Someone was wiping her forehead with a cool, gentle touch. Around and around she went in this tumultuous ride of dreams. Each time she felt herself surfacing from the land of slumber, she was sucked back in again. At one point, she heard someone pleading with her to break the surface.

Open your eyes, Charlotte. Just for a moment.

She tried, but she could not.

∞∞∞

It was worse than Benjamin had feared it would be. Even Doctor Price's face this morning when he had come for the first of his twice-daily check-ups, had been flat and resigned.

"It is the way of fevers. Sometimes they are more than the body can handle. She is young, so I hoped she would pull through. But young people die of fever all the time. Perhaps her body is just too tired. Prolonged stress, or underfeeding." He tilted Charlotte's wrist in his hand as he took her pulse. The sharp bones looked small and fragile in the old man's thick fingers. "If she has already worn away her reserves, then her youth may not be the saving grace we would hope it to be. Time will tell."

Time will tell.

The doctor's words ricocheted around his skull like a death knell in the stuffy room. Long after the man had left and come and left again, Benjamin could hear those words.

Time will tell.

Why? Why did he have to wait for time? Why could he not just fix it now? Wield some strategic force and will Charlotte to stave off the infection. He had seen the fire in her. She was a woman of unparalleled spirit. Why could she not just burn the fever out?

He began speaking to her.

She would not leave if she knew there was an argument to be had. He was sure of it.

"I really do not think women should be writing news columns. It is a waste of feminine energy." Even as the words left his mouth, he expected a slap. His own pulse jogged at the mischievous thrill of getting a certain rise out of her.

But then: nothing.

The utter and complete lack of response knocked the breath from his lungs. It took him a number of moments, head down on the counterpane beside her limp hand, to regain his breathing and marshal his feelings.

"Ladies do not belong in the Seven Dials, and you were foolish to risk your neck like that for some frivolous hobby." Again, he braced. Already sure he knew her well enough to know she would not stand for his domineering or any belittling of her craft.

Again, nothing.

The disappointment this time—though expected—was more acute than before. He had to push his fist into the hard plane of his breastbone, willing the pain to pass. He could not do it again.

"Truthfully, it is a noble thing you are doing." He scowled at the basin of water beside the bed, warm now that he had bathed her brow so many times, trying to get her temperature down. He should ring for it to be changed.

"The people there…we are hard. Life makes you like that out there. The things you see. The things you have to do— just to survive. It is like an axe suspended over your head at all times. Just waiting to drop. And it feels like even if you do everything you can, even if you scrape something together, that effort might not actually stop it. It might not even matter. That swift drop is just coming at you always—and yet you never know when." The fire crackled in the hearth, and somewhere, far beyond the windows, a dog started barking.

"It is not something you can understand unless you have faced it. And actually, I am sure you have a better idea than most with what your family has lost." This time, he did not expect her to reply. "But even before then, you cared. I cannot fathom why. Or how. But you did. And not in the way that the missionaries do—when they come in preaching about poverty and redemption. Even the good ones who bring food—they don't really understand. It does not help in the end. A full belly is a gift. But why are the children starving to begin with? It is not because of some original sin. And it is not through any fault of their parents—the vices on the street are a symptom, not the problem." The words were picking up speed, but his pulse slowed, his breathing evened out—almost as if he had fallen into a trance.

"And you do something. You care. You listen." He could not even see her chest rise and fall with the shallowness of her breath anymore. "And you give those people a voice. Something they never had. And miraculously, people read it. I do not know if you know this. Or have realised it in your employer's leniency. But your column has attention. People are reading it. People are talking about it. You are doing something. Just by caring."

The room was cooling. He needed to put more logs on the fire. But his face was wet, and he could not look away from Charlotte's impassive face. "Your humanity is doing something, Charlotte. Do not let it slip away. Do not abandon this. You cannot. I cannot let you."

He could not breathe. "I will not let you leave, Charlotte. Open your eyes now. Come back to me, please."

Chapter Twelve

Benjamin did not dare stay out for long. For the last two days, he had been gripped with an overwhelming, roaring anxiety that he could only quiet by watching Charlotte's chest rise up and down. Each time it faltered, he felt his own throat threaten to squeeze shut. Her condition had only worsened.

She had not fully awoken since she collapsed in his office, only drifting from sleep, restless, eyes hazy and asking for nameless people—comfort Benjamin could not figure out how to give. Occasionally, she thrashed and cried, afterwards quieting to a near-deathly stillness that had him begging, begging her to resurface. Promising to find whoever she needed—be whoever she needed.

Finally, tonight, she had said a name. Freddie. Sleep-deprived and desperate, Benjamin seized it. Freddie. Frederick Aston, ninth Earl of Elford. He could find him for her.

And so, with Lizzy stationed by her side with orders to send for him immediately if something were to change, Benjamin set out. In common workman's clothes and soft-soled boots, he took to the streets that had once chewed him up, spit him out, and made him whatever he was today. It was strange how easily his body remembered. How quickly he took to the shadows and sounds of London's night.

It had not taken him long to find Freddie's destination; his network had been watching closely for the movements of the young earl. Freddie should have been in Mayfair, spending an evening at one of the insipid ton balls. Or in St James', at a club, maybe even one the likes of Elysium. Maybe even at one of the early spring evenings in the Vauxhall Pleasure Gardens, though it was still a bit cold for those attractions to hold any real draw. But no, much to Benjamin's distaste, it seemed Frederick had chosen to spend his evening much further east than was wise for such a young lordling.

Benjamin stood in the alley across from the roiling house. Shifting light spilled through the dilapidated shutters to reflect off the putrid puddles in the street as the sticky smell of tar smoke drifted through the air. Patrons of all sorts were stumbling in and out. Sailors, merchants, roughened factory men, and men that none so respectable as the former would dare to associate with. Benjamin knew this place. And did not care for it.

He waited and watched as the seedy assortment of evening goers passed in and out of the establishment, remaining one with the shadows. It was all he could do to hold himself there still, as each moment ticked by, reminding him of Charlotte fighting the infection he had inflicted upon her. He could not think about it. The feral, fragile way she made him feel was untenable. He felt foreign to himself. A danger.

But he forced himself to stand there as still as death as the minutes slipped by, then turned into hours. And finally, his grit paid off.

A carriage rolled up the small, dirty street —far too fine for this side of town. The idiot did not even have the sense to visit such a pit with the appropriate deference. The patrons of a place like this—and, more importantly, the proprietors— could scent a stuffed hen a mile away. They would fleece Freddie for all he was worth— admittedly not much—and leave him stripped to nothing, potentially bleeding into the pools of muck his carriage wheels now stopped in.

The street was too dark to make out the crest on the carriage. It must belong to one of Elford's other well-heeled friends. Was there no end to the arrogant idiocy of this class of young lords? Benjamin was baffled at their inability to sense their own limits. To know when they had stooped too low, risked too much. But to them, he supposed, in their manicured town homes and ancestral estates, there was no such thing as the squalor that could steal everything from you. That could end your life. For them, each destination was just another chance at revelry. Another set of people and places from which to squeeze some sort of pleasure and move on.

Before he could run through the list of which of the young earl's wealthy, titled friends might be irresponsible enough to escort Elford to a cesspool like this, the carriage's owner stepped out. And Benjamin's stomach dropped

Lord Reuben Deering was dressed below his usual standards of pomp and circumstance. His heavy wool coat covered most of his clothing, but the boots and evening trousers that emerged when he descended the steps were not ostentatious enough to draw much attention from the passersby in the street. He stepped gingerly across the puddle in the gutter, face contorted at whatever foulness wafted up to him from the dark pools.

Benjamin watched, his guts hot and seething as the light from the den played across the baron's face. He had aged since the last time Benjamin had seen him. But the hatefulness in his manner made him appear unchanged, his stretched, sunken features a mask of sick humanity. Hot fury flew through Benjamin's veins and thrummed in his head. Flashes of Delia—of her downcast eyes when she had told him she would live in the main house now that she was no longer a kitchen maid; her quick, distracted manner when he would come around back to visit her—to check on her when he felt something was wrong; her tear-stained face, mottled in bruises when she appeared at the boarding house, bag in hand, and told him she had lost her post. He saw her misery when she knew she was carrying the babe.

And then he heard the landlady, felt her kick in his ribs when she told him to get the body out so she could let the room.

He had failed her.

Shame rose in his throat, burning and acidic as he disgraced himself on the wall of the back alley. Wave after wave of hot bile splashed off the bricks onto his boots. He only just managed to look up and see the back Deering as he disappeared into the smoke-filled interior, Frederick Aston nowhere in sight. The rough, bawdy, miserable singing spilled out the door and followed Ben as he slunk back into the night.

He would not fail Charlotte.

∞∞∞

"You look like shit."

"Care to bring up a new point? You are becoming a bit repetitive." Benjamin was not in the mood for idle chat.

Elkington shared a concerned look with Wells that made Benjamin want to break something. "He is right, you know. I don't think I have ever seen you like this. Have you slept at all this week?"

"When did you two turn into such mother hens?" Benjamin was signing off on his latest receipt of kegs of ale. He had impatiently overseen their delivery and was anxious to be finished with the matter so he could return upstairs.

"Since you stopped eating, sleeping, and drinking."

Benjamin stood, ready to leave the room, when he was met with the obstructive forms of his two closest friends. Their arms were crossed, and they were partially blocking the doorway.

"Get out of my way."

"No. Not until you tell us what is wrong with you."

Benjamin could commit murder. "What is wrong with me?"

He tried to press past them, but they did not budge. "What is wrong with me is that I shot a woman, and now her life hangs in the balance."

"Because of her own idiocy, not yours."

Benjamin clenched his fists. He did not have many friends. He could not afford to kill these two. "She was not being idiotic. She was being noble."

Wells was regarding Benjamin thoughtfully. "The two are not mutually exclusive."

"You can't help her if you are dead." Elkington tilted his head. "What is it to you anyway? She is not your responsibility. Whether you shot her or not, she chose to take her brother's place in the duel. If you had shot him, you would not be playing nursemaid."

"If I had shot him, he would have been facing the consequences of his own recklessness. The duel was his idea, and now his sister is on death's door while he is off, likely gallivanting around town, causing more trouble for his family."

His network still had not tracked down the young earl again. The boy obviously needed to be set straight, but judging by the company he was keeping with Deering, Freddie was likely frequenting the lowest establishments London had to offer and Benjamin would not allow his boys to venture after him. Even children from the streets deserved to be sheltered where possible.

Freddie would have to be ironed out another day. Benjamin would nurse Charlotte back from the brink and then fix her family. It was the least he could do for her.

"You have not told him?" Elkington looked mystified.

"I have my scouts trailing him. I made sure he has been barred from all the institutions that gave him such lenient credit to begin with." Benjamin ground out the response as quickly as possible, hating each word that kept him here downstairs while Lizzy was watching over Charlotte upstairs.

"What about her other brothers?"

"They are at school. And I am not a secretary. I cannot spend my days tracking down members of the Aston family. Not while I am trying to keep their sister alive." Benjamin's tone was like acid, but truth be told, he felt guilty for not reaching out to Charlotte's younger brothers. Somehow, he was sure she would not want to worry them, and he did not want to admit his own role in her condition. "If you two want to be a help, you could do that. I don't see you slaving over the club."

With that, he pushed past them and made his way back up the back stairs to his rooms.

There she was, just as he'd left her. Pale and unmoving in the middle of the large bed. He hated the mix of emotions he felt seeing her there. She looked like a shell of herself against the silk sheets, but he had seen nothing so right as Charlotte Aston in his bed, golden hair pooling about her beautiful face.

He walked carefully to the side of the bed and placed a hand on her cheek. Still too warm. The fever had broken and returned twice in the last five days. Price had shown him how to spoon water and broth down her throat the few moments she was relatively lucid, saying that, if the fever did not get her, dehydration would. He would not let that happen.

He twirled a silky strand of hair between his fingers and then took her hand in his, holding it to his cheek. "Come now, Charlotte. It is time for you to come back to the land of the living."

Chapter Thirteen

Charlotte felt warm air blow across her knuckles. She was not sure whether she was awake or not. The pain in her shoulder had subsided to a dull throbbing, and her body felt exhausted. She could not remember falling asleep.

She took one more moment to take stock of herself before opening her eyes. She was not in her bed. Again. Where was she? The canopy over this bed was also plush and rich and seemed to be of the same style as the last strange bed she woke up in. Benjamin Scarsdale's bed.

As if she had conjured him, she looked down and realised the feeling at her hand was his breath, gently blowing across her knuckles as he grasped her fingers in his own—only inches from his lips. If she stretched a finger out, she could touch his lips. As if of its own accord, her index finger did just that.

With a feather-light touch, she traced the soft bow of his lower lip. He had a wide, masculine mouth, and here in sleep, his lips looked so soft she could not take her eyes from them.

He looked more dishevelled than the last time she had seen

him. Dark stubble shadowed the strong planes of his face, and his short hair was sticking up in strange ways, as if he had repeatedly run his hands through it.

She watched him sleeping, still tracing a finger along his jaw and trailing a scar she had not noticed before that ran from his ear down his neck.

He stirred at that, and she smiled. He really was the most beautiful man she had ever seen. She was almost grateful to her idiot of a brother for challenging this man to a duel. Her brother. *Damn.* She still had solved nothing.

Before her mind could catch up with her, though, Benjamin stirred again and opened his eyes. For a moment, she was trapped in the depths of those beautiful, deep blue irises. The dark fringe of lashes only made them more striking.

Her heart began thudding against her ribcage, and she caught her breath.

"Charlotte?" It was like hearing her name for the first time. Without warning, he jumped up and took her face in his hands, pressing his forehead into hers. "You came back." He whispered it so gently, she was not sure she had heard him.

Then, he was kissing her. His lips were soft and tender at first. She was stunned motionless. But then, as if it were the most natural thing in the world, her body responded, and she kissed him back. It was raw and involved, and it felt like her mind had been wiped clean of all of the clutter. This was what mattered. This was what she should be doing.

Benjamin leaned in further, and the kiss became more heated. His strong arms wrapped around her and gently lifted her to him, even as she stretched toward him. Her body revelled in the action, twisting and grasping for more contact.

His fingers moved to the nape of her neck and curled in her

hair as he pulled her closer, careful not to jar her shoulder. He made a sound at the back of his throat that made her want to crawl onto his lap and wrap herself around him. Who was this man? What was this pull she felt toward him? It was beyond anything she had felt before and grew with every interaction she had with him. She wanted to explore it. And her uncluttered mind could not find any reason not to.

A harsh knock came on the door, and he broke away, chest heaving as he looked at her, eyes drifting back down to her lips.

The sharp rap came again, and he cursed under his breath and shouted towards the door, "What is it?"

"Ben, you are going to want to come out here."

"No, I am not."

"The Earl of Elford is here."

"Fuck."

Charlotte was nearly twenty-seven and had heard the word before—and many worse. Still, coming from his lips, it sent an electric jolt up her spine, and she found herself wanting to hear him say it again.

Benjamin stalked over to the door and threw it open. Charlotte realised she was wearing nothing more than a chemise and pulled the bed covers up to her chest.

A man was standing on the other side of the door. The Duke of Wells.

She pulled the cover higher.

"Ah, welcome back, Lady Charlotte. We were not sure you were going to make it." He made a polite bow, and Charlotte racked her mind for the polite gesture for greeting a duke from bed. There wasn't one.

"Thank you, Your Grace." She did not manage to tamp

down the uncharacteristic blush rising to her cheeks.

"How long has she been awake?" Charlotte could hear the duke despite his lowered voice as he arched an aristocratic brow at Benjamin, whose hand flexed on the door frame. He was clearly resisting the urge to slam the door in the duke's face.

"My brother is here?" Charlotte interrupted whatever was passing between the two men.

"Yes, my lady. He is in the office and demands to see you. Lord Deering is here as well."

At that, Benjamin's knuckles turned white, and Charlotte thought she heard the door squeak in protest. Her own body had gone stiff as a board at the sound of Deering's name, and she desperately wished Benjamin would close the door again. If only to keep that vile man as far away as possible.

"I will be down in a moment."

The duke nodded, and Benjamin shut the door.

"I should go down and see him. I am sure Freddie has been worried sick about me. How long was I asleep?"

"Six days. Maybe seven?" Benjamin was still glowering.

"Seven days?" Charlotte could not keep her voice down. "I have been asleep for a *week*?"

Her mind was racing. Seven days on top of the three before? Or was it four? The days following the duel were still jumbled in her mind, and she felt a well of panic rising within her. Who had taken care of the household during that time? Surely, no one had been keeping an eye on Freddie and his reckless spending.

She began pushing herself out of bed and then stopped. "You." She looked up at Benjamin pacing in front of the door like a caged lion. "You paid off his debts." Everything from that last night was flooding back to her now. "You bought out his debts from under Deering. He was furious." She remembered the scene in the study when Freddie had shown her the papers. "I came to repay you and you—" She stopped, suddenly acutely aware of him standing not two strides away and her wearing next to nothing in his bed. "You made me a proposition."

He had stopped pacing, but his face was completely inscrutable.

"To be your mistress. To cover the debt." There, her memory became foggy. "I did not accept, did I?" It did not seem like something she would accept, though she did not feel the indignation she would have expected at such an offer. No, in fact, she was intrigued.

"You did not accept." He betrayed nothing.

"But I did not say no, did I?"

"No, you nearly died before you could." He had taken on a whole new persona.

Gone was the relieved, unrestrained man she had woken up to. Now he held himself upright, apart. His features were arranged in a snide, unbothered mask as he shrugged back into his waistcoat.

"But the offer still stands," he said it casually, as if he did not care what her answer was one way or another. "However, I will have to take my leave of you now. I will send Lizzy in to help you bathe and dress before coming down to meet your brother and—" He stopped before saying Deering's name. A small mercy. "Maybe utilise some of the tooth powder standing on the shelf over there. Your breath is terrible, darling."

With that, he shut the door behind him, leaving Charlotte

perched on the side of the bed, gaping at the spot he had just left.

∞∞∞

It had sounded so vulgar when she had said it, offering that she be his mistress for money. Making her no better than a common whore. She had not said it, but Benjamin had thought it. And it made him hate himself.

He had put her in this situation. He bought up her brother's debt, and when she came to try to make it right, he'd offered to make her a whore. He had not planned it that way. Had he?

When the opportunity presented itself, he did not resist. The idea of having her was too overpowering not to take. And at the possibility of her rejecting the offer, he had turned cold and cruel. He was absolutely disgusted with himself.

He stormed downstairs and out the back door. Charlotte could meet with her brother alone. Lizzy would stay by her side, ensuring her reputation and Wells would appraise him of any developments. Benjamin could not bear to be in the building any longer and steep in his own shame. Moreover, he was not sure he would not lose himself and try to shake some sense into the stupid young earl. Charlotte did not need that right now. She did not need him.

He alerted his entire staff to ensure Deering was gone in moments. The man was not welcome in any establishment of his. They would remove him before he could harm Charlotte. She did not need him hanging around.

∞∞∞

Lizzy helped Charlotte bathe and dress, cooing over her the whole time. The poor woman had been scared out of her wits when Charlotte up and disappeared in the middle of the night. Charlotte felt guilty for not having considered her new friend's feelings before her ill-advised flight. So certain had she been that Lizzy would not be sacked, and so consumed by her own woes, she had not stopped to consider the distress she might still cause.

Perhaps if she had told Lizzy, she could have saved herself this whole ordeal. It had been foolish to jeopardise her health like that. She knew that now. Though she could not come to regret the whole experience. She touched her lips absentmindedly as Lizzy brushed out her hair and pulled it back into a loose chignon.

She still could not make sense of his behaviour when he had left the room. He was the one who had proposed the agreement, not her. But he had acted as if she had offended him. That must have been why he was so suddenly changed. But she could not make herself understand. Still, his words had stung and made her feel embarrassed about their kiss—his intention, she supposed.

But why would he want her to feel embarrassed? *He* had kissed *her!* She shook her head, giving up on rationalisation, still more fatigued and dazed than she would have liked to be able to devote proper thought to it. God save her from men and their mercurial moods and reckless whims.

"Do you want to wear the sling?" Lizzy had expertly changed her bandages and tied Charlotte into a high-necked dress that effectively covered the gauze.

"No," Charlotte replied immediately. Her shoulder did not hurt too much, and if she did not move it, there was no cause for worry. She would not injure it further by going downstairs. She did not want to have to explain herself to her brother and Lord Deering.

Although she had been here for days. Did they know that? How had they found out she was here anyway? What excuse would possibly negate the fact that she had spent seven days and nights in the private rooms of a bachelor? Private rooms attached to the most notorious gaming hell in London! And a bachelor who was just as notorious.

She had to put her head in her good hand for a moment to let the swirl of frenzied thoughts subside. "What am I going to say, Lizzy?"

"I think I can help with that." A low voice came from the door, and Lizzy bobbed a deep curtsy while Charlotte turned over her shoulder to see the Duke of Wells standing in the doorway again.

"Apologies for the intrusion. I just came up to fetch you. Scarsdale has abandoned you then?" He clearly knew the answer to that question, but Charlotte found herself wincing at the comment.

"No apologies needed, Your Grace. I am sorry to keep you waiting."

"Please call me Wells. Most beautiful women I meet do." It was an absurd thing to say, and Charlotte almost rolled her eyes at the flirtation. Somehow, she knew he was not sincere. Not because she was below his notice—though she was the spinster sister of a nearly ruined earl and had no aspirations to become a duchess—but because she had seen the bond of genuine friendship between him and Benjamin. And she knew that there was too much respect between the two of them for Wells to try anything with her. It was a strange position to be in, and she was not sure what to do with the unprecedented familiarity. And certainly not sure what to do with the implied proprietary nature of her relationship with Benjamin Scarsdale—if one could even call it that.

Did she want to call it that?

"But I could not help but overhear your issue. I assume you are trying to find a way to conceal the fact that you have been in Scarsdale's room unchaperoned for nearly a week?"

Charlotte nodded, eager to hear any solution.

"Well, it may help to know, your brother was only notified of your condition earlier this morning. He has not been to your townhouse in that time, and unless someone here has been talking—which I doubt very much—then there is no way for him to know that you have been here for more than a matter of hours. Though—" He eyed the strip of cotton in Lizzy's hand. "He was informed that you had taken ill, so maybe play that up."

"Sling it is then, my lady." Lizzy looked smug as she gingerly tied Charlotte's arm up in the cotton wrap.

"Thank you, Your Grace."

"Why, of course. We do not want any more duels on our hands, now do we?" He winked, and Charlotte laughed out loud. It was a strange relief to know there were at least a few people from whom she did not have to hide the truth of her injury.

Downstairs, Lizzy showed her to Benjamin's office, where Wells stood with her brother. Deering was nowhere in sight, and Charlotte experienced a moment of dizzying relief before she noticed Freddie was pacing in front of the desk. He looked agitated and sleep deprived. There were rings around his eyes, and his face was somehow red and sallow at the same time. He looked worse than the last time she had seen him.

When he saw Charlotte enter the room, he shot towards her. "Charlotte! What in the world have they done to you?"

"Careful, Lord Elford. I would not go throwing accusations around like that." Wells' cultured voice easily crossed the room to meet them at the door. Freddie looked visibly intimidated and faltered a step back. "Lady Charlotte was out for a walk in the park this morning and tripped over a root. Mr. Scarsdale and I were riding in the vicinity and escorted her here for medical treatment. The doctor suspects she only sprained her shoulder, and she should be on the mend in no time." Charlotte was relieved at his smooth explanation. She was not sure she could have convinced her brother of their lie.

Freddie's eyes narrowed at the mention of Scarsdale. "Lord Deering seemed to think Scarsdale had been keeping Charlotte here for inappropriate reasons." He blushed at the accusation and glanced uncertainly at the duke.

"Why would Lord Deering say something so maligning about your sister's character, I wonder? Surely you are mistaken." Wells' tone was steely, and Frederick shuffled his feet.

"Oh yes. I must have mistaken him. You see, he was the one who brought me the letter at—" he broke off, "—my club," he finished vaguely. "Yes, I must have mistaken him in the din."

Charlotte closed her eyes. What was Freddie doing at "his club" at nine in the morning? Did he not see the reprieve he had been granted for what it was—an unheard-of opportunity to change his ways?

More concerning was Lord Deering. He clearly knew she

had not been at home for the past few days. Had he been watching the house? The thought sent chills down her spine. Even now she could see his gaze in her mind's eye. Those beady, appraising eyes that shone like a viper's despite the low light of the Aston study. Still, he would not be able to refute this claim to Freddie because that would expose him as well.

"Well then. We thank you and Mr. Scarsdale for your invaluable service to my sister." Charlotte was not sure who he meant by *we*. Was he referring to himself and Charlotte or to himself and Deering? She was worried it was the latter. It seemed, for some reason or another, Freddie had thrown his lot in with Lord Deering.

"Charlotte, shall I escort you home?" Freddie was holding out his arm and, unsure of what to do, she took it.

The idea of leaving Elysium was suddenly horribly daunting. She had not realised it until this point, but this was the first place in ages where she did not feel like the fate of the world rested solely on her shoulders.

But of course, she had to leave. She did not belong here, and she could not rely on others to resolve her family's problems. That was up to her.

Chapter Fourteen

"That was very badly done, Scarsdale."

"Which part?" Benjamin dodged a fist thrown at him by Elkington.

His friend had found him at their preferred boxing club, Jackson's, shortly after he left Elysium. Wells stood below the raised ring, leaning between the ropes, berating him.

"All of it, I guess. Principally, abandoning Lady Charlotte to the care of her good-for-nothing brother. Who, inexplicably, seems to be in the thrall of that cursed Lord Deering. The baron clearly has some plot for the earl, and I would not hesitate to wager it includes the fine lady as well."

Benjamin lost his focus for a moment, and Elkington caught him in the arm.

"I would also wager you said something hurtful to the lady in question as well. She had a wounded look when I mentioned your name, and I can only assume you were an ass in some misguided attempt to distance yourself from her. Though, if I were you, I would be doing everything in my power to have as little distance between her and myself as possible."

At that, Benjamin snapped his head towards Wells. "How

dare yo—" His budding tirade at Wells was cut short as Elkington's fist collided with the side of his jaw hard enough to make his ears ring.

"Aha! Thank you, Wells. I have never been able to land such a solid hit on him before."

"Damn it, Elk. That is going to bruise." He rubbed his sore jaw, making sure it was not dislocated.

"Serves you right." Elkington swung out from under the ropes to join Wells below.

"Oh, so now you're against me too."

"No. You are against yourself. We," he gestured between himself and Wells, "are firmly in your corner." He laughed at his unintended pun and nodded at the opposite corner of the boxing ring, "Though not literally."

"I am not against myself. I just do not want Lady Charlotte getting the wrong idea."

"And what would the wrong idea be?"

Elkington was now leaning against the ropes beside Wells, wiping sweat from his brow with his discarded cravat. Benjamin always wondered if Elkington's valet was prone to fits. It would take a steeled retainer to be able to put up with the man's carelessness with his attire. A byproduct of a carefree existence, he supposed, was a disregard for the fine trappings of such a life.

"That you are interested in her?" Wells asked pointedly.

"I'd say he is more than interested."

"No one asked you," Benjamin snapped.

"So you are not interested?" Wells stepped aside to let Benjamin duck between the ropes and join them on the floor.

"Of course, I am. A man would have to be dead not to be." Saying it out loud made him feel terribly vulnerable. He poured himself a glass of ale from a pitcher at the side of the room and turned back to look at his friends. "I asked her to be my mistress."

The twin shock on the two men's faces would have been amusing in any other circumstance. He took a swig from the glass while waiting for them to process the information.

"You *what?*" To Benjamin's surprise, Wells sounded appalled.

Angry even. He had not expected such a reaction from the man known far and wide to be a womaniser of the highest order.

"It was not some salacious and unprompted proposition." *Not completely true,* he thought. "She came to me wanting to work off her brother's debts. The services she offered were of no use to me, so I offered an alternative." He kept his tone as matter-of-fact and business-like as possible.

"You want her to be your mistress to pay off a debt that is not even hers?" Now it was Elkington's turn to look appalled. "Jesus Christ, Benjamin. She is a lady."

"Perhaps." He felt like a cad and did not know what to do to make it better. "But she is also the spinster sister of a man who owes me a great deal of money. I would say she is getting the better end of the deal."

For a moment, he thought either one of his friends would pull him back into the ring and pummel him to a pulp. He found he did not like being on the receiving end of their disappointment. Still, he was fully within his rights to behave as he had. They were not saints themselves.

"If I had known that was why you were buying up Elford's debt, I never would have helped you." Wells had been instrumental in unravelling some of the trickier accounts with his elite Mayfair connections. If it weren't for him, Deering would still have a significant stake in the Elford fortune—or what was left of it.

He had also made the arrangements for the Eton payments. Despite all his London power, Benjamin could never dream of understanding the politics that went into the premiere school for posh toffs.

Feeling defeated and rather disgusted with his behaviour, or at least Wells and Elkington's perception of his behaviour, he tried to explain. "That is not why I did it. I swear to you. I did not even call the debts in. I did not intend to either."

"So what was this? A charity case with an unexpected bonus?" Wells still looked unimpressed, but Benjamin could tell he was softening.

"No." Although, at the core of it—yes, that is exactly what it was. "It was not my plan. I don't even know how she figured out it was me." *Liar.* Once he paid off the youngest Astons' school fees, he had known she would realise it was him—had hoped for it. In fact, he had expected her to figure it out from the start—though that was not why he did it.

The admiration he felt for that strong warrior of a woman, along with the lifelong contempt he had for the injustice of someone suffering for the misdeeds of others, had driven him to help. She deserved to be free of her brother's foolishness, and he had the means to free her. There was never a second thought about it.

"It was just—" He struggled to find the words to justify what he had done in that moment. "It came out before I had even thought about it. She was sitting across from me, and she looked so—"

"Unwell?"

"Feverish from infection?"

"Shot in the shoulder?"

Benjamin gave them a quelling look. At least they had recovered their humour.

"Beautiful."

It was not an adequate word for how she had looked in that chair illuminated by the glow of the fire. No word could describe the pure gravitational pull she had exerted on him in that moment and every other moment he had spent in her presence. Even when he was not with her, he felt the same draw to her—possibly even stronger in her absence.

"You horse's ass." Elk stared him down. "Beautiful or not, that is no way to approach an innocent lady!"

"She is not." The words slipped out before he could clamp his mouth shut. Some perverse need to justify himself and the undermining of his usual control. God help him.

The two men stared at him in stony silence. "I trade in secrets." He spoke in a flat, matter-of-fact tone, doing nothing to hide his weariness.

Wells' dark blue eyes were cold as granite, the full force of the duke present and menacing. "I say this as your oldest friend and as perhaps one of the few people in the world who knows you are not this man. But in the absence of her family—as her brother is even less honourable than you pretend to be—I will say this: another insult like this will not go unanswered. Not because of her virtue, not because of her status, but because that woman does not deserve to be toyed about by one single man more."

Benjamin felt a deep, abiding respect for the man. "I agree."

The words were quiet and full of apology. Wells stared him down a moment longer and, apparently satisfied he had made his point, backed down. Silence stretched between them.

"All that aside, why in the world would you proposition her?" Elkington still looked mystified.

Benjamin scraped a hand over his face, unable to explain the longing that was already far beyond lust. The fear he had felt when she was thrashing through the fever that went far beyond guilt. "I just…have to have her." The words were paltry.

Elkington gave him a fond but pitying smile. "Why not just marry her then? You have money. She needs security—and certainly to be removed from her brother's purview. Matches have been made on less."

It was Benjamin's turn to stare in shock. "Out of the question."

Elkington pursed his lips. "I just don't understand how you could make her your mistress like that. Especially after your mother—"

"Don't. Do not speak of my mother." Benjamin felt like his body had become encased in a block of ice.

"But—" Wells stopped Elkington with a hand on his arm, shaking his head. Elkington had only known Benjamin since he had fought his way off the streets. While he knew the story of Benjamin's past, Wells had actually seen it firsthand.

"You know how we feel on the subject, and ultimately, it is Lady Charlotte's decision—though she should be allowed to make it of her own free will and not some misinformed impression of obligation." He gave Benjamin a pointed look. "Though if you even try to play one of your sordid games of secrets and blackmail, it is you who will have a bullet hole in your shoulder. And I will not wait to meet you on a damp field to put it there."

Benjamin was relieved to have the matter dropped and his friendships still intact, but he did not leave the boxing club feeling any lighter than he had when he had gone in.

∞∞∞∞

Charlotte sat beside her brother in a loaned Elysium carriage. It had been sitting waiting for them as Freddie escorted her out one of the various side exits of the club, ready without a word to carry them away to their townhouse. Had that been where Benjamin had rushed off to? To arrange a carriage for her departure after kissing, insulting, then abandoning her? No, that was too dramatic by half. He owed her nothing and thus, could not abandon her.

"Where is Rowley Calthorpe?" Charlotte found it odd to see her brother without his friend. They had been attached at the hip since they were in school.

"I don't know. I have not seen him much this week." A sickly-sweet stench had begun to fill the carriage, and Charlotte realised with growing chagrin that it seemed to be emanating directly from her brother's person.

"Why not?"

Freddie shifted on the squab, clearly irritated by her questioning. "He has been such a fuddy-duddy since last week. He was not game for any of our usual haunts, and so Deering and I left him behind."

Charlotte found it odd that Freddie would voluntarily pass his time with a man nearly forty years his senior. He was always going on about the young set he ran with, and Freddie was nothing if not conscious of his social perception.

There was a lapse in conversation until Freddie offered

amiably, "I am sure we can arrange to have a nurse brought in to keep an eye on your injury, Charlotte." He was listlessly looking out the window, likely sobering up a bit and feeling the discomfort that accompanied such an experience in a moving carriage.

"That will not be necessary." Not to mention, impossible. She was not even sure they would have the funds to feed themselves this week, let alone pay a nurse's salary.

"It is no bother, Charlotte. Lord Deering has generously offered to pay the expense."

Charlotte's eyes narrowed. Freddie was still looking out the window, pointedly not meeting her gaze.

"Why would he do that?" She fought to keep her voice pleasant and even.

"Actually, Charlie, I wanted to talk to you about that." Freddie turned back into the coach and hesitated, as if aware of the delicate risk he was taking in that moment. "Lord Deering has offered to support the rebuilding of the Elford estates in return for…" Clearly, her brother was not fool enough to think she would welcome his news. He squared his shoulders and started again. "In return for your hand in marriage."

It was as if all the air had been sucked from the coach. Charlotte seriously considered opening the door and flinging herself from the moving vehicle—if only for the chance of a breath.

She could not think of a word to say as the carriage rattled up to the front steps of their townhouse. Freddie also seemed disinclined to speak, preferring instead to precede her out of the carriage and up the front steps. Charlotte gave a thin-lipped smile to the young driver and followed Freddie inside, fighting the urge to slam the door behind her.

Charlotte rounded on Freddie. "How could you? How could you, Freddie?"

He frowned and straightened his shoulders, clearly upset that that had not been the end of the matter. "I do not know what you mean, Charlotte. I have made you an advantageous match. That is the duty of a brother, especially a titled one. You should be wed, and considering your age and our financial situation, I would say Lord Deering is a very respectable option."

Charlotte gaped. "You insult me and our family by insinuating we should have any benefit to gain from Lord Deering. And I do not say so because of his rank."

Freddie sniffed and made a show of re-pinning the clasp of his pocket watch—their father's pocket watch. "I am the man of the house now, Charlotte. It is up to me to make sure this family stays afloat. Lord Deering understands this and has offered considerable help. I would think you, of all people, would understand the value of blunt in the maintenance of large estates. And I hesitate to remind you, you are not exactly in a position to be turning down offers. Father told me of your… indiscretion, shall we say, with *Signore* Rossi."

Charlotte stared at her brother, mouth hanging open.

Signore Rossi had been a painting instructor hired by her stepmother, Veronica, to teach Freddie the way of the Italian masters.

Despite Veronica's disinclination to dirty her hands with mothering, Freddie had always been her pride and joy, and she believed he had an artist's soul that should be nurtured. Their father had scoffed at the idea, insisting Freddie be raised understanding the duty he had as heir. Veronica would not hear of it and sheltered and spoiled the boy.

Not much better than her stepmother, eighteen-year-old Charlotte had doted on Freddie as well, sitting in on his lessons with the young, handsome artist, hoping to absorb any knowledge she could so that she might help Freddie along in his studies if necessary.

Signore Rossi—Luca, he had insisted she call him—was kind and warm. He paid her such special attention. It made her feel like a shining star, his muse. She had never felt so adored in her life.

She still did not know how her father had discovered their affair, though with the cynical hindsight of maturity, she could not rule out the possibility that Luca himself had exposed them. The earl had called her to his study one morning, summarily announcing that *Signore* Rossi had been dismissed and his silence secured with her dowry. *"I hope you feel the shame you have brought to our family, Charlie. The loss of a dowry is a fair price for the loss of your respectability."*

She had been heartbroken, arguably more so by her father's censure than Rossi's abandonment. And the worst part was, she had not even done what Rossi had extorted their family for. Certainly, given time and more devoted attention, she may have given up more than a few kisses and stolen touches. But she had not, and she had been left in limbo—a ruined virgin, the scorn of her family.

That day, in the hall outside the study, she had vowed to herself that she would never again risk her family like that. She would spend the rest of her life making up for her catastrophic failure.

Now, however, standing just steps away from that very same hall, she felt the familiar sting of her shame eclipsed by the blow of betrayal. Her father's betrayal of her secret, her brother's betrayal of her autonomy. She felt a burning fury toward every man who had ever deigned to power-play her. It was all-consuming.

She sputtered for a moment, and then the dam broke. "How *dare* you try to humble me with that? I have done penance for that mistake every day of my adult life." She felt the skin of her knuckles stretch tight as she clenched her fists violently in the folds of her skirts.

"Oh yes, Frederick. I understand. Far more than you ever had. It is because of you and your self-absorption that we no longer have an estate. The Elford Earldom is nothing but an empty title now. The only reason you still have a roof over your head and a bed to return to after your debauchery is because of me. I have taken on real employment in order to bring in the funds necessary for survival. We would have sold this house years ago if it were not for me."

She was really getting going now.

"And have you forgotten about your younger brothers? Your heirs until you find a woman stupid enough to take you on. You have stolen from them directly, and yet you have the audacity to claim you are responsible? To pretend you have an ounce of authority when it comes to this family? You don't have a leg to stand on, Frederick Aston. Don't you dare try to sell me off like just another heirloom."

Freddie's face was florid and scrunched like a sour-faced child. Charlotte half expected him to stomp his feet and yell.

"You took on *work*?" His right hand twitched, and she saw him eyeing the nearly empty whisky decanter he had left on the sideboard. "Don't you see, Charlotte? That is completely unacceptable. Of course, you need a husband. No respectable lady of the ton takes on work. It is unseemly and could tarnish the family name."

"I do not need a husband. I need a brother who can acknowledge the fact that his behaviour has done far more to tarnish the family name than my work has."

"It does not matter, Charlotte. It is already done."

Charlotte pinned him with a withering glare. "How much have you lost, Freddie? In the last week?"

Finally, he had the decency to look somewhat chagrined. "It is nothing for you to worry yourself over. Deering is good for it."

"I did not ask if Deering can cover the sum. I asked for the amount."

Freddie waved his hand. "Nothing. Nothing. Somewhere around five hundred."

Charlotte wanted to cry. That was more than she had made in the last year with her writing.

"Don't look so down in the mouth, Charlie. That is a drop in the bucket with Deering's shipping wealth."

"Do not call me Charlie."

For the first time that day, Freddie looked truly shocked. Finally, something had rattled his cage. "Charlotte, don't be like that. I am your brother."

"You are no brother of mine." With that, she marched straight out of the room and down the back hall. She needed to get some air before she was sick on the bare parquet floors.

Chapter Fifteen

Charlotte sat on a stone bench in the rose garden until the rain began again. She took cover in the small pavilion surrounded by cedars. It had always been a favourite spot of hers when she was a child. It felt like a small slice of the country nestled among the bustle of London.

Oh, how she missed the country. She sat for a while on a bench watching the rain roll down the glass walls of the structure before she kicked off her slippers and lay on her back in the middle of the smooth mosaic floor. For a moment, she felt like a child again, watching the wind blow the branches overhead and whistle through the metal frame.

As the world churned on around her, she was safe in this little haven, free from time.

"Mind if I join?" The low voice made her jump, and she quickly propped herself on her good elbow. "Please don't get up. I would rather come to you."

Charlotte slowly lowered herself back down. "Who let you in?"

Benjamin came to sit beside her, taking his boots off one by one—she caught herself admiring his stockinged ankles and his masculine feet as he lay down beside her.

"No one, in fact. I doubt I need to remind you, but there is no one in your house to open the door. When I knocked and received no answer, I checked around the mews. Your back garden gate is unlocked, by the way."

"I stopped locking it. There is nothing left to steal."

"You are still here, are you not?" He was very close. She could feel his warmth all down the side of her body. It was all she could do not to roll into it.

"No one is going to bother to steal me."

There was silence beside her, and she turned to find his face inches from hers, dark blue eyes full and watching. "I beg to differ."

Her heart flipped behind her sternum, and she forced herself to look back up at the cedars leaning over them, their silhouettes distorted in the afternoon rain pattering on the glass roof. Silence stretched again as she tried to school her humming pulse. She was acutely aware of every breath he took beside her. Of the warm, inviting smell of him, made deeper and more complex by the overlying smell of rain.

"I came to apologise." He spoke without looking at her, eyes fixed on the rain hitting the glass roof.

"Oh?"

He nodded.

"And?" She tried to keep the smile from her voice as she prompted him.

"I am sorry. I have treated you unfairly and spoken to you with contempt that you did not deserve. Not to mention insulting your honour."

Charlotte sighed, mesmerised by the lulling patter of rain and his body heat. "You would not be the first." She thought ruefully of Freddie but then pushed him from her mind. Those troubles did not belong in this moment. Here, she was free of all that. "I forgive you, Benjamin." It was easy. Maybe it should not have been, but it was.

In her periphery, she could see him turn at that and regard her, but she did not look away from the rain. He was still watching her, gaze intent. "No, I need you to know. I did not plan to hold you to any agreement. Those debts are not yours. I will not ask that of you."

She turned and gave him a sad smile. "Thank you. For doing what you did—buying up our family's debts." He seemed shocked that she would say such a thing. "Strange as it sounds, I feel much safer being in debt to a man like you than…" She did not want to bring his name into this space. So she did not.

"That does not excuse the proposition. I was taking advantage." He sounded angry, and that made her want to smile.

"Benjamin Scarsdale, I was comatose in your bed for *days*. You nursed me back to health. You saved my life." His eyes were wide when she looked back at him. "Lizzy told me how you hovered over my bed for a week, trying to coax me back from the brink of an infection I caused with my own pigheadedness. You are the last man in the world I would worry about taking advantage." Miraculously, hints of colour rose on his cheekbones—as if her words drew something out of him he was not familiar enough with to contain. This man, who always wielded explicit control over himself and his surroundings, seemed to be flustered. By her.

Charlotte wanted to reach out and touch the rising colour of his cheeks—see if they were as warm as she suspected. "I know the damage my brother has done…or suspect I do. I will make it right."

It looked as if he was going to argue. She could already anticipate the words he was going to say—could hear his low voice whisper the promise: *You don't have to.*

But he did not speak. The rain filled the silence, lulling the pavilion back into a peaceful hush.

He eventually turned back to the ceiling, and she felt his fingers brush hers. "This is beautiful."

Charlotte nodded. "I used to come out here when I was young. It feels like an escape from the city. Reminds me of home." She felt a melancholy ache in her chest at that word.

"Where was home?" His voice was quiet. It seemed a silly question for such a man to ask. She was sure he knew every last morsel of information about her and her family. But she answered anyway, happy to share something with him.

"Staffordshire. Our country estate, Lamdel Manor." She sighed. "It is long gone now, but it will always be home. Anyway, after my father remarried, we spent most of our time in town. My stepmother could not abide the quiet of the country."

"Did you so dislike living in London?" The backs of their hands were touching, their fingers gently intertwined.

"Not everything. I will never forget the first time my father took us to the opera. It was like a dream." She let herself drift back into the sparkling awe of the night. She had been fourteen and had heard nothing more than the country quartets that were hired for local fetes. The grandeur of the opera house and then the power of the soprano's voice had made her feel otherworldly. Then, life had seemed so possible, an endless potential for delight and joy. It was partly this newfound optimism that had made her such a fool for Luca Rossi. Then, it had all changed. "But the realities of society were enough to dim even that joy."

He nodded but remained silent.

"Where is your home?" She could feel him stiffen slightly. He was not used to sharing his own secrets. But she waited, happy to be patient with him in this little world they inhabited.

"Also in the country. Near Devon. I grew up with my mother and sister on the Bowring estate. That is how Wells and I met. His father's estate ran along the Bowring one. He and his father did not get along, so he spent much of his time with us."

"Your mother was in service?" She had not expected that from a man who seemed to have all the polish and education of a consummate gentleman, despite his rough reputation.

"In a way." His answer was toneless.

"When did you move to London?" He had fully laced his fingers with hers while he spoke, and she was scrambling to grasp at conversation, the intimacy of their joined hands drawing in all her attention.

"When I was eleven." He said no more, and judging by his tone, Charlotte decided it was best to leave it.

"Do you ever miss the country?"

He did not hesitate. "Every day."

"So do I."

They lay in silence for long, peaceful minutes. The rain continued to patter, and Charlotte thought to herself that, given the chance, she would stay in this moment forever with this strange, intriguing man by her side.

"My sister and I used to talk about finding a cottage back

in Devonshire."

She did not turn to him, as if he were a wild creature and any movement might startle him and break the spell they seemed to have slipped under.

"Cordelia. She was two years older than I. After my mother passed, she got work in a great house, and I was scraping together odd jobs at printers, tanneries—I could read, so that helped. We thought that between the two of us, we might save enough to get a small place in the country. Get out of the soot and grime of London. We did not need much—just a kitchen garden. I could work as a farmhand." He trailed off, and even though she was not looking at him, she could see he was worlds away; in another life where he was not the Master of London's Secrets but just another simple farmer, tending his land and living in peace. She could see that life for him—and yet, she was glad he did not have it. Otherwise, they would not be here now.

"Delia did not tell me her secret at first. I guess she thought she was still protecting me from the harsh realities of the world. But she grew nervous—always jumpy, always looking over her shoulder. She was promoted from scullery maid to upstairs maid and had to move into the servants' quarters. I did not see her as much. But she sent money and made sure I was fed."

Charlotte waited again as he fell into silence. The rain pattering on the glass made their little sanctuary seem removed from the entire world. She wanted nothing more than to ask him what had happened next. But she held her tongue, knowing the silence of this moment would draw it out.

"Then she showed up on the steps of the boarding house

one day. Bag in hand. Her jaw was swollen; her entire neck was black and blue. She refused to tell me what had happened. I was only thirteen at the time, and small for my age. But if she had told me, I would have murdered the coward myself. Then and there."

The way he said it so matter-of-factly made Charlotte shiver. What must it be like to have a man like this willing to defend you so absolutely? It was a tantalising thought.

"It only took a week to realise she was with child." His voice was flat again. "She tried so hard to find more work, but the babe made her so ill, she could hardly stand most days. I took on extra jobs. I was out from dawn till dusk, sometimes through the night too." Charlotte closed her eyes for the thin young boy that he must have been. Terrified, fighting to keep himself and his sister afloat. She could remember Freddie at that age. The twins were only now twelve. Her heart ached for the unfairness of it all.

"It was not enough, though. Another boarder got sick. He was old—not even on our floor. But it swept through the place quickly. I was ill first. I tried to stay out longer so I would not pass it to her. I slept on the back stoop for a week, hoping she would be safe in the little room we let."

He was breathing heavily, and the words sounded like they were being sawed from his chest. Charlotte felt moisture on her cheeks, but she did not dare wipe the tears away lest he see her and stop. She had to hear his story as much as he needed to tell it.

"One of the nights, the landlady kicked me awake on the stoop. She asked me to do something with the body so she could fill the bed. I did not even know Delia had fallen ill. She died alone in that tiny room while I was just outside, below the window. The babe died with her, of course. Probably for the best. The father would never have acknowledged the child."

Silence settled over them again. Charlotte did not ask who the father was. She had seen enough of the world's cruelties to know exactly how the rich and powerful treated those they felt were inferior. In fact, she knew Benjamin and his sister's story was not unique in the slightest. She had written about the conditions children and women lived in after they had been chewed up and spit out by their employers and "benefactors." The editorials had not been run and had been sent back by Mr. Keiler, who requested something of more general interest. That he had even paid her for those weeks had been a surprise. But she had saved each one. They were the work she was most proud of.

Still, hearing the story firsthand, her heart broke anew. Despite the dire straits her family found themselves in now, at least they had started with the privilege of birth that had largely protected them from a similar fate. Though there was always time to fall further, she supposed. It could come to the point that she was no better off than his sister.

"Charlotte?" When Benjamin spoke her name, she felt his voice in her bones.

"Yes?" She turned toward him and could only get the word out on a whisper. His nose was only inches from hers, and the look in his eyes was so vulnerable and unguarded, it was as if she was seeing him for the first time. He reached a hand up and gently brushed tears from the curve of her cheek.

"I did not mean to upset you." The words were muted and apologetic. She shook her head, lifting her left hand up to clasp his warm hand to her cheek.

"Thank you for telling me. I am so sorry you lost your sister like that. I cannot even imagine…"

She stopped as he traced his thumb across her lower lip. Charlotte made a decision at that moment. There was no knowing what was in her future—it was likely not a bright prospect. But here, in this moment, she had him. This beautiful man, who had fought for his family. This man who dealt in secrets yet had shared his with her. She wanted him. Whatever her future held, she could cling to this.

He must have read her thoughts in her gaze, for the atmosphere of the little glass pavilion changed. It was suddenly so charged she expected her hair to stand on end or static sparks to shoot from her hand if she reached out to touch him.

Without thinking, she bridged the gap between them and touched her lips to his. Gentle at first, only a hint of pressure. Then closer, a proper kiss. He matched her immediately, reaching his fingers to her nape and unspooling the loose chignon, letting her hair fall free. He scratched his fingers along her scalp, sending shocks of pleasure to the base of her spine.

Charlotte pulled at his cravat and slid her hand under the collar of his shirt. The heat of his bare skin was glorious, and she felt like she could not get close enough to him.

Having the same thought, Benjamin rolled over and propped himself above her, careful not to touch her shoulder. He did not break his lips from hers as he trailed a hand down the sensitive length of her rib cage and back up to cup her breast over her bodice.

She let out a gasp at the sensation and tugged his shirt from his waistband, pulling it up as he struggled to shrug out of his coat and waistcoat. After he had rid himself of the offending garments, he settled back down over her, breathing hard as he recaptured her lips.

Slowly, Benjamin drew up the hem of her gown and chemise, trailing a warm hand up the back of her thigh until he met her hip. She had never come to embrace the fashion of wearing drawers under her dresses. At that moment, when Benjamin's hand met naked flesh and he let out a strangled moan, she was supremely happy with her decision.

As Benjamin drew his fingers through the slick folds of her most intimate place, she sucked in a sharp breath. She had not imagined it could feel like this. Her entire body was on fire.

He moved from her lips and trailed kisses down her neck until he reached her bodice. With one strategic pull, he exposed one breast and then another, taking one nipple into his mouth just as he sank a long, thick finger into her core.

She let out a small gasp of joy and surprise and gripped his hair, holding him to her. It felt as if a taut chord travelled from her breast down to her core, and the feeling of him strumming at both ends was maddening. Charlotte needed more.

She had a general idea of where this was meant to go, information pieced together through the years, along with her work speaking to the straight-talking women outside her sheltered society upbringing. Fumbling for the fall of his breeches, her hand brushed over his length, eliciting a deep moan as Benjamin bucked his hips into her hand. She buzzed with the gratifying realisation that he was just as affected as she was. Emboldened, she freed the buttons of his fall. She recaptured his lips in hers, wrapping her hand around him and smiling as he gasped into her mouth. She ran her hand up and down his length once, then twice, revelling in the power she wielded.

"Charlotte," he let out in a strangled gasp. "Charlotte, you have to stop. I will not last much longer if you continue like that."

She grinned, kissing him again and pulling him over her. "Then stop me."

He let out another strangled noise that sounded something like a laugh. "You will be the death of me."

"Turnabout is fair play." She reached down between them, but he stopped her, gripping her wrist and pushing her hands above her head, twining his fingers with both of hers and settling between her legs, the rough hair on his legs deliciously scratching the soft, oversensitive flesh of her spread thighs.

He hesitated, looking down at her with searching eyes.

She panted, her bare chest brushing against his and sending waves of sensation through her. "Please, Benjamin."

She watched as her words washed over him with devastating effect. His head dipped, and he let out a tortured groan. She felt the blunt tip of him line up with her entrance and felt the pinching pressure as he sank deep within her.

She caught her breath at the miraculous intrusion. He remained perfectly still at first, letting her adjust to him. It was not what she had expected. The pain was minuscule—fleeting. Overwhelmed by something more, growing from deep within her and spreading through her chest. They were together, part of one another. She was not alone. He was there with her. The thought alone welled up inside her, carrying her forward. Then, as if her body could not wait any longer, she shifted her hips, urging him on.

Slowly but surely, he began thrusting. Shallowly at first, then deeper and deeper, until they were both panting. The rain had picked up even more, and the clatter of droplets against the glass mixed with the sound of their lovemaking. Nothing existed in Charlotte's entire world beyond this little pavilion.

∞∞∞∞

Benjamin hooked Charlotte's leg over his arm and thrust deeper. The fire in his body had reached a fever pitch, and it was all he could do to keep his movements steady. Beneath him, Charlotte writhed. Her hair was splayed around her like a golden fire, and Benjamin was not sure if he had not died and gone to heaven.

He had wanted this to go differently. In his fantasy, he would take his time, draw the pleasure out of her slowly. Watch as she came apart for him again and again before he joined her. They would be in his townhouse—privacy and comfort assured for however long they wished to remain abed—weeks preferably. He would savour her and worship her.

But what had taken them now was nothing like that. Something within him had cracked open in the quiet idyll of this garden pavilion. Charlotte had unwittingly broken through the hard, calcified layers of armour he had not realised had grown so brittle. And out had rushed truths and pains that he had not revisited in decades. It had been saturating, weighing him down and hollowing him out. And Charlotte had stayed.

More than that.

Charlotte had seen him. Touched him. Kissed him. What had followed, he had no power to stop. Perhaps they had both always been propelled by this current—dragged forward until they collided. But rather than crash and dissipate, they joined and grew and had now reached an irresistible force and intensity that they could only fly forward together. The current that took them up was strong and steady and completely overwhelming. Benjamin was lost. He could feel the water cresting over his head, threatening to drown him.

Using the slip of mental capacity he had left, he reached between them and stroked Charlotte with the pad of his thumb. Within seconds, she was clenching him so hard he could not see straight. With a sudden laughing gasp, she exploded around him, and he bent to catch her cries in his mouth as she rode out her climax, crashing around him in a glorious, obliterating wave.

His own thrusts were becoming increasingly erratic, and he pressed his forehead against hers, eyes shut tight as he plunged into her silken heat once, twice more, and then pulled out, spilling his seed on her soft thighs.

They lay there in silence for a while. The only sounds in the pavilion were their pants and the rain.

Benjamin could not get a foothold. He was lost. Out to sea. But somehow, the crack in his soul did not feel so gaping. The hollowness was no longer gnawing at him. In fact, he felt light. Buoyed by Charlotte's tickling breath at his neck and the warmth of her languid body beside him.

Finally, worried the chill of the tile beneath them might start an ache in Charlotte's shoulder, Benjamin roused himself.

He tucked himself back into his breeches and withdrew a handkerchief from the breast pocket of his coat to wipe the mess from Charlotte's legs. Charlotte still had a hand thrown over her eyes, and he could not help but smile at the sweet tilt of her lips.

He folded his handkerchief again and stopped cold.

There was blood.

But surely not.

He knew about her affair with the Italian painting instructor. It was information easily bought if one knew who to pay. And he had made a career of knowing whom to pay. He stared at the smear of blood on his handkerchief, dumbfounded.

That was her secret. The one he knew he could wield. The one that made her his. And he had. That was why she had considered his proposition in the first place. That was why she had not distanced herself completely the second she came to. He had used her brother's debt to bend her, but this secret had been the one to make her break. It was the only thing he had over her. And it had been a lie.

She was a virgin—or had been.

Unaware of his realisation, Charlotte went about putting her bodice to rights and then lay her head back against the tile floor of the pavilion. Too shocked to say anything and scrambling to make sense of what had just occurred, Benjamin followed her lead, hoping she would not see all the ways he was spinning and disoriented and unsure. Vulnerable.

He pulled back on his shirt and lay down beside her, pulling her up against him and pressing a kiss to her hairline.

She had been a virgin.

She had been a virgin and had chosen him.

His secrets meant nothing.

Chapter Sixteen

"I guess this makes me your mistress now." Charlotte regretted the words the minute she said them. She meant for it to be a joke, thumbing her nose at his absurd proposition. Instead, she felt Benjamin stiffen beside her. She could kick herself. Why did she have to shatter the beautifully delicate thing between them?

Something had changed.

She had no experience with this. But she was sure that what had passed between them had not been usual. Or had it been? Was she the only one shattered and burned anew by what they had just shared?

She had been unsteady. Scrambling for something to say—something to acknowledge what they were to each other now. But the words had cheapened the entire experience—made it feel sordid and transactional. She wanted to sink into the tilled floor and disappear forever. Instead, she turned her head to Benjamin.

His jaw was clenched tight, and he did not meet her eyes. Her heart squeezed at the distance she saw in his posture. He was gone again.

"I am sorry. I didn't mean—"

"If that is what you would like. It is certainly preferable to years of paperwork." With that, he pushed himself from the ground and pulled on the rest of his outer garments. He reached down to help her up but refused to meet her eyes.

Part of her wanted to grab his face and make him listen to her. That she did not mean it that way. It had been said in poor judgement, and nothing about what they shared had anything to do with the debt she owed him. But the walls were back up between them. She could not bridge the gap any more than she could take back her words.

"I will have my solicitor draw up the contract," Benjamin declared brusquely.

"Contract?" she squeaked.

When he looked at her, his blue eyes were cold. "Yes. Contract. You would be surprised how quickly mistresses lose sight of their agreement once involved in the affair. Especially when they feel they can get more out of it than originally planned."

Charlotte did not know whether to be affronted or miserable. She considered contradicting him or maybe delivering a well-placed slap. Instead, she held her chin high and said nothing.

Is this what it was like, then? Intimacy and trust traded in some sick game for power? He thought she was a Jezebel—ready to bleed him dry for her own gain. Using the precious thing that had just passed between them to enrich herself. The thought stung her pride and broke her heart.

∞∞∞∞

Charlotte stared uncomprehendingly at the document before her. The lines of impersonal text were so baffling and infuriating that she could not bring herself to sign at the bottom.

"What am I supposed to do with this?" she spoke the thought out loud, forgetting there was another person in the room.

"Sign, my lady."

The solicitor had arrived at the door shortly after nine in the morning. If the Aston house still had a cook, she likely would have been in the middle of her breakfast. Luckily, she had tossed and turned all night until she gave up and clumsily dressed for the day. She had been in the study before the sun rose, with a measly tray of stale oat cakes and an especially weak pot of tea.

Since the November before, when she had run out of money for flour after buying the other household staples, she had taken to reusing tea leaves once or sometimes twice to make the purchase stretch longer. Thus, when she had offered the unusually young and handsome solicitor tea, she was supremely relieved when he politely declined.

Looking down at the contract again, her vision swam. She had spent the entire morning trying to tally the sums paid to each of Freddie's creditors so she might have a more accurate view of the debt they owed to Benjamin. She must have been doing a terrible job, for the number listed under the debt exchanged for *one month of services rendered* was enough to make a nun swear.

Even with the sale of the house and the income from her writing, they would barely be able to make up the cost. There would be only just enough to cover the price of a small flat across town, not to mention the boy's tuition, which she fully meant to repay to Benjamin with interest.

And then there were the new debts. She did not know how much Freddie owed Deering. It was likely a king's ransom if he was only willing to forgive it in return for a wife.

The idea of marrying that snake of a man was enough to turn her stomach. She would go to debtor's prison before she submitted herself to him for the rest of her earthly existence. But it was not only her well-being she had to consider.

The paper was still clenched in her hands when a polite cough from the solicitor caught her attention. Mr. Colwell? No, Mr. Collier? Was that what he said his name was?

Her eyes focused again. Debtor's prison was a genuine possibility. As real as being left destitute with two growing twelve-year-old boys to care for. As real as being forced to marry Lord Deering.

Perhaps it was these horrors mounting one after another that compelled her to pick up the quill beside her and hold it over the document. Then again, perhaps it was the memory of the previous afternoon in the pavilion that moved the quill to touch the page. This was the last thing she could do for her family. Or was it the last thing she would allow herself to do for herself? Either way, she watched as the sloping lines of her name flourished from the tip of the pen and onto the paper.

It was done. It did not matter why.

Chapter Seventeen

"Yes, but how did she seem?" Benjamin was pacing the length of his office, clenching and unclenching his hands. He had expected to be relieved that the contract was properly seen to. He hated getting bogged down in legalities, and diligent contracts were the best way to avoid it.

Elliot Collier watched him impassively from his place beside the desk. "I was not aware part of my job was to report on ladies' comportment."

Elliot Collier, though younger than the seasoned geysers that normally served peers and successful businessmen like himself, was the best solicitor Benjamin had ever had. He was likely the best London had ever had. He was hardworking, methodical, and brilliant. What Collier could not do with the law was not worth doing.

"True, but you are a man with all his functioning faculties. All you have reported to me is that the contract signing was successful and legally binding. I am asking you for more. I damn well pay you enough for a bit more insight."

Collier arched an eyebrow and clasped his hands. "I do not

think it would be professional of me to comment on such things in the capacity of your solicitor. However, if I were just a friendly acquaintance who occasionally makes house calls to your female associates, I would say I have never seen a woman so reluctant to enter such a profitable agreement."

Benjamin stilled at that. "Reluctant?"

Collier nodded. "Yes, sir. The lady looked like she was signing her soul away."

Benjamin frowned. What a strange reaction for a woman who had shown no reluctance the day before. She had given him her virtue, for Christ's sake. That was not the act of a reluctant woman. Despite himself, he revelled in the memory of her beautiful body on the floor of the glass pavilion, the sound of rain patter twining with her gasps and sighs.

"Well, that must have been a pretty act. She knew what she was getting into. She planned for this."

Benjamin did not know why he was so mad about the whole ordeal. After all, it had been his rash idea to begin with. Who was he to look down on Charlotte for taking him up on the offer? It was not as if a better solution was likely to come along.

Collier gave Benjamin another sceptical look. "I doubt it was an act, sir. From what I could tell, she had all but forgotten I was in the room."

"From what you could tell? What makes you think you are such a good judge of a lady's motives?" Benjamin was being rude and pig-headed, and he knew it. He took a deep breath and forced himself to drop his shoulders. "Apologies, Collier. You find me a bit out of sorts today."

"I will take my leave, then." The man gave a small bow of his head and turned on his heel, leaving Benjamin alone with his thoughts once again.

If he was not careful, he was going to lose his best solicitor. And Lord knew it would be damned difficult replacing such a competent man as Collier. He strode across his office and yanked the bellpull.

"You rang, sir?" Boyd tried to press down the ever-errant tuft of hair that sprang from the back of his head.

"Yes, thank you, Boyd. Have a case of scotch sent to Mr. Collier's offices."

"The good stuff, sir?"

Benjamin could not help smiling. "Yes, Boyd. The good stuff."

∞∞∞

Charlotte stood outside the entrance to Elysium, uncharacteristically uncertain. She had waited all afternoon and evening until she was sure the doors to Elysium would be open. She had planned to storm in full of righteous fury at Benjamin's audacity to serve her that accursed contract. Through a stranger, no less! She would demand he burn it and forget the whole thing.

But now, she stood outside the elegant building and considered going home. Had she not signed that contract? Was she not just as culpable in these sordid dealings as he was? It was all a muddle now, anyway. She could not reconcile the depth of the experience she had had with him and the cold dealings of such employment that followed. He should have laughed at her mention of the proposition. Surely they had surpassed that—meant more to each other now.

It had not felt sordid in the pavilion. His hands on her

under the blanket of rain had not made her feel cheap and base like signing that paper in the drawing room had. But now it was done. She had agreed to his proposition, and she could not put any more blame on him than she deserved herself. And why should there be blame at all? Work was work. She could use the funds to clear the way for the twins and ensure Freddie would not get thrown in the poorhouse. Then maybe she could leave London and start her own life.

It was a tempting vision.

The only concern she had—though her upbringing really should have fostered more than the one—was that she was not sure she could pretend this was *only* a job.

There was nothing professional or detached about the way she was drawn to Benjamin Scarsdale. If she did not tread carefully, she would find herself in a world of trouble and heartbreak. If she were to do this, she would have to keep the man at arm's length and keep her wits about her. He had sent over a contract, for goodness' sake! After what they had shared in the pavilion, he had served her legal documents. No good would come from letting such a man past her defences. She would have to be as cold as he if she had any hope of surviving this. She wanted to survive this. And more frighteningly—she wanted to do this.

She had spent her adult life living under the strain of her own shame—her family's shame. And it had done no good. Nothing had been solved by her making herself small; hiding from the mistake bred only by innocent naivete. It had not stopped her father from dying. It had not stopped Freddie from ruin. She had given everything to make amends, and it had left her with nothing. The life of a ruined spinster was long and lonely, and she knew the years ahead would be much the same. So she would seize this chance. A chance to be held, to be touched, to *live*. And then, after their month was done, she would set off into the rest of her life.

She battled through these thoughts as she stared up at Elysium's elegant facade, well-sprung carriages pulling up and depositing well-heeled and common patrons alike. It was imposing in its vibrancy—this world of secrets and vice, filled with her own peers and yet completely foreign to her. A part of her knew that stepping into that building tonight would be the making or breaking of her. And yet, her fear was miles away, eclipsed by anticipation.

They would proceed only on her terms. She was here to set that straight. She would not be a concubine or a whore. She was an equal part of this—contract or no. Charlotte squared her shoulders and faced the doors of Elysium, refusing to let the past pull her away from fixing the future.

∞∞∞

There she was.

Benjamin had been prowling the gambling floor as he was wont to do on restless nights. It did him good to be amongst his patrons—seeing the fruits of his labours: cheering patrons, spinning roulette wheels. The living cloud of cigar smoke and laughter that hung over the floor on a busy night brought him a measure of solace. It made him feel like all the suffering that led him here had been for something. He had succeeded.

Tonight, he had taken to the floor with more pent-up agitation than usual. And to his dismay, the routine was not bringing him the calm that he had hoped. Instead, he felt more and more like a caged lion, ready to bolt. He resisted the urge to do so because he knew where he would bolt. And that was not acceptable.

He refused to be the one to push. She would come to him when she was ready. He could not bear the thought of forcing her hand any more than fate already had. Fate, and himself.

She had agreed to his proposition because she thought she had no other options. She did not know that he would never let her fall into the hands of that villain, Deering. He had purposely withheld the fact that Delia had been employed in the Deering household. He had not explained that Deering's son had been her attacker, and that before his death, he had always been the rotten apple fallen from the baron's cruel and twisted tree. Deering had been the one to beat Delia for her "transgression" when his son was through with her. And he had been the one to throw her out of his house with no reference and no pay, condemning her as he had to countless maids who had met the same fate at the hands of him and his son over the years. Deering had concealed his son's crime and punished his victim in the worst possible way, and Benjamin had spent the better part of a decade collecting secrets with the express intention of toppling the baron and his legacy.

Benjamin knew that if he had told her of his vendetta against Deering, it would have changed how she saw the situation. He was not sure if his revelation in the pavilion would have been enough to show her he would never let her fall into his clutches. He would pay off all her family's debts and find them a safe means of support. No questions asked. Or maybe she would assume, according to his ruthless reputation, that he was playing her as a pawn against the lecher. Either way, she likely would not have surrendered her virtue with only the promise of a cheap contract—though that truth had settled more comfortably than the idea that she had given him such a gift for nothing at all. Preposterous.

The clarity should have been a comfort. But the hollowness was back—washed away only for a moment before the cynical reality closed back in on him. Nothing was given for free. Everyone had an angle. Charlotte's was better than most: to rescue her family. But it was there all the same.

Still, she did not play the game well. She had thrown away a coveted advantage as if it were nothing. Society traded virtue above all else. She could have demanded anything from him— even marriage. She could have—and should have—demanded he absolve the debt and never speak to her again. And she had not even tried to use such leverage; she had let him think her the sum of a few suppressed rumours. It was baffling.

In the pavilion, she had said he was not the type to take advantage, but he had. He had withheld his secrets, and she had paid the price; and for the first time in his life, that did not sit well with him.

But there she was.

She was standing in the same place she had been when she came to offer him payment. The night all this nonsense began. It had only been a few days, but Benjamin felt like his world had somersaulted again. Everything was different.

Tonight, she did not have the sickly spectre of death hanging over her shoulder. She was resplendent.

Her hair was pulled back in the sensible coronet she seemed to favour, but she had allowed a few curls to hang down, framing her beautiful elfin face. Her gown was a dusky lavender that, while clearly a few seasons behind *la mode*, suited her so perfectly, she outshone even the most fashionable ladies in attendance.

Her soft colour in the middle of the rolling den of rich-hued vice was like a breath of spring air. Looking at her, Benjamin felt an acute yearning for the quiet of the country. He wanted to enjoy the quiet of the country with *her*.

More striking than anything, though, was the healthy rose flush of her cheeks when she caught Benjamin's eye and held it. He could not help the grin that split his face. Who cared about that blasted contract? In that moment, there was nothing between them again. Benjamin felt his lungs expanding in a way he was not sure they ever had. He had never breathed before today.

Then reality came crashing back in. Was she mad? What was she doing here in his hell again? She was the unwed sister of an earl. She could not just appear on the floor of a gaming club and not send the gossips aflutter.

He snapped one of the footmen over, quickly dispatching instructions to lead Charlotte off the floor immediately.

Benjamin made his own way to a concealed exit and traversed the twining back corridors to the spot he knew the footman was leading her.

"Lady Charlotte." He offered a courtly bow when she appeared around the corner, letting his lips brush her ungloved knuckles with a featherlight touch. "You are looking well. I am glad to see you so recovered from your illness."

She arched an eyebrow at him, and he bit back a smile. Her scepticism was delightful. "Small talk? Really?"

Benjamin realised he still held her hand in his and forced himself to release it. "As you wish. I see you have no interest in my manners and charm." He gave a mocking smile and then grew serious again. "Charlotte, have you no care for your reputation? Being seen unmasked in my establishment once was already courting disaster. Doing so a second time makes me wonder if you care about ruin at all?" He knew he sounded imposing, possibly patronising, but the thought of her tossing away her good name for him had his gut churning. He knew the arrangement they had struck risked all this and more, but he could be careful. He could be circumspect and protect her. But not if she did not take care, herself.

Charlotte only shrugged.

That shocked a disbelieving laugh from his chest. "You do not care for yourself or your reputation?"

"Wise of you to differentiate the two, Mr. Scarsdale. I am less and less convinced that what benefits my reputation lends any benefit at all to my person." She spoke low enough that only he could only just make out her words, and though she used his formal address, the intimacy of it made his pulse thrum. In the dim corridor, even with staff bustling by them, it was as if they were completely alone. "Besides, I am a spinster with very little stake in the *ton*. I doubt anyone will care much what I do. And I am not sure I care what they think. I find my recent brush with death has vastly changed my perspective on all this nonsense."

She was pensive for a moment, and he wanted to do anything, offer anything to have a glimpse inside that mind.

"As to your manners and charm—and I am sorry to be-labour the point—I have found that being shot by someone greatly diminishes the effect of their vacant flattering."

She spoke so sternly. Benjamin thought wryly that she might have missed her calling as a governess. Though considering her family's status, that might very well still be an option. The thought doused his humour, but when he glanced toward her, he found her eyes sparkling with it.

"Dear me, Mr. Scarsdale. Have you finally felt the pang of remorse for shooting a defenceless lady?"

"Lady, yes. Defenceless, no. I beg you to recall, Lady Charlotte, you were as armed as I." Her lips quirked at his response, and he desperately wanted to kiss her.

"Touche. But I beg *you* to recall that I aimed clearly for the sky. Not your person."

"True. A very noble move. Nobler than many a gentleman in your place."

"Nobler than you, in my place." Though she gave him a sly smile, she unconsciously rolled her shoulders back, wincing ever so slightly, as if her body could not forget the wound he had inflicted.

"I do."

She looked up at that. "You do what?"

"I do feel the pang of remorse." He spoke earnestly, and he watched as she furrowed her brow, clearly taken aback by the change of tone.

"While I appreciate your contrition, I hope it is not on account of my sex. Someone was bound to be injured in that foolish duel, as they are in any foolish duel. It is of no consequence that it was me."

"It is of every consequence." Benjamin was finding it increasingly difficult to maintain his pleasant facade. He wanted to grab this woman and haul her away from here. His rooms were only a few floors away.

"Not in the slightest," she said. "Playing with guns is irresponsible, and you cannot possibly be surprised or truly remorseful for the course of events. In fact, I would say any injury caused in a duel is the product of deliberate intent."

Benjamin heard the true message in her voice. *You intended to hurt me—my brother*. She could not forgive that so easily.

She glanced away and Benjamin wanted to take her hand in his. "I believe one can feel remorse about something they intended to do." Charlotte sighed, and Benjamin wished she would lean further into him—rest her head on his shoulder as they dodged a passing serving tray full of champagne flutes.

"If I am being completely honest," she said. "I would be tempted to shoot him too, if I had the chance." That was it. He caught the eye of a footman and nodded him over.

"Marks, please escort Lady Charlotte to the back. I will be there in a few moments."

Charlotte looked surprised. "The back?" For a moment, he regretted his impulsiveness and considered staying here, loitering in the liminal space of the corridor for the remainder of the night just to talk with her.

"Yes, m'lady." Marks gestured towards the intersecting passageway, politely forcing Charlotte to follow without further question.

Benjamin gave her a brisk nod and turned, making a show of passing back through the gaming floor alone and generously topping up patrons' drinks. If they had caught a glimpse of Charlotte, they were unlikely to remember the next morning.

∞∞∞∞

This was why he thought she had come. Charlotte pressed her hands to her cheeks to cool her blush.

Marks had discreetly led her down a dark corridor and around to a small flight of servants' stairs, depositing her in a dimly lit room with nothing more than a by-your-leave. She realised immediately what the well-rehearsed process was once her eyes adjusted to the low candlelight in the room. Really, she felt like a naïve schoolgirl for not realising sooner.

Of course, he assumed she had come there to consummate their agreement. Why would he not? He could not have known that she had stomped up to the front steps to confront him and tear up that contract. Especially when she had decided against that before she even entered. Why had she come in here, anyway? She had wanted to set her terms. To put them on an equal footing.

But how had she thought she would manage that? The idea of seeing Benjamin Scarsdale, of talking with him, of touching him, had been too alluring to resist. Then, once she was inside, she had been so swept up in the glory of his kingdom that she had lost her wits.

What must it feel like to have such power? Such wealth and influence? Even if it was from the outskirts of society.

She had lived on the outskirts long enough to know they were no less valuable than the centre of the *haute ton*. If anything, they were more important, connected to the real world, where one could see the truth of it all. And Benjamin had the power to change it, bend it to his will.

This man had far more power than she ever dreamed. And she was out of her depth. Worse, she was being sucked in deeper with each look, each touch. The ghost of a smile had her heart hammering and her skin flushing. She would need to steel herself to match his control.

She wanted to be here, she admitted to herself. She wanted to be nowhere but here, standing in the middle of Benjamin Scarsdale's bed chamber, staring at his silk-draped bed— funny that she had lain there just days earlier under such different conditions.

Charlotte wanted nothing more than to be a part of his world, even just for a moment. But she was not sure she was sophisticated enough to pull this off.

Chapter Eighteen

He was stalling. He had done two laps around the gaming floor on his own, making a casual inquiry about one gentleman's new stallion, another about a particularly slanderous wager placed in his betting books, and had generally spent the last fifteen minutes subtly scanning for any mention of Charlotte's appearance on the gaming floor.

It was for her reputation, he repeated to himself. He could not abide the lady being dragged into malicious gossip regarding himself. She had managed to keep her family's name above reproach, even as her fool of a brother did everything he could to tarnish it. Benjamin would not be the straw that broke the gossip mill's back.

It was a flimsy excuse, though. The truth of it was, after days of yearning for this exact moment, Charlotte had returned to his rooms and was awaiting him. He found himself filled with trepidation. He had never been one to be thrown out of sorts by a woman. Even as a boy, he had not been intimidated by the fairer sex, as some might. But now he was terrified. Or was that elation?

Damn it, he could not even think straight since she had

come in the door. But enough was enough. He rounded a Grecian marble and slipped through a door behind one of the tapestries. Even if someone had been watching, he had left the floor on the opposite side of the room from Lady Charlotte.

When he finally stood outside his bedchamber, he paused, trying to catch his breath. Should he knock? No, these were his rooms.

He pushed open the door and shut it behind him.

Charlotte looked up from her seat by the fire. She was perfectly calm, relaxed even, leaning back in the plush chair and running her finger over the lip of a glass.

"I hope you don't mind. I helped myself." She took a sip of brandy, and the moisture left on her lip shone in the firelight.

"Not at all." His voice sounded hoarse. "Sorry to have kept you waiting."

"Not at all." She smiled and took another sip from her glass.

He pushed off the door and poured himself a glass from the decanter, throwing half of it back before refilling it.

"How are you feeling?"

"Again, really? Small talk?"

He turned and was pinned by her raised brows. Benjamin shrugged and made his way to the seat across from her. She had a folio of papers across her lap, reading through them at her leisure, as if she were his man of business and this was a normal evening appointment.

"I don't consider it small. I did watch you almost die. Twice. Seems a fair question."

She waved the comment away, and he considered how strange it was that she had been asleep during some of the most harrowing days of his life. She had no idea of the investment he felt in her and her well-being.

"Your pub is being embezzled." She said the words casually, as if commenting on a bonnet while passing a shop window.

Benjamin started and then frowned, leaning forward to see the papers she had on her lap.

"Where did you get that?" He saw that she indeed had a balance sheet from the Trident's Hull.

"From your bedside table. Do you often go to sleep reading stories of cunning barmen stealing funds from under their swashbuckling thief lord?" She said it with a teasing smile and pointed at a row of figures as she passed the packet over to him. Sure enough, the entries for ale were listed as one number, when, just a few pages later, the supply cost showed a significantly lower sum.

"It looks like they are charging for more expensive ale than they ordered and pocketing the difference." He looked up, jaw slack as she sipped her spirits calmly, the hint of a smile playing across her lips.

"How did you catch that?" *How had he missed it?* He was usually so meticulous in his bookkeeping. That is why he did not leave it to a steward or Bell, his man of business.

She shrugged. "I have gotten very good at keeping accounts. Though I have to admit, yours are much more extensive than mine."

"I cannot believe I missed this," he said, somehow sure she would not use the admission against him.

"As I said, your accounts are extensive, if this is any indication. That is far too much for one person to keep track of. Though I admire the diligence." She was so forthright. He knew how much the compliment meant coming from her. It did strange things to his chest as he regarded her a moment longer.

He watched as she worried her lower lip between her teeth, clearly winding up to say something. "Benjamin," she said his name on a whispering exhale, and he almost vaulted himself from his seat to reach her.

But he restrained himself. It was clear she was working herself up to say something important—likely to call off this sham.

"I recognise that following this contract." Her nose screwed up at that, like she had more to say about his cowardly delivery of that accursed document, but she carried on, "I recognise that you are technically my employer."

It struck Benjamin as a strange idea, but she was correct. That is exactly what he was. A mistress was just another employee. It was his turn to purse his lips; the thought left a sour taste in his mouth. How pathetic.

"But even though I am now under your employ, I expect to be treated with the respect of an equal in this arrangement." Benjamin kept his face impassive. It was a bold declaration, and her pride warmed and shamed him simultaneously. "I know it is not the done thing, but I have never acted as a man's mistress before and find I have no regard for the customs of such an arrangement. I do not wish to be obligated by a contract, and I do not wish you to think I act out of an obligation either. I find myself at a crossroads in my life where this arrangement suits me as much as it suits you. Though I know the matter of money is unavoidable, I would ask that we both disregard it as much as is within our power during our time together. That means no gifts. No trinkets. No buying of affection."

She sat there with all the dignity of a queen, and Benjamin

could not tear his gaze from her. Her words hummed within him. She wanted to be a part of this. Beyond his blasted contract. It was too much to believe, and the deep-seated, cynical voice in his ear urged him to exercise caution. She must have an ulterior motive.

But he could not find it in himself to care. "Agreed. It would be my honour." The words were sincere.

Charlotte's lips quirked at first, then broke into a full, delighted smile.

Benjamin held his breath as she leaned over, bridging the distance between their chairs, suddenly set far too far apart for his liking. Finally, her lips met his, tentatively at first, only a caress. The immediate relief and exhilaration were dizzying, but the moment she deepened the kiss, Benjamin thought he might die.

She was warm and accommodating, matching every move of his lips with her own. She smelled of rosewater and the rainy pavilion. Benjamin felt like he was there and here at the same time. She combed her fingers through his hair and moaned into his mouth as he pushed her back into the seat, wrapping his arms around her.

In the hours following their encounter in the pavilion, Benjamin had convinced himself that he had imagined the electricity shooting to the base of his spine at her touch, or the heady pull of her mouth and the yearning thrum of her body. It had never felt this way before.

He had chalked it up to the time elapsed between the encounter and his last mistress. He had never been one to enter liaisons impulsively—life on the streets exposed the ravages of unanticipated infection—and he had dismissed his last mistress almost a month prior. Benjamin had hoped it was this bout of abstinence that had intensified the experience with Charlotte.

He had been mistaken.

Here, now, pulling Charlotte as close as physically possible, he could not get enough. She was like a drug, and a frenzied haze had clouded his mind so that all he could do—all he could think about—was the touch of her lips, the silken feel of her skin, the warm sweetness of her mouth…he might spend then and there, like a randy stableboy, if he did not regain some control.

He broke from her lips and began tracing kisses down her neck to the exposed ridge of her collarbone, then to her shoulder, pushing the delicate sleeve of her gown down the curve of her arm. He could feel her warm breath fanning over his neck as she panted.

He drew his tongue along the skin just below her clavicle and smiled into her sternum as she gasped. Her breasts were straining against the edge of her bodice, and with one decisive flick of his wrists, he freed them. His breeches felt impossibly tight as his cock throbbed at the sight of her breasts flushed pink with desire.

With one hand, he cupped one of them, running a thumb over the already puckered nipple. He leaned down and laved the other with the flat of his tongue.

She let out a strangled groan.

Encouraged by her frenzied reaction, he reined in his control even more and moved his tongue in a slow circle around her breast and up to the tip, sucking it in between his teeth before passing another broad lick. He switched and began paying the same attention to the other side.

She was clawing into his flesh now, head thrown back for

him to admire. She really was the most beautiful thing he had ever seen. It defied logic how breathtaking she looked just then in the firelight, skin flushed and chest heaving.

But he was not even close to finished. "Easy now, Charlotte. I want to take my time," he purred into the soft skin of her abdomen.

He reached down and grasped her ankle, running the other hand up the back of her calf, then the inside of her thigh, until he reached the top of her stocking. Slowly, he undid the tie and rolled the worn-softened fabric down her equally soft leg. When he got to her foot, she let out a breathy gasp that sounded almost like a laugh. Ticklish. Interesting.

Propping one leg on his shoulder, he reached up and brought her other stocking down, glancing up to see her watching him with hooded eyes, a finger caught on her lips. The look of her heavy lids and desire-dilated pupils shot straight to the base of his cock, and he had to bend further to accommodate the almost painful bulge in his trousers.

With her stockings removed, he was free to slide his hands up her legs and push back her skirts. He revelled in the movement, watching as his hands revealed more and more of her long, shapely legs. The sight was unbelievably erotic.

He began placing kisses along the length of her leg until he had her skirts folded at her midsection. She tried to push her legs closed, but he held them up, baring her to the firelight and his feasting gaze.

"Wh-what are you doing?"

"Shh, love. Do you trust me?" It was a natural question, but when she nodded without hesitation, he had to dip his chin against his chest to catch his breath, momentarily overwhelmed.

When he looked up again, he let out a groan. She was already so wet that her womanhood glistened in the warm light. He felt like a man starved, but he restrained himself, savouring the look of surprise and anticipation in her eyes as he lowered his mouth to her core. He laved his tongue up the length of her, smiling as she shuddered in response.

Benjamin pulled her other leg to rest on his shoulder and wrapped his arms under her thighs, pulling her to the edge of the chair and closer to him. He licked again. She moaned.

His restraint snapped at the throaty sound, and he buried his face in her glorious wet heat. Never had he experienced such bliss. He kissed and sucked, running the flat of his tongue over her clit again and again and then plunging it into her entrance. As she writhed against him, he brought a hand around and slid his middle finger into her heat.

His head swam as her muscles contracted around him. Pumping his finger in time with his tongue, he latched his mouth around her mound, sucking as he slid another finger in.

She was grinding against him now, rocking her pelvis against his face as her pants filled the room. Benjamin sped up his thrusts, reaching up to pinch her nipple as she ground into his mouth.

"Oh—oh God, Benjamin."

He felt every word throb in his loins. Her fingers were wrapped in his hair, and every tug brought him closer to his own release. And then she was spasming around him, holding his head tight between her legs as she let out a glorious stream of expletives no town debutante might know, let alone use.

He did not wait for her to come down from her high before picking her up and carrying her to the bed. In a flash, he had removed her gown and pulled off his waistcoat and shirt. Before he had the fine linen shirt over his head, though, he felt a caress over his breeches.

He let out a choked groan as he ripped the fabric from his face and looked down in awe. Charlotte had slid to the edge of the bed in front of him and was slowly undoing the fastenings of his breeches. She looked up and gave him a wicked smile, making his heart stutter. His magnificent elfin queen.

Her hair had escaped from its bindings and curled enticingly around her temples and down the back of her neck. He wrapped one around his finger and pulled gently, marvelling at the soft texture as it gently sprang back into place.

Quickly, his attention was drawn back to his own lower anatomy as he felt a warm hand grasp the base of his cock and stroke once, then twice. He immediately grabbed her wrist, stalling her actions.

Charlotte frowned. "I would like the opportunity to return the favour."

He gave a strangled bark of laughter and leaned to capture her lips in a kiss. "Next time, I promise. I just need to be inside you. Now."

Next time, there would be a next time. She was his.

She smiled at that and kissed him back, twining her arms around his neck.

Still standing, Benjamin lifted a knee to the bed, spreading her legs wide. Without breaking the kiss, he aligned the throbbing head of his cock with her entrance and slowly pushed inside.

He felt his eyes roll back as her heat enveloped him, drawing him further and further in. Beads of sweat began gathering on his brow and the back of his neck as he stood perfectly still, grasping for the last threads of self-control.

"Ohh." Charlotte tilted her hips forward, pushing him further inside her. "Benjamin." She moaned his name in a plea that was enough to break him. He drew slowly out and then, just as slowly, thrust all the way back into her tight, wet heat. His thrusts were long and deep, and as he began to pick up the pace, he looped one of Charlotte's legs up over his arm, going deeper and drawing moans from both of them.

He pushed her further onto the bed and climbed on after her, rolling his hips against her pelvis and sending shock waves through his body.

She wrapped her legs around his waist and pulled him closer, deeper. There was nothing but their two bodies. Together. Charlotte matched his thrusts, awkwardly at first, then more and more in sync with him. They were racing for the same edge, pushing, reaching. With one hard grind of his hips, the strength of her own legs pressing him into her, they both fell off it together in a blinding burst of release. Benjamin felt his pulse beating through him and into Charlotte, her own body thrumming in response. A harmony of limbs wrapped together and singing with the same euphoria.

It was long moments later that Benjamin began to regain his senses. He was lying atop Charlotte, their chests still heaving together. She trailed a finger lazily down his spine, and he buried his face further into her hair, inhaling deeply the smell of rose soap and satisfied woman. He felt lighter than he ever had—as if his bones had been replaced with some effervescent material.

"Benjamin." Her voice was a small, playful whisper, and it

sounded far away.

"Mmm," he hummed into her hair.

"I cannot really breathe." He felt her laughter under him as he nuzzled his face against her cheek, reluctantly rolling off her.

"Have I hurt your shoulder?" He drew a careful finger over the puckered skin just beside the roll of her shoulder. It was a fading red mark against her otherwise creamy skin and, while no longer an angry wound, was not yet a proper scar.

"Not more than the first time." She gave him a teasing grin, and Benjamin was immediately, impossibly hard again.

"Imp." He brushed a curl from her forehead. "Really, Charlotte, you would tell me if I hurt you."

Her smile softened. "Of course. Really, it does not bother me. It is only really sore in the mornings or if I swing my arm around."

"Do you have much call for swinging your arm around?"

"Oh yes. Besides being an accomplished duellist, I dabble in pugilism as well."

"I will keep that in mind when antagonising you."

"You plan to antagonise me?"

"Only marginally." He prodded her in the ribs, and she jumped with a squeal, breathlessly swatting at him to stop. Her laugh was infectious, and when she tried to wrestle herself away from him, he felt his own chest begin to rumble with laughter.

∞∞∞

Benjamin Scarsdale had a glorious laugh.

It was warm and rich, but the gruff way it emerged from his

throat made Charlotte wonder when the last time was that he had really, truly laughed. Now that she was thinking about it, though, stroking a gentle finger through the smattering of coarse hair on his sleeping chest, she could not remember the last time she had laughed like that before meeting him.

They had made love again before lounging in the warm glow of the fire-lit room. Charlotte had dozed off first, waking an indeterminate time later, tucked into Benjamin's side, the slow rise and fall of his chest moving her head while his long, muscular arm wrapped around her back.

She should leave now. The city would be waking soon, if it had not already, and Charlotte did not want her new situation to become common knowledge. It would take only one early-to-rise kitchen maid peeking out a window to see her alighting from Scarsdale's coach for all of Mayfair to know she had taken up as his mistress.

She was his mistress.

The thought did not fill her with the shame and disgust she would have expected. She was disappointed that it had come about as a result of insurmountable debt, but the reality of the exchange itself was unexpectedly wonderful.

Lying here in Benjamin Scarsdale's arms, in his wide four-poster bed, Charlotte could not think of a time she had felt more content. If she could stay like this for the rest of her life, she would.

But alas, she knew this moment was just a passing dream, and their arrangement would be over quickly as well. Perhaps Benjamin would consider keeping her on for more than the agreed month, but no. Charlotte would not watch him tire of her. She would savour these weeks and carry them with her forever. The memory of this moment, curled against his relaxed muscular form, would warm her in the long, cold years that stood before her.

With that, she slipped from under his arm and dressed herself as best she could and slipped out into the night.

Chapter Nineteen

lk and Wells watched from atop their mounts as Benjamin growled at a mousy stable hand in the mews behind Elysium. After the boy finished scurrying around, tacking his horse, Benjamin flung himself into the saddle, throwing a whole guinea down to the boy in lieu of an apology for his surly behaviour.

The boy seemed suitably pleased by the compensation and disappeared into the back stalls.

"What's got your knickers in a twist today, dear Mr. Scarsdale?" Elkington leaned over the neck of his horse to give Benjamin a sardonic look.

"Trouble with our fair Lady Charlotte?" Wills said her name in a singsong, such a boyish taunt completely at odds with his ducal hauteur.

"None of your business," Benjamin bit out.

He knew his friends were only teasing. If it were one of them, he would do much the same. Still, at the mention of Charlotte's name, he was plunged into another wave of frustration and irritability.

The night before had been heavenly—beyond words, really. And the thought of Charlotte in his arms sent sensations coursing through him again and again. But when Benjamin had awoken an hour ago—far later than usual despite his late hours—to a cold, empty indent in the sheets beside him, he had been cast into a foul mood that he simply could not shake.

Benjamin pulled at the reins, turning his horse down the mews toward the path they took to the park. The three of them met almost every day for a ride when they were all in London, and though he had slept late, Wells and Elkington were waiting for him when he came down from his rooms above Elysium.

"Ah. She did not go for it then?" Wells asked in a sympathetic tone.

"Of course she did. She would be a fool not to." Despite the self-aggrandising nature of the statement, Benjamin knew it to be true. He had offered Charlotte an impossible lifeline— saved her from ruin and likely destitution. While the concept of genteel poverty was something that he had always scoffed at, at the rate at which the young earl was blowing through the family coffers, the poorhouse was not an unlikely destination for his dependent relatives.

"Jesus, then what's all this about?" Elkington nodded to Benjamin's stiff posture, likely referring to his overall surliness.

"I don't know what you are talking about."

"Well, to start with, you are behaving like a bear with a sore paw."

"Not the behaviour one would expect after taking on a mistress. Is the anticipation driving you to distraction?" Wells levelled him an assessing glance. He was a master at teasing information out of people—a useful skill for such a powerful man. "Surely, once you bed her, you will be put to rights."

Benjamin could not stop his ferocious scowl, immediately regretting the reaction. He knew that was Wells' goal all along, but had been unable to stop himself. "Do not speak of her that way."

Judging by the expression on his friend's face, Wells already knew of Charlotte's visit. Damned duke, sticking his damned nose into things. Both he and Elkington clearly thought they already knew all there was to know. Benjamin would not mention the pavilion. That moment was too sacred to share, even with his closest friends.

Elkington looked surprised. "Well, judging by that reaction, I cannot imagine what you are grumbling about. Wish fulfilled! Now you can stop mooning over her and playing the tragic villain. Clearly, she forgives you for shooting her."

Benjamin frowned ahead, not taking his eyes from the park entrance they were approaching. It was still before the fashionable hour for Mayfair to descend upon Hyde Park to see and be seen. Still, there were enough coaches and single riders about that he found himself scanning for a certain pair of fair, arching eyebrows. But he knew he would not find them. From what he could gather—quite a lot—Lady Charlotte Aston had all but retired from the *ton*. She did not make public appearances. She did not attend parties or routes and had long since stopped being invited. For all the status of her birth, Charlotte lived much like the working classes she wrote about—though with a significant degree less freedom. Her life had been stripped away from her. And Benjamin felt a compulsive need to restore it.

All this only made him surlier, and he did not want to

examine why. While his day began with disappointment upon waking and finding an empty space beside him where Charlotte had been, he was pretty certain the thorn in the bear's paw was heavily laced with guilt—an emotion he buffeted at all costs.

"You are right, of course. I am merely tired."

"Oh-ho. Kept you up all night, did she?" Elkington waggled his eyebrows in an exaggerated gesture, clearly fishing for a reaction.

Benjamin could not suppress a smile. "A gentleman does not kiss and tell."

"No, and neither does Benjamin Scarsdale." With a wink, Elkington gave his stallion its head and left Wells and Benjamin to race after him.

∞∞∞

Dear Lord, Charlotte thought to herself, as she stood in the corridor that led back to the servants' stairs and down to the kitchen, pulling at a curling strip of paint that was peeling from the wall; she had not realised just how bad things had gotten.

Over the years, she had watched with detached pragmatism as the vestiges of her family's wealth were slowly stripped away. Now, however, the reality of their great fall was staring her directly in the face. This hall, being part of the invisible background that kept the facade running, even in the best of times, had been neglected the longest and now was in true disrepair. The sight was a blow.

After a few hours of tossing and turning after arriving home shortly before dawn, Charlotte had finally gotten up, donned her increasingly worn-out wrapper and with pencil and pad in hand, climbed to the attic rooms, and methodically made her way down through the house, taking inventory of necessary repairs and blemishes which would need to be seen to before the house could feasibly be put to market, and trying desperately to put the memory of Benjamin's touch far from her mind.

After their night together, Charlotte felt a renewed hope for her future. She would give herself this month—a month of joy and discovery—and then she would set out to build a new life full of purpose.

In the hours since she had slipped out of his bed, she had made a plan. She would put the house up for let. The income from that would be just enough to carry on paying the boy's tuition until they were out of school—maybe even into university if they were lucky. Freddie could take rooms at his club—maybe with a mistress. Charlotte could not escape the feeling that she must have failed him. Perhaps she should have taken a firmer hand with Freddie. She had known from a young age that Veronica was not interested in taking anything beyond a flying fancy to her sons.

Maybe Charlotte should have tried harder to balance that— to be the structure where her stepmother was a fleeting source of vacant praise and periodic neglect. But Charlotte had not had it in her to discipline the boys when they misbehaved. She could only do what she could to set things right after the fact. Besides, helping her brothers made her feel good—necessary. But in retrospect, she saw that shielding Freddie from the consequences of his actions had not helped. Her coddling until this point had only caused him harm.

The only thing she could do for her family now was wipe the slate clean and move on. And maybe, just maybe, it would be the right thing for her as well.

She would retire from London publicly, claiming a summons from an elderly aunt up north—Liverpool, perhaps, or maybe even Scotland. There, she could take a position as a governess, or perhaps even engage herself as a journalist—they were not so against women working for a living there, and she knew for a fact, the working conditions in some of those new factories up North were deplorable to the extreme. A woman sent to investigate and report would be much less remarked upon than a man.

The idea filled her with hope. There was nothing as empowering as taking hold of one's destiny after a lifetime of catering to others.

∞∞∞

After receiving a brief, yet informative note just after midday, Charlotte was ready when a high-quality but blessedly non-descript carriage had pulled up outside the Aston townhouse around seven that evening, and a liveried footman knocked on the door to collect her. He had masterfully concealed his surprise at the lady of the house answering the door herself, but Charlotte had noted the young man's curious look into the empty foyer as he had dutifully pulled the door closed behind her.

The carriage left their street in the direction of Benjamin's townhouse, and Charlotte peeked out the window to watch the evening bustle pass by, careful to keep her face hidden in the shadows of the dimly lit coach. It seemed strange to be among the fashionable traffic of Mayfair after being apart from it so long. For her, evenings of show and excitement had been the first luxuries to go when funds had grown thin. She thought wistfully of the delicious hum of anticipation as the theatre lights dimmed and the curtains drew, or the first dissonant chords of an orchestra tuning up one final time before the performance.

That was the life of another woman—a girl, really. She missed her, but, as she knew all too well, dwelling on the past only wrought heartbreak. It was best to save those memories—keep them apart like a distant fairy tale, just like she would the nights to come.

So momentarily lost in her musings was she that Charlotte missed the coach taking an unexpected turn. They were no longer heading south, but east, with the flow of traffic. When she realised the mistake, she knocked on the roof of the coach to draw the driver's attention to their intended direction. He, however, did not stop the carriage or even look down through the window beneath his seat, and Charlotte felt a moment of unease.

Surely the driver knew where she was going? She had mentioned nothing when she had come down the front steps in the name of discretion, of course. Is that not how these things were done? A lady surely could not be expected to shout the direction of her paramour up to the coachman from the walkway of a bustling residential street. Although Charlotte would not know how these things were done, this being her first and only true liaison. Already, she was reasonably sure she could never do what she had done with Benjamin last night—and in the garden—with another man. It would only ever be a game of comparison. A losing game.

But of course, that was the nature of all things—transient. She squared her shoulders. Life was long. Who knew what it had in store for Charlotte Aston? One thing she was sure of was that she would no longer let others hold the reins. She raised her fist again to knock on the roof—this time harder— she would be let out of this wayward carriage at once and make her own way to Benjamin's home.

Before she could knock, the door flew open, and a footman unfolded the stairs, silently offering his hand to help her alight. Stunned by the seeming preternatural power of her own thoughts, Charlotte gawked at him for a moment, fist still aloft. Realising the relative crush of people gathered behind the footman on the torch-lit steps of the marble building, she quickly composed herself and accepted his assistance out of the carriage.

There were men and women flocked around the entrance in the height of evening finery, waving fans and leaning around others to get a glimpse inside the palatial establishment.

When a woman passing by gave her an assessing side-eye, Charlotte remembered the seasons-old evening gown she had donned before leaving the house. It was not one of her finest pieces, but it had a high neckline that covered the puckered scar at her shoulder, and she had reasoned—rather smugly to herself—that she did not intend to keep it on very long.

Now, however, she felt acutely aware of the gown's deficiencies. The silver satin had worn over the years and faded to a rather dingy grey. The cloak she wore over it was not much of an improvement either; she, having selected the worsted wool travelling cloak for its concealing hood and protection against the early spring chill, now looked precisely like a chilled traveller rather than a lady on the town.

"Right this way, my lady."

She started at the footman's voice. His thick East End accent was punctuated by the telltale crack of boyish adolescence. Taking a closer look at his face, she realised he could not be older than fourteen. Still, he comported himself properly as he gently led the way to a side street much less crowded with bustling theatre goers. Catching a breath at the realisation that she and her lacking wardrobe would not, in fact, be subjected to more scrutiny, Charlotte followed the young footman to a door set in the side of the large, unfamiliar building.

The man at the door waved them in without a second look, and she followed the footman down a vaulted marble hall, the echoes of chatter filtering in from an adjoining hall around the corner. As she gazed around at the towering Corinthian columns and gilded frescoes, she noted they were in an opera house. This one must be new, though. She had never visited it before. Still, how could she not have even heard of it? Until now, the obscurity of the mire she was caught up in had never felt so substantial. She knew more about the market schedule in Covent Garden than she did about even the most notable events in Mayfair.

"Here, my lady." The young footman gestured to a door she had not noticed until he opened it, so well set it was between the elaborate wainscoting.

She looked at the door and then back at him, about to question her destination once again. Charlotte thought of the resolution she had made just moments ago. Here she was, being led blindly into the unknown by a man. She should turn around and march right back out, picking her own direction. Her curiosity, however, got the better of her.

The young footman gestured again but did not meet her eyes, demonstrating that he could not provide further information. Sparing him one more sceptical look, she stepped inside, her eyes struggling to adjust to the dim light of the room after leaving the hall full of brightly lit, glittering chandeliers and crystal sconces.

"Oh, there you are, my lady!" Charlotte drew her head back in surprise. What was Lizzy doing here?

"How is your shoulder faring, my lady? And your health? Are you well?" The girl was not pausing long enough between questions for Charlotte to answer her, and she had to raise her hand just to get Lizzy to take a breath.

"I am very well, thank you, Lizzy. And I thought I asked you to call me Charlotte?" With the direction her life had taken, the honorific felt hypocritical. She was no different from any other working woman.

"Yes, of course, my l—" Lizzy corrected herself, "Charlotte. I am ever so glad you are doing well."

Before she could get started again—Charlotte had learned that it was best to interrupt Lizzy's monologues before they began—she looked around the room and asked the obvious question, "Where are we, Lizzy? And why are you here, not that I am not glad to see you," she added, worried the question could have seemed terribly rude and high in the instep.

"Oh, of course!" Lizzy's face brightened as if she had wholly forgotten their surroundings. "Follow me, my la-Charlotte." She turned and pulled aside a curtain that led to yet another concealed door and a flight of stairs.

"Why all the secrecy? This is an opera house, is it not? I do not think it needs quite so many smugglers' tunnels."

"I'd say many gentlemen of the *ton* have a need for much

more secrecy than the average smuggler." Lizzy winked over her shoulder, the candle she held aloft casting shifting shadows on her face that lent the small winding staircase an extra layer of Gothic intrigue.

At the top of the stairs, Lizzy led them into a small chamber filled with racks of clothes. Large hats sat stacked atop the racks, and prop swords and pistols hung along the wall, interspersed with Shepard's crooks and dainty parasols.

"Just here." Lizzy reached up to a rack on the far side of the room.

"Are you going to dress me in a costume? I do feel much improved, but I fear no amount of improvement would prepare me to take to the stage." Charlotte was not sure whether she should be amused or alarmed. Forget about the unknowns of the future; what in the world was in store for her tonight?

"No…" Lizzy drew the word out evasively until she turned and saw Charlotte's raised eyebrows, "Well, not exactly." With a flourish, she turned, a length of shimmering gold fabric draped over her arms.

"Oh my." Charlotte touched her fingers to her lips.

"It is not a costume, not technically. This is a gown made for a fine lady, and you really are the finest lady of my acquaintance."

Charlotte looked up and smirked at Lizzy. "High praise indeed, Miss Lizzy. Thank you." She reached out and touched the fabric, watching in wonder as it slipped through her fingers like water. "It really is extraordinary."

"Come now, we can't spend all night ogling over a bundle of fabric in my arms. It *will* be extraordinary once we get you in it."

Charlotte felt the urge to protest. She had worn nothing this nice, not even when her mother and father were alive. Now, looking at the decadent material, Charlotte could not help but tally all the things she could pay for with the price of this single frock—not least of them being that Lizzy could get her little brother out of the workhouse and sent to school.

Despite Charlotte's hesitation, Lizzy had already discarded her cloak and unfastened the first row of buttons down the back of her bodice. She remembered the effort it had taken to button them herself and despaired at the seemingly useless pain she had put herself through, contorting this way and that to fasten them all.

"Step out." Lizzy passed her another slip of fabric and turned to properly hang Charlotte's cloak and gown.

When she looked down, what she thought was a gauzy wrap was actually an impossibly thin silk chemise. The fabric was so cool and feather-light on her skin, she almost blushed at its caress, then did blush when she thought of the man who most assuredly purchased it for her.

Tamping down her flush, she pulled her sturdy cotton chemise over her head and quickly donned the new one. A standing mirror peeked from behind a rack of clothes, and Charlotte caught a glimpse of her reflection and tried, for Lizzy's sake, not to look completely scandalised.

The undergarments left nothing to the imagination. The silk clung indecently to her curves and was practically translucent. In one glance, she could see the faint V of hair at the apex of her thighs, only a few shades darker than the hair on her head, as well as the pink shadow of her nipples. She could not bring herself to look Lizzy in the eye as she helped her step into the gold-shimmering gown itself.

"Oh my, Charlotte." Lizzy stepped to the side after lacing up the back of her dress.

Oh my was right, Charlotte thought as she looked at her reflection in the mirror. The woman looking back at her was another being entirely.

Throughout her life, she had shied away from gold and yellow hues, remembering her stepmother's warning that the colour would wash her out and make her look ill. She had been mistaken.

The gold satin of the dress shimmered like champagne in the dim candlelight. The colour was nearly a perfect match for her hair, and rather than making her look flat and pale, the blend made her eyes glow. She stood transfixed.

"Could you bend, my lady?" Lizzy was reaching up to undo the pins that held her braids tightly to her head but could not reach the ones on top.

"Oh yes. Sorry, Lizzy."

Lizzy proceeded to unravel the plaits and brush out the waves, only pinning a few bits back from her face and letting the rest tumble down her back.

"Surely I should wear it up." Charlotte had not worn her hair down in public since she was a girl. It just was not done—except by the truly daring ladies, who still made sure the loose tresses were curled to perfection. Charlotte had never been one of those ladies, preferring to have her hair out of her face and off her neck so that it did not dip into her food, or more importantly, her ink.

"This is better, my lady,"

"Charlotte."

Lizzy rolled her eyes. "This is better, Charlotte. You look like an angel."

Charlotte laughed. "Do angels often have bullet holes in them?" She fingered the puckered skin, feeling a phantom twinge through the muscle.

Lizzy screwed up her mouth in thought, then reached around to pull the length of her hair over the scar. "There. Good thing it did not go out the other side."

Charlotte thought ruefully of the blistering pain she had awoken to as the doctor fished the bullet out of her flesh. She was so blinded by it, she could not remain conscious, and then, when the laudanum had kept her subdued, she had still felt the pain. She would have taken a matching exit wound if it had meant not enduring that nightmare.

"Well? Are ye' ready?"

"Ready for what?" Charlotte felt her trepidation return.

Lizzy just gave her a cryptic smile. "You'll see."

With that, she ushered Charlotte down a small corridor that attached to the costume room. She could faintly hear voices on the other side of the wall.

Without a word, Lizzy stopped and opened a door, waving Charlotte ahead. When she stepped out, she found herself in a lushly carpeted corridor wider than the one she had just left. There were ladies and gentlemen in gorgeously elegant finery milling about the corridor, some stepping in and out of padded doors that lined the hall.

"My lady." The voice caught her attention, also belonging to a footman, this one only a few years older than the other. He held open one of the elaborately cushioned doors, and she lifted her skirts to step inside, careful not to trip on the few small steps that led into the space.

"Champagne, my lady?" The second footman had followed her into the room, which she now saw was a sumptuously appointed opera box, and held a platter with a single glass of champagne out for her.

"Yes, thank you…" she trailed off, prompting his name. In her shock, she had not asked the last footman his name. She now felt badly about it.

"Carons, my lady."

"Carons. Thank you." She took the glass he offered. "Might I be expecting company here tonight, Carons?"

"I could not say, my lady." With that, he bowed out of the box, the door shutting behind him almost silently.

Charlotte sighed and looked around the box. The floor was carpeted like the outer corridor, but it was thicker here. As she stepped around in a circle, her slippered feet sank into it like stepping onto lush grass. There were elegantly upholstered seats at the front of the box like any other, but behind the first two rows were a matched pair of chaise lounges set around a low table like a small sitting room. Ornate lamps sat sporadically throughout the space, giving it an intimate air despite the open banister that overlooked the still-curtained stage.

As she took it all in, Charlotte absently sipped from the glass she held. Then she sipped again. The Astons had not been able to afford something so decadent as champagne for a long while, even the cheaper sparkling wines that imitated its effect. Despite that, she was reasonably sure that this was the best champagne she had ever tasted.

It was light and dry with a true effervescence that lingered on her tongue and spread through her limbs after each sip. Between the delightful lightening effects of the drink and the soft spring of the carpet, she felt like she was walking on air.

Still alone in the box, and mostly concealed from the

crowded auditorium below, Charlotte indulged in a little spin, giggling at herself and revelling in the pure elation of the simple moment.

Chapter Twenty

She was breathtaking.

Benjamin stood silently in the doorway of the Duke of Wells' box at the newly built English Opera House. Wells and he had been key investors in the theatre's renewal, and the opening night turnout seemed to indicate the investment's success.

He watched, mesmerised, as she twirled gleefully before him. The dress he had commissioned from Madame Renaudin, the most exclusive *modiste* in London, swirled around her like a wash of stardust. He could not look away as the gossamer skirts swished and clung to the outline of her legs.

Charlotte let out a small yelp and stopped spinning when she saw him in the doorway. She held a hand to her chest, the other still balancing the delicate, rounded champagne glass. "You startled me, Benjamin." Her casual use of his given name sent a delicious sizzle up his spine. "You really should not lurk in the dark like that, spying on women. It is most ungentlemanly and rather disconcerting."

She had a warm flush to her cheeks; he noticed as he stepped further down into the box. Her golden hair lay in silky swaths over her shoulder, and he itched to reach out and twine it between his fingers.

"I was not lurking overly long." To give his hands something to do other than touch her, he stepped to the side table where Carons had left a glass beside the cool *seau à champagne* and poured himself a glass, bringing the bottle to top hers. "And I seem to remember you asserting most emphatically that I was not a gentleman. So it is of little concern that I behave in a gentlemanly manner."

Charlotte met his silent toast with her glass and regarded him with an arched brow. Benjamin felt decidedly uncomfortable under her scrutiny, especially when her sweet lips pulled into a slow smile as if she had come to some conclusion about him—solved a piece of the puzzle.

"You seem awfully against being identified as a gentleman for someone who adheres to the general code of conduct. Ah—" She lifted a slender finger from the glass and pointed at him. "Before you try to contradict me, remember you speak to someone who has faced you on the duelling field, the pinnacle of a gentleman's code of honour—no matter how foolish it is."

Benjamin could not fight the answering smirk that tugged at his own lips. "A man can have honour without being a gentleman. Is honour among thieves not equally well known as that of their gentleman counterparts?"

"The two are not mutually exclusive." A shadow passed over her face for a moment, dimming her glow.

"That is true enough."

"So you are saying you are a thief then?" The playful spark returned to her eye as quickly as it had vanished.

"No, I am not a thief." *Not anymore*, he amended silently. "Though I have quite the reputation as a rogue and a scoundrel."

"Yes, we have spoken of your notorious reputation before. I still believe you delight in it, having cultivated it intentionally."

Benjamin lifted his hand to his chest in mock affront. "You believe me to be capable of such artifice?"

∞∞∞∞

Charlotte took a slow sip as if contemplating deeply. "Perhaps not. It is quite roguish of you to lure a lady to an opera house without her knowledge." Though it was considerably less roguish than luring her to his bachelor lodgings. In fact, standing here in this box, sipping champagne was one of the least untoward things they had done together. A night at the opera escorted by a beau was even appropriate for the purest of society debutantes—though a severe and dowdy chaperone was conspicuously missing from their company.

The thought of Benjamin as her beau sent a startling wave of bashfulness through her. She had to look away towards the stage as she took another sip rather than meet his dark blue gaze in the soft shadows of the box.

"Lure." He said the word thoughtfully with an audible smile. "I like that. I am happy to be the rogue who could *lure* Lady Charlotte Aston."

Wanting to make a quick retort but still feeling flustered by her own thoughts, Charlotte was saved by the sudden hush that fell over the audience as the stage curtain began to part.

Wordlessly, Benjamin gestured to the row of seats at the front of the box, but Charlotte hesitated. "Would it not be tantamount to declaring our arrangement if we were to be seen in a private box together? *Sans chaperone?*"

It felt silly to be concerned about such things. She was well and truly an old maid; no one much cared for what the spinsters of the ton got up to. But the impact the revelation would have on her family, she could not add to their troubles further.

"From up here, the crowds below may see that the box has occupants, but they would not be able to discern precisely who said occupants are."

Benjamin had sent footmen earlier that day to ensure just that. With the strategic lamp placement and large curtains framing the box and casting shadows from the stage lights, no one would be able to make out their identities. "Besides, we are not *sans chaperone* as you so elegantly put it." He gestured to the back of the box, where an elegant dowager sat in a plush wing/backed chair. Fast asleep.

Charlotte gasped. "Has she been there the whole time?" Her voice was lowered, trying not to disturb the elderly woman. As if their previous conversation was not proof of their companion's deep sleep.

"Do not worry. She is Lady Elsie Wylde's aunt, Lady Iona Gordon. She just travelled down from Edinburgh with her ward for her niece's wedding. She was glad of the respite from the wild Wyldes." He winked and took Charlotte's hand, turning it over to press an open-mouthed kiss to her palm. "We are the picture of respectability tonight, my lady."

∞∞∞

Her sharp intake of breath was like a caress down his whole body, and he was equal parts frustrated and glad as the orchestra drew their attention back down to the stage with the first notes of tuning.

Benjamin did not much care if anyone saw him in the Duke of Wells' box, but he would not risk Charlotte's reputation any more than he already had. In fact, he had almost decided against bringing her here tonight, but after his inquiries and seeing the state of her life first-hand, Benjamin yearned to present her with the finest experiences money could offer—particularly those she had been deprived of by the faults of her brother.

The way she had spoken of the opera that afternoon in the pavilion—Benjamin had taken one look at her face and sworn he would be the one to give this part of her life back to her. He had persuaded Wells to skip the opening night of the first opera hosted by their new venture so that Charlotte could experience the excitement without having to expose herself to the humiliation of their acquaintance—or worse, feel she must explain herself or her presence to his friends. Elkington had insisted he bring Lady Elsie's aunt as chaperone—though he suspected it had been a ploy to catch his dear fiancée alone for the evening.

More than anything, though, Benjamin wanted to be alone with her; to enjoy her pleasure at the experience wholly and unreservedly. He was doing it now; he watched the anticipation in her eyes as the curtains receded and the orchestra awaited the conductor's cue.

Even as the first soprano took the stage and began singing a heart-wrenchingly tender overture, Benjamin could not look away. He sat like that, leaning back in his chair, knee pressed against hers, watching her face for the entire first act. Charlotte did not even notice his gaze; she was so transfixed on the performance.

When the curtains closed for the intermission, she broke from her reverie and looked at him, cheeks damp but a glowing smile in her eyes.

"That was magnificent." She took the handkerchief Benjamin offered her and dabbed at her cheeks. "I forgot how much I enjoy the opera. It's one of those things you do not think about…" she trailed off. "When there are other things to worry about."

Benjamin resisted the urge to pull her into his arms then and there. The idea of proud Charlotte, alone in her draughty, empty townhouse, trying to scrounge together enough money to feed herself and protect her brothers, made his chest constrict. He wanted Charlotte to never worry about anything again.

"Yes, it is very nice." Benjamin felt as if he were seeing the opera through fresh eyes.

He had enjoyed music as a boy but had never been to London until his mother moved them there. Even then, before she passed, they did not have the money or connections to do something as lavish as attending the opera—and his mother would not have dared return to such a life. After her death— well, it was just as Charlotte said; it was not something one thought of when there were other things to worry about.

The opera and the other extravagances of the London elite had become a beacon to him through the cold, hard nights. The figure of a wealthy gentleman dressed in evening finery, an elegant woman on his arm, riding in his landau through a summer twilight on their way to the opera, had transfixed Benjamin. If he could achieve that, his comfortable childhood in the country and a future glory of true riches and independence would be reconciled, and he could forget the intervening years of suffering.

Thus, the opera had never just been the opera for him. It had been an achievement—a sign of wealth and success. Now that he was a part-owner of this opera house, he was so far beyond his wildest dreams. And yet, seeing Charlotte experience it with a simple appreciation for the art and beauty of it all, he felt as if a veil had been lifted from his eyes. The place was new, and all the more dazzling for the woman sitting before him.

"Benjamin?" Charlotte's voice broke him from his reverie.

"Sorry, what was that?" He tried to focus on her words and leaned in. A mistake. Her sweet breath fanned the side of his face, and she set a light hand on his arm in a casual gesture that made his heart thrum.

"I asked, why did you bring me here?"

Unable to summon a clever response, he replied honestly, "I thought you would like it."

Charlotte pursed her lips in an assessing way that made him want to fidget. He suppressed the impulse and met her warm, sparkling gaze. "I do like it. Thank you."

Chapter Twenty-One

Charlotte was unsure what to do with his sudden candour. In all actuality, it was a simple gesture. If they had been engaged in a real courtship, it would even be expected—a matter of course. But Charlotte found herself taken aback by the sweetness of it. This man had arranged a lovely evening for her because he thought she would like it. She could not think of another time someone had done something for her simply because she might like it—she was not sure there had ever been one.

She placed her hand on his, his fingers turning and twining through hers as if it were second nature to him. Looking at their clasped hands, she felt something well inside of her. She opened her mouth to speak but was not sure what she wanted to say. There was something important to be said, but when she looked up from their hands, she met his gaze, which then flitted to her mouth, and all rational thought was lost.

A muted knock came from the door at the back of the box.

"Damn it." Benjamin released her hand and stood, muttering further expletives under his breath. There was something delicious and intimate about the way he seemed to forget the courtesies owed to a lady in her presence.

∞∞∞

"Yes, Carons?" Benjamin tried to curb the annoyance in his voice at being torn from the spell in which Charlotte's warm, low voice and smiling eyes had caught him.

"Sorry to disturb you, sir. There's a man here who says he wants to see you."

"I say, Wells! What is it with this guard dog you have out here? Can't a man drop into a fellow's box without having to answer these riddles three?" A grating, self-aggrandising laugh followed the man's overly-loud comment—likely intended to be heard by neighbouring opera-goers.

Benjamin recognised the foppish, affected accent of Clarence Nisbet, Marquess of something or other—Benjamin was sure he knew but did not really care. The man owed a considerable sum at gaming establishments all over London, including his own, and had the tragically common trait of men of the aristocracy, believing himself to be above both reproach and consequences. He was also a miserable social climber, touting his own title as a means to rub elbows with those titled above him—like the Duke of Wells.

Benjamin stepped out into the hallway, hoping to deter the young insipid Marquess from his course—likely aiming to be seen in a duke's box on opening night.

"The Duke of Wells is not attending tonight." He kept his voice polite but stern, hoping the fop would see the absence of social cache available to him and leave.

"Scarsdale? That you? Oh, you sly fox. Using your connection to our esteemed friend tonight, are we? Well,

I cannot fault you there. Best box in the house. And what a place to be seen, eh?"

Benjamin had to clench his jaw. Best not to engage with the man; he would wind himself and adjust course soon enough.

"Betty, darling?" A woman's voice sounded from the dim corridor, her cultured accent drawing her words out lazily in the luxurious way only the truly rich and fashionable did. "Oh, there you are. Where did you get off to? You left me with that droll woman, Lady Effing. I cannot say I understood a word that came out of her mouth. That headpiece was truly a monstrosity. Feathers spewing in a most alarming way." The woman finally appeared from around Nisbet, and Benjamin's stomach dropped.

Lady Catherine Beaumont was the beautiful young widow of a French count, who had conveniently died only a year into their marriage. She was a relaxed, confident woman with shining black curls and hooded grey eyes, which enticed any man to imagine her in considerably more intimate surrounds. More to the point, she had once—not very long ago—been Benjamin's lover.

"Benji, darling. How good it is to see you." Catherine held out her slender hand for him and gave him a lazy smile that could drive a man mad—as she well knew. "Betty and I were speculating about who was occupying the duke's box this evening. Of course, he thought it must be Wells himself, it being opening night and all, but I was not convinced. His shadow reads much differently than yours. Much more prim and upright." She trailed her eyes over his form as she would a physical caress. "You have a predatory lounge about you."

"Indeed. Indeed." Nisbet seemed put out by the direction of the conversation and Catherine's clear preference for the other man in their company. "Well, who is it, then? Who do you have hidden away in there?"

Benjamin gave him a steely glare, hoping to compel the man to sway from his curiosity.

"Yes, do introduce us to your guest, Benjamin. Spare our craning necks this long second act." She waved a hand as if it were a passing request born of idle curiosity and not the sole purpose for their presence outside the Duke of Wells' box.

Benjamin ground his teeth. He did not want to let them into the box and expose Charlotte without a word of warning. Denying them, however, would ensure the gossips fixated on the matter, ferreting the truth out eventually and making it all the more sensational for it. This night had been a colossal mistake.

After another beat of silence, during which Catherine and Nisbet watched him with barely concealed curiosity, Benjamin gave a single nod and turned toward the door of the box, opening it but preceding them into the dim room.

Charlotte stood from her seat, where he had left her, and gently shook out her skirts as if she were not already a perfectly pristine image of sophisticated beauty. She met his eyes and arched a delicate eyebrow, but other than that, acted fully composed and unruffled at the entrance of the two unannounced guests.

"Lady Charlotte, may I present to you, Countess Jean-Beaumont and Lord Clarence Nisbet…"

"Marques Lagsten." Nisbet filled in his title proudly, eyes roving Charlotte's form.

"Right." Benjamin clenched his fist at his side. "This is Lady Charlotte Aston."

Charlotte executed a polite nod and curtsy, her shimmering

gown catching the light of the small table lamps and the wide chandelier suspended above the audience behind her.

After the requisite pleasantries were exchanged, Catherine turned to Benjamin with a new glint in her eyes. "Oh, but there is no need to introduce Charlotte and myself. We have known each other for quite a while, have we not?"

She turned back to Charlotte with an overly sweet smile that put Benjamin's teeth on edge. Standing there beside Charlotte in the dim booth, he was suddenly at a loss for what charms had attracted him to Catherine to begin with.

Her beautiful face seemed cold and jaded beside Charlotte's intelligent sparkle. And though both women had likely seen more of the truths of life than their peers, Charlotte carried none of the calculating bitterness that hid behind Catherine's lazy, seductive stare.

"The countess and I made our debuts the same season," Charlotte spoke politely in her low, cultured tones, and Benjamin was struck by the thought of young Charlotte, just eighteen, full of hope and promise that a first season may bring. He wanted to go back in time and protect that girl from the future of hard truths that filled the eyes of the woman staring back at him.

"Yes, what fun that was. Such a whirlwind of a time. I felt I could hardly keep my head on straight with all the excitement. I could not even imagine how you fared." She turned conspiratorially towards Nisbet and Benjamin. "Charlotte had a number of beaux following her around like lost puppies. She was quite a hit. I always imagined your father barricading his study to keep them from beating down the door." She gave a tinkling laugh and touched her fan to his sleeve.

He was unfairly gratified to see Charlotte tense at the action. But then, he realised, the proud confidence of her posture had transformed ever so slightly. She was uncomfortable—more so than one flirtatious tap would engender. Still, she gave them all a serene smile.

"The countess is merely deflecting the truth of the matter. It was she who was the true success. Her marriage to the Count was quite the *coup de gras* for the rest of us young ladies. None could hope to outshine her stunning victory."

Benjamin watched the ladies exchange smiles. There was another battle being waged here, right in front of him.

"I was ever so sorry to hear of your father's passing. My condolences. Your brother is now the earl, correct?"

Charlotte gave a tight smile. "Yes, he is. And my condolences for your loss. The Count seemed a…commanding man." Something in that comment had another meaning.

It could have even been sympathy. Did Charlotte know of the Count's heavy-handedness with his young wife? There was no way for her to have known the truth of Catherine's life on the continent. It had taken Benjamin a while of concerted digging to find the proof of the Count's treatment of women. Although having met him during their debut, he would not rule out the possibility that Charlotte had seen the man's viciousness firsthand. The relief at knowing she had not been the one to fall into the man's clutches was as overwhelming as it was ungenerous.

Judging by the iciness of Catherine's gaze, she did not appreciate the note of empathy in Charlotte's voice.

"Thank you, Lady Charlotte. That is ever so kind of you. Though I must say, I find the life of a widow suits me now. I could not imagine returning to the days of the starry-eyed debutante flanked by dour chaperones." She flicked a smug glance toward Lady Elsie's still-sleeping aunt. "To have one's own home. One's own place in the world. It is a joy of its own. Though I miss my husband dearly."

Charlotte smiled, this time more genuinely—though Benjamin could not understand why. "I am happy to hear that, Lady Catherine."

Catherine's gloved hand tightened on her fan. "So how do you know dear Benji?" Benjamin cringed at the nickname he had many times asked her not to use.

Charlotte arched an eyebrow and regarded him briefly before turning back to Catherine. Those damned eyebrows—they would drive him mad.

"Mr. Scarsdale is an acquaintance of my brother. He was kind enough to invite me to the opening night when I had mentioned in passing my interest in the opera."

"Yes, Benji has always been quite *considerate*." Benjamin wanted to roll his eyes at her blatant innuendo. This was not how he wanted Charlotte to think of him; in the arms of this—now he could see—petty and vindictive woman. "But you must feel quite at home here, Benji." She turned her gaze back to him again. "Your mother was an opera singer, if I am not mistaken."

Benjamin felt his chest seize at that, a cold, prickling hand gripping his neck and spreading down his back. He nodded only once, and Catherine smiled, turning back to Charlotte. "I hear she was the voice of her age. So enchanting that the Duke of Winden could not help but whisk her off to his country home and jealously guard her from her other admirers."

Charlotte's gaze flicked to his. He could see she had not known about his mother. The thought of discussing her now was enough to make Benjamin sick. He wanted to bolt out of the claustrophobic box.

"Indeed?" Charlotte's smile was cool. "You must know so much about these opera legends. I know your father is also a devotee of the opera."

Benjamin fought to keep his mouth from falling open. Not only did Charlotte know of the Viscount's long-standing mistress plucked straight from the stage, but she had also wielded the knowledge with the cool precision of a master swordsman cutting the opponent down to size in one elegant swoop.

There was a tense silence in which the two women regarded each other with cool, assessing stares behind the masks of politeness. After a moment, Benjamin considered stepping in to diffuse this standoff, but the blundering Nisbet saved him from the task.

"I cannot say I recall the last time I saw you out, Lady Charlotte. Have you been out of town?" Well, this was worse.

"What is all this chattering?" A grumbling voice came from the back of the box. Lady Iona Gordon pushed herself from her seat and frowned at the gathering before her. "Is the opera not a place for quiet reflection?"

"Lady Gordon," both Nisbet and Catherine gave the chaperone respectful greetings. Despite her eccentricities, Lady Iona Gordon was a formidably elegant woman who had spurned the nonsense of English society and come out victorious. Her whole family was uniquely immune to the scorn of the *ton* and lived by their own rules, yet still somehow managed to retain a degree of respectability in their varied society circles. In that moment, Benjamin was relieved to have landed her as their chaperone. Perhaps her indifference to scandal would go a long way in shielding Charlotte as well.

Lady Gordon gave the box's guests only a cursory glance before proclaiming, "Now, was that the gong? You had best return to your seats before we miss the second act."

"Quite. Quite." Despite the interruption, Catherine gave Nisbet a fond smile. The two were clearly relishing the prospect of returning to their seats, but not, Benjamin wagered, to enjoy the second act. The social capital they had just secured would be priceless as they sat to mingle with their fellow operagoers. "Lady Charlotte, it has been a pleasure to see you again. Perhaps I may call on you tomorrow? You are still in residence at the same address, are you not?"

A tendon in Charlotte's jaw twitched. "Yes. I am. Though we are having some renovations done at the house. Unfortunately, I will not be able to receive callers."

"Oh, that is a pity." Catherine gave a serene smile as she looped her hand through Nisbet's outstretched arm. "Then perhaps we will meet again at some function soon. With the season in full swing, there will be so much excitement. And it is never too late to catch someone's fancy." With that, she smiled over her shoulder as Nisbet guided her from the room.

When the door shut behind them, Benjamin strode to Charlotte, grasping her hands in his, an unreasonable urge to comfort her seizing him. He hated the pinched look around her eyes and between her brows that appeared the second the door closed behind the intruders.

"I am terribly sorry. I should have turned them away cold."

"No, no." Charlotte shook her head and extricated one of her hands to rub between her brows. "That would have just fanned the flames. It was bound to come out, eventually. One could have only wished it were not Catherine Sutton to make the discovery."

"Quite right, my dear." Lady Gordon settled back into her chair, clearly with every intention of returning to her nap. "They will batter it about. But they cannot do anything if you don't let them see you blink." With that, she gave Charlotte an audacious wink and settled back, the first strings of the orchestra picking up again.

∞∞∞∞

"Your mother was a singer?" Charlotte sat across from him, surrounded by the satin cushions of his carriage. They had deposited Lady Gordon at her sister's home and carried on through Mayfair. The question was soft and kind, as if she wanted him to know he could decline to answer if he so chose.

"Yes." It came out too sharp—too raw—and Benjamin had to take a few deep breaths to collect himself again. Charlotte only waited, letting the unhurried silence wrap around the two of them as the carriage rolled on. He was starting to understand how she managed to get all those stories from even the most untrusting, jaded residents of London.

He rubbed a hand over his face, years of sour memories crowding in on him.

"My father was the Duke of Winden. We lived on his estate, in a small house away from the manor, until his death. He had been relatively generous with us, as far as dukes and their bastards go. Delia and I had tutors and riding instructors." He had to stop; his breathing was already choppy. But he wanted to get this out—wanted her to know the truth from him—not the dregs the gossip mill might turn up.

197

Charlotte just sat there, her face open and warm, her skirts touching his legs where they stretched alongside her. One of his feet was tucked between hers, his boot covered by gold satin.

"After he died, the Duchess threw us out. Fair enough, I suppose. It was an insult to her and her children that we even existed—let alone lived on the same grounds."

He could sense her question before she asked. "We did not know his children. They were kept far away from us. I suppose they are my half-siblings, but I do not even recall their names."

Lie. He knew every minute detail about each of their lives. Had watched as the new duke had ventured into London, timid and rather dull. And as his two sisters had married equally timid and dull peers, moving along through each step of their aristocratic lives, blithely unaware of his existence. No inkling of the fact that their half-sister had died alone and destitute in a flea-infested boarding house.

The memories made his jaw clench, but he pushed more words out. "Our house was on the property line with the Wells estate. I spent more time with Jonathan than with any of my blood siblings."

"Jonathan is the Duke of Wells?"

Benjamin only nodded, carrying on. "My mother was an opera singer. A successful one too. So, when she packed up what little was ours in the house that now belonged to my half-brother and moved us to London, I was eleven, and I thought she wanted to go to London to sing again. That we would live in an opera house, and she would sing and all would be well."

He could still feel the crushing disappointment when he

had realised that would not be the case. That they had left their quiet country life behind for nothing. "But she did not sing. We stayed in a rented flat for a time. Delia tried to get her to take us to the opera house where she had once worked. But she refused. She spent the days in bed. Would not get up for anything. It scared me."

He was there again, in their modest little flat with fading green wallpaper and worn-down furniture, begging his mother to return and replace the listless figure that lay in her bed and stared at the ceiling. She had been such a warm, vibrant woman, always quick with a joke and a comforting embrace. They had left that woman in Devonshire.

"Delia went out for work. She tried for a few governess posts, but without a name or a reference, she could not find any. She was a child herself. Families did not want a fifteen-year-old for a governess. Finally, she got an interview with a housekeeper in Mayfair. With her education and bearing, she thought she might be a lady's maid. But again, she had no experience, so she was put in the kitchens. But it was something.

"One day." He felt the bile rising in his throat. "One day, Delia woke me and told me we must leave." He could still feel the confusion, wanting to lie back down in his small, warm bed. Delia's strained cheerfulness as she tried to conceal her panic. "She took me to the front room, grabbed my coat, and packed some of my clothes. She told me not to go into our mother's room."

But he had. He had wondered why she was not coming with them on this strange, early-morning trip. Thinking to help her get ready, he had walked to the door, giving it a gentle knock before pushing it open. Delia had burst from the other room, grasping for him and shouting for him to stop. She had yanked him back and pressed his face into her chest. But not before he had seen the blood. Dark red streaks, already drying after dripping down to the rough wood floor.

"She had killed herself." The words were flat, matter-of-fact, as if recounting figures from a ledger he had read.

Charlotte let out a whooshing breath, reaching across the space to grasp his icy hands in hers. He expected the empty, comforting words that people said now. The scrambling for something in the face of horror.

But she merely held his hands in hers. "Oh, Benjamin. How old were you?"

"It was two days before my twelfth birthday." She only nodded, a calm, quiet understanding giving him the space to continue. "And you know what happened after—to Delia." How had he already shared so much with this woman? Things he had told no one. She nodded again. "I know it was beyond her—my mother. That she was suffering. But somehow, I cannot forgive her. Her foolish love for a man who did not care if she lived or died. It killed her. It killed Delia. She chose that dead love over us. And I cannot forgive her."

It was a simple thing to say, but somehow, it stunned him. He had never said those words. Had never spoken to anyone about his life and how he had come to be here. Wells knew his life before they left. And he knew his life once he had found him again when he was sixteen. But he knew nothing of the time in between. And Benjamin had never wanted to tell him.

Telling Charlotte brought it all back together. For years, he had pretended he had lived two lives, his childhood and the life he lived now. The years on the street, the other life to be secreted away, even though it haunted his every move. Now, however, they had fitted back into place. The different parts bleeding together, spilling over one another in a painful, raw mix. But they were one—whole. In telling her, he had restored a part of himself he had not realised was missing. And it was too much.

"We have arrived," he said with a relieved gasp. They had indeed pulled up in front of the Aston townhouse.

"Benjamin." Charlotte was still holding his hands, infusing life into his numb fingers.

"Thank you for accompanying me, my lady. The night was a joy." He beat the footman to the door, unfolding the steps and handing Charlotte down in a swirl of golden silk.

"Benjamin." Her voice was soft and almost pleading.

"I will see you again soon. Do not hesitate to call if you wish."

He paused, the formal words sounding strange in his voice. Charlotte was looking up at him, the glow of a streetlamp gilding her features and making the tenderness in her eyes sparkle. He felt his shoulders soften. He leaned in to press a soft kiss to one cheek, then the other, and then a lingering, chaste kiss to her lips. Her eyes fluttered open as he pulled away.

"Will you not come in?"

"Good night, Charlotte."

Chapter Twenty-Two

The next morning, Charlotte sat alone in the study, a cold cup of weak coffee beside her as she shuffled through documents and correspondence. Somehow, the running of an estate remained a laborious task, even when there was no longer an estate left to run.

Benjamin had returned her to her home and not followed her inside. She tried to conceal her disappointment as she made her way up the steps to let herself in the front door. This was not how the night was meant to unfold, but she could not bring herself to feel remorse for the evening's events. There was something deliciously satisfying in the world connecting her to Benjamin Scarsdale, for however brief a time. And after his confession in the carriage on the ride home, she felt as if she now held a priceless gift—a piece of the man she was growing to care for. More than was wise.

A clatter sounded from the front of the house and broke Charlotte from her reverie. She listened as she heard the familiar tread of her drunken brother slowly advance through the unlit corridors toward the study.

"What is the meaning of this, Charlotte?" It surprised her

how much Freddie sounded like their father just then. He even stood in the doorway, feet spread wide, just as their father had done when he was particularly cross.

No, she realised, he was not affecting the bravado of their forceful sire. He was bracing himself so he would not stumble forward in his drunken state. She rubbed the headache forming between her eyes.

"Good morning, Freddie."

"Good morn—ing?" he stuttered the question, pulling out his pocket watch. "But it's hardly—Oh. So it is." He shook his head as if releasing that he had strayed from his initial purpose. "What is this I hear about you being seen at the opera with Mr. Benjamin Scarsdale? The well-known gangster and underworld scoundrel! I mean, the shame of it! He is not fit to be seen with Charlotte. Think of your reputation. Our family's reputation!"

He was really starting to get himself worked up into a froth again when Charlotte held up a silencing hand, and he stilled, giving her a sceptical and condescending stare—or his best drunken approximation of one.

"How dare you?" Her voice did not rise above a whisper, and some of Frederick's swagger dropped away as he turned to see the quiet fury in his ever-doting sister's eyes.

"What do you mean, 'How dare I'? I am the head of this—"

"Stop." Her voice was like an icy blade slicing through the stale air of the study, already perfumed with the smell of whisky, smoke, and her unwashed brother. "Do not say another word to me about this family." She had his full attention now. "This family has been left destitute. We are virtually penniless. Would you care to venture why? Hmm?" She pressed herself up from the old leather chair that had sat behind the fine mahogany desk her entire life. "I will tell you why. Because of your cruel and thoughtless selfishness."

Frederick's lips moved as if he were trying to form words to argue against her accusations, but not a sound came out.

"You have put me and your brothers directly in harm's way, not to mention our family's reputation. And you have the unmitigated gall to caution me about my behaviour? I have *literally* taken a bullet for you." She could see that was where his sodden mind stopped absorbing her meaning, but she soldiered on. Now that the words had started, she could not stop the flow any more than she could dam up the Thames with a sheaf of parchment.

"You are as much the head of this family as the King of England is a cherry pie. I am the head of this family, and I say, we are done with you. I am done with you. I have decided to lease out this house so that the boys may finish their schooling. I expect you to find lodging elsewhere. If you want a single penny more out of this family, you will have to earn it yourself."

"Wha—what… You can't!" Freddie finally found words upon hearing that piece of information.

"Freddie, I have tried for years to keep this ship afloat while you time and again shoot cannonballs directly into our hull. Perhaps I am partly to blame. I coddled you. My precious baby brother. I thought you could do no wrong, so maybe you just never learned the difference. For that, I apologise. Truly."

She could not read the expression on his face—likely shock. "It brings me no joy to do this to you. But I am done. I have to do right by our family," *and by myself*, she added silently. "And this is the only solution left to me. I hope one day you will see it was for the best."

She remained standing, staring at the washed-up shell of her brother as the silence stretched between them. They stood like that for so long she thought perhaps he would say nothing. Finally, he shifted his weight and straightened his horribly disordered cravat.

"I can see you have got yourself quite worked up about all this. Inevitable, really. All these worries should not be the concern of a lady. Not to worry, Charlie. I will sort everything out." With a self-important sniff, he turned on his heel, noisily making his way back down the corridor and then out the front door.

Charlotte stood unmoving as she absorbed what had just happened. There was no going back from this, she saw. Of course, she had already made many decisions over the last few days that had drastically altered the course of her life. This, however, was the final nail in the coffin—a morbid phrase for the liberation she had felt at finally taking her life by the reins—appropriate, though, for the sense of foreboding at Freddie's resolute response to her tirade.

∞∞∞

Later that afternoon, the ring of the front doorbell drew Charlotte out of the study. When she peeked through the front windows to ascertain who was calling, she saw a beautiful, well-sprung curricle with jolly yellow wheels and two matched bays. Seated in the vehicle was the dashing figure of a woman dressed in the height of elegance for an afternoon ride through the park.

From her vantage point at the window, Charlotte could not

make out the identity of the woman, and the second ring of the bell, along with her curiosity, compelled her to the large front door.

"Good afternoon. May I help you?" Charlotte asked the liveried groom standing on her doorstep.

She held the door open only wide enough not to seem wholly rude without exposing the vast emptiness of the foyer.

"Lady Amelia Cartwright, Countess of Danvers, here to collect you for your ride in the park."

The groom gave a graceful bow and handed her a calling card, with the same name printed across in elegant gold leaf.

"Our ride?" Charlotte looked over the man's shoulder to the woman seated high in the curricle. She smiled and waved.

"Yes, madam. We will wait while you collect your things."

The servant decorously stepped aside, and Charlotte was left with no other option but to close the door and collect her riding hat and pelisse. Though they were a touch out of style, they were still both in rather good condition, considering their lack of use in recent years.

"Marvellous vehicle, is it not? I love driving the curricle—though I have yet to be able to goad anyone into racing me in it." The Countess of Danvers gave a mischievous smile as Charlotte settled in the seat beside her and the groom hopped on the back.

"It is quite dashing, Lady Danvers."

"Oh, please, call me Amelia. We shall have no need to stand on ceremony."

Charlotte smiled and nodded, but was a bit taken aback by the young countess's familiarity. She seemed to be about her own age, but they had never been formally introduced—the countess only arrived in Town after Charlotte's own withdrawal from society.

"I don't imagine you expected a call from me, did you?" The genteel young countess gave her a sly smile as she twitched the reins.

"No, I must admit you have caught me quite by surprise this afternoon."

"Ah, well, I can assure you this will be a pleasant surprise. I have come as a favour to our mutual acquaintance, the Duke of Wells."

"The Duke of Wells?" was all Charlotte could echo. She felt as if she had been playing catch-up since this woman's conveyance arrived in front of her house.

"Well, he was the one to make the request, but I imagine it was really on behalf of his business partner, your Mr. Scarsdale."

Charlotte was appalled by the blush that crept up her face at the phrase *your Mr. Scarsdale*. Had word already spread so quickly? It had been less than a day! But of course it had. The mouths of the ton spread gossip like wildfire.

"And what was this request?" Charlotte was pleased with the steadiness of her voice after the embarrassing reaction her body had had to her previous comment.

The countess looked ready to bounce in the curricle seat like a schoolgirl. "That I act as your chaperone! Lady Gordon will not be available during the days since she has her young ward to tend to, not to mention all of Lady Elsie's wedding preparations." She had to make a sharp pull on the reins to catch the turn she had almost missed in her giddiness.

Clutching the railing so she did not fall from their high and increasingly precarious perch, Charlotte eyed Amelia Cartwright with unconcealed surprise. "What use have I of a chaperone? I am nearly seven and twenty. I may even be older than you."

"Oh! I am five and twenty. How about that?" Amelia smiled and waved at a couple as they pulled into the park.

"Quite. But doesn't that make you a rather unusual choice for a chaperone? Besides, last night was an isolated incident, I am sure. I am a verified spinster, and going about my business unescorted will hardly draw gossip."

"Oh, nonsense. You were seen on the arm of the most notorious bachelor in London. You have all eyes trained on you, my dear. Besides, I am a titled widow. And what I lack in respectability of person, I make up for in pure charm and social connections." She gave Charlotte a cheeky wink. "Besides, I hardly think my purpose is to glower down at some young whelp wanting to take liberties. I rather prefer to think I am aiding you in taking liberties with a certain rogue about town, who will of course, not be named."

"I think you have already named him." Charlotte met Amelia's gaze, and the strange amusement that had been building since the start of this unusual encounter began to bubble over. The two women shared a conspiratorial grin.

"Really, Amelia. I cannot see the need for a chaperone. I believe the damage to my reputation is already done—and really, I cannot bring myself to care overly much."

"A friend, then. Surely you could find a use for one of those." Amelia smiled warmly, and Charlotte could not help but return it.

She thought of all the girls with whom she had made her come out. Now titled and tucked away with their broods of children. Or the women she had indeed considered friends, who, after the death of her father and the shame of the family's financial decline, she had seen less and less of until she saw them not at all. Although now she was beginning to suspect she had been, while not responsible for their poverty, the author of her own isolation.

"Yes, I believe I could use a friend," Charlotte agreed.

"Actually, I will admit, I already feel like I have been friends with you for years." To Charlotte's surprise, Amelia elaborated, "I hired your former lady's maid, Anna, a few years ago. When I read your letter of recommendation, I hired her on the spot—never had I seen such a glowing reference for a member of staff before. Then, once I got to know her better…" Amelia flicked her eyes back to the road. "She told me her story. From then on, I could not help but admire you."

Charlotte had found Anna curled up beneath a hedgerow on the edge of Regent's Park on a particularly foggy morning. From her torn-up clothes—nearly rags—it was clear to her that Anna had been employed as a prostitute, and the blooming bruises and contusions on her face had been truly alarming in the dull morning light.

Despite the few years she had worked diligently with charities in the aid of the poorest of London's inhabitants, Charlotte had never seen anyone so close to death. At that moment, kneeling in the mud of the walkway, trying to convince the skittish Anna to rise and come home with her, she had realised how hollow her efforts had been. It was that week, after bringing Anna home and helping her recover from her injuries as well as installing her as her new lady's maid—her last one had left to marry a country lad at the end of her first season—that Charlotte began writing.

Two years later, she had been forced to let Anna go. Despite the deep trust—nay, friendship—that had grown between them, Charlotte could no longer pay her wages and would not hear of her sacrificing any more opportunities to remain by her side.

"Oh, I cannot tell you what a relief that is to me," Charlotte said. "I have worried about her so much, but I was not sure where she ended up. She would never write; I know she does not like to draw attention to herself or her whereabouts." While she never knew why, it had been clear to Charlotte that Anna was hiding—from whom, she never knew, nor would she pry. "But it is an immeasurable relief to me to know she has landed in a good home."

Amelia nodded, a solemn look in her eyes at the unspoken knowledge they shared about the woman. "She is safe with me, I can assure you. And the most wonderful lady's maid I have ever had."

"Looking back, I am glad she got out of my house when she did. It would not do to have her attached to our family's damaged reputation," Charlotte said the last quietly through a gritted smile as two matrons passed them in a gig, giving polite but icy nods.

Amelia gave a smile and a wave, too, and then turned back to Charlotte after the old biddies had passed. "Anyway, damaged reputation or not, you could hardly go striding into Elysium tonight without a suitable companion."

Charlotte laughed, remembering the two times she had done just that.

∞∞∞

Benjamin had spent the morning crouched over papers across

from his long-trusted man of business, Bell. The man had worked for him for the last eight years, but Benjamin was reasonably sure Arthur Bell had been born sixty years old. Never once in all the time he had known him, had Bell exhibited anything but the retiring, determined patience of a harried history tutor, wire-rimmed spectacles to match.

"With this, there is enough for at least a corruption charge, sir. There is a surfeit of evidence that he is trading in fraudulent goods through his shipping company."

Benjamin did not look up from the document he was reading. "I cannot see how it would be prudent for someone such as myself to be alerting the authorities about corruption schemes, Bell."

"You do not actually operate so far out of the bounds of the law, sir." The quip was uncharacteristically acerbic, and Benjamin made a mental note to give Bell a larger-than-usual Christmas bonus for putting up with him all these years.

"What do I always say, Bell?" Benjamin leaned back and stretched his neck, the morning already trailing long behind him.

Bell let out a long-suffering sigh. "Treason gets the gallows."

Benjamin nodded. "Precisely." He had heard whisperings of a shipper smuggling spies across the channel. After digging further, he was sure that Deering's company was the one responsible. Since then, he and Bell had been keeping meticulous track of the cargoes and transactions the Deering shipping house conducted.

Looking down at the document Bell slid across the table, Benjamin could feel that budding excitement that came just as the pieces slotted into place and he could see which string to pull to have it all crumbling down. They had found it.

A shipping log marked the duty paid on the cargo, but there was a telltale mark at the bottom. Sometimes, if it were a particularly cold night, or the port control officer had a hankering for the pub, they would flag a manifest anomaly on the night's bill of landing to circle back to the next day. It was a sloppy sort of work—and one that got officials into trouble more often than not. But it was also an easy spot for leverage. If the ship's manifest was a few bodies short, it would only take a well-placed question to find out. Benjamin knew just how to pull that string. The lazy port control officer would be fretting away all the ship's secrets in no time.

∞∞∞∞

The entry hall of Elysium was dazzling. Charlotte had not remembered it looking this fine. There were gas lamps along the walls and elegant chandeliers overhead. Their steps were muffled by the ornate runner that stretched the length of the hall where they stood behind the sizeable crowd of patrons weaving their way onto the main gaming floor.

It was an impressive place, and Charlotte could hardly believe she had not noticed its extent before. She had been a bit preoccupied on her previous visits.

Amelia looked around at the swarming crowds, basking in the excitement of the atmosphere. "There's nothing like the joy of being at the place to be. It always feels like a triumph. Quite an establishment your Mr. Scarsdale has here."

"Keep your voice down," Charlotte implored. "Besides, he is not *my* Mr. Scarsdale. Stop saying that."

Amelia snapped her fan and arched her eyebrow at Charlotte. "My dear, a man who sends the most stunning evening gown to your home on a moment's notice, arranges for a suitable evening companion, and sends an elegant carriage to fetch you and said companion to come to his unbearably popular establishment as special guests, is most certainly under your purview."

Charlotte blushed and, satisfied she had made her point, Amelia flicked open her fan again in order to wave it flirtatiously as she batted her eyes at a handsome young gentleman across the hall.

It was the most stunning evening gown. A package had been delivered to the Aston townhouse earlier that afternoon. Luckily, Charlotte had been passing through the kitchen corridor at the time and had heard scuffling on the back stoop beside the empty mews. Thinking that perhaps it was a debt collector come to take the house by force, she peeked through the small window beside the door only to see a little street ruffian scampering away, a finely wrapped box left in his wake.

Upon bringing the box inside, she found a small, embossed vellum card atop the delicate tissue paper with only one line scrawled across, in bold, rushed hand: *Her skirt was o' the grass-green silk.*

She had puzzled over the words a moment, clear who had written them but not exactly their meaning. Her curiosity got the best of her though, and she unwrapped the tissue paper to reveal the most sumptuous material she had ever seen. The silk was the colour of grass—but not the bright sun-drenched grass of a country spring. It was a deeper, more subtle, shifting colour. Like the shade of dusk in an early summer meadow. The gown had long sleeves and a high neck, and, truth be told, it would be unfashionably dowdy if not for the scandalously low back, seemingly tied closed with only a simple silk sash.

Now that she was in it, it was a relief to know the dress's construction was deceptively secure, fastening all the way up the side and in no danger of coming undone at a simple tug of the bowed sash. Still, the illusion was effective. Charlotte could feel eyes on her from all sides as she and Amelia made their way down the corridor. The matching green silk domino had been secured long before they arrived, and its guarantee of relative anonymity, along with the noticeable appreciation for her ensemble, made her feel nearly invincible. Even as a debutante, attention had always felt unseemly—as if she should make herself smaller before drawing the male gaze. She certainly was not meant to enjoy it.

But now, she was a woman grown. She was saving her family and taking hold of her future. And had the attention of the most magnetising man she had ever encountered. It was enough to make her head lift just a little bit higher.

"I say it is a sign of good sense that he tries to spoil you so." Amelia gave a smug look at the group of gentlemen who made barely an attempt to mask their lingering gazes as they passed. "Clearly, he is not the only prospect a dazzling lady such as yourself might have."

Thinking of the warmth of Benjamin's hands in the rainy pavilion—the glow of his skin in the firelight of his chambers—Charlotte could feel her cheeks heating. How could she possibly consider another prospect after being touched by a man like Benjamin Scarsdale?

"What about you and the Duke of Wells?" Charlotte did not want to continue a conversation centring on her romantic—

not romantic, she reminded herself—situation. She did not know how much Amelia knew of their arrangement, and it was mortifying to imagine having to explain it to her.

"Oh, there's nothing in that. He took a flash fancy to me sometime last year." She waved her hand dismissively as if the attention of the wealthiest, most eligible, and elusive bachelor on the market was of no consequence. "I do not think we had even met! He must have just glimpsed me across the room at some event or another and been struck. Is that not the most terribly romantic notion?" She sighed, gazing up at the frescoes on the ceiling. "Anyway, it all came to naught. He followed me to a house party in Oxfordshire, and after a few false starts, we came to the mutual conclusion that a civil friendship was more in our cards. He is surprisingly good fun, once you get past that haughty ducalness."

Though he had been cordial—helpful even, in their previous encounters, Charlotte could not really imagine anything past said ducalness.

They had arrived at the front of the queue.

Chapter Twenty-Three

"She is here, sir." Boyd's face bobbed into the door frame and out just as quickly as he hurried by to carry the news to the other back-room employees.

Elkington looked up from the game of chess he had been frowning over for the better part of an hour. "What does he mean, she is here?"

His fiancée, Elsie, was leaning back in the other masculine leather chair placed before the hearth in Benjamin's office. Her round face was rosy from the warmth of the fire and her imminent victory over her intended's abysmal strategy. Elk would stand a better chance if not for his utter fixation on the woman before him at the price of his focus. Benjamin had already played out what moves Elk was likely to make that would put him right in her well-laid trap while he was checking over the invoices for the club's next month's foodstuffs.

"Oh, who is *she?*" Elsie perked up, glancing over at Benjamin.

She really was glowing. Benjamin narrowed his eyes at his friend. Perhaps there was more to this swift engagement than the couple's obvious infatuation.

"*She* is an acquaintance of mine. Lady Charlotte Aston." Even sharing that much felt tawdry. "And," he addressed Elkington while glancing back down at the stack of receipts before him, hoping his hammering heart was not visible to his friend. "I imagine when Boyd said she was here, he meant that she is here."

"Here. At Elysium?" Elsie's voice was almost affronted.

Benjamin tried to maintain a cool, unaffected expression when he looked back up. Elsie's too-intelligent eyes were scanning his face, and he knew she saw too much. Benjamin pushed himself from his desk and made a show of straightening his evening finery—sometimes even the costliest fabrics chafed.

"Benjamin, please tell me you have not invited an unaccompanied, unmarried lady to your gaming hell for all the *ton* to see?"

Benjamin resisted the urge to straighten his cravat. "Do not exaggerate. The season has not even started yet. Your precious *ton* is still largely off rusticating in their country piles. Besides, are you not an unmarried lady in the very same hell as we speak?"

Elsie gave him an exasperated look and stood from her chair. "Do not split hairs with me. You know my situation is different. The Wylde family is beyond scandal at this point. Being seen with my fiancé." Despite her rising indignation, her voice softened as she said the word, looking down at Elkington with a fond smile. "In his own establishment is hardly the same as a respectable young lady."

"Darling, you do not know the whole of it," Elkington spoke from the chair as he moved another chess piece closer to defeat.

"Oh, and I am sure he does. London's Master of Secrets." Elsie played another piece without so much as looking down, glare still fixed on Benjamin. "You cannot play fast and loose with a young lady's status. Women are given so many fewer opportunities in this world, maybe especially those of the *ton*. By risking her reputation, you take from her what little power she has." Elsie was working herself up into a true froth, Benjamin could see by the vein pulsing in her forehead. "It is the greatest injustice to rob someone of what little options they have. She likely cannot afford damage to her stainless reputation." Benjamin cut her off before she could whip herself into a full fury.

"Oh, there is a stain, believe me." He hated himself just a bit more at that. Especially since he now knew there was no truth to the sordid secret that dogged Charlotte Aston's steps.

Still, truth had little bearing on secrets and gossip.

Silence descended as Elkington gaped at him with the awe of a man who had just seen someone sentenced to the gallows. "Scarsdale."

Elsie clamped her jaw. "No, Alex. Everyone has something to hide. Benjamin just makes it his business to find out what it is."

The words he had said to her upon their first meeting all those years ago. He had confided it then, as a show of his respect for her. Now, the memory shadowed by her censure hurt more than he would care to admit.

She crossed her arms and regarded him evenly. "Well, I suppose I will just have to get the measure of the situation myself. Alex, dear, please escort me down to the floor?" It was clearly not a question, and Elkington stood, gallantly offering his arm to his intended, and giving Benjamin a speaking look as if to say *I told you so,* before the pair preceded him from the room.

Despite his frustration at Elsie's rightful scolding, he found himself dizzyingly elated at the prospect of seeing Charlotte again.

∞∞∞

A footman had only just appeared to offer the ladies champagne in delicate little glass flutes when Charlotte looked up to see him. His face stood out above the crowd—hard, calculating, indescribably handsome. He stood on the landing just above the wide gaming floor, his keen eyes missing nothing as he surveyed the ordered chaos of the crowd. Footmen bearing trays of drinks and *hors d'oeuvres.* Musicians playing lively string pieces that would not have been out of place at Almacks. Dealers shuffling cards and raking in markers. Gentlemen and ladies mingling above the baize tables. And him.

The moment his eyes landed on her, she was caught. It was as if the room had fallen away, and they were lying side by side in the pavilion in her garden. His wide, full lips quirked in an infinitesimal smile, revealing a dimple just above the line of his jaw. Then, without warning, they hardened into a firm line, and Charlotte watched the permanent furrow between his brows grow deeper. He was not looking at her anymore but tracking the progress of someone through the crowd. She looked down just in time for a striking, dark-haired woman to emerge from the throng before them, followed closely by the Marquess of Elkington, who looked rather harried after following the woman through the melee.

"Dear, you need not run." His voice was low and teasing as he bent over the smaller woman.

She gave him an arch look and turned back to Charlotte and Amelia, who both stood clutching their newly acquired glasses, a bit taken aback by the sudden approach.

"I was not running."

If it were not for her elegant coiffure—though a few springy chestnut curls had escaped their fastenings—and her flattering sapphire gown, this lady would be exactly what Charlotte's stepmother had always called a *hoyden*. Charlotte was disposed to like her immediately.

"Oh, Lady Elsie Wylde!" Amelia was almost shrill in her glee. "For a moment, I did not even recognise you. How long has it been? Not since we were girls, surely."

Lady Elsie turned to Charlotte's companion with surprise. Strange, she did not even seem to have noticed the other woman. Then what could have been her purpose in rushing towards them?

"Amelia Barton?" The surprise turned into a smile. "Of course, it is Amelia Barton. Even a mask cannot disguise that hair. Whatever are you doing so far from Northumberland?"

"I married an old stodger and got my ticket to London. I am Lady Amelia Cartwright now. Countess Danvers. Can you believe it?"

Lady Elsie laughed out loud, drawing some curious looks, and her strange, mixed brogue rose to the fore. "Oh, Amelia, dinnae say you did it. Just as you said you would."

Her smile was infectious, and the two women's girlish exchange had Charlotte feeling amused and an outsider all at once.

"We are forgetting our manners, I fear." Amelia turned to Charlotte. "Charlotte, may I present Lady Elsie Wylde, and Alexander Burke, Marquess of Elkington? my lord, mylady, Lady Charlotte Aston. Lady Charlotte is my guest tonight. I am dragging her down my sordid road of wicked pursuits."

Lady Elsie glanced back at the handsome marquess hovering above her.Charlotte noticed his hand linger at the small of her back—a quiet, intimate gesture that had her looking up at the landing again. Benjamin was gone.

"Lady Charlotte, Lady Danvers, good evening," a familiar low voice rumbled beside her, and Charlotte's head snapped from the landing to find Benjamin.

It felt as if her thoughts had conjured him, and she was suddenly breathless. He was of a height with the marquess, but his dark colouring gave him a wicked appeal against the other man's bronzed appearance.

"I hope you are enjoying yourselves." Benjamin bowed to each of them, and it did not escape Charlotte's notice that he did not greet the marquess and Lady Elsie but gave the latter a pointed look she could not decipher. It was clear that the three had already spoken this evening.

"Yes,we are enjoying ourselves very much, Mr. Scarsdale," Amelia tittered. "Lady Elsie and I are old girlhood friends.What a lark to have run into her."

"Yes, almost literally." The marquess smiled mischievously atLady Elsie, but she did not catch it.

She was too busy looking back and forth between Benjamin and Charlotte—quite fixedly, as if teasing out a riddle.

There was an awkward pause as another look passed between Lady Elsie and Benjamin, but Amelia was too consummate a socialite to allow it to linger long."The marquess

221

is a co-owner of Elysium with Mr. Scarsdale and the Duke of Wells." She waved her closed fan between the two men. "But how are you *acquainted* with Lady Elsie, my lord?" She put extra emphasis on the word acquainted.

"Lady Elsie and Elkington are engaged," Benjamin answered before the duke had a chance.

"To be married?" Amelia clapped her hands together, nearly upsetting the champagne in her glass. "Oh, what a *coup*, Elsie! How is this the first I am hearing of it?"

"Oh, we just travelled down from Edinburgh only a few weeks ago. Alex has not even had the chance to send the notification to the papers yet. He has been run so ragged with the wedding preparations."

Elsie gazed fondly up at him, and Charlotte fought an uncharitable wave of envy. She had long since abandoned the notion of marriage, or at least of a love match. But it stole over her just the same, seeing Elkington and Elsie so clearly devoted to one another. She was painfully aware of the man at her side and fought the direction of her thoughts as they slid towards the intimacies they had shared.

"Lady Elsie exaggerates my role," the marquess replied. "Her mother has shouldered most of the planning. I have onlybeen lending a hand where I may."

"I am afraid I have been terribly neglectful. I am working to start a school, you see." Elsie's dark eyes practically glowed with animation as she explained to the ladies her plan for a school for young girls of all backgrounds, hoping to rival Eton's curriculum. "Since I am hardly ever in London, I had to take this opportunity to seek out interested sponsors for the venture."

Charlotte was thoroughly charmed by the woman. Her

obvious passion for the cause and her genuine warmth and intelligence were a joy. Maybe she would welcome a renewal of their acquaintance once Charlotte was settled up north. Perhaps she even had the connections that Charlotte would need to find a position as a governess—or with her progressiveness, maybe even ties to journalism. The thought was buoying despite the heaviness that came with the thought of leaving. Leaving Benjamin.

She glanced toward him and found him already watching her, his face inscrutable but fixed all the same. For a moment, their eyes held, and she felt the rush of feeling she was beginning to associate with his presence—or even the idea of him.

"Amelia, Lady Charlotte, you must come to the dinner my parents are hosting next week." Elsie had clasped Elkington's hand and was practically beaming at both of them. "It will be an intimate affair, really. Only some family and friends to celebrate our engagement. It would be so lovely if you joined us. Even Mr. Scarsdale will be there."

Benjamin narrowed his eyes at that but said nothing.

Amelia was already nodding when Charlotte froze. "Oh no, I could not possibly." It was the height of impoliteness to decline such a generously offered invitation, but Charlotte could see no way around it.

"Nonsense, you must come. If you and Amelia get on so well, you must meet my sisters."

Charlotte could not accept. It was one thing to be squired about to the dark corners of a theatre or masquerade through a gaming hell as Benjamin's mistress, but it was a whole other thing to attend an intimate family function celebrating the love of his dear friend. That was not something a mistress did. She opened her mouth to protest again.

"Yes. You should come." Benjamin's face was unreadable, but she sensed a challenge in his words.

A moment passed as she tried to get a better read of his mood. His intentions. She could not. "That is a very generous invitation. Thank you, I will gladly come."

She bowed her head slightly, stealing another look at Benjamin from beneath her lashes. He was still watching her.

"Oh, is that Lord Rippon? Excuse me, dears. I must go say hello." Amelia flounced away in a swirl of mauve silks. "See you next week, then."

Elsie chuckled and waved goodbye.

"I believe that is our cue to go. You may still be able to read Helen another story, darling." Elkington gently guided Elsie toward a break in the crowd. She looked up at him with hopeful eyes.

"Do you think it is not too late? I am worried she is still tired from their journey down."

"Not if we make haste." He smiled down at her and nodded to Charlotte and Benjamin. "Until next week."

Elsie gave them both a little wave before disappearing into the crowd, leaving the two of them alone in the middle of the crowded gaming floor.

∞∞∞

She was beyond magnificent. Standing there in the deep green dress Benjamin had chosen for her, it was all he could do to take his eyes off her and scan the surrounding room, conscious of not allowing their exchange to draw too much attention. Even with a domino, the gossips of London were sharp and eager to jump on the smallest whiff of scandal.

"Would you care to join a table? Hazard seems to be popular tonight." He nodded toward the back of the floor where ladies and gentlemen were gathered over a particularly high-stakes game in progress.

Charlotte did not follow his gaze. She seemed quiet—withdrawn. Had something upset her?

"I do not approve of gambling, Mr. Scarsdale."

He watched transfixed as she took a sip of champagne. The delicate glass tilted between her soft, bowed lips. Could he squire her away to his rooms already? It seemed hasty. He did not want to rush her—wanted her to have a night of leisure and entertainment. But the idea of having her in his rooms—in his bed. Beyond the demanding physical desire, he craved being alone with her. Being allowed to watch her and speak to her without monitoring their surroundings. It all culminated in a physical ache that almost made him miss her question.

"Might we retire?" She was looking up at him, hopeful, almost timid, as if gauging his interest.

The force of his reaction was like a physical blow, knocking the air from his lungs. Did she realise how desperately he wanted to haul her over his shoulder and run from the room that very moment?

"We—" He coughed, his words caught in his throat. "Of course, my lady. If that is what you would prefer."

With that, he gave her a bow and turned into the throng of patrons, nodding to a footman who precipitously wound his way to escort the lady through the club.

Uninterested in delaying the encounter as he had the last

time Charlotte had come to him here, he made his way directly to the other side of the floor and slipped through one of the many concealed doors. He could only pray no sharp eyes had followed their subtle separation—for they would have seen the truth in every inch of his being.

Desperate longing.

Chapter Twenty-Four

The footman guided Charlotte to an alcove where he reached behind a curtain and pulled a corner of moulding to reveal a door very similar to the one she had been shuffled through last time. "Boyd will show you the way, my lady." With that, the noise of the crowded gambling floor was shut out behind her, and she stood a moment, almost blind, as her eyes adjusted to the dimmer candlelight of the small corridor.

"G'd evening, m'lady," a bright voice came from just to her left, making her jump.

"Oh." Charlotte put a hand to her chest, hoping to steady her racing heart.

It was just the fright, not the anticipation of her illicit rendezvous. Not rendezvous. Appointment. As far as Benjamin was concerned, she was a paid employee. The thought was lowering and made the champagne in her stomach turn.

Her eyes had adjusted, and she saw a young boy before her. "Good evening."

His face was cleanly scrubbed, and he was dressed in a tidy miniature version of the footman's livery, but his straight black hair was obstinately sticking up at odd angles. He absentmindedly smoothed a patch at the back, only making the cowlick more pronounced. His cheeks were full and rosy as if he ate well and often, but he could have been no older than ten. Maybe eleven. Certainly not old enough to be working in a gaming hell.

"Did not mean to frighten you, m'lady. The name is Boyd." He bowed chivalrously but teetered a bit on the ascent.

"Pleasure to meet you, Boyd. I am—"

"Lady Charlotte, I know. You are the master's new friend. Not like the ladybirds, though." From the mouths of babes. Leave it to a child to cut straight through the fat. "If you will follow me, my lady." He scampered down the corridor, and Charlotte was left with no choice but to follow.

"Is Boyd your family name or your Christian name?" Charlotte asked, following the ever-moving shadow through the rabbit warren of the club's inner workings.

"Dunno, m'lady. Both, I s'pose."

Upon her first visit, she had taken little stock of her surroundings—likely already battling the infection. The second, she had still been too stunned by the novelty of her new situation to much care what things looked like.

Now she looked around the bare halls, hoping for more insight into the institution and, more specifically, the man running it. A footman crossed their path here and there, but the back halls were mostly empty. It seemed there was far too much to do for employees to be loitering in the corridors.

Boyd pushed a swinging door and held it so it would not hit her as she followed through.

"Thank you." Charlotte caught her skirt's hem before it snagged in the closing door. "What do you mean you do not know?"

"Just that. Don't have no family. And can't think of a Christian name. Everyone just always called me 'boy.' Was not until I got here that Sir says I need a proper name. So we choosed Boyd. It is easy for me cause it sounds the same."

The child's rosy countenance did not waver, but Charlotte felt her world tilt a little on its axis.

"That is a very fine name, Boyd." She wanted to know more about how he had come to be here and what his life was like working under Benjamin. "How do you like living here?"

"Oh, it is just swell, innit? Cook lets me eat all I want, even though he is French and grumbles when I get my 'dirty street mitts' in his sauces. And the other footmen say I can be out on the floor one day if I keep my toes straight on the line. I even have my own bed upstairs. I never had my own bed before. No bed at all, actually. Not one I can remember." His little dark head was bouncing ahead of her as he rattled off his excited list. "Sir said I could even get reading and writing lessons and maybe work in the offices with him."

"That all sounds very nice, Boyd." It was clear the boy idolised Benjamin. She would have to tread carefully if she wanted to get any real information about his employer out of him. "How did you come to work for Mr. Scarsdale?"

"Here we are, m'lady." Boyd pointed to a staircase that led to a landing above them. "Sir's rooms is up there."

He gave her another lopsided bow and bounded down the hall, leaving Charlotte to consider the information she had gleaned and look up at the door that the man waited behind. How in the world had life brought her here?

Before she could get lost in her introspection, the door at the top of the landing opened. "Coming up?" The low, gentle roll of his voice sent gooseflesh prickling along her whole body, starting a low simmer in her abdomen.

"How did you know I was here?"

"Boyd's stomping." His mouth curved in a slow smile as he crossed his arms and leaned against the framework. He had abandoned his evening coat, and his cravat was already untied, hanging loosely around his neck. "He has not yet mastered his exuberance."

"I should think not." Charlotte collected her skirts and proceeded up the stairs with her chin high, as if she entered her lover's abode in the bowels of a gaming hell as a matter of course. "He is only a child, after all."

Benjamin stood, allowing her to pass by him and enter the suite of rooms while he closed the door behind them. "Childhood does not last long on the streets." The certainty in his voice made her turn, searching his face for more clues about his history.

"No, I suppose it does not." She folded her hands together, unsure of what to do with them. "It was good of you to hire him." *And house him, and feed him, and name him,* she added silently.

He just nodded. "I saw many—When I was…" He stopped and chewed the inside of his cheek. "I have the means to get them off the street. It is cheap labour anyway." He waved a hand and made his way over to the sideboard. "Would you like something to drink?"

Knowing he was evading her interest, but unsure of how these arrangements usually went, Charlotte let the deflection go. If he preferred her to think of him as an unfeeling opportunist, then she would let him. It did not change the fact that she suspected there was a lot more to this man than he was letting on. Already, she knew that what had happened to his mother and sister had shaped him deeply. Clearly, whatever had befallen him afterwards had changed him as well.

∞∞∞

Benjamin poured two tumblers of scotch and handed one to Charlotte. She was regarding him with a slight furrow in her brow. Of course, she would be curious about his unconventional staff and their hiring methods. He knew enough about her nature and interests to know she could not resist poking her nose into any proverbial dark corners.

Truth be told, he admired that about her. She had a heart for justice and a head for words. It was a noble streak that motivated seemingly every one of her decisions. Unfortunately, he was less noble, motivated by the pure ambition of survival. Though it had been some time since he was truly at risk of being on the streets again, or even of approaching material discomfort, it was not a switch one could simply turn off. The thought of her weaselling her way into his empire, his secrets, his heart, was enough to have a cold sweat break out across his neck. Her presence in his world alone was a threat—why could he not just be rid of her?

But watching her delicate neck move as she sipped the spirits, and the rosy flush that coloured her cheeks in its wake, he could no sooner fathom expelling her from his life than he could cut off his own arm. He just needed to distract her from further investigation. That he could do.

"The dress fits." It was a deliberate understatement, and he

231

let his roaming gaze belie the passive words.

She glanced down, as if only just remembering what she had on. "You would know." She arched a teasing eyebrow up at him, making his breath catch. The minx.

"I had Lizzy get your measurements when you were staying at the townhouse." He leaned back against the sideboard, balancing his tumbler in the crook of his elbow.

"You mean when I was a captive in your home?" She gave him another challenging glance and took a sip of the scotch, moving to survey the sitting room that adjoined his bedchamber.

It was still strange seeing her in his rooms. The furnishings were distinctly masculine. He rarely had female company here, and the more muted tones were soothing to his senses after long nights in the revelry of the club or his other holdings.

Seeing her lithe, silk-swathed form floating through the space was almost jarring. A blinding shaft of sunlight after living for years with his eyes adjusted to the darkness.

"I do not usually have female guests here." Where had that comment come from? She looked over her shoulder at him, the exposed skin of her back soft and tempting in the candle and firelight, but did not say a word. "I mean—" What did he mean? *Dammit.* "I usually prefer to go to them."

He could not say why it felt so important that he tell her this. Some part of him wanted to assure her that this was different. She was different.

Charlotte just nodded. "But my home is hardly fit for entertaining."

She had misunderstood him. She thought it was her family's circumstances that made this different from his other liaisons. Unable to think of a better explanation that did not relinquish an unacceptable amount of power, Benjamin let it go.

"The dresses are too much." She spoke to the landscape on the wall instead of to him.

He frowned. "You do not like them?"

Charlotte glanced toward him and back again at the painting. "I love them. But they are too much." She seemed almost… nervous? It was not as if they had not already done this before. *This* being increasingly all he could think of.

Standing there across the room from him, she was too far away. He needed to reach out and touch her hair, the satin of her skin. He could hardly drag his thoughts from trailing his mouth across her whole body.

"No, they are not." The words came out too forcefully, and he had to cough to clear the gravel from his throat. "These are precisely the type of gifts a mistress would expect to receive. In fact, they are paltry compared to the fare of a usual arrangement such as this."

He expected her to balk at that. He knew the arrangement needled her. But she surprised him and kept her face serene, not looking away from the landscape.

"I would prefer it if you did not give me such lavish gifts. Prototypical or not."

Instead, it was his turn to be needled. "But it is no less than you deserve."

She raised a cool eyebrow at that, and he could not stop himself from crossing the room over to her. Reaching a hand up, he unfastened the silk domino from behind her head, revealing her lovely face. Despite the smooth fabric, she had a few lines pressed into the tops of her cheeks from where she had fastened it too tight. Those lines reminded him of how precarious her situation was. Only a scrap of fabric standing between her and scandal. He knew already there were rumblings about their association. Catherine had ensured that after their run-in at the theatre. But no one knew the whole of it yet. It was wise of Charlotte to take such precautions, fastening the domino firmly against it all. Still, the fine indentations tugged at his conscience.

He drew a fingertip along the line, running it lightly outside one side of her eye, over the bridge of her nose, and across the other cheek. She did not say a word, but he saw her eyes widen and her pupils dilate. For all his misgivings, it was supremely gratifying to see that she wanted to be here as much as he wanted her.

"Charlotte?" Her name was barely a whisper, but her lips parted in response.

"Yes?"

"I am going to kiss you now." The words fanned over her lips just before he lowered his head to hers.

Chapter Twenty-Five

His kiss was gentle, tender—not what she expected in that moment. It was coaxing and reassuring, making her knees go weak. His hand had trailed sparks over her skin as he traced some invisible line over her face, and now it had followed the curve of her ear down to her neck, spinning her concentration away with soft warmth.

She knew it was a tactic; he was trying to draw her out of her thoughts—her reservations must have been clear to even him. He used one hand to take the nearly full tumbler of scotch from her and set it on the fireplace mantel, then used the other to tilt her head and deepen the kiss.

His mouth was warm and smoky—the lingering scotch on his tongue making her own lips tingle with sensation. His kiss was insistent but not hurried, as if he had all the time he could ever wish for.

She, on the other hand, felt a real urgency building under her skin. It was as if his calm, methodical pace had her growing ever more desperate to lose control. Why did he not feel the same? Frustrated, she slid her hands up his lawn-clad arms and down his sides, pulling him closer.

The man had the unmitigated gall to smile into the kiss. But he did not relent, even pulling away when she tried to deepen the kiss again. She let out a frustrated puff of air through her nose, and she could feel the beginnings of laughter in his chest. The feverish frustration that had overtaken her body made her combative.

She pulled away enough to start to speak, "What are you about, teasing—"

"Patience, my love."

He pulled her back into the embrace and gave her a searing kiss, enough to distract her from her course again. Then he proved willing to compromise, still maintaining the slow plunder of his kisses but allowing them to build in intensity. She could not get close enough to him. Her breasts felt uncomfortably confined by the low stays under the gown, and the warmth radiating through the layers of clothing they both still wore was a teasing torture. Tempting her with more.

"Ben, please." He froze for the briefest of moments, and she wondered if she had spoken too familiarly.

It seemed beyond the intimacy of the moment to care about such things, but she was still unsure how he expected this liaison to go. Before she could work herself up over the slip, he had pulled back, tearing off his waistcoat and shirtsleeves in one fluid movement, then clutched her to his bare chest. The contact drew a delighted sigh from her just as he brought her lips back to his.

His kisses were even more intense now. He pulled her arms up around his shoulders so he could work the hidden clasps down the side of the dress. He could have been the modiste himself for the intimate knowledge he seemed to have of the article's construction. In the span of a few breaths, he had the entire side unlaced and a hand already under the back of the bodice to undo her stays. The fluttering of his fingertips as he pulled the laces looser sent shivers over Charlotte's entire body. Then suddenly, he had both layers pushed down her shoulders, trapping her arms to her sides and baring her breasts.

"Oh," she let out a surprised gasp as he splayed his large, rough palm down her chest and over her sternum.

"God, Charlotte." His voice was not much more than a growl, and when she looked up into his eyes, she saw her own raw need reflected back at her. "I meant to go slow." His eyes flashed over her bare chest, flushed now up to her neck. "But, damn, Charlotte. I do not think I can."

She returned his stare boldly and confessed, "Neither can I."

With a groan, he bent and captured her left nipple in his mouth, laving the flat of his tongue over it again and again until she threw her head back in pleasure. Her nails dug into the taut muscle at his shoulders, unable to contain her own moans.

"God, woman. What have you done to me?" He punctuated the words by wrapping a steely arm around her waist and hoisting her to him.

She could feel his hardness pressing against her. As if of their own accord, Charlotte's legs wrapped around his lean waist as he carried her through the open door to the bedchamber.

She let out a short squeal as he tossed her onto the mattress as if she were no more than a bundle of linens, following her descent with his own body until she was trapped under his delicious weight.

She wiggled under him, causing him to groan into her hair. "Charlotte, I want to take my time with you." He sounded so raw and desperate, it made Charlotte thrum with feminine pleasure. She had reduced him to this.

"You have all night to take your time." She nipped the shell of his ear and felt his hissing breath on her neck. "I want you now."

It was possibly the most brazen thing she had said in her life, but rather than feel abashed, she felt absurdly powerful. Womanly. Especially when he wrapped both hands around her waist and pulled her to the edge of the bed, her skirts bunched around her abdomen. She watched as he hastily undid his falls, hands almost shaking in anticipation.

When he kicked them off, it was her turn to suck in her breath. He looked like the devil himself standing there over her, framed by the sumptuous scarlet bed hangings and illuminated only by the banked fire. He ran his hands up the smooth planes of her thighs and up under her buttocks, kneading and rubbing as he went.

"Charlotte?" It was clear he was hanging on only by a sliver of self-control. Luckily for him, she had lost her own self-control a while ago.

She nodded, reaching for his forearm to pull herself closer. In a single breath, he lined himself up and pushed inside. The stretch was unbelievable and delicious, stealing her breath until she moaned in exhale. Looking up through the haze of lust, she saw that a sheen of sweat had already broken out across his forehead.

Charlotte rolled her hips to try to get him to move. He let out a pained groan before taking her invitation and thrusting forward again before withdrawing almost completely. This time, they both moaned in unison when he pushed forward again. He set a slow rhythm at first, until it was clear neither of them could stand it much longer. Both of Benjamin's powerful hands gripped her hips as he drove into her in increasingly rapid thrusts.

It was all Charlotte could do to draw breath. Their frenetic movements shook the bed, and she could hear herself groaning with each new intrusion. When he slid his hand down and lifted one leg against his chest, she almost screamed in pleasure. "Oh God, Charlotte. I cannot—" He thrust again, even deeper. "I am so close."

She was not sure if it was the words combined with the look of sheer, pleasurable torture on his face or the next, particularly fierce roll of his hips, but she felt her eyes roll back as liquid fire rolled from their joined bodies, washing over her in wave after delicious wave. She could distantly hear the guttural shout of her name as Benjamin arrived at his own climax, and it was not for many long, ecstatic moments that she felt herself return to her body.

∞∞∞

"My mother called me Ben." Charlotte looked up from his wide chest, where she had been lightly tracing scars. They had made love again and were lying tangled together atop the sheets. Charlotte had been close to falling asleep again until he had broken the silence with the unexpected admission.

"Hmm?" she hummed drowsily up at him, but he was still looking up at the bed's brocade canopy.

"When I was a boy, my mother called me Ben. She was the only one. Delia always called me Benjamin."

"And your father?" She followed the line of a particularly ragged scar up his chest and over one shoulder. She wanted desperately to know where each and every one of them had come from and marvel at the man who had survived them.

"I do not remember." He spun a strand of her hair between his fingers. "We did not really have much cause to see him. I think when Delia was younger, he visited more. She was named after his great-aunt Cordelia. I know he always called her Delia." He frowned as if he were trying to remember how he knew that. "I do not recall him calling me anything. When he died and the duchess threw us out of the estate cottage…" His bitterness was plain to see. "I only found out later that my mother had had offers for a new position." He paused on the word, clearly battling complex emotions around the reality of his mother's *position*. "But she declined. Even when she knew Winden's health was failing. She said she loved him and could not bear to leave."

The resentment in his voice was vicious, and Charlotte stopped her tracing. She knew their arrangement was not born of tender feelings—and was relieved for it, really. It was the only sensible way to proceed. But as she grew to care more and more about this man, his clear contempt for even the idea of love was frighteningly disappointing.

"And you feel that you and your sister wound up in dire straits because of her decision." It was not a question.

"As a direct consequence of it, yes."

Charlotte splayed her hand over his chest, feeling the rapid beat of his heart. She did not know what to say. Did not know if it was her place to offer comfort for all that he had suffered as a result of his mother's decisions. It was not fair to any of them. Even though she may have loved him, his mother had no power as a duke's mistress. Her illegitimate children had even less. It was indicative of the duke's disregard for all three of them that he had not provisioned any security for them in his will.

"Benjamin." Charlotte looked up at him, willing him to meet her gaze. When he did, she reached up to trace the rough stubble that had cropped up on his jaw. "What happened to you after Delia passed?"

The idea of Benjamin as a young boy, suddenly alone in the world, broke her heart all over again for him.

His eyes were shuttered when they met hers. "It does not matter." She had pushed too hard. Once again, she had broken the tenuous thread between them with her probing. "I fended for myself until I was sixteen. Wells found me and offered me a job. I took the position. And from it, I built this."

Charlotte only nodded and looked down again. She did not want him to see the disappointment in her eyes that he did not want to confide in her. Or the anger at herself for jeopardising the gentle haven they had found themselves in. He had already given her so much.

He seemed to misunderstand her silence as censure. Defensively, he said, "Now that I have this, the past does not matter."

Charlotte suspected that he was trying to convince himself more than her, so she just nodded, her cheek rubbing along the dark hair of his chest.

"Why did you start writing?" he asked. She felt him pick up a tendril of her hair and wrap it around his finger. "And do not say to pay off your brother's debts. I know you have been playing the journalist since before your father passed."

Surprised by that, she looked up. She had been eminently

discreet about her investigations into the working and living conditions of the poor before she had begun selling her work for publication.

"Everybody talks, Charlotte. It is just a matter of asking the right people." For a moment, with the flickering shadows of the night dancing across his hard-planed face, Charlotte could see him as the lethal, calculating underworld kingpin he was reputed to be. The Master of London's Secrets. Then he smiled, a gleam of mischief in his crinkling eyes, and she wanted to tell him every secret she had ever had.

"My lady's maid inspired me to write," Charlotte said quietly.

It sounded spoiled and vapid after the revelations of his own misfortune. That it took seeing another suffer for her to realise there was a world outside of her quaint Mayfair existence was humbling.

His brow quirked at that, and she propped herself on his chest, hands folded beneath her chin, rising and falling with his breath. "I found her. I was on a morning walk in Regent's Park, without a groom or chaperone of any kind. I thought myself quite rebellious."

She smiled at that and was surprised as he gently tucked a curl behind her ear. She looked up to find him watching her intently, and she momentarily lost her train of thought. Benjamin nodded, encouraging her to continue.

"I just saw the hem of her dress in the bushes. I thought it was a lost parasol or something. I was not even going to stop to pick it up. But then, something came over me, and I had to look closer."

She was back in the park on that rainy morning. The spring had been cold and damp, and her stepmother had moved the family back to London; she was so stir-crazy in the dreary countryside. The boys had been driving their nanny to distraction, and so Charlotte had taken to occupying Freddie or the twins while Nanny took the other. When she found herself with a rare morning alone, she had struck out to the park—a young lady with no real occupation besides entertaining her half brothers, the idea of a solo trip to the park seemed a true adventure. So she had gone, bundled in thick country wool against the damp, and determined to walk as far and wide as possible.

She was tiring by the time she reached the hedgerows of Regent's Park. Her toes had also begun to freeze, and she planned to head back for luncheon soon. When she approached the hem of the skirt protruding from the bushes, she did not know what she would find.

Anna Witton was so battered, one could hardly make out her face. Her tattered clothes were torn from her body in graphic fashion, and dried blood and bruises were visible in the exposed places.

"She was not even crying. It was as if she had crawled under there to die."

The hollowness in Charlotte's chest upon looking down at the woman's broken form was just as sharp now as it had been that morning. She felt a warm, rough hand cup her cheek, and she looked up. Benjamin was there. He was with her. He stroked her cheek gently and allowed her to continue.

"I tried to wake her up, but she was fading in and out. Finally, I was able to pull her mostly upright and get my walking coat around her. I do not know how I managed to get her to the street, but I hailed a hackney cab and brought her home. Luckily, my lady's maid had just left to get married, and my stepmother was not much bothered by the hiring of the household. It took a week for Anna to be well enough to walk again. And even then, it was nearly a month before she spoke. I made do with making myself up and covered for her until she was ready for the position." Charlotte smiled nostalgically at the memory of the bond that had grown between them. Anna had become a true friend. "I realised that morning in the park that I was wasting my life if I was not using it to try to help people like her.

"I tried publishing a few of my pieces on children's living conditions in the Dials with some charitable organisations I am part of, but the ladies would not hear of it. They were scandalised that I had even ventured to such a part of town. After that, I do not think they even had the energy to be scandalised by the conditions themselves." Her lips twisted in a rueful smile. "It was not until the desperation of our financial predicament that I even thought of publishing under a pen name."

"Necessity is a powerful motivator."

Spoken like a man who knew.

Chapter Twenty-Six

"Where are you going?" Benjamin looked up at her from the bed, the soft morning light filtering over his handsome face, still half asleep.

"I have an interview today. Mary Kaur works in a stall in Covent Garden, and she only has time to speak after the morning rush while the lunch pies are baking.

"I am coming with you." He flipped the covers off his legs before she could protest.

"No, you have things to do, I am sure. Besides, I don't know how to get people to talk if there is someone else around. Especially you. You will scare her witless." Charlotte tried to fasten the sides of her bodice again. The gorgeous dress was still immaculate, despite having lain on the floor all night, but she needed to go home and change into less conspicuous garments.

"I do not like you going out on your own. It is not safe." He batted her hands away and helped her finish fastening the clasps, still fully nude.

"It will be the middle of the morning. And besides, I will be careful. I always am." He scowled at her, and she scowled back before breaking into a smile. "I have been doing this since long before I met you. I can hold my own."

"You do not have to."

It was a casual comment. One he threw out as he turned and rummaged for a new set of clothes, pulling them on with casual haste. They were not his usual gentlemanly attire, but the rough-spun wool still suited him—as everything did. For a moment, she could see him clearly in another life. The most handsome farmer in his little village. But then he looked up at her perusal and gave her his devilish grin, and he could be no one but her underworld king.

"Come along, we will stop by your house so you can gather what you need."

∞∞∞∞

Benjamin surveyed the corner, where sellers hawked their wares to passing workers, and pickpockets darted in and out of the crowd like fishing birds, plucking their catch with surgical precision before returning to their nests.

He gave Charlotte some space, standing close enough to hear, but not so close as to unnerve the young woman whose dark face was covered in flour and sweat from an already long morning spent before the oven.

"Why did your family come to London?" Charlotte kept her voice subdued, making her cultured accent less noticeable.

With her heavy grey work dress and her tightly fastened bonnet, she could be any passing worker—one with an education, but certainly not a lady. The transformation was impressive, and Benjamin had to grudgingly admit she knew what she was doing.

"We fled Palashi when the East India Company attacked.

246

My aunts and uncles were all killed." The young woman spoke with a thick, lyrical accent, some of her words blending into an almost French pronunciation. "Five hundred people were killed. We were lucky to make it out. My mother knew a friend who had married a Frenchman and moved to Europe. We followed her. But my father and sister died in France when a fever came through the town we stayed in. My mother brought us here."

Charlotte just nodded, allowing the woman to speak.

"We lived in a flat near here, the four of us packed in with three other families." Benjamin well knew the arrangement. "We were, all of us, young. But we found work. Until my brother fell in with a bad crowd. He was stealing. It is not good, but it kept us fed. One day, a man came and knocked on our door. He dragged Rabin out and beat him. He was only fourteen. My mother cried for two days. Then, one of the boys he ran with came by. He was older and said he knew where he could get Rabin help. His arm had been broken, and we could not afford a doctor."

Benjamin continued to scan the street, but he felt the story tugging at the back of his mind.

"The boy and I brought Rabin to a back door in St James's. I had never been that far west before, but he knew where we were going. Inside, there was a cook who brought a doctor down, and they set Rabin's arm. My brother did not scream, but I saw the tears on his face. Afterward, a man came down. He was dressed in fine clothes, but he spoke to everyone in the kitchens as if they were his friends. He said Rabin should stop stealing and come work for him. I was scared. You hear of the work they make young boys do. But I was wrong. He was a good man. I never got to thank him for saving my brother."

Benjamin was frozen in place. He knew the story.

When he turned to see why the woman had stopped talking, he saw that both Mary and Charlotte were staring at him. A moment passed, then he gave the woman a nod. He could do no more. He did not want thanks.

As if in silent agreement, both women returned to the story. Charlotte asked questions about Mary's work. How she'd found the job, and whether it was enough for her to support her family. Then she asked strange, irrelevant questions: what Mary missed from her home in Bengal, what she dreamed of doing with her life. And Mary had an answer for all of them. Despite the hard life she had lived, the young woman was surprisingly full of hope.

"Thank you so much, Mary. Thank you for sharing your story with me." Benjamin watched as she pushed a coin into the woman's hand.

"Thank you, Miss Charlotte, for listening." She turned, and Benjamin thought she would duck back into the shop where the ovens were pumping out heat, but she paused, facing him. "And thank you, Mr. Scarsdale." She gave him a bow and disappeared beyond the shop window.

Charlotte joined him again, quiet for a moment. "Your reputation is not as black as it seems." Charlotte smirked up at him as they walked side-by-side back through the streets of Covent Garden.

"I do not know what you are talking about." Benjamin kept his eyes ahead, warning off potential thieves with merely a look.

"It is okay. You do not have to be embarrassed on my account. But I think you are far less feared than adored out here."

"And how would you know?" He felt surly in the face of her teasing, which only seemed to delight her more.

"I have heard tales of you far before our fated meeting, Mr. Scarsdale."

That intrigued him. What had she heard? Had he lived up to her expectations? Or had she been disappointed when she met the man behind the myth? He fought to let none of his curiosity show.

"You would be surprised how eager people are to whisper about the legend of Scarsdale. A mythic being that may bless you or curse you, but only on the merit of your soul."

Benjamin scoffed at that. "And how am I to know what is in the depths of a fishmonger's soul?"

"You know everyone's secrets. That is a window into their soul."

He glanced down at her, their gazes catching. "Not for everyone."

Her warm brown eyes searched his, as if she, in fact, was the one who could peer into his soul. "Grumble all you want, Mr. Scarsdale. I think you might have a beautiful soul, after all."

The words robbed him blind, and it was all he could do to navigate them back to the main road and call a hackney.

Chapter Twenty-Seven

Come away with me. The words were written in a familiar cramped, forceful hand. Charlotte had read them from the missive delivered to the townhouse as she pored over the paperwork for letting the house and doing what she could to ensure the twins' stability, and her heart had sped, an eager flush stealing through her.

Where did he intend them to go? For how long? The note gave her none of the answers, so she had sent back a missive by way of the young urchin who had delivered it.

I can hardly drop everything at one cryptic note, now can I?

The response had come within an hour.

Please? I can make it worth your while.

She was sure he could. Thoughts of the previous night invaded her senses, and she found herself fanning her rosy cheeks before considering her response.

When? Where? For how long?

Not long after the errand boy left, she heard carriage wheels rolling up outside the townhouse.

∞∞∞

"You cannot just spirit me away at a moment's notice, Benjamin." Charlotte crossed her arms and leaned back against the squab of the well-sprung carriage. Benjamin lounged negligently across from her, his long, muscular legs taking up more than his fair share of the small space.

"I think you will find I can do precisely what I wish to do, when I wish to do it." His tone was imperious, but the twinkle in his deep blue eyes made her lips quirk.

It was hard to maintain her air of exasperation when, in reality, she was humming with excitement. It had been years since she had escaped London's smoggy streets, and frequent glances out the window confirmed that they were leaving the crowded city behind. Benjamin still refused to share the particulars of their journey with her, but she could not bring herself to care overmuch as she pressed the folding glass window open and breathed in the heady smell of warm earth that never quite made it to Mayfair's cobbled streets, no matter how beautifully the spring thawed.

"Will you tell me our destination if I guess?" She had already determined it must be close.

He had not requested that she pack anything for the journey, so they would not be venturing more than an afternoon's ride away. They were headed west, she was fairly certain, so that would also eliminate many possibilities—though her knowledge of the geography around London was considerably lacking.

Benjamin only shrugged, as if he were only half interested in their conversation and more intent on working his booted foot casually under the hem of her dress to caress her ankle gently. It was supremely distracting.

"Are we going to have a picnic?" Charlotte could not imagine Benjamin Scarsdale lounging like a fashionable London gentleman amidst a variety of delicate finger sandwiches— though the course of his foot up her calf had her considering the other things they might do on a blanket under a shaded tree in a secluded corner of the countryside.

"We may if you would like to." He watched a field pass, filled with sheep and lambs gambolling behind their mothers.

"But that is not the primary purpose of this excursion?" she asked.

He shook his head, and Charlotte's brows furrowed in thought. "We are heading west…"

Benjamin leaned further towards the window, the warm side of his knee pressing against the inside of hers, as if to ascertain the sun's position. "Yes, we seem to be travelling in that general direction."

"Are we going to a village fair?" Charlotte was growing more frustrated, both from the lack of answers and the restlessness inspired by his proximity.

"No." He shrugged again.

"Well then. How long will it take us to arrive at our destination?"

"A few more hours, I imagine."

"Hours?" Charlotte squeaked.

They had left Mayfair just before noon. Unless they arrived at their destination and then promptly turned back around again, they would not be back in London before nightfall. And Charlotte was loath to travel by night, even with the formidable company of Benjamin Scarsdale.

"Do not worry about it, Charlotte."

Her brows drew together at that. How like a man to dismiss her concerns. If she did not worry about it, who would?

He reached out to press his thumb to the furrow between her brows, rubbing with a soothing pressure that forced them to relax. "Trust me, love. I have everything under control."

She felt herself relenting but could not bring herself to fully relax. She was not quite reconciled to the strange and foreign experience of trusting someone else to care for matters…yet. No. Would never be. Their arrangement was temporary. She would be back on her own in only a few weeks' time. The heavy mantle of her responsibility, which had somehow seemed lighter in the last days, would settle back squarely on her shoulders, and she would be away in some new place alone to battle her way through. It was liberating, but it was daunting. She hoped the weight of it all would not crush her.

"Charlotte," his warm voice was a warning. "I can *see* you worrying."

She let out a huff. "Well, what do you suggest I do? I do not know where we are going. You will not tell me. And now I know there are hours between us and this mystery destination, so now I have to just wait. I would say worrying is a very good use of my time. There is always a good number of things to worry about. The principle of which is that we will likely need to be travelling back after nightfall, which is asking for trouble out on these country roads. What if a horse throws a shoe, or we are set upon—"

"Charlotte," he interrupted her with his broad hands splayed above her knees, the warmth of his bare palms seeping through the layers of her skirts. "I believe I can propose a better way to spend the next few hours than worrying."

"Oh?" Still cross, she jutted her chin out in a mulish line.

Benjamin's face cracked into a slow, wide smile, and

Charlotte's mouth softened watching the expression light up the inside of the carriage.

"Oh."

∞ ∞ ∞

Two hours later, it took both Charlotte and Benjamin a considerable amount of effort to put her hair and clothing to rights, an endeavour that was derailed twice by Benjamin's wandering hands as he did up her stays. Finally, after multiple assurances, Charlotte was confident her hair and travelling dress were appropriately restored.

For the last ten minutes, they had been rolling through the streets of a town. So busy was she righting her attire, she had not yet made out which town. It was bigger than a coaching town one might find on the Great North Road, where the buildings sprang up around an inn and thrived off the passing traffic. There were people milling around the streets, much like any other town—but she could tell there was something different about this one—though she could not yet tell what.

"'Ere we are!" The coachman shouted down at them just as they rolled into the mews behind a row of buildings.

"Where is here?" Charlotte craned her neck to see more of their surroundings while she waited for the footman to fold down the steps.

"Welcome to Eton, Lady Charlotte."

Benjamin's voice was right beside her ear, and the warmth of his breath on her cheek had her blushing and touching her coiffure, hoping any passersby would attribute any stubborn flyaway curls to the length of their journey. Then his words sank in.

"*Eton?*" She stood frozen in the carriage's door. Eton.

They were in Eton. Marcus and Henry were here. Close. She could see them. She had not seen them since the start of last term, and even then, it had only been for a few days after they returned from summering with the Chesterfields. The Chesterfields had three boys. One of them, Simon, was the same age as the twins, and the three had been nearly inseparable since they began school. While not titled, the family was wealthy and well respected and, frankly, considering the Aston's fortunes, a godsend.

"I have arranged for a room at the inn just here." Benjamin waved up at the brick building that fronted the mews as he gently lifted her from the carriage and placed her on the cobbles. "We can go inside and freshen up—" he stopped when he saw her face, "*or* I can escort you to visit with your brothers now."

Charlotte jumped at the suggestion. "Yes! Please!"

"Alright, let us be on our way then." He offered her his arm, and she took it, the strong steadiness beneath his coat keeping her tethered despite her suddenly racing heart.

When they arrived outside the boarding house, Benjamin gently extricated himself from her grasp.

"What are you doing?" she asked. "We are here."

He put another step between them and nodded. "Yes, I sent word ahead. Your brothers are expecting you. You have a reservation at the coffeehouse down the street here for six o'clock. Carons here will escort you and your brothers there and ensure everything is in order."

"And what about you?" Some of the wind had gone out of her sails.

She realised now that there would be no genteel way to

explain her travelling with a bachelor of ill repute, let alone dining with him and her brothers in public. Still, the thought of him slipping away now had her chest caving in just a little. She wanted him there. With her. With them. She wanted to introduce him to the boys. He would love them—so young, clever, and spirited. And they would adore him, she just knew it.

"I will see you later." He only smiled and tipped his hat to her. "We are staying at the Royal Arms. Carons will see you back."

Charlotte could only nod as he turned to return the way they had come. She gave him a sad little wave that he did not see.

Chapter Twenty-Eight

Charlotte could not believe her eyes—or her ears. The boys before her were like strangers—joyful, jubilant strangers.

Their precious youthful faces had grown and stretched, in that awkward way of adolescence—full of echoes of their childhood selves but not yet the adults they would soon become. It was jarring, and Charlotte had spent the whole first hour of their conversation looking back and forth between the two, trying to reconcile her memories with the people sitting across from her in the little coffeehouse.

As promised, after the boys had come down and given Charlotte exuberant embraces, Carons had led them to the little shop where the proprietress greeted them warmly and brought them to a quiet table in the back. She plied them with tea and cakes, and chocolate. Sweets aside, the boys had hardly stopped for a breath since setting eyes on Charlotte.

"And Randolph is going to lend me his cricket paddle because it is wider than the other one—"

Henry interrupted Marcus for what seemed like the hundredth time since they sat down. "The tutor would not even let me explain my reasoning. He just marked me wrong and—

"

"But I do not think cricket is even that sporting, and they won't let us try for the polo until we are—" Marcus cut back in as if Henry had not said a word.

Charlotte had forgotten just how dizzying the two of them could be. When they were young, she had prided herself on juggling conversation with the two of them better than anyone else in the household. It was sweet to do it again, but she felt an ache in her chest to realise she was out of practice.

And would remain that way. Reality was hovering only a few weeks away, casting a pall on the joy of the moment, of the day, the week. This would probably be the last time she could see the twins for a while. Years maybe. Her work up north would help support them. She could care for them but not be near them; she could not await their return home from term every summer at their country estate like the other families of the *ton*. But she would not let that spoil the moment—or the twins' happiness at getting to talk to—at—her again.

"Thank you so much for the accounts, Charlie." Henry had stumbled his way into a new topic, and Charlotte was not sure she had kept track.

"Yes, thank you, Charlie! With our allowance now, we can keep up with the other boys. But I promise we'll only use it for school or sport. No betting, just like you said."

Marcus seemed to be suddenly on the same subject as Henry. They did that every once in a while, their meandering paths criss-crossing over each other here and there.

"What accounts?" Charlotte asked.

She hated that they had felt the pinch of the purse strings the last couple of years. Not that they did not have everything they needed here at school, but she knew the social price of not having an allowance. Burdened estates kept other boys from titled families in check, she was sure; theirs was not the only family that faced the spectre of genteel poverty. But she wanted more for them. She wanted them to live their carefree boyhood to the fullest—though that same wish had not done Freddie much good. What accounts were these that were dispensing allowances to her young brothers? She was sure she already knew.

But the topic was already forgotten, the boys forging onwards into different subjects of interest, and Charlotte was left reeling, trying to keep track of the two again and give them her full attention.

∞∞∞

After bidding the boys goodbye and promising to visit them once more before she left—though she was not entirely sure when that would be, not having been involved in the planning of this surprise trip—she followed Carons back through the quaint streets to the Royal Arms. It had been presumptuous of Benjamin to procure lodgings, but the idea of travelling back to London that evening, no matter the company, was wholly unappealing.

The inn was a respectable red-brick building with a cheery crown on its sign and a convivial rumble coming from the supper room on the ground floor. Carons held open the carved oak door and bowed her inside. The smell of stew and meat pies and the yeasty waft of ale came on a warm gust that rushed past her into the cool evening air. Carons stepped inside and guided her to the staircase at the back of the establishment.

"Oh, one moment, Carons." She placed a staying hand on the boy's arm and turned back to the bar, where a woman stood polishing glasses.

"Excuse me." Charlotte gave the woman a smile, trying to snare her attention from where her sharp eye roved the dining room.

She seemed the type of no-nonsense proprietress who ran a tight ship in this town overrun with privileged young lordlings.

"Yes, madam? How may I help you?" Upon spying Charlotte, she turned all things solicitous, but her address confirmed she did not know her true identity.

"I wondered if perhaps you could send a bath up to my room?"

"Why, of course, it is already done. Your husband requested one to be ready for your return."

"My—" She stopped herself short. Her *husband*. The words struck her so squarely in the chest, she could barely manage a breath, let alone a thank you and good night.

She followed Carons up the narrow staircase to the first landing and down a hall where the footman knocked on a door and, following a summons she had not heard, opened the door and bowed her inside.

"Is there anything else you may need, my lady?"

Charlotte surveyed the room, prim but well-appointed with faded striped wallpaper and heavy wood furniture, all orbiting a large, four-poster bed piled with pillowy linens. A copper slipper tub sat before the hearth, and lavender-scented steam wafted from its basin. The room was empty.

"No, thank you, Carons, that will be all." She wanted to ask where the boy's employer was, but something told her the footman's loyalty would prohibit him from sharing what was not his to share—if he even knew.

Besides, Benjamin would appear eventually. For now, the tub was crying too strong a siren call to resist.

Not long after Carons shut the door, a knock had Charlotte jumping, arms tangled in her pelisse as she tried to wriggle free on her own—a feat that was still tricky with the stiffness that settled in her shoulder at the end of a long day.

"Yes?" It was a silly squeak of a question, but she could not think who would be knocking. Benjamin would surely come straight in—it was his room, after all.

"I am here to help you with your bath, ma'am." It was a woman's voice.

"Oh, alright then."

Charlotte was not sure what to do. She could not turn the maid away, but she also was not used to having the help of a lady's maid. Even with Lizzy, she had still bathed alone, except for the cleaning of her shoulder.

A young woman stepped in and closed the door behind her. Her face was pert and freckled in a charming, country-lass way, and her dark hair curled becomingly from her mobcap. And yet, when she looked at Charlotte, there was something sour about her countenance. Charlotte was sure she looked foolish; the travelling companion of such a well-heeled gentleman—his *wife,* as far as this girl knew—wrestling her way out of years-worn travelling clothes without the help of a lady's maid. It was enough to make her cheeks warm.

She fought the urge to explain herself as the woman dipped a shallow curtsy and crossed the room, silently helping her out of the layers of her wool gown.

When the maid, who had not given Charlotte her name,

hung the garments in the wardrobe and returned to lift her chemise, Charlotte almost shied away. But that was foolish.

The maid offered her a hand as she stepped into the bath and sank into the warm, fragrant water. It was heaven. Charlotte was sure she would continue to melt straight through the floor.

"Oh!" The maid's voice drew her gaze back up where the woman's eyes were fixed on the gnarled scar at her shoulder. *Damn.*

"Thank you, that will be all." The masculine voice came from the door, and Charlotte did not need to look over her shoulder to see who stood there.

Relief surged through her. She would not need to explain the scar to the maid—and, more importantly, Benjamin had not abandoned her to the night as she had feared. He was here. And she was stark naked in a bath with a beautiful woman between them.

Charlotte watched the familiar expressions play across the woman's face. Surprise—Benjamin was arrestingly handsome. Desire—it was a natural step. And then, calculation. The maid dropped Charlotte an assessing look and then turned back to Benjamin as if she were nothing more than a loose cushion, fluffed and deposited on a sofa, free to be disregarded. The maid dropped into a deep curtsy, her full bosom on display in the firelight.

Charlotte had to admit, it was a beautiful display. The maid had a womanly shape that commanded the men of London— and beyond. She sashayed towards the door, her hip brushing Benjamin's leg as if the doorway were too small for anything else.

"G'night, sir. If ye be needing anything, just come find me.

Anything."

If Charlotte did not feel the humiliating burn of embarrassment, she might even admire the woman's boldness. As it was, sitting naked in the tub, the day's grime still clinging to her, the bones of her hips protruding more than was fashionable after months of lean grocery budgets, and a gnarled scar at her shoulder, Charlotte felt decidedly foolish.

When Lady Catherine had appeared in the box at the opera, Charlotte had known that there had been something between her and Benjamin. It was obvious. Whether she had been his mistress, just as Charlotte was now, she was still not sure. The encounter had stirred a similar burning in her chest. The natural jealousy of a woman who had captured the attention of a man who had so captured her own. But that was nothing compared to this now.

She had not loved him then. *Christ.* She loved him. This mercurial man, who had already given her so much. Who shouldered his responsibilities and eased the lives of others, no matter how blackened his reputation may be.

It was good that this arrangement with Benjamin was only a month long. She could not imagine the pain and humiliation that would come when he tired of her and moved on to a woman more like this maid—or Lady Catherine. And she was sure it was just a matter of time. A man like Benjamin Scarsdale could not possibly be satisfied with a woman like her for long. She knew her self-pity was misplaced. The weariness of the journey and the slow gnaw of change had her feeling heartsick.

She knew she was passably pretty, if in a rather strange way, and had attracted enough admirers in her first season. But that was another life—another woman. That young belle had not seen the truth of life yet. She had not been hardened by loss and made cynical and plain. No, it was best they leave all this behind before he understood all that and saw her for what she was—the veil of novelty stripped away. Before he could break her heart.

∞∞∞

There was no air in this room. It was all lavender steam and Charlotte. Benjamin stood braced against the door, trying to catch a breath.

The water had darkened her fairy-light hair, and the fire caught the deep golden hues spilling down her narrow back. She watched the maid leave, and Charlotte's gaze lingered on him, turning his knees soft and his heart tripping forward, towards her. He had to loosen his cravat just to get a full breath of air.

She rested her sharp chin on her shoulder.

"Good evening, Benjamin." Her voice was quiet, as if she were far away. He should be closer to her.

"Good evening, Charlotte." He toed off his boots, making every effort to appear calm and patient—not as if he were burning to climb into the small slipper tub right beside her, legs tangling together in the silky water. "How was your afternoon?"

She had a smile for him then, one that gripped his chest and had him nearly delirious with joy. "It was wonderful."

She reached her hands out to catch one of his between hers, pulling him down and holding it to her lips. He could feel his heart pumping in his throat as her warm breath fanned over his scarred knuckles, the softness of her lips tracing the ridges of the bones and somehow finding places between that were still soft and sensitive—that had not been hardened by the cruelty of the streets. It was a wonder to him that there was any softness left at all—that she could find it.

"I should be cross with you." Her faint brow arched, and the familiar governess quirk of her lip exposed the dimple he was coming to recognise as a reward—it only appeared when she made that precise expression.

"Cross?" He was swimming through a daze—fixated on kissing that dimple.

"We agreed, no gifts."

At that, he frowned, momentarily snapping out of his trance. If she only knew the amount of restraint he exerted in not buying every single diamond and silk he came across— every filly and coach and townhouse and slipper. He wanted to give her *everything*. But he had respected her damned rule. He had not commissioned more gowns. He had not opened a line of credit for her in every fashionable establishment he could think of. What more could she possibly want? Or not want, as it were.

"I—"

"Shhh." She still held his hand and pressed it to her cheek— where he so desperately wanted to place his lips. There was something Shakespearean about the moment, but he was too far in her thrall to recall. "I said, no gifts. And you have just given me the most precious gift I could have asked for."

Her eyes were wide and dark in the firelight, and Benjamin was so close, he could lean in and drown in them. "It was nothing." The words were strangled by her proximity—her gratitude. Didn't she know she need not be grateful? He would give her anything. He could not help it.

"It was not nothing, Benjamin. I have not been able to see Marcus and Henry since last year. And even then, it was only a moment. And now…" She seemed far away again, and Benjamin leaned even closer, compelled to keep her with him. "Well, with my circumstances as they are, I will likely not see them for another long while…maybe even years."

Her voice caught, and he watched her throat work as she valiantly fought the wave of emotion that had taken her, not allowing the undertow to draw her back out to sea again. Didn't she know he would dive in after her and pull her right back?

"So today was an unbelievable gift. To see them—they are not even boys anymore. And now, when I meet them again, when they are men." Her eyes were misty, like the whips of heavy fog that rose from the fields in the cool summer twilight. "Perhaps they will not be strangers to me."

The loss in her voice was enough to cleave Benjamin in two. He knew what it was like to lose a family—one by one, like strips of flesh being peeled away. A part of yourself gone with each one. And now, she was in the middle of it. A slow splintering of her family—of herself—despite all the selfless battle she had waged to prevent it.

Looking into her sharp, open face, which sparkled with dewy steam and firelight, Benjamin made his decision. He would not let this happen to her. He would restore her to the life she had been robbed of, and maybe, that could mean he could keep her too. Just a little while longer.

"Charlotte." He brought his other hand up, framing her face between his palms, the linen of his shirtsleeves dampening as she gripped his forearms, clinging to him as much as he was to her.

An errant tear escaped and slipped down her cheek, and he brushed it away. He could see the chinks in her armour cracking, and he wanted to tell her he could hold her together if she needed to fall apart. Instead, he kissed the side of her lip, precisely where the dimple would appear given the right provocation.

There were so many things he wanted to say. Words that were bubbling up inside of him, mounting a pressure that he likely should not ignore. But he did not dare release them. Instead, he pressed another kiss to the tip of her long nose. Then another to the other side of her lips. These words would have to do for now. The words of his touch—of his kiss.

"Thank you, Benjamin." Her voice was quiet, filled with a reverence that stunned him.

And then she kissed him. Her warm lips were a soothing pressure on his. Her hands pulled him closer, until his forearms were pressed to her chest and the linen at his elbows submerged in the warm, lavender water that had so temptingly obscured her bare body.

The kiss turned deeper, the hot wet of her mouth drawing him in further until his shirt and waistcoat were drenched, her fingers scoring his scalp and sending shock waves down his spine. Somehow, he managed to shuck his buckskin breeches before doing precisely what he had longed to do the moment he arrived in their room and saw Charlotte in the bath. Even as Charlotte was trying to peel his wet shirt off, he climbed into the small tub beside her, sending Charlotte into a peal of surprised laughter as water sloshed over the edges of the tub and onto the hearth rug beneath.

"The landlady will not be pleased if we make a mess." Charlotte was still laughing, and despite the forceful desire that consumed him, the sound of her laughter loosened something in his chest.

"Let her rage," Benjamin growled through a feral grin as he took her in—the flush of her breasts and the glow of delight in her eyes.

He almost said something then—the words almost bubbled out of him. But something stopped him. Some dam honed from a lifetime of survival. So instead, he just pulled her closer, her legs wrapping around his waist as he lifted her onto his lap, a hiss of blind pleasure escaping through clenched teeth as her silken heat caressed him, one shift of her hips taking him deep within her.

They moaned in unison, and Benjamin watched through heavy-lidded eyes as Charlotte's head tipped back, the flush on her neck and chest growing a deeper, more enticing red. Benjamin placed his lips there, pressing open-mouthed kisses down the column of her neck and to the tender peaks of her breasts, nipping and sucking until she was rocking against him, more bath water splashing out of the basin and onto the floor.

Charlotte let out another cry of pleasure as he laved his tongue over a love bite already beginning to bruise. She rode him expertly, drawing pleasure from both of their bodies, the steam of the bath mixing with their heavy breaths. Neither of them would last long like this; Benjamin already knew. Her hips on him rolled and bucked, making his eyes roll back in his head as she pushed further and further, reaching for the pinnacle they were careening towards.

And then she gasped, a delicious, shuddering shout rolling from her. Her clenching pleasure blinded Benjamin just as he managed to pull her off of him, pressing her to his chest as his own release took him.

Their hearts beat as one, as their breath slowed, chests rising and falling together until the bathwater cooled around them—or what was left of the bathwater.

Benjamin forced his muscles to work again, though they had suddenly become languid, uncooperative things, and pushed them out of the water, using a length of towelling to dry both of them off before laying Charlotte down on the bed.

After dousing the candles, he crawled in beside her, pulling the worn but clean quilt around them and drawing her warm, sleepy body in beside him, fitting her back to his chest and twining their legs together.

As he lay there, the warmth of her seeping into his skin all the way down to his soul, the words were there again. He wanted to say them. Needed to whisper them into her hair— even if her slow, heavy breathing proved she was already asleep, pulling him down with her.

But they would not come. He could not let them.

Chapter Twenty-Nine

izzy had appeared at the Aston townhouse that afternoon with yet another new gown in hand for Charlotte to wear to the Wylde dinner. She insisted that this had already been purchased with the other gowns and thus did not violate her "no gifts" rule. And Charlotte did not fight her on it. She could not bring herself to care overmuch even if Benjamin was flouting her stipulations. She had been in a dreamy daze since returning from Eton a day ago. It was the first time since feeling the first pinch of financial strain that Charlotte had felt like someone other than a shrewish estate steward. In fact, she felt like a woman—not a bluestocking—not a spinster; a woman. It was elating.

Lizzy had helped her dress, and Charlotte fought the urge to preen as she watched the maroon silk swish and sway in the lantern light of her room. It had been embarrassing to let Lizzy in to see the faded glory of her family home. The night she and Amelia had gone to Elysium, Lizzy had been at the countess's home, ready to help her prepare.

But the young woman had simply smiled and gone about her business, never once mentioning the sorry state of Charlotte's nearly worn-through bedspread. Judging by the stories she had told Charlotte of her family, it was likely Lizzy had lived in much worse conditions. It was rather self-centred of Charlotte to worry about such appearances when she knew of the real suffering in the world. And thanks to the patronage of Benjamin Scarsdale, neither she nor Lizzy would have to worry about falling into squalor for a long time to come.

"What's this, my lady?" Lizzy pulled the small embossed card from the frame of the mirror where Charlotte had sentimentally tucked it.

It was the note that had come with the emerald dress and, silly as it might be, it warmed her heart to see the scrawled message. Though she did not know what it meant, she cherished the thought that Benjamin had taken time from his day to write down the line on top of commissioning such a dazzling gown. It was fanciful in a way she would not have expected from a man so hardened by the world and reminded her of the soft spots she kept teasing out the more she got to know him.

"Oh, that is nothing." She took the card from Lizzy's hand, but her blush gave her away anyway.

Lizzy's face broke open in a grin. "Ah, I see. Sending you love notes already, is he? Well, 'tis as he should."

"It is hardly a love note. Just a short missive." She tried to tamp down the girlish glee that Lizzy's waggling eyebrows stoked up.

"No, no. I know that look. You two are right smitten."

"Ah!" The mock outrage was completely undermined by the high pitch of her voice. Charlotte cleared her throat and strove for equanimity. "That is enough of that. Such ridiculous talk will only lead to trouble. Now, if you are done with my hair, I will make my way down to the carriage. I do not want to be late to the Wylde home."

Lizzy pressed her lips together and mimed turning a key and tossing it over her shoulder. The woman's knowing smile was only made worse by a cheeky wink in the mirror before turning to pack the dress's wrapping back into the box.

Thanking Lizzy for her help, Charlotte slipped the card into her reticule and made her way downstairs to the waiting carriage.

∞∞∞

"How is your neck, Elkington?" Wells, Elkington, and Benjamin were sequestered in the Wylde family library, enjoying a pre-dinner sherry and awaiting the rest of the family to come down before the guests arrived. "Feeling a little close around the collar as the noose slips tighter and tighter?" Wells rubbed his own neck in mock discomfort, only for Elkington to snort at his antics and give him a good-natured salute with his glass.

"Not at all. I would not expect you to understand, what with your utter phobia of matchmaking mamas, but the prospect of being tied for life to a woman like Elsie is enough to make a man giddy." He leaned back and crossed his long legs, sinking further into his soon-to-be father-in-law's rich leather upholstery.

"It was not long ago, you shared the phobia," Wells grumbled.

"Then consider me cured. Maybe someday you will stumble upon a woman to relieve you of such an ailment."

"I stumble upon plenty of women who provide ample relief

for my ailments. None of them need involve the church and state and irreversible mistakes."

"Bold of you to claim none of them were irreversible mistakes."

Wells and Elkington both chuckled at that.

"Scarsdale? Are you with us?" Elkington spoke to Benjamin, who was standing at the window that overlooked the square.

Benjamin gave a noncommittal grunt.

"Cat got your tongue?"

"Or is it a rather more feminine beast?" Wells eyed him keenly.

"Neither." It was not entirely true; his thoughts had been straying to Charlotte—when she would arrive, how she would look in the maroon silk, how her eyes would flash at his continued flouting of the gift rule. But those gowns, made for her brilliance and enough to steal his breath away every time, were more a gift to him than anyone else.

But the real draw of his thoughts was an uncharacteristically risky plan he had set into motion today. He had spent the last decade, ever since his rise from the streets, collecting every bit of useful information he could on the Deering family, most specifically the baron himself. The discovery he had made with Bell was the tipping point. He had the chip of information he had needed and was biding his time until the day he could wager the Deering empire into dust. He had not planned for that day to be today.

"Does this have something to do with the bruisers being sent out?" Wells posed the question casually, but when Benjamin turned on him, his face was carefully observant, catching every nuance of his reaction.

There was no point in denying it. "How did you know

about that?"

"Stopped by the club this afternoon. Young Boyd could not keep his mouth shut for all the meat pies in Covent Garden."

"You have taken to interrogating my staff now?" Benjamin never felt defensive about his business decisions. He knew well enough to trust the instinct that had delivered him this far.

"Our staff," Wells corrected, gesturing at himself and Elkington as well as Benjamin, "have no reason to hide anything from me. Besides, I am far more pleasant to talk to."

"You are a duke; they feel obligated to indulge your loneliness."

Wells scowled at that, and Benjamin knew the jab had struck a chord.

"Boys, boys." Elkington raised his hands to corral them. It was still easy for them to fall into their boyhood bickering despite all the years that had passed between them. "We still do not know *why* Benjamin is so wrapped up in the matter that necessitated the bruisers."

Benjamin turned back to the window, still a bit piqued. "The Earl of Elford has somehow racked up even more debts. And Deering bought them all. He has the leverage to force the young fool into pretty much anything to keep him from debtors' prison." Benjamin shuddered at the thought of Charlotte having to visit her brother in such squalor.

"Again?" Benjamin could hear the frustrated sigh as Wells' reflection in the window rubbed a hand over his face. "I thought you already solved that problem?"

Benjamin sighed too. "So did I. Of course, I did not account for the fact that the boy is categorically stupid. I should have made more of an effort to track him down and talk some sense into him. Barring him from his favourite haunts clearly did not do the trick."

His friends only grumbled behind him, clearly waiting for the rest of the story.

"Not long ago, Bell and I stumbled upon…a key bit of evidence against Deering." He did not articulate just how key their bill of landing discovery had been. Like he had hoped, it had taken only the slightest hint to the port control officer on duty about the unfinished manifest report for him to discover there had been four unregistered passengers on the Deering ship, the *Lilla*, on the night in question. It had taken only a menacing look more to discover the extra passengers had each paid healthy fees for the officer to overlook their illegible, water-logged documents.

"With the leverage Deering has fabricated against the earl, he is angling for a marriage contract. With Charlotte." He forced the words past the bile crawling up his throat.

"The key bit of evidence in question would be enough to get Deering locked up. So it was no surprise that, when Clarence and Full arrived at his townhouse this afternoon, he relinquished all claims he had on the Elford fortune and promised to discontinue any association he had with the family."

That confession was met with stunned silence. Benjamin refused to turn to read their reactions. He did not need to justify his choices to them. His skill in business had nearly doubled both of their fortunes. It had been a disproportionate trade—he knew that. The information he had bartered with was beyond a simple warding off of an unwanted suitor. It was the tipping point in the quest he had dedicated his life to. Still, neither of them spoke.

Finally, Benjamin was forced to turn, if only to exit the library at the telltale sounds of the Wylde sisters descending upon the party.

What met him was wholly and completely unexpected. Elkington was grinning so wide, Benjamin was not sure he would not injure himself. Though always more reserved than their well-dispositioned friend, Wells also wore a look of clear amusement—some may even have called it a smile.

"What?" Benjamin demanded sharply.

"Nothing." Elkington could barely get the word out right. Wells pressed his lips together in a suspiciously tight line.

"What is it?" Benjamin was feeling completely disconcerted now, and his voice came out harsh.

"Nothing! It seems like a sensible move."

Benjamin scowled at that. "No, it does not. It was a foolish use of leverage for the useless debt of a useless earl. I cannot even fathom why I did it."

Elkington's countenance had not dimmed a fraction. "Completely foolish. Likely the most dimwitted tactic I have ever seen you take."

"Then what do you two find so bloody delightful?" He was close to bellowing now, but he could not stop himself.

"You did it for her," Wells answered, with a foreign twinkle in his eye. The cynical facade he usually wore momentarily cracked.

Benjamin felt as if he had just crashed a carriage head-on into a brick wall. Of course they were right. He had done it for Charlotte. The idea of Deering having something over her had driven him to distraction, and he had sacrificed all the years of blackmail, over a decade of carefully curated information that he had meant to use for the downfall of the man who had killed Delia. And he had thrown it all away for Charlotte. The realisation was like a bucket of ice thrown over his head.

"You can never tell her. She cannot know," Benjamin said sternly.

While he already knew the only reason Charlotte had condescended to their agreement was because she felt indebted to him—an impression he had encouraged, damn him—the idea that she would feel tethered to him by her brother's debt any longer than already agreed upon made his stomach roil. Truth be told, it made him no better than Deering, the scumbag. At least Deering had offered her the respectability of marriage, even a title. Jesus, in that way, Benjamin was worse than Deering. The thought was nauseating.

His only comfort could be found in the fact that he knew she enjoyed their liaison as much as he did. It may have come about through sordid means, but he had given her pleasure in return.

Knowing how deeply her brother was indebted to him, Charlotte would certainly insist on repayment. The idea of their arrangement continuing indefinitely made Benjamin feel almost lightheaded. But no, he would not have her stay because she felt she had to. Though if she chose to of her own free will, Benjamin would never deny her. Perhaps in these next short weeks, he could convince her of the benefits of maintaining her position as his mistress. Of staying with him.

Wells' face had grown serious again. "Ben, you are playing a dangerous game."

∞∞∞∞

The Wylde townhouse was positively buzzing with activity. When the butler let her into the foyer, Charlotte could already hear the animated chatter of feminine voices.

"No, Helen, you absolutely cannot join us downstairs." One voice could be heard over the banister above.

"But why?" a higher-pitched voice whined plaintively.

"I am sorry, dear. Children can not join a meal when guests are present."

The third voice was more conciliatory. "I only just got to join formal dinners, pet. You will have to wait a while longer."

The first voice again. "I promise you can join us for tea tomorrow."

"Can I please come down to see the ladies after dinner? I just want to see all the gowns. We never have just fancy dinners in Edinburgh!"

"Maybe, pet." One of the two older voices.

The butler motioned Charlotte toward the hall as if the conversation audible through the front of the house were not out of place at all.

Just as Charlotte turned to follow him, a small, chestnut-haired head peeked over the banister. "See! What a beautiful gown!"

Charlotte could not help but smile and gave the small girl a little wave. Two more chestnut heads popped out from behind the girl and seemed surprised to see her, then mildly embarrassed before disappearing along with the first. It was immediately clear that the three were Wylde daughters. Lady Elsie shared their twinkling eyes and silky chestnut curls.

"I told you guests were already arriving. We must make haste; otherwise, Mama will have our heads. Helen, no sneaking, do you hear me?"

Charlotte could not hear the reply as she and the butler arrived at a well-appointed drawing room already half-full of people. When she was announced, a pause fell over the milling group as all eyes turned to her. While she had been bracing for this moment all day, she was surprised to be met with what seemed like only passing interest—nearly polite indifference. It might have taken the wind out of her sails if it were not such an overwhelming relief.

She had not been to a dinner party such as this in years. She had been invited, of course, but once the clumsy mending of her dresses became more pronounced, she had found it easier and easier to decline invitations. Until they stopped coming altogether. That, combined with the notoriety that was surely being attached to her name after being linked to Benjamin Scarsdale, was enough to have her pacing her chambers in her moments of downtime since Lady Elsie had sent the formal invitation earlier that week.

As if conjured by her thoughts, Lady Elsie appeared from the side of the room and rushed forward to greet her. Suddenly, Charlotte could well imagine how a family of spirited ladies with their looks could quickly come to some notoriety. It made Charlotte stand that much straighter. She was in good company.

"Charlotte, I am so happy you could join." Elsie had dropped the honorific immediately, and Charlotte felt flattered but a bit dazed. What had she done to invite this woman's obvious warmth and affection?

"Thank you so much for inviting me, Lady Elsie."

"Just Elsie, please. I detest titles on principle." Charlotte stopped herself from pointing out that the woman was on the cusp of marrying a duke and was not likely to be able to brush off the heavy title of duchess so easily. "I know it sounds very disingenuous of me considering my position, but I could never stomach the thought of a whole swath of society being revered and rewarded for an accident of birth."

She spoke with such forthright conviction, almost as if she were a man. It was quite refreshing for Charlotte after years of playing the respectable lady in person and dropping the very same pretences in her writing. Not that she even half believed the majority of ladies of her acquaintance could not hold their own in discussions of substance, it was that they were never given the chance, and if they were, the consequences of their daring were usually far too dire to be worth a single dialectical victory.

"Well then, Elsie, I am happy to be here." The words were truer than she had expected, and she smiled as Elsie looped arms with her and began making introductions. "These two here are my sisters, Corinne and Joanna." The two women bore a striking resemblance to Elsie, though Corrine was smaller and Joanna had slightly darker hair than the other sisters. "The other two should be making their way down to join us any minute—ah, speak of the devils." Two young women appeared at the doorway, and Charlotte immediately recognised them as the ladies in the foyer. Both were taller than Elsie, nearly as tall as Charlotte. "Jane, Loretta, please come meet Lady Charlotte Aston."

"Oh, we saw her as she came in. Your gown really is beautiful, Lady Charlotte." The one named Jane curtsied and looked almost abashed at their earlier pseudo-interaction.

"Jane is making her debut this season; that is why the family is down from County Durham."

"It is rare to see us five in one place." Corrine gave Elsie a playful jab in the arm.

"The Wylde sisters are too busy causing scandal to settle in one place long." Joanna gave Charlotte an audacious wink, and Charlotte had to stifle a laugh.

Their cheery mischievousness as a group was highly infectious, and she felt herself relaxing into the evening by greater and greater increments.

"Has Elsie told you about her school? I think she has taken the cake for the most audacious scandal yet with that one," the youngest, Loretta, piped up—eager to contribute something to the exchange.

"I think that is hardly a scandal at this point," Joanna said placidly, scanning the room's occupants.

"Not nearly so much as chartering a yacht to ferry you to the continent unchaperoned." Jane beamed at Joanna.

"Do not be absurd, Jane; it was not a yacht. It was a schooner."

Elsie scoffed at that. "That is nothing compared to the way Corrine ended up with a husband."

"Oy!" Corrine made an unladylike interjection and gave her sister a pointed glare. "The less said about that, the better." Her countenance softened when she turned back to Charlotte. "My apologies; we tend to get a bit competitive."

"I imagine all our antics will pale in comparison to the scandal of Mama having an outright conniption when she realises she has both the most eligible gentleman bachelor and the richest rogue of London at her table tonight." Joanna smirked over to the doorway, and Charlotte turned to see Wells and Benjamin enter beside Elkington.

Her heart stuttered, skipped a beat, and then started thumping in double time—just his presence in a room was enough to have her completely elated and absolutely out of sorts.

"Goodness, what a handsome pair." Jane sounded as if she could not contain the thought, and Charlotte was reminded of the breathlessness of being a new debutante swamped with all the handsome young bucks of the *ton*. It was a sweet memory of girlhood, but it paled in comparison to the thrill racing through her veins now, a woman grown, looking upon the man who made her world turn upside down. "Your Elkington is handsome too, of course, Else. But my, those dark features are striking."

Charlotte could not help but agree. She only had eyes for the rougher of the two, but standing there, side by side in their evening black, Benjamin Scarsdale and the Duke of Wells looked like a perfectly matched pair of dark-haired devils. Charlotte tilted her head—really, they could be two sides of the same coin.

"Yes, they are all three quite striking, are they not, Charlotte?" Elsie gave her a conspiratorial smile, and Charlotte had to fight the blush that rose in her cheeks.

It was one thing to be Benjamin's secret mistress. It was quite another for his business partner and friend's future wife to know of it—and… approve? It was enough for Charlotte to almost feel like she might belong—an absolutely ludicrous and devastatingly tempting idea.

"Well, Charlotte, we should finish the rounds before dinner begins." With that, Elsie swept Charlotte away from her chattering sisters and introduced her to the rest of the guests she had yet to become acquainted with.

∞∞∞

The dinner was a delightful whirlwind of Wylde family antics. By the time the ladies withdrew, Charlotte's spirits were buoyed by the sisters' easy repartee despite both of their parents' censorious demeanours. They flouted the common dinner convention of speaking only to the guest on their right or left and chatted across plates and through courses to each other and their guests alike, making one feel very much part of the warm, familial atmosphere. It had not been since her stepmother's passing that Charlotte had been part of such an informal gathering of family, and even then, she had always been acutely aware of her own otherness in her stepmother's home. She had come to think that a mother was what rooted one in the world and gave one licence to occupy space. But now, seeing the Wylde sisters do that for one another, perhaps it was not a mother necessarily but the giving and receiving of this messy, unconditional love that carved out one's place in the world. Maybe it could give one a sense of belonging. Perhaps one day that love might find her again—but that was a dangerous thing to hope for.

"Elsie, you are looking positively green." The ladies had hardly reached the salon before Loretta Wylde made the pronouncement in front of all the female guests.

Corinne made a hissing sound through her teeth at their youngest sister and nearly hauled her off to the pianoforte, where the other ladies politely followed.

Charlotte hung back, watching Elsie through her lashes. From her seat just opposite, she too had noticed that Lady Elsie had touched little of the rich courses that diligent footmen had set before her, seeming to balk specifically at the salmon dish as well as the fig pudding served just before they made their withdraw.

"I am feeling uncommonly fatigued after such a rich meal. Perhaps you would like to join me on the settee beside the window?" Charlotte made a show of eyeing the plush settee, and Elsie gave her a knowing, but grateful smile and followed to the other side of the room, out of earshot from the other guests.

Charlotte dug around in the surprisingly spacious little silk bag. She made a point to bring all practicalities with her wherever she could. "I keep some peppermint oil in my reticule, if you would like. I find dabbing some on my wrists helps the nausea pass."

Being caught out unprepared was a recipe for disaster when one was out researching. After rifling through and depositing several items on the cushion between them, Charlotte finally found the small glass vial she had been searching for.

Elsie took it gratefully, uncorking the stopper and inhaling deeply. After a few long breaths, the colour began to return to her cheeks, and her lips curved in a self-deprecating smile. "Thank you, Charlotte. It would have been poor *ton* of me indeed to cast up my accounts in front of my guests—at my own engagement dinner, no less. Goodness, that would give them all something to talk about."

Charlotte fought the urge to ask the question burning in her throat, but the journalist in her and the easy familiarity the two of them had fallen into won out. "How far along are you?"

It was a horribly crass thing to ask. No well-bred lady should ever broach the subject—or even notice its symptoms—and she had forgotten her place. She was more out of practice in polite society than she had realised.

Charlotte was swamped with mortification. "I apologise

profusely—I do not know—"

Elsie raised a hand, effectively silencing her blabbered apology, and Charlotte was surprised to see a smile growing on her clever, expressive face. "Please, I appreciate the candour—and the eye for detail. The only other one who has figured it out is Corinne." She looked over to where her eldest sister stood over the pianoforte, singing an old lilting Scottish ballad that had the other ladies staring on forlornly. "I believe I am just shy of a quarter of the way there. Alexander is rushing the wedding, so I do not begin to show before the banns are read."

Charlotte thought back to the lovesick looks she caught passing between the two of them during dinner and refrained from pointing out that he likely had an even more compelling reason for rushing the wedding.

"So he knows about your condition too. How did he figure it out?"

Elsie laughed out loud at that. "Oh, he figured nothing out. I told him immediately." Her face grew more pensive, and she placed her hand absently over her midsection.

Charlotte felt a twist of pain in her chest at the tender intimacy of it all. The budding joy of family and connection beyond the mere coupling of bodies. She thought of the man she would like to share such joys with and was met with an even more sickening twist at the truth that it would never happen. She thought Elsie must have read something in her face, but when she looked up, the other woman's eyes were miles away as she stared at the door that led down the hall away from the entertaining rooms to the family's private chambers. "Trust me, Charlotte, keeping secrets from the man you love can only lead to heartbreak." She took another whiff of the peppermint oil and lay her head back on the settee. "Christ, it was not this difficult the last time."

It was a passing comment, made almost under her breath, but Charlotte felt a flickering of the intuition that had guided her through countless stories to the truth of a matter. "There are only five Wylde sisters—are there not?" Elsie's gaze followed Charlotte's to the four nearly identical dark heads gathered amongst the guests.

Elsie tilted her head at the question, turning back and giving Charlotte a speculative stare—as if her agile brain could unpick the mystery of the person before her if she just looked at it from the right angle. It was a strangely gratifying sensation from another woman—as if she saw Charlotte and considered her equal.

"Yes…" Clearly, she knew that was not the end of the question.

"But there was a sixth in the hall when I arrived."

Elsie stared at her in silence for a beat longer than was comfortable. But Charlotte had learned time and again, vague statements prompted details. She just had to hold her nerve longer than the other. Lord, perhaps she could not lay the blame entirely at Freddie's feet that she had not been welcome in polite society for an age. Here she was grilling her hostess, not a full day into knowing her.

But then, just as her cheeks began to heat from the impropriety of her implication, Elsie's lips quirked into a rueful smile. "You are good, Charlotte. Very good. Her name is Helen." She smiled wider, her face glowing with joy even at her name. "My least-concealable secret. See?"

She spoke as if she and Charlotte had had this discussion before, and her point was being proven once again.

"This is why we must live in Edinburgh. You get one look at her and know she is one of us. If the *ton* caught sight of her, everyone would know immediately that she is not my Aunt Iona's ward. Or some distant cousin."

Charlotte considered herself to have gained a fair amount of worldliness over the last years—she certainly had shed the foolish vestiges of maidenly innocence, or ignorance, that was enforced in ladies of the ton—but she found herself awed by Elsie's casual dismissal of sure ruin in favour of lighthearted, but very earnest pride for her illegitimate daughter.

"So, your family knows?" Charlotte could not keep her surprise out of her voice.

"It would be hard for them not to, considering she is an image of me when I was her age." She was an image of Elsie now, Charlotte could have pointed out. "My parents do not speak of it—though I believe my stodgy father is secretly delighted by her. And of course, my sisters know. I told them after she was born. It was meant to be a secret, but holding that baby in my arms, I could not deny her the warmth of her own family."

It was deeply admirable the way Elsie seemed unconcerned for her own ruin in the face of her daughter's comfort and joy.

"And the marquess?"

Charlotte expected Elkington to be a kind and reasonable man, considering his friendships and his relationship to this woman, but the idea of a future duke accepting another man's by-blow in his home, with his own children—that was a stretch.

Elsie's lips twisted in a wry smile. "He knew the moment he met her. When he proposed, he said Helen would be to him like his own daughter." Her eyes were suspiciously misty.

Charlotte was floored by the generosity of his love for Elsie—it was beyond what she had thought men capable of. But then, while the idea of Benjamin with other women stirred that foreign jealousy in her gut, the knowledge that he had had lovers before did not make her care for him any less. Why could a man not experience the same? It was quite a new revelation to chew on.

"So, Charlotte. What use have you for peppermint oil? You do not have the look of the expectant about you."

Charlotte blushed at that, though it was the thought of carrying Benjamin's child that had her aflutter rather than the forwardness of the question itself.

"I find I get quite nauseous if I skip a meal." She felt it only right to meet candour with candour, but she could not bring herself to spell out her family's dire situation.

"You do that often?" Elsie's gaze was assessing again, and Charlotte knew she was not hiding anything from this woman.

"More and more. Though not so much since—" She waved a hand towards the door, hoping that Elsie knew more than she was letting on, because, to her everlasting shame, she could not articulate her own ruin as well as Elsie had.

"Ah." Elsie looked off to the door through which, presumably, the gentlemen would be rejoining them soon.

Elsie seemed to let the topic drop, and Charlotte breathed a sigh of relief.

"Oh no, you keep it." Charlotte smiled as Elsie offered the peppermint oil back to her. "You have more use of it than I." She began shuffling items back into her reticule.

"What is this?" Elsie picked up the embossed card.

Charlotte fought to keep from snatching the little paper

from her hand. The scrawled words had become frighteningly dear to her, and it felt raw to have another read them.

"*Her skirt was o' the grass-green silk.*" The words sounded right in her lilting accent, and Charlotte watched as she frowned down at the card and then up at her.

"You know it?"

"It is Thomas the Rhymer." Elsie was watching her with some surprise. Seeing that Charlotte did not know what she was referring to, she explained. "Thomas the Rhymer was a Scottish Laird of old. Legend has it that as he lay out beneath a tree in the Eildon Hills one day, he heard the tinkling of silver bells, and a beautiful woman approached him. It turned out that this woman was really Queen of Elfland, and Thomas fell under her spell, following her deep within the hollow of the Eildon Hills to the fairy Otherworld. He lived there with her for seven years before returning to the mortal realm without her—though his eternal love for her had granted him immortality."

Charlotte took in the tale, staring down at the bold script on the thick white card. Why in the world had he written a line from such a tale—for her? The thought filled her with an elated sort of panic, and she tried to suppress the frantic need to hear more.

"All hail, thou mighty Queen o' Heaven," Elsie mumbled the words under her breath as she thumbed the card. "He gave this to you?" Her intelligent eyes were piercing when she looked back up at Charlotte, handing it back to her.

"Y—yes." Charlotte was not sure what to say in the face of the woman's sudden intensity.

Surprisingly, Elsie only shook her head and almost smiled, looking back at the door. "Damned fool."

Chapter Thirty

"What are your intentions toward her, Scarsdale?" While the men chatted over port and cigars, Wells had leaned over with a dark scowl on his face.

Surprised perhaps not so much by the question but the place and method of delivery—while the other men were wrapped up in a heated debate about the optimal rotation of crops and livestock on their country estates, it was still overly public to broach such a topic—Benjamin sat and stared at his friend and business partner.

"Lady Charlotte," Wells repeated. "What are your intentions toward her?"

"Trying your hand at playing protector?" Benjamin tried to deflect the inquiry with his usual jaded passiveness, taking a sip of port to wet his suddenly dry mouth.

The overly rich liquid only made it worse. Despite his meteoric rise in the ranks of society—informal, to be sure—there were some tastes he had never been able to adopt; this thickly sweet wine being one of them. He had to mask a grimace as he swallowed.

"Well, it is not as if her good-for-nothing brother will step up to the task. And though she may have kept herself upright thus far…" The pause in his sentence was enough to make Benjamin want to squirm. They both knew that her dealings with him had driven her to the very brink of ruin in the eyes of society. "I feel it is my duty as a gentleman to ask what it is you are about."

The emphasis on *gentleman* cut even further. Leave it to Wells to wield the sharpest barbs in the things he did not say.

"Do not mistake me," Wells said. "I believe women of all creeds should be free to make their own choices and take their pleasure—and money—where they may."

"The Duke of Wells, a closeted Wollstonecraftian?" Benjamin muttered into his glass and considered braving another swallow of the foul liquid. "What *will* they say?"

Wells ignored him and continued, "It is one thing to make a lady your mistress in return for her financial freedom. While I have disputed the ethics of the inherent coercion in such an arrangement, it seemed to be mutually beneficial." Benjamin tried not to roll his eyes at a duke delivering such a lecture on power inequalities but knew any interruption would be thwarted by the man's single-minded tenacity. "But this? Ben, what is this?" The bewildered tone of his voice was enough to make Benjamin look away again, unnerved by how much Wells' disappointment hurt. It cut too close to the quick of his own feelings. "Bringing her here, or out to the theatre? Think of the position you put her in. You are not courting the girl. Nothing can come of this but her own ruin. It is unusually cruel—even for you."

At that, Benjamin's head snapped up. He had spent years hardening his heart, cultivating a ruthless, powerful image. It had served him uncommonly well in his dealings and protected what little was left of his soul on the streets. But now, hearing his closest friend—the only family he really had—call him exactly what he had set out to become? It was enough to make him taste bile. What *was* he playing at?

"So, I ask you again, Ben: What are your intentions regarding Lady Charlotte?"

Suddenly, the answer was obvious. The idea that there was no future for them was absolutely untenable. She would not be left out in the cold, her reputation in tatters, and her family's safety only secured until the fool of an earl found his next vice. She certainly would not be alone for Deering to swoop in and destroy her, the way his son had destroyed Delia.

"My intention is to marry her." The moment the words left his lips, he knew he was right. It was as if decades of sodden weight were lifted from his shoulders. He suddenly felt so light, he feared he might float away right there in the Wylde's dining room.

Wells regarded him closely, as if he was not entirely sure he recognised the man in front of him. Then, a grudging smile tugged at his cheeks. "Jesus, I am surrounded by lovesick fools."

∞∞∞

As the footman closed the carriage door, Charlotte sank back against the squabs. The evening had been full of laughter and excitement and—dare she think it?—belonging. After the men had rejoined them in the parlour, there were rounds of lively card games, music, and singing—the Wylde sisters working their magic and pulling everyone into their convivial mood. It had been a treat to watch Elkington dote on Elsie and, later, after the majority of the guests had gone, even little Helen was allowed to join the revelry—Elkington had insisted, despite Elsie's protestations, that it was far too late for a girl of her age to be up and about. When the sprite of a child had bounded in directly following Elsie's capitulation, it became clear that she and Elkington had been in league from the outset.

Even more than that, Benjamin had been by her side the whole time, solicitous and warm in ways he had only ever been in the privacy of his chambers. It was almost embarrassing to know the others could see him clearly favouring her, pairing with her in a game of whist, flirting over sherry, brushing her arm as he turned the pages of her music when she had played at the pianoforte. It was enough to make her dizzy.

It had been a warm, sparkling night that would stand out in her memory as a shining glimpse into a life that might have been. But now, alone in the quiet of the carriage, no longer distracted by the cheerful Wyldes, Charlotte could feel the ache in her chest growing.

"Did you not enjoy yourself?"

Charlotte squeaked at the familiar voice, suddenly in the dark space with her. Benjamin had opened and closed the other carriage door and vaulted himself inside without breaking her from her reverie. Either he was magnificently stealthy, or she had been far more lost in thought than was good for her—likely both.

"Apologies, I did not mean to startle," he added.

There was only a slight glimmer of light from the carriage lamp shining through the window, but Charlotte was still able to make out the uncharacteristically boyish glint in his eye.

"Yes, you did." She could not keep the smile out of her voice.

"Yes, I did."

He grinned, and she felt the look like a gust of warm seaside breeze. He removed his hat, tossing it haphazardly onto the cushion beside him before stretching out his long, sculpted body in the small space, his legs inevitably tangling under her skirts as he rested his hands on his midriff.

With the shadow of a night beard and lines of comfortable fatigue around his eyes, he looked for all the world a noble gentleman ready for the short carriage ride back to his family home after a long night on the town, where he would retire—with his wife. The strange thought knotted the tendons in her chest further.

He watched her with the deceptively lazy stare that she knew concealed a wealth of cunning and what seemed like all the world's secrets. "So, did you enjoy yourself? The Wylde brood can be a trifle overwhelming at times."

"Not at all; they were delightful. I enjoyed myself very much." Too much.

"Then why the long face?"

It was not like him to ask such direct questions. It was a testament to how relaxed he was after the ease of the evening that he seemed content to chat with her, tease out her thoughts and musings. The casual intimacy of it was a knife to her gut.

"Merely tired. How did you find the evening?" She gave him a soft smile, which she hoped hid the swirling roil of emotions inside.

"I admit, I usually find nights like this to be tedious affairs—

but I think I actually enjoyed myself." He had a far-off, yet speculative gleam in his eye. "I think the Wyldes have taken a liking to you. Elsie especially."

Charlotte tried not to preen at the comment. She considered it the highest compliment to have found favour with such women. "I like her too. All of them, in fact. Miss Helen was a delight."

Charlotte had played a silly children's duet with Helen on the pianoforte until they both had to stop for their fit of giggles. She was not sure she had felt such lightness and joy since the twins were young—and even then, her responsibility to them had often loomed over the merriment of their play.

They sat in silence as the carriage pulled along the quiet streets of Mayfair, both basking in the evening. "You charmed her. I think it will be that much more difficult to keep her from the evening entertainment the next time."

Charlotte's heart stopped and stuttered, picking up to a sickening speed. Next time. He spoke of the future so casually, as if it were a given that she would continue her acquaintance with the family and remain part of his world. A world they both knew she was only borrowing time in. Less than a few more paltry weeks. Not that she had been counting.

"Elsie seemed fairly familiar with you. How did you meet?" It had been clear even the night in Elysium that Elsie and Benjamin had been acquainted longer than her betrothal to Elkington.

"We met some years ago—I did her a favour." The characteristic evasiveness returned, and Charlotte feared she had pressed too far.

She arched her brow at him sarcastically. "Is that all you

will share?"

Surprising her, he shrugged and grinned, the boyishness returning as quickly as it had left. Her heart swelled to see him so comfortable and at ease. "Not my secret to tell."

Charlotte huffed at that. "Are not all our secrets yours?"

He smiled at that and took her hands in his lovely, large, warm ones. "Shall I tell you a secret of mine?"

His words were light and teasing, but the look in his eyes was full of something elusive. Charlotte found herself leaning forward to try to capture whatever well of truth was hiding just behind his beautiful, deep eyes.

"Yes." The word was hardly more than a breath, and she watched as his wide mouth parted and his pupils dilated.

Her own heart sped, her breath coming fast and short. She could sense that they stood on a precipice, side by side. It would take only a word to blow them both over together.

His eyes flitted over her face, drawn to her lips and up to her eyes, as if cataloguing every angle of her face in the dim lantern light. "I…" She could do nothing but hold her breath as he paused and traced the curve of her chin with a long index finger. "I would very much like to take you home."

The teasing glint in his eye had returned, but suddenly, somehow, he seemed farther away, as if he had drawn away from her even though their noses were only a carriage jolt away from touching.

Charlotte felt foolish for the devastating way her stomach dropped—she had fallen off the precipice alone.

"I would very much like you to take me home, Benjamin." To her relief, the catch in her voice sounded almost husky with passion. He would not guess she was swallowing back her tears.

∞∞∞

He was going to marry this woman.

The revelation set his soul on fire. Seeing her laid out on his bed in the underused chambers of his townhouse—their house, if she wanted to live there—everything was right. The nagging sensation that she belonged there, with him, wherever he was, was finally laid to rest.

He crawled up the bed beside her, both of them completely bare in the firelight. Her skin was warm and inviting as he pulled her to him, greedy just to hold her.

"Hello, there." Charlotte's voice was soft and heavy—as if she knew the magnitude of what lay between them.

"Hello, my love," Benjamin whispered back, placing careful, reverent kisses on her cheeks, then her temples, the curve of her chin, and her delicate eyelids. When he pulled away again, her eyes opened, and he was caught in their swirling depths.

For a moment, they regarded each other, so much hanging between them that Benjamin did not dare break the silence. Instead, he traced the faint arch of her eyebrows—how he loved the expressive feature. He could tell exactly what was going on in her busy mind by the set of those brows. Now, they were relaxed; her face a serene pool, full of depth but content to absorb the surrounding light.

Benjamin smiled when she brought her own hand up, running a gentle caress down his cheek. He caught her fingertips in a kiss and saw her smile.

Now was the time for words to be said. He could feel it. They were pressing up his throat, caught up in his tongue behind his teeth. The silence begged him to speak—to tell her how he felt. But he knew once those words—that had been simmering in his chest for weeks now—came out, it all would. He would admit his love for her—how she made him weak in ways he never knew he could be and somehow stronger than he had ever been without her. This love that was eclipsing his grief, making it spill over, and cleansing the putrid cave he had trapped it in. The light such a love brought—that had grown almost blinding and had him imagining life in a way he had never even thought to consider.

Now was his chance, with her looking up at him like he could do no wrong. But the cold, familiar fingers of shame wrapped around his throat. He could do wrong. He *had* done wrong. More than wrong—he had done terrible things. He had been a monster, even if he was starting to think he might not be anymore. He could not tell her of his feelings—propose marriage—without first sharing the full truth. She deserved to know. He would not wield secrets in this. He could not have her accept on the back of his dark shadows. Even though the mere thought that she might accept him sent tremors of raw elation through his body.

No, he could not allow himself to be carried away by hope just yet. He had to tell her the truth. The full truth, and let the cards fall where they may. Even if that meant she refused him. Even if that meant he would have to watch her dear face crumple with disgust. He loved her. He would do that for her.

But not now. Not when she was staring at him like that, the whole heavens in her eyes. He would not dare disturb this holy peace between them.

So instead, he kissed her.

What he could not say in words, he poured into his body.

Neither of them spoke. They were beyond words as they held each other. He worshipped her with kisses and caresses, and somehow, he felt she was doing the same.

Their breaths mingled as their hearts beat as one. She met every stroke with her own—their slow rhythm perfectly aligned with an unheard symphony. Benjamin did not have to think. They were there together, beyond it all, suspended above themselves. He had never been so close to another soul in his life. And he knew there would be no separating himself from her from here on. They were one. He could no more tell where he ended and she began than he could pull down all the stars in the sky.

It was a wondrous, whole feeling. There was no fear, only simple, pure joy.

And as they came back down to earth, and their breathing slowed, until sleep threatened to pull them under, he was sure she understood.

Chapter Thirty-One

This was foolish.

Charlotte stood looking up at the manicured facade of the white stucco townhouse of the Countess of Beaumont and considered abandoning this ill-advised mission before it began. It was born of desperation, and thus, not well considered or particularly safe. In fact, Charlotte had felt significantly less concerned for her well-being on any number of her ventures into the stews. Then, the only risk had been to her person—and she knew how to be careful. Now, she faced a much more devastating risk—that her own suspicions might well prove true.

Before she had the chance to go through the merits of her fact-finding mission again, the front door opened to reveal an imperious butler. "May I help you, madam?"

"I was just about to knock." Charlotte refused to feel small and foolish for dallying on the front step. "I am here to call on her ladyship. Is she receiving?"

It was unacceptably early to be calling upon a lady. After Benjamin had sent her home in one of his carriages with a sweet kiss and sleepy eyes full of promise, Charlotte had come straight here. The previous night had stripped her bare, and she did not know what else to do.

The officious man only inclined his head, the afternoon light glinting off the peaks of his perfectly smooth forehead, giving no indication of the lady's inclination.

"Who, may I ask, is calling?"

"Lady Charlotte Aston."

The butler's flat, assessing demeanour did not shift, but he waved her into a receiving room just off the foyer anyway.

"I will see if she is home for callers. Please wait here."

Charlotte nodded and perched on a small, wildly ornate chaise—the height of Paris fashion, she was sure. This piece alone could feed her for a year.

She smoothed out her skirts—clean and pressed—but not one of the lovely creations Benjamin had bought her. And she waited.

And waited.

When the clock above the mantle struck half past, she considered rising to leave. She had already been there for nearly half an hour. If Catherine was expecting callers, another one was sure to arrive soon. And if she were not, Charlotte should just abandon the idea altogether.

But something—some last hope flickering in her chest— forced her to stay just five minutes more.

Her patience was rewarded when Catherine Beaumont swept into the room, a picture of costly elegance in a deep pink silk day dress. The bold colour flattered her dark hair and smooth complexion, and Charlotte briefly wondered what exactly had possessed her to make this call.

"Charlotte, what a lovely surprise!"

Catherine greeted her with a familiarity that spoke to a much closer acquaintanceship than they had ever enjoyed, and yet still carried the underlying coldness that had been present in the Duke of Wells' opera box.

"Catherine, thank you for receiving me."

"Of course, we are old friends, are we not? I am happy to see you circulating in society again. It feels like an age since we last crossed paths before meeting at the opera." She gestured for the maid, who had preceded her, to set the tea service.

Charlotte only gave her a faint smile. "It is actually that meeting that I wanted to discuss."

"Oh?" Catherine's beautiful oval face was the perfect picture of inquiring surprise.

"Since, as you put it, we are old friends, I would like to speak to you plainly about our mutual acquaintance."

The mask fell away, and Charlotte could see Catherine's wariness take its place. Her sparkling hazel eyes watched with a newfound interest and calculation.

"You were once intimately involved with Mr. Scarsdale?"

Charlotte posed the question as a means to inform; she knew the answer. She had known immediately, from Benjamin's discomfort and Catherine's angling, that the two of them had some kind of history together. She would let Catherine fill in the blanks—a task the countess would likely relish—but she did not need further details.

"Yes. We were lovers." Catherine surprised her with her simple candour.

Charlotte nodded.

"It has not continued. We parted ways last winter. A mutual decision." Charlotte doubted the last was true, but she did not push. "But I assure you, we have not been involved since. You need not worry." Catherine's posture shifted. She was now leaning forward, a real earnestness in her eyes. "I would not be party to such an arrangement, I assure you."

Charlotte nodded again, her lips pressed in another wan smile. "Thank you, I appreciate you saying that."

She believed her. That was not what she had come to discuss—Benjamin's fidelity was not something she had once worried about—but Catherine's sober assurance was surprising. Perhaps that would make the next question easier.

"What I came here to ask was more nebulous in nature." Charlotte frowned down at the teacup in her hand. This was proving harder to articulate than she had thought.

"Please ask." Charlotte looked up to see the countess's face furrowed in uncharacteristic concern. "If I can be of help to you here, please dispense with all pretence. In our coming out—when the Count was courting me—you cut through all our differences to warn me. Even though we had always been in competition—and I know I could be…unpleasant towards you—you still approached me at the Powell's Ball to warn me what kind of man he was. I was so quick to dismiss you. I thought you were just trying to undercut me. And honestly, I wanted to ignore my own misgivings as well. He was such a catch. My family were thrilled, and I had won—not that you can win a season." She shook her head and looked down at her own cup and saucer, balanced impeccably in her hands. "I ignored your warning. And I paid the price."

Charlotte watched as the woman across from her—one she had once been girls with—was dragged back through time.

The years of unspoken pain played across her face. "If I could return the favour…please. Ask."

Charlotte blew out the breath she was holding. And stopped short. How could she ask? "Do you…" She stopped.

For once, the words were not coming. "I know this is beyond all boundaries of propriety. But I had a feeling you might have an insight that could help me make…a decision." She sucked in another breath. "Do you think he could…that he is capable of…" The words petered out as she fought the alarming knot crawling up her throat.

Catherine gave her a bleak smile. and in that moment, she knew she did not have to say more. "No, Charlotte." Her voice was gentle, a shared sadness pulling between them. Catherine was just on the other side.

The countess set down her cup and saucer and took a deep breath, clearly setting her mind to something. "Benjamin and I met at a gaming evening hosted by the Marchioness of Donnelly last May. I will spare you the details, but we became involved quickly. It was exciting and daring and romantic. In retrospect, I should have gone in much more guarded, given my experience. But he is handsome, clever, and shockingly kind."

Charlotte could only nod. Every fibre of her being wanted to bolt—to reject anything she heard. But she was fixed to the spot. She had to know. Even if it was excruciating.

"After the first month, I was enthralled. After the third, I had fallen for him. Hard." Catherine cringed at that and put her hands to her cheeks. "I was not foolish enough to tell him, thank God. I preserved part of my dignity in that. But he must have known. He became distant. I pushed. I could not resist it. I wanted more of him. More he was not willing to give. By December, he had called it off."

Charlotte wanted to slink away from the idea of Benjamin being so involved with another woman—this woman. But she also saw the real heartbreak on Catherine's face. She now knew the same heartbreak was hurtling towards her.

"I would like to say the pain has passed—that I am beyond the rejection of it all. But I think my performance at the opera would make that lie abundantly clear. I hope you can forgive me for that bit of nastiness, if not the rest. I was surprised to see him with another woman—and an unmarried one at that. He never deals with marriage bait."

"I am hardly—"

"And the way he looked at you," Catherine carried on as if she had not heard her. "It all seemed so serious and proper. He got you a chaperone, for goodness' sake!" She stopped, clearly fighting to rein in her emotions. "What I mean to say is, I thought you had caught him. And it crushed me. So I acted out." There was real regret in her eyes when she looked back up at Charlotte. "But if you are here now, asking me. I have a duty to warn you: do not expect anything from Benjamin Scarsdale. And above all, do not lose your heart to him."

Charlotte felt the floor drop out from under her.

She had heard what she came here to hear.

∞∞∞

Benjamin had walked back up the garden steps to the kitchen door, feeling lighter than he had since he had come to London. Last night had been a revelation. Every touch, every kiss was full of import and promise. Charlotte must have felt the shift, for she had met him at every stroke. It was as if more than their bodies had been in communion; the frenetic, deliberate current had carried them forward together. He had woken with Charlotte in his arms, soft and warm from sleep, and

305

made love to her again before bundling her up to the mews behind the garden and sending her and his coachman back to the Aston townhouse. He would have liked to have kept her here, holed up together in his chambers for the rest of the day—forever, really. But that would come soon enough. First, he had some matters to settle.

After a quick wash, a change of clothes, and an interminably tedious shave by his young valet, Rand, he headed over to Elysium, where he closeted himself in his office with his man of business, Bell.

Boyd appeared at the door of his office. "Mr. Collier and the Duke of Wells."

Benjamin had sent for Collier the moment Bell had shown him the incriminating document, but Wells' appearance was a surprise.

"Jesus, Benjamin, what on earth has happened here?" Wells stood at the door while Collier entered with his characteristic equanimity, seemingly unbothered by the sprawl of papers across Benjamin's desk and the second table he and Bell had pulled over to catch the spillover.

Benjamin looked up from a folio of documents he had been poring over and took in his friend's riding breeches and crop. "It is late for you to be out riding, is it not? The mamas of the ton will be out hunting already."

Wells snapped the crop against the leather of the top of his boot absently. "I told Elk we would be going out later today. I assumed you would still be wound up with your…intended." He said the last with a sarcastic quirk of his mouth, as if the turn of events was supremely ironic.

Benjamin supposed in many ways it was.

"But it seems perhaps you are more touched in the head

than I previously gave you credit for. It is not a sane man who would elect to spend the morning with Bell and a dusty stack of papers. No offence, Bell."

The owlish middling man quirked a brow before returning to a pile of correspondence he seemed to sort into multiple distinct categories apparent only to his own esoteric mind.

"She is not my intended yet." Benjamin took a sip of coffee before realising it had gone cold since he last touched it. Grimacing and setting it back on the mantle, one of the last empty surfaces in the room, he turned back to his work. "Sorry for the wasted trip. I cannot join our ride today. Besides, it is Elk who you should expect to be occupied with his intended—it is clear he and Lady Elsie are anticipating more than just their vows." He grinned absently at Wells, who was observing him with such a confounded look, he stopped his shuffling of papers and looked at him again. "Surely, you noticed her condition as well. The poor woman could not even look at the fish course."

Wells waved a dismissive hand, still regarding him as if he had woken to find a goat standing in his dressing room rather than his valet—a prank they had played on his father, the former Duke of Wells, when they had been boys. One that had ended in dire consequences for Jonathan, as any prick of his father's temper inevitably did. "Of course I noticed. What I am confounded by is you."

"Me?" Benjamin crossed his arms, an echo of a defensive habit he had acquired over the years.

"Yes, you. *Master of London's Secrets.* You just joked about a detail that could turn a whole life if wielded properly."

Benjamin frowned but waved it away. "They are friends. I would never use their secrets against them. I need not hoard them. Coffee?"

He gestured to the pot of ostensibly cold coffee and hoped Wells would drop the subject. His friend's adept scrutiny made him uncomfortable—mostly because he himself could not reconcile the change the last days had wrought.

"What are you doing here?" Wells stepped further into the room and fingered a few cards teetering on the edge of the second table. "After our conversation last night, I assumed you would be discussing more important matters with the fine Lady Charlotte."

Benjamin found the document he had been searching for and passed it over to Collier, who had been sitting patiently beside the table since he had been announced by Boyd. "I need you to determine the legality of this."

Collier took the page and crossed his long legs, settling back to read through the tight script.

"I have not informed her of my intentions yet."

Benjamin's heart thrilled and stuttered at the idea of such a conversation. Would she accept him? It was clear there was something between them. Last night had been even further confirmation of her feelings, even if no words were spoken. But would she agree to marry him? He could not be sure without asking. That was why he was doing everything he could to sweeten the deal.

"You have not? Ben!" The tone was admonishing, and Benjamin had the feeling Wells would have been a domineering elder brother if the duke and duchess had been blessed with any other children. "You had best do that sooner rather than later."

The warning set off alarm bells in Benjamin's head.

"What do you mean by that?" His words were sharpened

by fear.

"Nothing. Just that she is in a precarious position, and the longer you wait, the more dire her circumstances become. You would not want to lose her to your own hesitation."

"I am not hesitating." He waved at the mess his usually meticulously ordered office had become. "What do you think I am doing here? I am trying to buy her family's seat back for her. And not for the earl to sell it right back out from under her. It will be hers. The manor will be in her name, so she will never have to worry about losing it again." Benjamin had seen how much she missed her home. How she had been set adrift in the world by all the twists of fate that had robbed her of her mother, her security, and, in many ways, any sense of family. He would restore that to her. And then she would never turn him down…right?

"It will be tricky," Collier spoke up from behind the document Benjamin had handed him and another he had drawn from the pile, and was now comparing. "The current owners have defaulted on a debt here." He pointed to one of the pages. "They mortgaged some of the farmland. You may be able to leverage that into an offer. As for transferring it to Lady Charlotte's name, it will be difficult to guard it from the earl. Though she has already reached her majority, until she is married, her brother still has some legal sway over her as her guardian *de jure*."

"What do you mean? Not possible? Collier, you are meant to be the most brilliant legal mind of your generation." Frustration made his voice harsh.

Collier only smiled mildly. "I said difficult. Not impossible. Of course, I can manage it."

Somewhat mollified, Benjamin turned back to the stack

of correspondence Bell had passed him and then up at Wells again. "Is there anything else you wanted?"

Wells just gave him a repressive look and swung his crop around his fingers as he turned to leave. "Do not drag your feet, Ben. There are always wolves in the wings—it is never good to give them a chance to strike."

∞∞∞

The mail coach was cramped and smelled strongly of cabbage and ale—both of which Charlotte suspected were emanating from the large man slumped in the corner of the conveyance. The matron beside him had wound her scarf over the lower half of her face upon boarding, ignoring the close warmth of the coach's cabin.

Despite her malodorous companions, Charlotte was glad for the tightly packed coach—the presence of strangers forced her to keep herself together and not give in to the sorrow that was tearing at her insides. If she had been alone, she would have certainly given over to retching sobs by now.

When she returned from Lady Catherine's home, she had bound through the bare halls of the Aston townhouse up to her room, packed a trunk with her wardrobe and books, and sat at her desk to pen three letters. One letter she addressed to Lady Elsie Wylde—it was presumptuous considering their short acquaintance, but after their conversation the evening before, she felt she could rely on Elsie for assistance. Another, she wrote to Freddie. And the last, she had not been able to finish.

The mail coach would depart at five sharp, and she had only filled the page with scored-out lines, for the first time in her life, unable to put her thoughts into words. How could she tell him everything in her heart? That it was the love she felt for him that meant she had to leave. That she could go no further in this arrangement, pretending it did not mean everything to her. That she could not allow herself to settle into this beautiful thing they shared any longer, lest she be forced to tear out her own heart when it ended. A man like Benjamin Scarsdale would not be receptive to such a sentimental display. So she abandoned the letter, praying the night before had been enough to convey all she felt for him.

The trunk had been impossibly heavy, and it was all she could do to haul it down the steps to the hackney, the scar at her shoulder twinging in the cold, early morning mist. She had planned to pawn the books and Benjamin's fine gowns before she left, so she would not have to carry the weight, but she no longer had the time. She would sell them when she arrived in Edinburgh. Surely the fine London fashions would fetch a better price up north. As it was, she had just enough saved to pay for her fare up the Great North Road and modest rooms in Edinburgh until she secured a position, hopefully within the next few weeks, with Lady Elsie's recommendation.

With that hopeful thought, she closed her eyes against the bone-deep weariness that had settled over her. She fought the drift of her memories of the previous night, the feel of safety upon waking to warm arms and long kisses. No, she had to keep her thoughts leashed to the present if she was going to scrape out a life for herself. Once she was settled, she could revisit the gems of her past, with the safe buffer of time between them and her. Not until then could she allow herself to dwell on what she was leaving behind.

Who she was leaving behind.

Chapter Thirty-Two

L*eith, Scotland*
June 1818
"I needed work. My sister had twa bairns and between the pair of us, we had not tuppence to rub together. She works inna tannery, but tha pay is shite. Our da' wis a fisherman. Dressit as A am, A get paid twice as much at the market. Na ane trusts a woman fishin." Davina Robertson gestured to her clothes—rough workman's ware—a heavy, cable knit jumper covering the shape of her torso. "A dinnae e'en neit tae lie aboot it. A juist say, ma name's Dav—it is after aw. An they see whit they want. Na ane expects a woman tae be strong enouch for the work. But fool's money spends an aw as the wise man's."

It had taken a few interviews before Charlotte could make head or tail of the lowland dialect, but in the end, her familiarity with cockney had done her well. They were completely unique dialects, but once she had keywords, she could piece the rest together. Learning their way of speaking gave her a whole new insight into the lives of the people she interviewed. It was not until then that she felt she could give their stories the depth they deserved. And after nearly four weeks, she finally felt as if she had gained her footing.

Edinburgh was a beautiful city. Charlotte had not expected the dark, moody crags of the medieval town to bring her such solace. But unlike London, the perpetual fog and mist were like a blanket in which she could wrap her broken heart. As each day passed, she felt more confident that she could move on from her heartache.

Her life here was already full and promising. During the day, she acted as governess for the two young sons of Lady McFadden, a friend of Lady Gordon's and a harried widow in desperate need of a quelling force for her rambunctious boys, who were only one year apart in age.

The small, dark-haired boys were fantastically intelligent—if bent on mischief—and she found teaching them to be a spirited challenge that reminded her of the days her own brothers were small. Thinking of the twins, however, always brought her melancholy back. They would be returning for their term break soon, and Charlotte had arranged for them to stay with the Chesterfields for the summer.

She would have given anything to bring them up to stay in Edinburgh with her, but her rooms were far too small, and while her reputation had not been publicly sullied during her liaison with Benjamin, she did not want to risk their futures with her proximity. No, she would make sure they were cared for from afar, her savings now almost just enough to cover the cost of their tuition—though the cheques she sent to the tuition office had never been cashed. Perhaps she could even send a gift down for their thirteenth birthday in July.

Her evenings often looked like this, standing on the docks or in the closes, speaking to women and men about their lives. The working class here faced many of the challenges she had seen in London. Poor working conditions, pitiful pay—women, as always, faced the brunt of the difficulties. In collecting these stories, she had begun chewing on an idea. An anthology—vignettes of each of these people's stories, pulled together to show just how common their suffering was—and how unnecessary it seemed next to the wealth of the nation.

The idea had been encouraged by her introduction to a radical whirl of writers, artists, poets, philosophers, and other such characters known to Elsie. Her friend's name had granted entrée into a whole other society in Edinburgh. One so entirely different from what she had known her whole life. Speaking to so many colourful minds, she felt herself changing, growing. Sometimes it felt as if she were becoming a whole new person yet had never felt more herself. It was a fantastic education that was proving immensely helpful to her plan of self-sufficiency and journalistic advancement. She had already had two articles printed, and while the alternative presses did not pay as well as her position in London, she felt she could really make a name for herself and her writing, and, most importantly, shed light on the concealed truths that desperately needed to be changed.

Fingers growing numb in the heavy, dense fog of the Leith docks, Charlotte tried to scribble down all the fascinating tidbits of Devina's story. At sixteen, the woman had dressed in her dead brother's clothing and signed up for a fishing vessel. When no one questioned her, and she was paid thrice what she had been when she worked with the other women up the dockyards gutting fish, she decided to make a go of it. Since then, she had managed to purchase her own boat and take on a small crew. In the two decades since then, she was one of the most successful small vessels on the water—and no one dared pay her a woman's wage for her catches. When the call of the pub finally dragged Davina and her crew up from the docks, Charlotte thanked the woman and slipped away.

Her mind swirled with the possibilities of this story, and how beautifully it would tie in to the story of the factory woman who had struck her floor manager when he had made unwanted advances and been cast out the same day. She had gone on to start her own cottage enterprise, making better quality garments than her previous employer, while her employees were paid and fed better than any factory worker. It could be a fair argument for the benefit of improving working conditions for all.

As the idea took hold, and her excitement mounted, as it always did when she grasped onto an idea, she completely missed the steady sound of boots on the misty cobblestones behind her.

It was not until she turned down Leith Walk that she realised her mistake. It was evening. The early summer light this far north always tricked her, staying light until much later than she would expect, but then once it dimmed, it was far too late to be out alone as she was. She should have hailed a hack the moment she came up from the docks. Edinburgh was not nearly as big as London, but she was not familiar with the streets, and she would be foolish to think it safer for a single woman at night.

The steps behind her had grown nearer. They were heavy. And now that she was listening, there were at least two of them. They might merely be workers on their way home, but Charlotte was not so naïve as to be hopeful. And the hair on the back of her neck prickled, not allowing her to ignore the sudden fear that settled in her bones and propelled her steps forward.

A hack drove by, but it did not slow down when she waved. At this time of night, few conveyances were passing on the road. She hurried her steps again, pacing wider so she could cover more ground, without it looking like she was fleeing. If she could just put more space between her and the boots behind her, she could slip off to a side street and lose them before they sprang on her.

The thought had her scanning each coming turn, mentally gauging the distance between her and her pursuers, for she was now certain that was what they were. How stupid of her to get herself into such a predicament. Benjamin would have railed at her for going out without an escort to a place like this, especially so late at night. She hoped he would forgive her now—if he heard of her foolish demise. It was that thought that propelled her even faster, eyes fixed on the next turn. That would be her only chance. If she got there, she could run. There was a cemetery down the next street. If she could get there, she could hide.

She would run in three…two…one…

A hand shot out and pulled her off the street. She could not even manage a shout as the long arms wrapped around her and covered her mouth, bundling her down the stairs and into the door of a cellar room.

Her whole body was screaming, muscles tensed and eyes frantic, desperate to make out what was happening—how she could run. This was it.

"Shhh. Please don't scream when I put you down." The voice sounded as desperate as she felt. "Please, please. They will hear us if you scream."

She could only frown in response. Her captor's hand still covered the whole lower half of her face.

"I promise I will not hurt you. But if you scream, he is going to have my hide. I promised to keep an eye on you, and I lost you for one minute, and you were nearly set upon by thugs!" The captor's voice was…English. And growing more and more agitated as he spoke to himself. "Please. You are safe. Please do not scream."

Charlotte was losing feeling in her arms where he gripped her like a vice above the dark floor. She nodded, if only to be released.

Seemingly satisfied with her response, her captor set her down gently, offering a hand to steady her as she regained balance.

"Who are you? What do you mean you will be in trouble if I scream?"

"Shhhh." Her voice had been rather loud in the small, dark room. Where were they?

"My name is James Smith. I used to work in London. My employer, Benjamin Scarsdale, sent me to Edinburgh for an apprenticeship last year. He wrote to me a few weeks ago with instructions to keep an eye on you. He gave me your address and an idea of where you might habit to venture. Boy, he was conservative in that estimate. You cover half the city every evening!"

Her eyes had adjusted to the dim light that filtered through some grimy windows on the street side of the wall, and she could see the tall young man who had grabbed her. He was well dressed, like a shopboy or perhaps a clerk.

He ran his hands through his hair, clearly agitated. "I would not have accepted the task if I had known what you would be getting up to. But I could never say no to Mr. Scarsdale. I owe him my whole life."

Charlotte could only stare. Hearing Benjamin's name in this little, neglected cellar flat, a country away, had stunned her speechless.

"We should get out of here. I have no idea whose flat this is. I think your pursuers are gone." James peeked out the door and waved over his shoulder, indicating that she should follow. Charlotte took the steps on wooden legs.

Back on the street again, they were the only two in sight. Somehow, James managed to flag down a passing hack and helped her inside.

"Please do not go off to the docks again so late. I only just got out of my shift, and only on a hunch managed to find you down at the docks. Thomas could not cover for me when I had to work late, and if you leave between seven and nine, we have no hope of finding you."

"Thomas?" Charlotte had been struck slow, her mind reeling to try to keep up.

"Thomas, Lucas, and I are supposed to watch you. We trade off so that we can all work, but between the three of us, we are usually able to keep track."

"Benjamin Scarsdale sent you to watch me?"

"Well, not sent. We were already here. We keep in touch with him—keep an eye on things here in Edinburgh that might be relevant…"

He stopped, clearly worried he had said too much. He was still running nervous hands through his hair and scanning out the hack window as if the adrenaline of the moment had not yet worn off.

The hack pulled up to her boarding house, where James

handed her down and walked her to the door. "Please don't go down to the docks again, Lady Charlotte. Not unless one of us is with you."

Charlotte opened her mouth to argue, but the pure anxiety on the boy's face was enough to stay her tongue. He had had enough of a scare this evening. And it was not his responsibility to worry about her, even if his master seemed to think it should be.

∞∞∞

As she crossed through the common room to the stairs that led up to the rooms, her landlady, Mrs. Walters, caught her attention, handing her a letter addressed to her. "It's awfie fine paper, Miss Charlotte." Since moving to Edinburgh, Charlotte had not used her title. It was a vestige of a life gone, and she wanted to make a go of building a life of her own merit.

Charlotte's heart did a flip at the familiar cream vellum of the letter. It was the Elysium stationery. After weeks of silence, Benjamin had come crashing back into her life. But when her trembling fingers broke the seal, she found the contents written in a rushed, cramped script that she now recognised as Elsie's. She had never met a lady of such breeding with such atrocious handwriting, but it fit the woman's constantly turning mind. Disappointment and relief warred within her.

The content itself was less of a surprise. Elkington and Elsie were returning to Edinburgh, where they planned to live until she had her school up and running. Charlotte knew that Elsie's Aunt Iona had returned with Helen only a week before, and she had expected the couple to be close behind. Elsie had invited Charlotte to join the four of them for dinner the end of the following week.

Returning to her room, Charlotte sat on the narrow bed and reread the letter by the light of the banked fire. Her room was modest but warm, positioned above the boarding house's common room. The convivial rumble of the other boarders coming up from the floor meant she never felt completely alone. Lady McFadden had offered her room and board, but Charlotte had preferred to receive all her payment in cash, allowing her to economise on her own expenses in favour of saving for the twins.

The letter was short and to the point—no opportunities to extrapolate hidden meaning from turns of phrase. And yet, Charlotte felt herself scanning the words over and over in the vain hope that they would give her some clue as to how Benjamin fared. That it was written on the Elysium stationery he kept in his office was her only clue—besides the sudden appearance of the boys tasked to tail her—that he must have some idea of where she was. She had not requested that Elsie keep their correspondence secret, but Charlotte had assumed that she had, for she had received no word from Benjamin since her flight north nearly a month ago.

She had lied to herself during the first days, telling herself that she hoped he would never find out where she was. Then the idea of him worrying over her had broken her heart anew, and she hoped he would use his vast network to track her steps—even if it was just to ensure she was well. That had kindled the small hope that once he found her, he might come and confront her—demand why she had left him and insist that she return to his side. That had been the most foolish hope of all, and it had taken days of distracting herself with work and discovering the endless maze of the city to quash the rising tide of longing.

It was not until now, knowing that he had indeed been keeping tabs on her and seeing a missive scrawled across his letterhead, that she realised all of that had been wrong. The truth was far more crushing. He knew where she was—really, she should not be surprised, considering the outsized sense of duty he felt to those he considered under his protection. It did not really matter how. He knew that she was here, and he had let her go. He was not coming to find her.

Chapter Thirty-Three

Benjamin was sitting behind his desk, working through some murky account books. He would have to find a new manager for the Trident's Hull, the pub he owned down by the docks. As Charlotte had discovered, the current manager seemed to be skimming funds from the establishment and covering it with the purchase of cheaper, poorer quality ale. Benjamin almost admired the man for covering it up so well, or he would have, if he could have mustered up any feeling besides the empty, numb indifference that had settled over him that day three and a half weeks earlier when Elsie had burst into Elysium a day before her own wedding, brandishing a scrap of paper in her hand.

He had read Charlotte's letter to Elsie as a curtain of detachment descended over him. Elsie had prodded him, likely hoping for some dramatic reaction to the news that she had thought must mean devastation for him. But surprisingly, he had felt nothing—no sorrow, no heartbreak, just a detached realisation of inevitability.

He had looked up at her and asked in a cool voice, "And what am I supposed to do with this? The letter is addressed to you, not me. If she had wanted to inform me of anything, she would have written to me instead."

Elsie had stared at him in disbelief before railing at him until she wore herself out and declared him impossible. After that, she had stormed out of his club.

Since then, he had gone about his business in a highly productive haze. His accounts had never been so scrupulously ordered, and the club, the Trident's Hull, the silk warehouse, and his three roadside boarding inns were all doing superbly. On top of that, he had only had to resort to blackmail once to sort out a small supply chain issue. In a strange, unresonant moment of clarity, Benjamin realised he had become a legitimate businessman. His entire empire could run smoothly and profitably with no need for him to throw his weight around. It might have been a hollow victory if he could bring himself to feel anything at all.

Upon their return from a comically brief wedding trip to the coast, Elsie and Elkington had stopped by Elysium to inform him and Wells that they were returning to Edinburgh to finally launch Elsie's school for girls. As a newly minted duchess, she now had enough backers to get the endeavour fully underway and was eager to venture back. Elsie had asked to borrow some paper to send out a correspondence— they were already packed from their travels and did not want to dally long in London.

"I am writing to Charlotte to tell her we are returning to Edinburgh. I would like to see how she is faring." Elsie had spoken to the room at large, but Benjamin knew it was directed at him.

The attempt was almost amusing because whenever he heard Charlotte's name, he could never make out a single word after that for the ringing that took up in his ears.

Today, he sat alone in his office, with only the ordered files of documents and the rattle of the Elysium day crew working through the halls below to keep him company. He looked back down at the Trident's Hull ledger. Perhaps he would not strip apart the pub's manager as he normally would. The idea of settling the score and exacting retribution held little charm for him now. He could just sack him. Or even allow the blighter to stay on, if only to see what kind of scheme he cooked up next. That might be entertaining.

Benjamin scrubbed a hand over his face. Christ, but he was tired. Tired of all this. What was it worth anyway?

"Sir?" Boyd's crackling voice caught his attention from the door.

"Yes, Boyd? What is it?" Was that a glimmer of hope in his voice? The prospect of anything to break this monotony he had fallen into was enough to have him sitting forward and waving the boy in.

"There is news from Laurens."

At that, his ears did prick up. Laurens was one of the young street youths whom Benjamin employed to be his eyes and ears around London. The Master of London's Secrets could hardly maintain his position without a vast network of invisible informants. Laurens specifically had been stationed outside the Deering household for nearly a fortnight.

Deering's behaviour had grown more and more erratic after Benjamin called in his markers to collect the Earl of Elford's remaining debts and warn the baron off the family. Finally, the baron had locked himself up in his townhouse and stopped leaving altogether. From what Benjamin's plants could discern through the household staff, the man seemed to be very nearly mad.

"What news?" It was as if he were waking from a fever, seeing the world again in growing detail.

"He sent a letter."

"A letter?" Already rising from his seat, Benjamin fell back into the chair with a thump. What was the importance of a mere letter?

"Yessir. It was franked express. Maxim got a look at it too." Maxim was another street urchin he had stationed outside the royal mail offices. "Express to Edinburgh, he said."

Benjamin felt his blood freeze. Edinburgh. Deering had sent a letter to Edinburgh.

"You okay, sir? Yer white as a ghost."

Benjamin vaulted out of his seat and ran past Boyd into the hall. "Summon the Duke of Wells at once, Boyd," he shouted over his shoulder as he tore through Elysium.

∞∞∞

When Charlotte arrived at the address Elsie had given her, she was surprised to find Helen answering the door after her knock. The young girl grinned up at her, revealing a new gap in her front teeth, surrounded by a haphazard smear of what looked to be raspberry jam on her rosy cheeks.

"Well, aren't you a charming butler?" Charlotte said.

Helen giggled and then shrieked when Elkington appeared behind her and swooped her over his shoulder like a sack of flour.

"Good evening, Lady Charlotte. Please come in. You will have to forgive us for the informality. It is Gordon's birthday, and Iona makes a point of giving all the help the afternoon off to celebrate the occasion. She claims it should be a national holiday for all the good Gordon does."

Assuming Gordon was the household's butler, or possibly the housekeeper, Charlotte found herself admiring Elsie's Aunt Iona even more than she had upon their first meeting.

"Papa! Let me down!" Helen laughed as she thumped ineffectually at Elkington's back. His face lit up at the endearment, but he did not respond to Helen or set her down. Instead, he turned back to Charlotte and gave her a pleasant smile. "Edinburgh truly is a spectacularly Gothic city, do you not find, Lady Charlotte? I swear I hear ghosts moaning and shrieking behind me at every turn." At that, Helen let out another girlish squeal, and Elkington spun, a look of patent horror on his face. "Do you see?"

Charlotte could not fight the grin that spread across her face and instead had to hide behind her hands, hoping—to the upside-down child—that she looked terrified rather than amused. "I have long heard tales of the spooks and banshees roaming through the wilds of Scotland. But since my arrival here in Edinburgh, I must admit to feeling an otherworldly presence. This house in particular seems to be desperately haunted."

Elkington smiled and winked at her, and Charlotte could understand how he had cut such a swath through London and the continent before being snared by Elsie. He had a delightfully unstudied charm about him that made one feel simultaneously part of an inside joke and also like one was delightfully impressive to him.

"Right then, Lady Charlotte. You ought to carry on to the parlour while I hunt down and vanquish this demon. I would not want to upset the ladies' sensibilities with such ghoulish mischief."

He nodded her toward the door down the hall and then turned and bounded up the stairs, a giggling, shrieking Helen still slung over his shoulder.

Charlotte smiled as she walked the short distance to the already ajar door. She had been rather apprehensive about coming here tonight. She worried that the collision of the past she had left behind with her new future would be off-putting at the very least, and heartbreaking at the worst. Being here now, though, she realised that had been foolish on her part. The Wylde-Burke family was warm and open and did not conjure more memories of Benjamin than already occupied her every waking moment. She was no different here than she was in her modest rented room or when she was tutoring the McFadden boys in history and mathematics. And just like those places, she would be able to hold herself together just fine.

Charlotte's confidence faltered as she stepped into the room, and Elsie looked up from a journal, her face transforming into kind, friendly concern. She would not be able to hold herself together if Elsie did not stop looking at her like that soon, as if she knew all the pain Charlotte was holding welled up inside her and would help her mop up the mess if the dam broke.

"Good evening, Charlotte. How happy I am to see you!" She stood with almost no discernible awkwardness, though Charlotte caught her placing a protective hand on her midriff. It was likely almost time she would start showing, and from there, if Charlotte's stepmother's experience was anything to go by, it would quickly become impossible to hide what was likely to be a six-month wonder. Judging by the warmth and love that radiated from the couple, their joy would be unmarred by any resulting scandal from their miraculously short pregnancy.

"How happy I am to see you, as well." Charlotte was surprised by the truth of the words.

She had not realised how trying and lonely it had been to move to a new city with only the ties of a few tenuous social connections. Seeing a familiar face—a friendly face—was a relief indeed. And so, when Elsie blew past the customary greeting and embraced her in a sisterly hug, Charlotte gladly returned the gesture.

When Elsie pulled back, she held Charlotte at arm's length and examined her. "You look well. Much better than he does." The comment was a punch to her gut.

It took Charlotte a moment to be able to draw breath again, and she remembered an afternoon when she was first learning how to ride at their country estate, only a year before her mother passed, the stable master had sent her out with a young groom tasked with walking her and her mare out around the corral. The groom had saddled her mount swiftly, wanting to get outside before the maids finished beating the carpets on the lawn—he had been sweet on one of them—and in his haste, had not measured the stirrups well enough.

When Charlotte turned to watch a bird flying overhead, her feet had not found purchase in the loose stirrups, and she had slipped off the saddle, landing hard on her back in the turned-up earth of the ring. The impact had made her bones vibrate like a tuning fork, and her mouth tasted of metal for the long moments before she was able to catch her breath again. She had been unharmed, but it had hurt.

This hurt more.

Elsie's eyes were searching, but she did not back down or demur. In some ways, that was a mercy. Charlotte would have gladly gone the whole evening dancing around the topic of Benjamin, but she was lying to herself if she pretended that it was not the only thing she could think about.

"He has been like a man possessed," Elsie continued, "and not in a good way. I do not think he sleeps. I doubt he eats, judging by the hollowness in his cheeks. All he does is work— and refuses to be questioned about anything."

It was like water in the desert, hearing of Benjamin's well-being. Or, not-so-well-being if Elsie's assessment was anything to go by. Charlotte would give up a week's pay just to hear whether he had gone out for the evening or stayed in. If he had been seen riding in the park or about town on business. And just like water in the desert, after one sip, she found herself only desperate for more.

"Is he really suffering so?" Her words were desperate, but she felt a secret thrill of relief that he might be just as affected as she was by her sudden departure.

"He would say nothing of the sort, but yes. I believe he is." Elsie had led them over to the sofa she had only just vacated, and Charlotte sat down. Hard.

"You must understand, I did not intend to cause him any distress."

Elsie was still clasping her hand, and she held on to it for dear life as she felt the tears she had not allowed since her flight north rise in her throat. Her nose prickled, and she rubbed it in a most unladylike manner.

"Of course, you did not." Elsie's voice was sure and strong. "You did what you had to do to protect yourself and your family. It was an incredibly brave decision, and you have set yourself up here with great success." She pressed Charlotte's hand between hers and pulled it closer so that Charlotte would be compelled to look away from the ceiling, where she had been valiantly fighting back tears, and down to meet her eyes. "I know how hard it is to rebuild yourself and your life after heartbreak. It takes a strong woman to take stock of her situation and move forward to make the best of it. You have done an incredible thing, and you are not to blame for any sorrow that has come from it."

And Benjamin was, she seemed to imply.

Elsie let the words sink in, and silence settled for a long moment. When Charlotte trusted herself to speak again, her words were soft. "Thank you, Elsie. For your continued friendship."

The two women smiled at each other, and Elsie withdrew not one but two handkerchiefs from her sleeve, passing one to Charlotte and using the other to dab her own eyes. "I stay prepared. Nowadays, it takes next to nothing to set off the waterworks. The other day, Helen properly excused herself after she sneezed, and I was nearly inconsolable."

She gave a wry, if watery chuckle, and Charlotte felt, even if the ache in her chest had not lifted, the burden of carrying it had been lessened by Elsie's support and acceptance.

"I find myself dreadfully appreciative." Elsie blew her nose like a barbarian, and the honking sound made both women break out in cleansing, belly-rolling laughter.

Elkington materialised in the doorway, Helen clasped onto one leg like a monkey in a tree, all traces of jam removed from her face, and a fresh frock to replace the pinafore that had been likely as jam stained as her cheeks after her purported escapades in the kitchen.

"*Mama,*" the girl whined as Elkington good-naturedly peeled her from his leg. "Am I really to have no supper? Papa said I have already had too many scones."

Elsie smiled at Charlotte's raised eyebrows. "Upon our marriage, Alexander legally adopted Helen, so we are now properly *Mama and Papa.*" She smiled, and the glow of her face was enough to light the room.

How happily things had turned out for the two of them, Charlotte thought with a remarkable lack of envy. Some people just deserved a happily ever after.

"He is teasing you. Of course, you are to have supper. What kind of mother would I be if I let my growing imp starve?" She smoothed back the riot of dark curls from the girl's face and planted a kiss on her brow. "Now, let us go find Aunt Iona so we can all have supper together."

Chapter Thirty-Four

Benjamin had been watching the Deering townhouse for three nights. The ghosts of the past were most alive here, and it was all he could do to keep himself alert and focused on reality. He had not slept more than a few hours at a time when Wells sent footmen to force him to change shifts. And when he did sleep, he was pulled further into the dark bleakness of the past that had seeped into his present. It did not do to give it any more hold than it already had on him, and so he avoided rest.

He had spent the last week combing the underbelly of London for any hint of what Deering might do. What he was plotting. The one letter the man had sent had slipped through their fingers, and there had not been another peep from the man's home. All his and Wells' investigating had come to nought—even the servants knew nothing. The baron had sent the missive and then holed himself up in his chambers, only opening the door to allow food to be passed through.

It was as if he were holding vigil for something. No one knew what. But Benjamin had a sick premonition that it was something terrible. And so, having learned to trust his gut, he had taken up this post three days ago, holding his own vigil and lying in wait to trap the snivelling worm the second he showed his hand.

Wells had sent a message up to Edinburgh to ask Elkington to keep an eye out for anything suspicious. Benjamin knew where she was staying; his informants kept a close eye on her to ensure she remained safe, but he felt it better to alert someone else of the danger she may be in, as he did not trust himself not to go charging up there to find her himself. No, it was better if he did not seek her out. Elkington and Elsie would be back in Edinburgh any day, and they would keep an eye on her—even beyond his faith in Elk, he knew Elsie had adopted Charlotte into her ranks, and he knew not to underestimate her loyalty. Besides, the manner of Charlotte's departure nearly a month earlier made it clear that his pursuit of her was not welcome.

She had cut ties with him completely, even instructing her bank not to accept money from his accounts. He had transferred it anyway. Charlotte was endlessly clever and had managed her family's finances with miraculous acuity, but she was no match for the innumerable loopholes that men like Bell and Collier could find when given the right incentive. He had also handed over the deed to her family seat to Collier to ferry up to his solicitor network in Edinburgh so they could present the document to her and explain the legalities. Benjamin had hoped to pass the gift on to her himself—the fantasy of her beaming smile and those faint eyebrows arching in surprise had dogged his every step—but he would not be the one to share the moment with her. She had made her choice, and he would respect the decision.

Besides, Deering was up to something, and Benjamin could not let him go. He was likely trying to cover up the slip with the shipping manifests. He would not put it past the snake to try to wriggle out of the consequences of smuggling spies, just when Benjamin was about to finally pin him down for good. Even though he had played his hand, Benjamin was not about to let him get away. There was more evidence. There always was. And Benjamin would find it. There was nothing else for him to do anyway.

After everything Deering had done to the people he loved—to him—he had to see this through to the bitter end.

∞∞∞∞

"A letter for you, Miss Aston." Mrs. Walters had caught Charlotte just as she returned from the McFadden household. She was in a bit of a rush. Elsie had arranged for her to meet with a publisher friend of hers, and there were hopes of discussing a book of her writing on the first measures that could be taken to alleviate poverty among women and children who lived in the London slums. A book! Charlotte could hardly believe it when Elsie mentioned it over tea on Sunday afternoon, her one day off from governess duties. The budding friendship between the two women had been well and truly solidified at dinner the week before, and Charlotte felt as if, though not yet, soon she might truly make a home for herself here—a life of meaning.

"Could you set it aside for me, Mrs. Walters? I am in a bit of a hurry," she called over her shoulder as she unlaced her bonnet and patted her hair.

Hopefully, it had not become too mussed over the course of the day. She would not have time to plait it again. Never mind, usually her customary crown of braids held up well enough to the trials and tribulations of a busy schedule.

"Are you sure, miss? It is fine stock again—looks like the kind your English lords use. Even has a crest on it. Besides, it is addressed to Lady Charlotte Aston. I did not know you were a lady!" She said the last with almost accusing disbelief. To be fair to Mrs. Walters, it would be quite a boon for her business if fine ladies began frequenting her boarding house.

Charlotte stopped in her tracks. She was not expecting a post from anyone who might have a crest on their stationery. And she had only just seen Elsie two days ago—besides, they had no use for the Royal Mail when a messenger boy could deliver a missive through the city in a thrice. She felt a tingle of apprehension along the nape of her neck. Had Freddie written? It seemed unlikely. She imagined he was still too piqued at her last letter to him, in which she had disavowed his behaviour and stated that it was high time he took responsibility for himself and the estate.

She had not told him that she would continue to look after the twins—she could not have abdicated that responsibility if she tried—but she doubted they were high on his list of concerns now that the full weight of his actions would come crashing down. It had been painful to write the words, but it was now clear to Charlotte that her coddling had only done her dear Freddie harm. This was the only way to show him love now.

"Thank you, Mrs. Walters." Charlotte accepted the letter with an almost steady hand.

It was a script she did not recognise, but she broke open the seal in haste, realising she had not checked the crest. Her eyes jumped straight to the bottom to see who the sender was, and her heart dropped in dread before craning back up to read the letter's contents. A cold sweat broke out on her neck, and for a moment she thought she might have been shot in the shoulder again.

"Are ye alright, lass?" The ageing landlady reached out a hand to steady her, but Charlotte's head snapped up, and Mrs. Walters jolted back in surprise.

"I must travel back to London for a spell. It seems there are some family matters I must attend to. I am sorry for not giving the proper notice. I assure you, I will pay through the end of the month." Her voice was falsely cheery and nearly manic. "I hope to return as soon as possible, but I cannot be sure when that will be."

Mrs. Walters looked concerned but gave her a reassuringly maternal look. "Aye, lass. Dunnae worry. You can always find a place here. I hope the news is not as dire as all that."

Charlotte's smile felt wooden as she gave a shake of her head. "No, no. I just need to be home to sort some things out."

She worried that if she stood there a moment longer, the older woman's kind gaze might reduce her to desperate tears. She did not have time for desperate tears.

∞∞∞

Charlotte sat in Elkington's carriage, watching anxiously as the scenery flying by the window darkened as night enveloped the countryside. The days were already getting so long here up north, and it was hard to believe she had only received the letter this afternoon. After packing her belongings swiftly—she had pawned some books but could not yet part with the gowns—she had left her trunk with Mrs.

Walters and hurried on foot to Lady McFadden's home.

Her employer had been kind and understanding, saying that she must take however long she needed to put her family affairs to rights and that she and the boys would manage well enough until she got back. She had then pressed an extra week's worth of earnings into Charlotte's hands, refusing all protests Charlotte could muster, and sent her on her way. Armed with the comfort of extra blunt, Charlotte made her way down Regent Terrace to the Wylde's residence.

A month earlier, Charlotte would have gone dashing back down to London upon receiving the letter without stopping to tell anyone what had transpired. Now, when Elsie hurried into the sitting room, Charlotte nearly burst into tears.

"Oh, Elsie. I have wrecked everything, after all."

Elsie traded a handkerchief for the letter Charlotte withdrew from her sleeve, ushering her to the settee where she skimmed the contents and looked back up just as Charlotte regained some control over her desperation.

"I cannot believe it." Charlotte sat miserably deflated as Elsie read through it again. "How could the Chesterfields have possibly heard of your association with Scarsdale? They notoriously never come to town. And to refuse to host your brothers during their term break? It seems rather harsh."

Charlotte's brows pulled together. Elsie was so uncommonly bright, she found it surprising she did not understand the voracity of *ton* gossip. "If it is out, it is hardly surprising that they have heard. Especially since the twins are such close friends with their son. Any number of people would have clawed to Derbyshire just to be the first to tell them the news."

Elsie cocked her head to the side as if puzzling out a particularly confounding sum. "But it was not out. Alexander and I were in London only a week ago. Of course, there was some talk of Benjamin's interest in you after you were seen together around town. But since your departure, there have been at least three more scandals for the *ton* to gnaw on. I cannot see how the Chesterfields would have found out only just now."

"Perhaps the post was delayed." Charlotte threw up her hands, frustration born of desperation giving her words an edge. "What does it really matter? They know—likely, so do many others. And not only that, I was seen to be entertaining a courtship. Look, there—" She pointed to the line but did not have to read it out from the page. It was already seared into her memory. "It has come to our attention that you have been conducting a highly improper affair with a man of ill repute. We are sure you can understand that, though it is not their fault, we could not possibly house Marcus and Henry over the summer after their sister behaved in such a vulgar manner. We expect no further correspondence from you or your family."

The words had cut through her like a knife the first time she read them, and they hurt just as acutely now. Her worst fears had come to pass. Her selfishness had ruined her family.

"Yes, well… That is rather damning, is it not?" Elsie was still chewing her lip, going over the letter again and again.

"Indeed." In any other situation, the understatement would have made Charlotte laugh.

"It does not much matter how they came to have this information. They do now. And now my family is ruined, and the twins are going to be left out in the cold in less than a week's time." Her voice rose with each word until the shrill tone hurt even her own ears. "The townhouse is let already. The new family is moving in the Sunday next. I cannot welcome them back there. I must return and find lodging for them—and I cannot possibly leave them alone in London, so I must stay until I can find something better. Certainly, staying with me will only make the situation worse for them. But I do not see what else can be done. Perhaps I will bring them back here. It will only be a few weeks until they can return to school."

Charlotte thought doubtfully of her small room at the boarding house—the all-female boarding house. Mrs. Walters was kind, but she doubted she would allow two rambunctious youths to run rampant through her establishment. No, she would have to think of something else.

"Charlotte. Charlotte!" Elsie's voice cut through the manic whirlwind of thoughts swirling around her head. "Charlotte. Why can your brother not take care of them? He is the earl, is he not? Would it not be best for you and them if he found an arrangement for them?"

Charlotte scoffed at the idea—tempting though it was. "I could not possibly trust Frederick to take care of them. He can hardly take care of himself. Besides, I do not even know where to find him. He never wrote a response to my last letter informing him that I was to leave, and the house was being let to pay for the boy's schooling. No, I must return to London and collect them. What I do from there..." The uncertain future yawned before her in a dizzying void. "Well, I am sure I will think of something. I always do."

She brought her hand up to rub the thrumming pain between her eyes.

Elsie did not look convinced. "I know you will not listen to me, but I am not sure a mad dash back to London is the most reasonable solution. If you would let us, we could write to our contacts back in London to discover more about the situation. I cannot imagine Benjamin—" She stopped at Charlotte's sharp inhale of breath. "Well, if it were that dire, he would have written to tell us. I am sure."

Charlotte shrugged her shoulders helplessly. "Even the Master of London's Secrets cannot know everything. Besides, you said it yourself; he was out of sorts. Maybe he has been off his game. He is not privy to every thought and private correspondence of the *ton*."

Elsie gave her a dubious look, but she stood to ring for a footman anyway. "Kelly, please have the marquess's carriage prepared for a journey to London. Lady Charlotte will be leaving this evening."

Any protests from Charlotte had fallen on deaf ears, and an hour later, she had been shown to the carriage with her trunk already strapped to the back and a pile of wool blankets, heated bricks, and a basket laden with food packed inside to ensure her comfort. Elkington and Elsie had bid her farewell, insisting that she write as soon as she arrived to apprise them of the situation.

Now, with the impenetrable dark of a Scottish night upon the conveyance, she had nothing to do but lie back on the generously upholstered bench and hope the restless fits of sleep that took her would somehow make time move faster.

Chapter Thirty-Five

"Jesus Christ, man. You look no better than the night I found you bleeding out on the street." Leave it to Wells not to sugarcoat his thoughts.

"That is an absurd exaggeration," Benjamin mumbled as he stumbled toward the washstand.

Considering his exhaustion, he should have just allowed himself to collapse on the bed. However, years on the streets, living in filth, had made him reverent of the fine linens and clean bedding he now had access to. And though he could well afford to replace the sheets ten times over, he could not bring himself to allow the grime that he had accumulated on his skin and clothes to soil such a pristine setting.

"That is what you think." Wells had followed him into the club, past the gaming floor, and through the halls to his suite without relenting.

When Benjamin looked up from the bar of expensive soap he was lathering, he saw that Wells was serious. Since becoming the duke, it was rare to see anything beyond the aristocratic hauteur on the man's face—an effective facade that kept the man far away from the title. But now, Benjamin could see genuine concern.

Wells straightened. "I have indulged this wild hunt long enough. It is time for you to give it up. The man has gone insane—some informants are saying they suspect he caught the French disease sometime last year during one of his romps in the gutter. It has eaten away at his brain. There is no one left on whom to exact revenge."

Benjamin watched the grey water trail down his forearms into the basin. This would not be enough. Perhaps he should ring for a bath to be brought up.

"There is nothing left for you there," Wells said. "He cannot hurt you anymore. He cannot touch Charlotte. You must let this go before it eats you alive. Ben? Are you listening to me? You should go to her. Be with her."

"I cannot!" Benjamin smashed his fists on the washstand, upsetting dirty suds onto the plush maroon carpet under his feet.

He whirled, heart hammering like a caged animal, and Wells stared with unconcealed surprise.

"I cannot." He repeated more quietly but no less forcefully. "You do not understand. I can never be with her. This—" He gestured wildly to his sullied clothing. "Is all I can do for her. I can never be with her, but I can do this. I can stop this man—the evil of his family. I can stop it." His voice was rising again, and the raw scrape of the words was tinged with hysteria.

"Why?" Wells' hands were held palm up, as if he was approaching a wounded animal. "Why, Ben? Why can't you be with her?"

"Do not call me that!" he roared again. "That is why! I am Ben, the son of a woman who was made a whore. The bastard of a man who never cared to acknowledge me or my sister. I am made of street rubbish, and I have been driven to unspeakable things. Things that would destroy her if she ever knew. I was fooling myself to think I would dare to keep her—to marry—" the words stuttered and stopped when his breath caught in his throat.

He closed his eyes and shook his head, trying to shake away the cloud of pain that enveloped him at the thought.

"That night—the one you found me, after all those years." He kept his eyes closed, his heart hammering as he was transported back in time to the cluttered streets off the docks where he had been working in a fish packing house by day and spent his nights carrying coal up from the barges to be delivered to the sleeping homes of London. "It was not just a footpad skirmish."

He knew Wells had been shocked to see his childhood friend as he fled the docks, so delirious with blood loss that he could not make sense of why Wells would have been in such a part of town at such an hour, he had not been able to come up with any more elaborate explanation for the seeping slash that ran down the side of his neck.

"I figured." Wells' voice came through the fog of memory, but Benjamin did not open his eyes.

"I was working the coal shipments, like I said." He could still feel the splintering cut of the rough wooden pallets they loaded the buckets of coal into the carts. "I had just filled my last cart of the night and was taking a shortcut through a back alley to the pub where we were paid. I had to be at the packing warehouse by five, and if you did not collect your coin the night of the work, the pub owner would withhold it, and you would never get paid."

He had learned that the hard way, and after a day without

food, he had never taken the risk again. Even with the funds from both jobs, he only ever had enough to buy an oatcake or two for breakfast and a pasty for midday. It was not enough to fuel the backbreaking labour, and he could not survive on less.

"There was a couple in the alley I cut through. Not uncommon for the docks. Sailors often can't afford more than a pinch and poke behind the tavern. But this was different." His skin began to crawl at the memory. "You get used to seeing violence on the streets. It is not pleasant, but it is a fact of life. You learn to turn your head and mind your business. But this—" He stopped as his gut turned at the memory. "He was brutal. She was not even crying anymore. I think she was already half dead by the time I arrived." He gritted his teeth. Watching the scene behind his eyelids was almost as real as the night itself. "I approached quietly, hoping I could take him by surprise. I could hold my own in street fights against other starving youths, but I had grown so thin. I did not have much hope against a robust gentleman. It was clear from his togs that he was a gentleman slumming around, finding his pleasure in the gutter." Benjamin's lip curled in disgust. "But then he turned—maybe he heard me coming. And I saw that it was not just some gentleman—it was *him*. Reginald Deering. The man who raped my sister and forced the pregnancy on her. The pregnancy that killed her." He stopped, his breathing rough and choppy. Wells simply stood, allowing the space and silence for him to continue.

"I wish I could say I attacked him right there on the spot. He had clearly beaten the woman in his arms to the brink of death before assaulting her. He had destroyed my sister, the gentlest soul I had ever known, and the only person I had left. But I just stood there. Dumbfounded." Benjamin fought back the bile of shame that rose in his throat. "He must have recognised me too. I had gone to the house when Delia came back bruised and battered. The butler had turned me away, but not before I threatened his master with some form of naïve retribution. Then, after she had died, I had sat outside the house for days. Waiting for my chance—to do what? I am not sure. But they must have taken notice because Reginald knew me. He sneered and said, *You?* He let the woman go, and she fell in a heap against the wall. I did not go to help her. I was frozen to the spot. And then Reginald laughed and called me a piece of scum. *No better than that dirty slut of a sister, are you?* he said." Benjamin's words were flat, as if he were reciting a story he had heard from another. "*For the best she died before she produced yet another dirty bastard like yourself.* And then I lost it.

"I was on him like a rabid animal. Clawing, punching, biting. He screamed and pulled out a knife. I should have seen it in his boot, but I had not had a single thought in my head after I realised it was him. He lunged and caught me, but I did not feel it. I wrestled the blade out of his hands, and we both fell to the floor. I had not even turned fully; one of my arms was trapped under his body. And then it stopped. He stopped fighting and just gasped. I pushed him off me, and that is when I saw his blade sticking out of his gut. I had stabbed him. I still do not know if I did it on purpose or not. It was just done. There was so much blood."

He could still smell the way the coppery smell of Reginald's blood mixed with the ever-present stench of fish and smoke. It took a few long moments of drawing breath through his nose before he could fight away the nausea. "Much of the blood must have been my own. I passed out for a moment, and when I came to, it was like I was awake, but in a dead body. But then I saw him. His empty eyes were still so full of hate, staring right at me. There were people coming. Men from the docks. I think one of them crewed for Deering because he knew Reginald's name. I can only hope he did not recognise who I was through all the muck and the blood. Otherwise, Deering knows that I killed his son. Some part of me must have realised I would hang for it. So I pulled myself up and ran. And ran and ran." His breathing was more even now, and he looked up at Wells, still standing in the doorway.

"And that is when I found you."

"And that is when you found me. And I tried to start my life over." He slumped into one of the chairs by the fire. "But I never really left it behind, did I? Nothing I can do will erase what has happened. And now, knowing that Deering had a hand in all of it, Reginald's abuse, Delia's death? And how he has fixated on Charlotte—this is the only thing I can do for her without dragging her down into the gutter with me. The blood is already on my hands. I can end this."

Wells came and sat across from him, his dark hair glowing like coals in the firelight. "What? You plan to kill him?" The words were blunt and practical, and Benjamin shook his head.

"I do not know. If it comes to that, yes."

"It will not win her. You know that, right?"

Frustration burned at the comment, said with the same condescending inflection Wells used with everyone. "Damn it, Jonathan. I know!" The infuriating man only arched an eyebrow at his given name. "I am not doing this to win her. Were you not just listening to a word I said? I have no hope of winning her. I love her too much to win her!"

He stopped at that, and Wells merely nodded, as if he was further confirming a conclusion he had already reached. "I do not know what you hope to gain from hunting a dying man. No—" He held up a ducal hand to stop Benjamin's retort. "I understand your motivation, but I disagree with your reasoning. This is no longer about the crimes of the Deering family—though there are many. You cannot run from your fear of love. I do not think it fair to Lady Charlotte for you to deny her the opportunity to return your love—that is really what you are doing. You are using your past and your vendetta against this man to wedge a shield between you and happiness. After all these years, all the wrongs done to you and losses you have suffered, it terrifies you to face true love. And trust me, that is what she offers you."

Benjamin could only sputter. Never in their lives had he known Wells to deliver such a monologue. Despite his ducal arrogance, or maybe because of it, Wells had always allowed others to talk and try to fill the space in their desperation to impress him. It was even more galling that his insight rang true. Benjamin felt scraped raw by the arrow burrowing through flesh to hit its target.

Benjamin sagged. "I like you better when you do not speak." His words were shaky, and the attempt at levity fell flat.

Wells merely quirked his lips in his self-satisfied way and leaned back against the chair, sipping whisky from a tumbler he seemed to have conjured out of nowhere. "As do I."

A crash in the hall outside his apartment had both men turning to the door. After a moment of scrambling, the knob turned, and a red-faced Boyd entered the room.

"He has left!" He was panting hard as if he had run all the way through Elysium's maze of corridors and up every flight of stairs at breakneck speed.

"What? Who?" The words were out of Benjamin's mouth before he could think. There was only one man Boyd would be talking about.

"Laurens was snooping around the back of the house—"

Benjamin exploded from his seat. "What! He knows he is not supposed to leave his post. This is not a game. Snooping around is dangerous. He has no idea what might happen to him."

Boyd gulped but admirably soldiered on, with only a slight tremor in his voice. "Aye, he knows. But he had a friend once who knew a boy who worked inna toff's house and said there was secret passages. Tunnels the toff used to sneak out and see his ladybird with no one the wiser." The boy kept babbling on as Benjamin's eyes grew wider. "So he says to himself, maybe this toff has got something too. Maybe them's why we ain't seen hide nor hair of him the last week."

Benjamin might have laughed at Boyd's use of the plural. He had made sure to keep the younger boys, such as Boyd, out of this investigation, using only the help of the older boys he knew had a good grasp of the intricacies of surveillance and would not be at risk out on the streets at night, even in the relative safety of Bloomsbury. Still, all the younger boys employed in Elysium had been following with rapt attention—excited by the boss's clandestine mission, and every time an older footman returned from a watch, he was swamped by curious urchins scrambling for every exciting detail.

"He'd climbed back through the mews and, sure enough, there is a cellar door that don't lead to no cellar. He left and got Conway—since he is so much smaller and a legend climber—to scurry up the back trellis and peek in the toff's room. Sure as salt, there's not a soul in there!"

Benjamin could only stare down at the boy with his jaw slack. How had this ragtag group of street youths figured this out before he did? He was torn between pride and fury that they would risk their necks like that. Fury won. They had deliberately disobeyed his orders to keep a low profile and only watch.

"I will deal with you lot later," Benjamin growled, and Boyd only swelled with barely concealed, delighted pride.

It sparkled in his dark eyes, and Benjamin resisted the urge to ruffle his hair. God, when had he gone this soft?

Still, the sense of dread gnawing at his gut spurred him into action. "Come along, Wells. Even after your gorgeous pontificating, you must admit this is suspicious behaviour. There is something else going on, and I mean to get to the bottom of it."

Wells merely sighed, drained his glass, and followed Benjamin out the door, ruffling the young footman's spiky black hair when he passed. "Good work, lad."

∞∞∞

As Benjamin and Wells raced through the streets, stopping at seemingly arbitrary corners and alleys to consult with Benjamin's network of informants, they slowly pieced together a path of Deering's movements. He had been slipping out of his townhouse at night—overly paranoid or perhaps knowing he was being watched—according to multiple accounts. Either was just as likely, as the man had gone visibly mad.

"French disease, it is. Can spot it a mile away," a beer maid shouted up at them as she dumped a pot of dubious contents down the alley gutter. "Rots away the good bits until there is nothing left but madness—not that there was many good bits to begin with with that one."

She spat away from their mounts as she hefted the pot back on her hip. From their interactions thus far, her poor opinion of the baron was not uncommon amongst the working class of the city. It seemed the Deering name had been soured for more than just Benjamin.

"Have you seen him recently? In the last days, to be precise?" The buxom maid smiled up at Wells with unmistakable favour.

"Can't say as I have. But a cousin o' mine works as a kitchen maid up at one o' them big houses in Mayfair. Said she thought she saw him the other night."

Benjamin had always prided himself on his underground network of informants and his singular ability to get information from nothing, but he had to admit, having a handsome duke by his side seemed to grease the wheels substantially.

"Where in Mayfair?"

"Up on Mount Street, she works." Benjamin's blood ran cold. The Aston house was on Mount Street.

"Thank you for your assistance, Miss." Wells flipped a coin down to her, and she plucked it from the air, smiling prettily as she tucked it into her generous bodice. "No trouble at all, m'lord. Do not hesitate to find me if you need more."

Benjamin was already turning his mount towards Mayfair, his pulse hammering in his ears.

"Easy, Scarsdale, we cannot just go charging in there with no plan. A madman is not one to be underestimated. They are even more dangerous than the sane ones." His grave tone brooked no argument, and Benjamin wondered if he spoke from experience.

Benjamin only nodded and followed Wells' lead. The only thought keeping the panic at bay was that he knew no one was in the Aston house. Freddie had fled to seedy bachelor lodgings, and Charlotte was safely tucked away in Scotland, where Elkington's family and Benjamin's street network were keeping an eye on her. No one else had any reason to be in the home. Benjamin was sure of this because he had leased the property himself.

No, there was no reason to believe Deering could do any harm if he was indeed secreted away in the Aston's vacant townhouse. They would go in, look around, and if the madman was hiding there, they would drag him out and bring him to the authorities at Bow Street—or Bedlam, whichever institution took him first.

Chapter Thirty-Six

It was strange returning to the townhouse. Charlotte had only said goodbye a month ago, but already, she felt as if she were stepping into another life. The familiar rooms and corridors in which she had spent much of her life were now empty of all sentiment. She would have thought the setting would bring back memories of, if not of better times, then of simpler ones. But there was nothing. It was just an empty house.

The new tenants were not meant to arrive for two more days, and she was not sure if there were even enough linens left behind to make a serviceable bed. Charlotte wondered if perhaps she should spend the night at an inn instead. But the journey had been long and without respite, and the idea of seeking out a suitable establishment and paying for it with her limited funds was too daunting. She would make do with what she could find.

The one part of the house Charlotte felt compelled to check was Freddie's room. Freddie had moved his things to the earl's chambers upon their father's death, but as he rarely spent time at home since he came of age, Charlotte found it funny that she still thought of them as Freddie's chambers.

No other part of Freddie's life had adopted the trappings of an earldom.

The heavy wooden door did not creak as she pushed it open. Despite the relative disrepair of the house since the staff had been dismissed, some things still bore the mark of the care and dedication devoted to them over the years. Charlotte felt the echo of guilt at the depths to which she had seen her family fall. She would not take any more of the blame upon her shoulders than she already had, but it had always been her self-imposed mission to keep the family standing strong through all of their trials and tribulations. But that was a lifetime ago. She had done what she could. And now she was doing what she must.

As she stepped into the bare room, she stood a moment, basking in the emptiness. There was no trace of the generations of earls who had laid their heads here. Even the ornate four-poster bed had been dismantled and sold off months before she left. Freddie had never even noticed. Or if he had, he had not said anything to her about its absence.

Looking around, she felt nothing; no stirrings of regret, no true guilt for her decisions. It was something of a relief to realise that she was free of the memories of this house—the bitterness of the past. It was liberating to be ruined. There was nothing left to tiptoe around, and the farce that her old life had become was now over.

She would collect the twins at the end of the week and find a solution for their situation, and then they would all move on with their lives. With a deep breath of the stale, dusty air, Charlotte felt the desperation of the last days on the road receding. Now that she was here, she could figure something out. All would be well.

And yet, there was something odd about this room. She felt a lingering sense of wrongness. After puzzling over it and scanning the room again, she could not put her finger on the sensation. Likely, it was just the weariness of the journey and the enormity of her life stretched out before her.

With that thought, she hefted the basket with what remained of the food from her trip from the doorway and made her way down the hall to her old room. Pulling her travelling cloak around her, Charlotte stretched out on the bare mattress that was once her bed and let the deep sleep of a weary traveller take her.

∞∞∞

She was not sure what woke her. Judging from the quality of darkness out the window, it was likely still an hour before dawn. It took a moment for her senses to adjust to being awake—she had not slept so deeply in quite a while, and it was disorientating to awaken in her empty childhood bedchamber.

And then, all at once, she knew precisely what had awakened her.

The figure in the corner was not moving, but its muculent breathing filled the room. Charlotte scrambled up as far back as the wall would allow. The figure did not move.

"Who are you? What are you doing here?" The words whooshed out of her as if panic was squeezing them from her chest.

A gravely laugh morphed into a cough. "My dear, you ask such silly questions."

Charlotte felt glued in place. Somehow, she forced her legs

355

to shift to the side of the bed. She stood and pressed against the wall, as if she could somehow get more space between her and the intruder. He was in the corner beside the door. If she were fast, she might have been able to jump over the bed and make it to the exit, but he need only reach out an arm to grab her. No, she could not risk that.

"What are you doing here?" she asked again, hoping to draw him out somehow, to buy herself time to get out of here.

This time, the voice was more perturbed. "Come now, Charlotte, do not play coy with me." And then she knew the voice. She recognised the condescending way Lord Deering whined her name. "It is a husband's prerogative to visit his wife on their wedding night." *Husband? Wedding night?*

"Lord Deering? What are you doing in my bedchamber? What do you speak of? We are *not* married." Her voice was shaky as she shimmied along the wall slowly, hoping to reach the window before he moved. Perhaps she could throw it open and scream for help before he pounced.

"Charlotte, I am growing tired of this game. Be a good girl and come to your husband. I am your master now, or do you not remember the vow you took to obey?"

"No!" Charlotte's urge for caution was overwhelmed by the desperation to convince Deering he was mistaken. "We are not—we did not wed!" Surely he was confused.

He could not think they were married—or that it was acceptable for him to be in her room, in her family's abandoned home. No, he was clearly out of his mind. She had to escape.

Deering stood and stepped toward her. Charlotte pushed herself even further back, the wooden panelling of the wall pressing into her back painfully. "I take exception to your tone, Lady Deering. There will be consequences for your impertinence."

He had always been a large man, but something about him had always given the impression of sloth. She could never have imagined he could move with such agility. In the blink of an eye, he was upon her, his hot breath fanning her face. There was a putrid odour, something like the stink of rotten fish, that made her gag. The streetlight from below illuminated his face, and Charlotte thought she must be dreaming—this could not be real.

For it was not Lord Deering's face above her but the rotting, lesioned visage of nightmares. The bridge of his nose had collapsed, giving his long face a skeletal air that propelled her back even further, though there was nowhere to go.

Too late, she saw him raising his hand above her, and when she tried to duck away, the back of one ringed fist caught her across the temple. The glancing blow would surely have felled her if she had not moved when she did. Even still, she was knocked off balance and fell to the side just as he raised his hand again. Hunched as she was, she saw that, though he had moved quickly, Deering did not seem terribly steady on his feet. Seeing her chance, she kicked out with her booted foot—thank goodness she had not seen fit to undress for bed—and connected with the flesh of his knee. The blow was effective, and the force of her kick sent him reeling and swearing.

"Damn you, you worthless slut!" he bellowed, and Charlotte jumped away just as he lunged for her neck.

She was over the bed and an arm's length from the door before he grabbed hold of the hem of her cloak, yanking her back by her neck. A choked scream came from her, and she scrambled at the fastening. By some miracle, and likely due to the garment's age and wear, she was able to tear the clasp from the seam, not stopping to gasp for breath as she tore open the door and sprinted down the hall.

"HELP! SOMEBODY, HELP!" Charlotte screamed at the top of her lungs as she took the stairs two at a time, nearly tumbling down the two-storey landing.

As if in answer to her prayers, the front door banged open and Benjamin Scarsdale stood there before her, pistol drawn and chest heaving in the streetlight. Never had she seen a more blessed sight in her life.

"It is Deering! He is here!" she screamed as she hurtled towards him.

Before she made it to the doorway, she heard a bellowing roar. It sounded as if a pack of wild boars was bearing down on her. She glanced over her shoulder at the diseased monster rampaging down the stairs. Benjamin was closing the distance between them, taking the stairs two at a time, but it wasn't enough. Benjamin made to fire, then appeared to change his mind. Deering was closing the distance, making the shot too dangerous with Charlotte in the lead.

She would not make it. She could not believe it. She would not make it.

Just as Deering's stride ate up the last steps between them, she heard another yell. This one was a vicious cry of a warrior flying into battle. Before she knew what was happening, Benjamin collided with Deering, and the impact of their bodies sent a gust of air past her face. The gun in Benjamin's hand clattered to the landing. The two men tumbled down the last of the stairs, blows raining as they wrestled on the bare marble floor of the foyer.

Just when she thought Benjamin was getting the upper hand, Deering's substantial form rolled over, pinning him to the ground. They both fought with a wild ferocity that made Charlotte certain that neither would stop until the other was dead. Charlotte's head was still ringing from Deering's blow, and it made it seem as if the fight before her was playing out in slow motion. She watched in growing horror as it became clear that while Benjamin was the more skilled fighter, Deering had the advantage of size and the frenzy of madness.

"You took my son." Deering punctuated the yowl with a punch to Benjamin's gut that Charlotte felt reverberate through her. "You will not take my wife!" he screamed as he pinned Benjamin's torso under his haunches, landing blow after blow about his face.

"STOP!" Charlotte screamed, her hands shaking as she jumped down from the stairs to grab the pistol that had been knocked across the hall. "STOP!"

She almost fired a shot in the air and then realised that this was a duelling pistol and she did not have another round to load. Luckily, her movement and shouts seemed to have drawn Deering's attention, for he lurched back upon seeing the firearm levelled at his head. "Stop, or I will shoot you!"

He truly was beyond sanity, for he just sneered and grabbed Benjamin from the floor, wrestling him up to hold before his body. "I would like to see you try. Shoot me, and you shoot your dear gutter rat."

Charlotte's breath caught as she saw Benjamin's face. His jaw was starting to swell, blood trickled down his lip, and his eyebrow was split, oozing blood over his left eye. As if he heard her gasp, his eyes opened, and she was caught in the familiar deep blue gaze. For a moment, time stood still, and Charlotte felt all they had left unsaid pass between them.

No, he was trying to get her attention. His lips were moving. She looked down and tried to make out the word. No, she must be mistaken. It looked like he was saying, *shoot*.

His eyes flicked to the meaty hand grasping his shoulder. Deering had his arms pinned to his sides so that Benjamin could not buck back and twist out of his grip. Benjamin looked down at the hand again, looking up at her and mouthing the word again.

Shoot!

He could not be asking her to do that. She could kill him! He could not be asking to sacrifice his own life just to save her from this deranged beast!

"You will come with me, Charlotte. Or I will kill you and this underworld bastard, right here and now. Do not doubt me. All it takes is a quick snap of the neck, and it is you and me, anyway. As a matter of fact, I might as well do it—"

Deering moved, and Charlotte did not have to think. She pulled the trigger. The powder lit and exploded in the empty hall, the recoil sending Charlotte reeling back, and the pistol clattering to the bare marble floor.

Then, all hell broke loose. Shouts were filling the hall, men streaming in from all sides. Charlotte could not see through the melee to Deering and Benjamin. Someone helped her up, leading her outside. She fought against the arms.

"No! No! Is he okay? Is Benjamin alright?" The stranger lifted her up and carried her flailing from the house until they set her down on the pavement beyond the front steps.

"Stay here, Lady Charlotte. We have him. Deering has been apprehended." The Duke of Wells put his hands on her shoulders to steady her and hold her in place so she could not bolt back into the chaos of the foyer.

"But what of Benjamin!" she wailed, unable to modulate her voice with the shot of the pistol still ringing in her ears.

"He was alive when I grabbed you. I will go back in and see to him. But you must stay here!" She was not sure if she had heard his words, but by some force of will, she was able to nod her agreement.

A crowd was forming on the street, neighbours craning their heads to try to find the source of all the commotion. A housekeeper from one of the neighbouring houses began fluttering over Charlotte's bruising face, but Charlotte did not pay her any heed. She could not tear her eyes from the dark doorway—the love of her life somewhere on the other side. Dead or alive. She did not know.

After interminable moments, she could not stand it any longer and began to make her way back inside. The Bow Street runners that Wells had appeared with were already beginning to file out of the house, and she could not stand to watch another man who was not Benjamin step out of that door.

But before she could take the first step, two figures emerged from the chaos. Wells' ducal profile was immediately recognisable, and he held up the slumped form of—"Benjamin!" His name tore from her chest, and she sprinted up the steps, her hands fluttering around him, not sure which injury to tend to first. Then she saw the blood seeping through his coat and felt her heart drop.

"Benjamin! Oh, God, Benjamin."

She did not know whether to grasp him or stand back, lest she do any more harm, and so she found herself floundering uselessly on the front stoop of her family's empty house.

"We are even now." The words were weak, and Charlotte thought perhaps she was imagining them.

But when she leaned forward, she saw the strained smile on his bloody face, and a strangled, hysterical laugh bubbled up from inside her. "W-what?"

"You shot me. We'revn." He gave her a full, dazzling smile, his face transforming. And in the next moment, he was gone—dropped away in a dead faint.

Charlotte let out a scream and rushed to catch him, the blood from his wound seeping into her bodice the moment she touched him.

"We need help here, now!" Wells shouted towards the group of runners, and two robust men hurried up the steps to help lift Benjamin's unconscious form.

The pain of being moved must have brought him back around, for he groaned and swore—though it was full of pure agony, Charlotte did not think a sound had ever made her happier in her entire life.

"Benjamin, I am here with you. Just hold on. We will get you help."

Chapter Thirty-Seven

Wells assisted her down the steps and into the cart that had pulled up alongside the crowd. The runners manoeuvred them all into the small space, and they had set off down the road to the duke's townhouse. In no time at all, Benjamin was set up in a plush guest chamber, a doctor tending to the bullet wound, which had, blessedly, been a clean hit, through and through, and would only need cleaning and sutures. A nurse had appeared to tend to the cuts and bruises on his face as well as the resetting of his nose.

Benjamin had been unconscious for most of it, thank goodness. Charlotte was not sure she could have endured watching him writhing in pain—especially knowing that she had been the cause. After he had come to when his nose was reset, swearing and growling at anyone who touched him, the physician declared that, judging by his spirit and foul language, he expected him to make a full recovery. Not even an infection would dare cross such a man. The nurse and maid had been dismissed, and then it was only Charlotte left in the room.

For a moment, the two of them just eyed each other.

Benjamin reclined with bandages on every visible part of his body, and Charlotte stood in the far corner of the tastefully appointed guest chamber, his blood drying on the bodice of her grey travelling dress.

"I am sorry I shot you." Her voice seemed small in the aftermath of so much uproar.

"Turnabout is fair play." He shrugged, clearly forgetting his whole torso had been wrapped in gauze. His already pale face turned a shade whiter as he grimaced at the pain.

"Don't! You will tear your stitches." Charlotte took a step forward as if she might need to restrain him if he got the idea in his head to disregard the doctor's orders and spring up from the sickbed.

As if reading her thoughts, he gave her a wry smile—though it did not reach his eyes. "Do not worry, I do not plan on being a difficult patient. As much as I hate to admit it, I do not think I have it in me just now to be gadding around town again—certainly not so soon after that quack had his needle in me."

He closed his eyes briefly as if warding off a wave of pain. Charlotte wanted to comfort him, to reach out and stroke his brow. Was this how he had felt when she was lying abed with the bullet wound he had inflicted? Surely not. They had not even known each other.

"I really think," he continued, "Wells should see about getting a new physician. Doctor Price is a charlatan—pouring perfectly good spirits onto my gaping flesh rather than down my throat. What a waste." He opened his eyes again, brow raising when he saw that she had moved closer. "Though I suppose he did a fine enough job with you." He eyed her right shoulder as if he could see through the layers of rumpled clothes to evaluate the state of her scar. "But I had enough of discussing bullet wounds with him the last time around. I cannot countenance another lecture on festering sutures."

That brought Charlotte up short. The Duke of Wells' physician had tended to her wound? And Benjamin had conversed with him at length during her convalescence? She supposed it should not surprise her. She had been unconscious most of the time. Still, it was strangely heartening to imagine Benjamin, still a stranger to her, worrying over her sickbed. There beside her, caring for her when she could not care for herself. It made her love him even more.

"I promise to ward him off." Charlotte had meant the words to be light. But Benjamin's face sobered, and the air in the room grew heavy.

"You plan to stay?" His voice was low and rough, and Charlotte felt her heart breaking at the hope in his words. She had never seen him so vulnerable.

She could not stop herself from rushing to his side and grasping his hand, lifting his bruised knuckles to her lips. "I cannot stay long. I am so sorry."

With that, his eyes shuttered, and Charlotte felt as if she were watching him slip through her fingers—all over again. The pain in her chest threatened to drown her.

"Benjamin." She tried to lean in to get him to look at her again, her voice desperate and pleading. "I am sorry for leaving without a word before. I just—" her voice caught in her throat, and she had to take a few deep breaths to loosen the knot. "I could not find the words." She looked down at his hand cradled in hers. She had been a coward for running—for not telling him why she had to flee. Now she had to make that right, or at least try. "I was terrified—am terrified."

Benjamin's eyes snapped open at that, and she was perversely relieved to see some spirit returned to his face. "I would never let anything happen to you. Deering is no longer a threat."

His brow was so furrowed, she could not help but reach out to gently smooth the groove worn by years—a lifetime—of scowling.

"I know." She spoke softly, and her fingers traced the swollen skin of his left eye. "It was not that."

She almost laughed at his scowl. "Then why did you leave?" The pain in his voice cleaved her heart in two as she saw the boy he must have once been—abandoned by his father, betrayed by his mother, and grieving his sister. She could not be another arrow in this man's battered heart. "I thought—" He stopped, lips clamping tightly shut.

"I was not afraid of Deering." She saw flashes of the rotting face above her bed and could not suppress a shiver. "That is not true—though I clearly should have been more afraid of him than I was. But that was not why I left." She let out a shaky laugh. "It was not for fear of my reputation either, though that too, I should have taken more care with." Benjamin frowned at that, but she soldiered on, determined to get the words out before they choked her again. "It was you—us. The promise of it—"

She shook her head and started over, the words making a jumble of themselves between her heart and her mouth. "The Wylde's dinner party. Being there with you—with your friends. Your family, really. It was too real—too much. I wanted it too much. I thought I could take our month together and be happy with it. Make it an experience, something I could carry into the rest of my life but comfortably leave behind. I did not even want to take your money, though it would have solved a lot of problems. But I wanted it to be something I did for me—not for anyone else. But I was fooling myself to think I could keep it wrapped up in my mind. The dinner party proved that I had not kept my heart apart. I mean, it is foolish, really. How could I? It was *you*."

She could feel the warmth of his hand and knew he was urging her to look up at him. But now that the words had started coming, they would not stop. "I realised I wanted it. All of it. All of you. And that scared me out of my wits. I knew I could never have it, and the realisation was crushing. It was the only thing I could think of doing. Run." Her breath was coming hard now, and the last words came out in a terrible, gasping jumble.

"Charlotte." His voice was hoarse, but the gentle touch of his fingers to her chin made her look up at him.

And she was robbed of breath. In his eyes—though one was almost swollen shut—she saw it all: all the pain and longing she had been trying to ignore, even as it gnawed away at her soul, was reflected back at her in his eyes. And more than that, she saw a tenderness she could not begin to name—or at least, could not begin to hope for.

"You did not need to run." His voice was still soft and almost admonishing. "I was going to take care of everything." She frowned and opened her mouth to argue that it was not his place to take care of her or her family—that she could not ask that of him, as he had already done so much for them. But he held his finger to her lips, sending a jolt of awareness through her and abruptly halting her contradiction. "I was going to ask you to marry me."

And then she had nothing to say. The words shot through her mind, numbing her with shock. For timeless moments, the only sound in the room was her heart hammering against her rib cage—for surely he could hear it too.

∞∞∞

"I have shocked you." Benjamin chuckled and sank back against his pillows, wincing at the pain of the movement. "It does not speak well of me or my behaviour that the mere idea of me proposing has left you speechless."

He closed his eyes, collecting himself and his strength, and then turned his gaze back to her beautiful, elfin face—still pale from the shock of his admission, save for crimson flags across her high cheekbones and a despicable bruise that had blossomed across her cheek and up her temple.

"It is I who must apologise. I took horrible advantage of you—the truth is, I was captivated the moment I saw you on the ground of that damned field, my bullet lodged in your shoulder. And then, when you were being treated, I was half mad with the knowledge that I had just found you, only to destroy you with my own foolishness. The idea of being so close to something and then watching it slip through my fingers—"

He was pulled back to the close confines of his study in his townhouse—a room he rarely occupied in favour of his offices at Elysium, pacing back and forth, awaiting the doctor's prognosis. The feral desperation that had gripped him as she wavered between recovery and the alternative— and then, when she had left, risking infection and fever—he could not revisit that panic, not if he wanted to get his words out.

"When you came back to me that night at Elysium, in that lavender dress—" She looked surprised that he knew the colour of her gown that night, as if he could ever forget it. "I was so relieved. And in my relief, I was desperate to make you stay, to grab some piece of you. And so I proposed that ridiculous arrangement." He shook his head in disgust. "I swear I did not plan it. I saw the opportunity, and after years of seizing whatever I could—grasping and reaching—I could not bring myself to pass it up. I was disgusted with myself the moment I said it. But then..." He laughed, his disbelief and joy from that afternoon in the pavilion bubbling up. "Then, you accepted me. I think I wanted to marry you then and there."

In saying the words, he realised they were true. He had not known what it meant at the time, but the joy of her touch, the foundation-shaking realisation that she had given him such a gift—he had experienced a visceral need to keep her with him always. "I just—" he faltered, "I could not have ever imagined you would want the same. I am..." He struggled to find the words to encompass the gulf between them, the corruption of his soul. "I have done bad things—terrible things. I shot you, for Christ's sake, Charlotte. You are so far above me."

Her lips pulled up at the corners, and he was enchanted by the elusive smile in her eyes.

"I hesitate to remind you," she said, her melodic voice dancing around his heart, "but I shot you too."

Benjamin laughed at that, and despite the pain and weariness hovering at the edge of his vision, threatening to engulf him, he felt lighter for it.

"Yes, my love, you did." Her breath caught at his endearment, and he took her hand in his, unable to muster the strength to lift his other across his body to take both. "I love you, Charlotte Aston."

The words had haunted him, toyed with him, and terrified him since their trip to Eton. But now that they were out, he could die a contented man, his soul at rest. Not that he fancied dying once he saw Charlotte's eyes light up at the confession. It was like he was meeting the woman anew; a brilliant light glowed from within her.

"Benjamin, do you really mean that?" Her eyes sparkled with unshed tears, and he fought the impulse to tease her that of course he meant it, he would hardly say such a thing if he did not mean it—hell, he had been ready to propose marriage. But the joy on her face was so pure, he could only smile and nod.

"Yes, I mean it."

Shocking him, she let out a sudden hiccupping sob. "I love…" hiccup, "you…too."

He did not think his ever-composed Charlotte could be reduced to such a blubbering mess, but then he felt his own throat working in response to her outpouring of emotion. If he had two working arms, he would have pulled her into his embrace. As it was, he had to settle for gently guiding her lips to his.

"Shh, Charlotte, my love. It will be okay." And then his lips met hers.

∞∞∞

Benjamin woke with a throbbing headache, his whole body feeling like a mail coach had run him over. He groaned as he tried to ride through the wave of pain until he gathered the strength to open his eyes.

The effort proved worth it when he was met with the tired, worried, luminescent face of Charlotte above him. As he regained further consciousness, memories began filtering back to him. It had been three days since the incident at the Aston family townhouse. After the first evening when he had confessed his feelings to Charlotte, he had fallen asleep clutching her hand and woken the next morning with a fever the likes of which he had not experienced in years.

"Infection," Doctor Price had proclaimed pragmatically as he hovered over Benjamin's flushed, scowling face. "Likely aggravated by all the other injuries. The body is trying to heal too many things at once. He will need to be dosed with laudanum—I do not trust him not to leave his sickbed. I have had trouble with that recently."

Benjamin's head had been on fire, but he had still seen the disapproving look the physician gave Charlotte, who had the good sense to look properly chastened. He was not a fan of laudanum or the sickly limbo it induced, but he had a distant desire to prove to Charlotte he could be a better patient than she was. It was a newfound competitiveness born of the secure joy of her love. And so, he let the doctor spoon the vile concoction into his mouth, and the days began to slide together in a vague haze.

Now, the cool cloth Charlotte bathed over his face seemed unnecessary. His skin no longer felt hot to the touch, and though his mouth felt filmy and dry, he did not sense that he was seeing the world in a fevered daze. The infection had passed.

"Here, have some water." Charlotte held a glass to his lips, and he drank greedily.

Now that he had awoken as a man again, rather than an insensible invalid, he felt the agitation of confinement buzzing through his body. He must get up. He had a new life to live. A life with Charlotte. Which was the most urgent matter he must attend to, in all the chaos and confessions of the night he was shot, Benjamin had not actually proposed to her. An oversight he meant to remedy today—as soon as he managed to bathe and change into something that was not stiff with sickly sweat.

"I have—"

"I wanted—"

They both stopped, chuckling as their words collided. Benjamin waved his hand, indicating that she should speak first. He found he was a much more patient man, knowing he had the love of the woman of his heart.

Charlotte smiled sheepishly, plaiting her fingers together and fidgeting with them in her skirts. She was nervous; he realised. That made him sit up straighter. "I know I said I would not go…" The words sprouted panic in his chest. Had she changed her mind? Was it all just guilt over shooting him that had spurred her words the other night? "I will be back," she said quickly, seeing his expression drop. That only partially placated him. "But it is the twins. I have to go collect them at Eton. Their term ends tomorrow, and they have nowhere to go for the break. The Chesterfields have rescinded their invitation on account of my ruin." She said this last to the bunched fabric in her lap, crinkled and stained from days of worrying in her clenched palms.

Benjamin frowned. This was news to him. "What do you mean? The twins left last week with Robert Chesterfield.

Mr. Chesterfield collected them a week early—just when their exams were finished—to go on a fishing trip. As far as I know, they are enjoying the Lake District for the next week and a half."

Charlotte's mouth dropped open. He could read the emotions flying across her face like words on a page. Shock at the information. Outrage that she should not have known of it. Indignation that he should. Resignation that he would likely always know more about anyone than she could. Some higher sisterly concern must have overridden her desire to take him—or someone—to task that she had not been informed of her brother's whereabouts, and instead she just asked, "Then why did the Chesterfields write me?"

He frowned at that too. "They wrote to you?"

"Yes! I received a letter at my boarding house in Edinburgh. They said word had gotten out that I had been…well, you know…" The blush that rose in her cheeks was so absurdly charming, he had to fight the urge to smile. "And they could not take the boys for the term break because of the family's tarnished reputation. That is why I came down to London in such a rush. I had to make new arrangements for them."

He could see the thoughts and worry spinning through her head as she tried to reconcile the new information.

He froze. His mind must still be sluggish from the laudanum; otherwise, he would have recognised it the moment he heard what she said. "The Chesterfields did not write to you." He sat up further, his body weak and stiff but thrumming with the energy of the realisation. "It was Deering." Charlotte's eyes widened. "We were watching the house, but he got a letter past us. The only thing we knew was that it was addressed to somewhere in Edinburgh. Wells sent word to Elkington to keep an eye on you to make sure he was not plotting anything, but it must not have reached him until after you left."

Charlotte nodded, the wheels turning in her head. "I left the evening I received the letter. They would not have had time to get your warning." She frowned. "But how did he know where I was? I did not tell anyone about my plans or how to reach me. Not even you. Only Elsie, so that she might help me find employment, and Freddie."

She stopped short, and Benjamin felt the icy grip of intuition.

Chapter Thirty-Eight

Freddie. It had been Freddie. Charlotte sat down hard on the edge of the bed, Benjamin's hand coming around her wrist in a steadying grip.

"We do not know it was Frederick who told Deering of your whereabouts." She heard Benjamin's voice as if from the end of a long tunnel. "Charlotte, we do not have the facts yet."

"No," she whispered. "It was Freddie."

The certainty was like a rock in the pit of her stomach. She had never known something so absolutely in all her life. Freddie had betrayed her—betrayed her family. And she could not, for the life of her, understand how he could have done it.

She stood abruptly. "I need to find him."

"Let Wells do it. You do not need to go running through the stews of London to find him. You would not know the first place to start."

Charlotte thought of the stack of letters Freddie had received when Benjamin had bought up all of his debts. The kiss of lip rouge on the bottom of one. "I think I have a very good idea of where to start."

Benjamin grumbled behind her, and she heard the sounds of his bedclothes being pushed aside. "What do you think you are doing?" she demanded sharply. "Get back into bed this instant!"

"I will not," Benjamin replied calmly, and Charlotte found herself distracted by the long expanse of bare muscled leg that emerged from beneath the sheets. The linen tunic he wore preserved his modesty—but only just.

"If you keep looking at me that way, I will indeed have reason to return to bed—though I would prefer it to be a fresh one. This one smells as if someone has been lying at death's door." He gave her a devilish smile that did funny things to her insides.

"Benjamin Scarsdale. You have been shot. You are still recovering from an infection. I insist you return to bed!" She was bordering on shrill now, but she could not seem to do anything about it. Worry for his health had eclipsed all reason.

Ambling over to the bellpull by the washstand as if he had not a care in the world, Benjamin tugged the pull. Then, to her astonishment, he stripped off his shirt and went about lathering a wash rag with all the leisure of a gentleman enjoying perfect health. Completely nude.

"Benjamin!" She was mortified by the missish squeal that came from her lips, even as she should have turned around. Somehow, she could not bring herself to tear her gaze away from his firm buttocks and demur to his privacy.

"What?" The insufferable man had the audacity to sound completely innocent, as if he did not know what his sudden disrobing was doing to her—as if he had not done it on purpose. "I must wash some of this sickly grime off of me if I am to accompany you on this foolhardy hunt for your worthless brother."

"I—I…" Charlotte did turn around then, if only to regain some use of her mental faculties. "It is not foolhardy. Freddie betrayed me and our family, and it is time he faced the consequences of his deeds. And—and…" She took a deep breath, her voice dropping with sorrow and uncertainty. "I need to know why."

"I understand." His voice was soft against her neck, and she sucked in a breath—surprised by his sudden proximity. She spun and found him there, a hairsbreadth away, and nearly fully dressed—that was fast. And then, when she looked up into his eyes, she knew that he did understand. There, staring back at her was a wealth of understanding, acceptance, heat, and—her heart soared—love.

"We will find your brother, Charlotte. But first, before I let you leave this room, I must ask you a question." Charlotte felt her body swaying towards him, completely in his thrall.

"Yes?" The word was barely a breath.

Benjamin's lips quirked before he grew serious once again. "I would have preferred to do this in a more idyllic setting, but I cannot wait." He took her hands in both of his, still cool from the water in the washbasin. "Charlotte Aston, my Elfin Queen, will you marry me?"

Charlotte could not breathe for a moment, sure she had been drawn into some faraway dream. Benjamin's eyes searched hers, uncertainty creeping across his face the longer she did not answer.

"Yes." She gasped the word out, the force of it somehow loosening her tongue. "Yes. Yes!" She let out a stuttering laugh. "Yes, Benjamin. I will marry you!"

His face broke into the most radiant smile she had ever seen and transformed him from handsome to unbearably beautiful. She could not take her eyes off him.

He let out a whooping, jovial laugh that she would have never expected from a man like him, and he crushed her into his arms, lifting her feet from the ground as he kissed her. For a moment, they were suspended there together, floating above the ground. Until he let out a surprised groan.

"Your shoulder!" she nearly shouted. "You idiot man! What are you doing hauling me up like that, days after you were shot?"

"I love when you scold." His smile was still a ray of sunshine on her face, and she found she could not maintain her frustration.

"Take care, my love. You are not mended yet."

He grinned and kissed her again, though more gently this time. "My love. I could get used to that."

"Eh-hem." The pointed clearing of a throat caught their attention, and they turned to the open door to see the Duke of Wells standing rather awkwardly in the threshold.

Perhaps it was on account of her very good spirits, but Charlotte wanted to laugh at the absurd picture of a duke looking uncomfortable in his own home. It was likely a rare occurrence indeed.

"You rang?" His voice was dripping with mildly amused sarcasm, and the urbane mask was back in place.

"The duke responds to a bell summons?" Charlotte could not mask her surprise.

"He does when his friend has been shot. My staff were instructed to alert me to any changes in the patient's health. The maid you did ring for has already come and gone, I assume by her rather flushed appearance when she came to inform me of your clear change in health…" he gestured lazily to the bed and Benjamin's obvious absence in it, "that she must have caught you in a rather more compromising position than I just have."

Charlotte felt a blush rising to the roots of her hair.

"Your Grace." Benjamin's sardonic delivery of the honorific title was somewhat undercut but his clear happiness. "You may be the first to congratulate us. Lady Charlotte has just agreed to be my wife."

A slow smile spread across the duke's carefully bored features before turning into an outright grin. It had a similarly arresting effect on the man's appearance, and Charlotte found herself able to imagine both men as the boys they once were. "Well, it is about damn time. My felicitations to you both."

∞∞∞

A half hour later, after nearly force-feeding Benjamin a tray of biscuits to try to fortify his strength after he made it very clear he would not back down from his decision to accompany her and Wells to find Freddie, Charlotte sat across from the duke in one of his lush carriages, Benjamin's good arm wound through hers, their fingers clasped on her lap.

"Will you move back to Derbyshire?" Wells asked conversationally as he flipped the curtain from the window to better see the carriage's progress.

Charlotte cocked an eyebrow. "I imagine we will live here." The new concept *we* sent a thrill of pleasure through her, undampened by their current errand. "What with Benjamin's business in London, it makes the most sense. Besides, we do not have a family residence in Derbyshire anymore—there is no reason to return." Though the idea of her quiet country childhood had her feeling unaccountably wistful. "Even if we did, it would by rights belong to Freddie anyway. He is still the earl." Whether he deserved the title or not.

Wells raised his eyebrows in response, but he was not looking at her. "You have not told her?"

"Told me what?"

Benjamin glowered at his friend but then turned an almost sheepish gaze to her. "I suppose it is hardly a wedding gift, considering I purchased it before I had actually considered marrying you to be a possibility—and if you had stayed in Edinburgh, you would have found out soon anyway—unless Collier's colleagues were somehow waylaid." None of this was making any sense to her, and if he had not been so endearingly timid about it, she might have badgered him to the point. "Still, in light of recent developments." He squeezed her hand in his and smiled. "I would rather have liked to tell you upon our marriage."

"Benjamin! Spit it out! A woman only has so much patience." The demand was only softened by her eager smile.

"I bought Lamdel Manor. It is yours now. Everything is in your name. As it always should have been."

Charlotte could not believe her ears. He had bought Lamdel. Her childhood home, which she had cherished so fondly. That Freddie had squandered. He had purchased it for her. In her name. And he had not intended to use it as any sort of leverage—simply bestow it upon her because she loved it.

Her eyes grew misty, and the two men's faces grew taut

with panic at the prospect of a tearful woman in their midst. The comically identical expressions made her laugh out loud.

"Apologies, I am just so—" She could not find the words. "Benjamin, I am touched beyond words. I cannot tell you what this means to me."

He grumbled some dismissive comment when she kissed his cheek. But she saw the flush of pleasure that had stolen over his high cheekbones. Wells cleared his throat uncomfortably.

"Ah, here we are." The obvious relief in the duke's voice was enough to make her laugh again. For such an unflappably powerful man, it was proving remarkably easy to disconcert him.

The three of them stepped out of the carriage, Benjamin offering her his good arm to alight, despite the fact that it pulled at the sling holding his injured shoulder immobile. It was foolish that he was willing to inflict pain for such a small gesture, but it warmed her heart all the same.

∞∞∞

The inside of The Velvet Hook was dark and thick with sweet, acrid smoke. In all her time sneaking around the corners of London as a journalist, Charlotte had never experienced such an oppressive atmosphere, and she had to fight to restrain her gagging coughs. Wells flagged down a woman holding a tray of drinks, her clothes practically falling off her well-rounded figure. She was beautiful—or would have been—had she not had a certain hardness about her. Charlotte had seen it many times. The only way to protect oneself—to survive out here by the docks, in any profession but especially this one—a person had to build up a hard shell.

"Do you know where we might find the proprietress of this establishment?" Wells' cultured tones sounded out of place here in the lounge of the east-end brothel. "A Missus Fannie Bulette."

The young woman—Charlotte could see now that she was no older than four and twenty, despite her world-weary appearance—looked up at the well-dressed, obviously powerful gentleman before her in mute wonderment. Charlotte was surprised when, rather than take the opportunity to flirt with or attempt to seduce such a well-heeled potential customer, the woman simply pointed toward a back room, the door ajar, more dark, sweet-smelling smoke drifting in a languid haze through the opening.

She and Benjamin followed Wells to the door and into a modest-sized room strewn with chaises and cushions, the upholstery worn and patched in places and soiled in others. There was a sense of dilapidation about the place, despite the fact that it was full of patrons.

The men, and some of the women lounging throughout the room, were of diverse origin, some clearly workers straight from the docks, and others in their evening finery, coming from the entertainments of the *ton*. It was a jarring mix, though that was not what was most arresting to Charlotte. No, the most shocking detail—though upon entering a known brothel, Charlotte had prepared herself for a number of shocking sights—was that all the room's occupants were beyond intoxicated, their eyes rolling back in their heads, the most lucid smiling dreamily at the ceiling, the least nearly comatose on the floor. This was an opium den.

Madam Bulette—or at least the woman Charlotte assumed was the proprietress, given her voluminous skirts and general air of authority—bustled toward them with an entrepreneurial glint in her eyes. "How may I be of *service* to you, good sirs?"

The emphasis on the word was accompanied by a fetching turn of her chin and a touch of her hair. Though she was likely nearing fifty, the madame had an ageless beauty that she wielded with precision.

Benjamin did not beat about the bush. "We are looking for one of your patrons. Lord Elford. We have reason to believe he is here." It was a bold statement, considering Charlotte had proposed the location after a brief glimpse at a letter, though she realised it was entirely possible Benjamin had long kept tabs on Freddie and likely had his own reasons to suspect he might be here.

The madame deflated slightly at the rebuff, but she was clearly an avid businesswoman who knew when to play her cards and, more importantly, when she should not. "In the back. Good, you have come to collect 'im. Was ready to toss him out—no one has come to pay his tab in nearly a week. Tar ain't cheap, and it is not as if I am running some sort of charity, am I?"

Charlotte's heart plunged to her toes, and it was only the force of Benjamin's hand at her back that propelled her forward. Despite her distress—or perhaps because of it— Charlotte was overwhelmed with gratitude for his solid presence beside her. It was selfish, she knew. He should be in bed recovering. But having him there beside her was the only reason she did not crumple to the ground when they approached a figure sprawled on the chaise lounge in the back of the claustrophobic room.

It was Freddie.

And it was not Freddie. His golden hair was greasy and stained from all the smoke. He had lost an appalling amount of weight since she had last seen him. His clothes were rumpled, and the air around him smelled of unwashed body and dissolution.

Charlotte gasped and shied away before compulsion took over and sent her to her knees beside her baby brother, stroking his cheeks and cupping his head in her hand, whispering his name to try to draw him awake. After long, miserable seconds, his eyes cracked open, but even then, there was no recognition in his blown-out pupils.

"Come, Charlotte, move aside," Benjamin said. "We have to get him out of here."

She felt his hands on her shoulders, and she allowed herself to be moved, watching in a daze as Wells, along with a footman he must have summoned from his carriage when she was fussing over the unconscious shell of her brother, lifted Freddie and carried him out through the maze of opium-saturated patrons. Charlotte followed, wringing her hands and taking hurried, uncertain steps behind them. When they crossed the threshold, some morbid impulse caused her to glance back over her shoulder at the wretched room that would forever haunt her nightmares.

Chapter Thirty-Nine

It was harrowing watching Frederick experience opium withdrawal. It was a protracted and miserable process full of tremors, nausea, restlessness, and delirium, made that much more dire by Frederick's already weakened state. From what Benjamin could discern, he had been holed up in the opium den for nigh on a month, Deering stopping in periodically to pay his tab and encourage further consumption until the man's own madness took full control. It sickened Benjamin that he had not kept a closer eye on Freddie in his sister's absence. It had hurt too much to even think of the Aston family, and he had—foolishly perhaps—thought that it would do the boy some good to be responsible for himself for once.

More painful than watching Freddie suffer through his detoxification was watching Charlotte suffer alongside him. She was at his bedside day and night, sleeping awkwardly in the upright chair for only minutes at a time, ready to spring into action at the slightest disturbance. She administered water and broth, mopping his brow and soothing his panic when a particularly vicious delusion set in. By the end of the first week, Benjamin was finally able to convince her to let him hire a nurse to see to Freddie so that she could rest.

"Just as it is your job to care for Freddie, it is my job to care for you," Benjamin had said sternly before Charlotte could launch another argument against leaving her brother for a single moment.

Somehow, it had worked. And like Charlotte had with Freddie for the last week, and likely had with himself the three days of his own convalescence, he watched her sleep. After eight hours, he climbed into bed alongside her and did not wake until she began to stir the next morning.

"Good morning," Benjamin said sleepily, eyes still a bit bleary from the shockingly deep sleep he had enjoyed nestled beside Charlotte's warm body.

"Morning?" Charlotte blinked, disoriented as time and events fitted themselves back into place in the sleep-jumble of her mind. "Oh, my. It is morning. How long did I— Oh, I must—"

Benjamin rested a stilling hand on her bare shoulder; her sleeveless cotton chemise was slightly askew from her occasional turning in the night.

It was a delightful sight, Charlotte sleeping warm and rumpled, the wrinkles of the pillowcase imprinted on one rosy cheek. It filled him with a decadent contentment that went beyond sensual desire or even aesthetic appreciation. There was a new satisfaction in his soul that Benjamin could never have imagined.

"He is alright, Charlotte. The nurse is watching him, and the doctor believes he is already out of the woods." He felt some of the coiled tension leave her body as she released a breath he did not realise she was holding. The air puffed across his face, and he smiled. "It is no guarantee that he will not fall back into use someday—it is a lifelong struggle for people to overcome the disease of addiction. And even if he can keep himself clean, he must live with the guilt of what he did to his family forever. It is not an easy path." He stopped when Charlotte reached a hand up to touch the beard-roughened skin of his cheek.

"Thank you, Benjamin. Thank you for saving me. Saving my family."

"You are *my* family." He held her soft hand to his cheek and then brought it down to his beating heart. Charlotte smiled softly and moved both their hands to the raised skin at his shoulder that was just starting to scar.

"And *you* are mine." She took his other hand in hers and held it to her own heart, his fingers splaying over her sternum and collarbone, thumb just skimming the edge of her scar. "Forever."

∞∞∞

Benjamin had never imagined he would have any sort of wedding. And he certainly had not imagined a large one that would be the talk of London. But their impending nuptials had already been written about in three different papers, and the Southwark Cathedral was the smallest venue that could host all the staff of Elysium, their friends, and Charlotte's family.

Despite his notoriety, Benjamin had always enjoyed a rather subdued relationship with society. He liked to think the high-flyers understood and respected the power he might wield over them, especially if they got too close. But upon marrying a society lady—even one that had long ago been labelled a spinster bluestocking—Benjamin found himself cast in a wholly different light.

Now, attached to Charlotte, he was a formidable business-man. Wealthy and well-to-do and, if the gossip rags were to be believed, a dashing catch indeed. That he had always had very public friendships with not one but two ducal titles, seemed suddenly a stamp of quality. He was a man about town.

In the weeks leading up to the wedding, Benjamin had been inundated with invitations to this soiree and that ball and another musicale. For Charlotte's sake, he had attended a few, but it did not take long for her to convince him that the insipid social whirl of her past was just that: her past. Neither of them put much stock in the hallowed circles of the *ton,* and the packed cathedral before him proved it.

There were urchins and street thugs and washing women and prostitutes lining the wooden pews. Elkington and Elsie had not been able to make the trip down from Edinburgh, but the rest of their friends and family were here, mingling without concern with the common guests, the subduing atmosphere of the church doing nothing to quell their eager chatter as the organist began to play and the tall carved doors opened.

Everything else fell away as Benjamin saw her.

Dressed in a diaphanous swath of creamy gold, and hanging on the arm of the Duke of Wells, was his Charlotte. Even across this distance, their eyes met and held—full of all the unbelievable joy and hope. He could not believe the stroke of fate that had brought them together, standing as many paces apart in a damp, misty field in one of dear Mother England's most miserable glooms to date. Charlotte. His Elfin Queen.

His wife.

Epilogue

London, England

January 1819

"It is here! It is here!" Charlotte looked up from her desk as Boyd skittered past the doorframe, overshooting the entrance and pulling himself up last minute in his haste, nearly bashing his head on the ornate panelling.

"Careful, Boyd. There is no need to rush."

"Of course, ther'is, Ma'am. The printer just dropped this off!"

He waved a paper-wrapped parcel above his head. The footman's uniform sleeve was already too short—it was the second one he had grown out of that autumn.

"OH!" Charlotte shot up, banging her knees on the underside of the desk. There was only one thing it could be.

Her book.

She rushed over to Boyd, taking the parcel and tearing it open so he could see too. Sure enough, it was a bound volume in deep red cotton. In ostentatious pressed gold leaf, the cover read: *The Secrets of London's Underworld.*

It was a sensational title she knew. She had wanted to title it something more straightforward like: *The Harrowing Conditions of Life Amongst London's Masses*, or something equally informative, but after the cajoling of Benjamin, Wells, Amelia, Lizzy, Elsie, and her publisher, Charlotte had agreed that this title would capture the attention of the London elite long enough for them to recognise the truth of the rest of their fair city—and perhaps, be compelled to do something about it.

Her book.

Here it was.

"Wow, ma'am. It looks better than plum pudding!" Boyd's exuberance cut through her haze of awe.

"Thank you very much, Boyd."

"Can you read what it says?" The low voice from the doorway caught their attention.

Benjamin leaned negligently against the door frame, cravat loose and one booted foot crossed over the other, dust from his morning ride still evident despite having spent the bulk of his day in the office right beside Charlotte.

"The Sec-ret-s ov London's-s Un-der-wo-rld," Boyd pushed valiantly through, "By Charle-s As-ton." He looked up to Charlotte and then Benjamin with a proud grin.

"Well done, lad." Benjamin gave him an affectionate pat on the shoulder. "Run along now. You have more lessons this afternoon, and I'd better not hear of you skipping out to follow the older boys around."

Boyd bobbed a bow and bounced out of the room. "Of course, Sir. Wouldn't dream of it, Sir." He called over his shoulder.

Charlotte smiled and leaned against the desk, looking back down to marvel at the book in her hand.

"Congratulations, my love." Benjamin moved to stand before her, his strong arms bracketing her hips as he leaned to look down at the volume in her hands.

"I cannot believe it is here." She flipped through the book, pages filled with type-set stories she had collected nearly her entire adult life.

He smiled as he pressed a kiss to her hair. "You did it."

"I did it," she whispered. A laugh bubbled up. "I did it!"

Then she was laughing and shrieking as Benjamin picked her up and spun her around the room. Their laughter mixed and filled the office that had seen so much of their story already.

"Wait!" Benjamin set her down suddenly. "Are you alright?"

Charlotte was still laughing, her head light and her cheeks warm from her smile. "Yes, of course. Why wouldn't I be?" She held the book aloft again, as if nothing could ever make her unwell after such a victory.

"Carons just said in the kitchen that Dr. Price was here this morning. What happened? Are you ill?" He pressed a hand to her brow, frowning and checking her over like a mother hen.

"Oh, that." Charlotte laughed again. "No, I am perfectly well. I just had a spell of dizziness this morning when I arrived, and the cook called for the doctor."

"What do you mean, dizziness?" Seeing Benjamin was ready to bundle her up and deposit her in bed for a fortnight, Charlotte put the book down and placed soothing hands on either side of his face.

"All is well. A bit of dizziness here and there is normal when a woman is expecting." She watched as the words filtered through his worry and their meaning settled.

His eyes were wide, and his hands gripped hers. "Expecting?"

She grinned and nodded.

"Expecting!" He nearly shouted, and then he swooped her up again. "Charlotte!" His joyful shout had her laughing again.

"Okay, okay. Let me down!" She swatted his shoulder.

"Not a chance, my love." He was already out the door and up the stairs to their chambers in the back of Elysium. She was sure their laughter could be heard throughout the building, winding in and out of the labyrinth of Benjamin's underworld palace.

"Benjamin, we have work to do!" she admonished even as she relished her husband's strong embrace.

"Indeed, we have to celebrate. I plan on being diligent in my duty indeed." With a devilish grin, he kicked the door to their chambers closed behind them.

* * *

Acknowledgements

This book, like any labour of love, did not come about through my own sheer force of will—though that was certainly a factor on those days the cantankerous author (me) was especially difficult and ill-tempered. But beyond my own wrangling of self, I would like to extend my heartfelt gratitude to all the other hands that helped mould this beast into the beautiful book it is today. Starting from the cover, thank you, Elizabeth Convis of Fitter Fang for the incredible cover design and for your endless patience with all my waffling. You are a fantastic artist and better friend. I would also like to thank my beta readers, who are too many to name— your ability to see through the early drafts of this to the treasure of a story concealed within was what gave me the encouragement to carry on unearthing it. To my editor, Sherri Shackelford, your eye for story and craft is marvellous, and your kindness and encouragement bring out the best in your authors. Thank you. Again, too numerous to name individually, I want to thank everyone who helped me publish this book with Lamond House Press. An indie author's road to publishing is fraught, and the guidance and advice you gave me along the way was like a lighthouse in a storm. Finally, I would like to thank my family and friends, who are at the heart of this book. To my mother and all her siblings, thank you for bringing me up in a bookish gang of bluestockings. I am endlessly proud of all the clever women I am related to. To Johannes, thank you for being a true partner and keeping me fed at all times. To my dearest friend, Erin, thank you for listening to obscenely long voice notes about the dramas of writing and life in general. I could not have written this book—or anything at all—without you. And thank you to all my other loved ones. You have filled my life with joy and love, and I am nothing without you all. And to you, Dear Reader, thank you for picking up this book. I have long dreamed of this day, that I might get to share it with you.

About the Author

Lydia Margett is a historical romance author and creator of the Dreamers and Dukes trilogy. Lydia was born and raised in the United States and moved abroad as a teenager. She studied International Relations and Spanish at the University of St Andrews in Scotland and completed a Masters in Political Science at the Technical University of Munich before settling down in Germany, where she is now a permanent resident. Lydia tries to incorporate her experience working in human rights and foreign policy into her work, weaving in social justice causes into what is otherwise a light and entertainment-driven genre. Learn more and follow along for updates on her work through her website and newsletter.

You can connect with me on:

🌐 https://lydiamargett.com

Subscribe to my newsletter:

✉ https://lydiamargett.com/mailing-list

Also by Lydia Margett

Dreamers and Dukes

Heavy is the head that wears the crown… or perhaps in better terms, strong are the shoulders that carry the title. Benjamin Scarsdale, Master of London's Secrets; Alexander Burke, Marquess of Elkington; and Jonathan Bradford, Duke of Wells all carry heavy titles that have shaped their lives. However, none of them could have anticipated how a dreamer might come into their lives and send them down a whole new path. Dreamers and Dukes is a collection of three standalone novels that follow each man's story on their broken road to love.

Titles in this series:
To Shoot a Sinner
To Love a Libertine
To Mistake a Maiden